Cat Schield has been reading and writing romance since high school. Although she graduated from college with a BA in business, her idea of a perfect career was writing books for Mills & Boon. And now, after winning the Romance Writers of America 2010 Golden Heart® Award for Best Contemporary Series Romance, that dream has come true. Cat lives in Minnesota with her daughter, Emily, and their Burmese cat. When she's not writing sexy, romantic stories for Mills & Boon Desire, she can be found sailing with friends on the St. Croix River, or in more exotic locales, like the Caribbean and Europe. She loves to hear from readers. Find her at www.catschield.net and follow her on Twitter, @catschield.

Maisey Yates is a *New York Times* bestselling author of more than thirty romance novels. She has a coffee habit she has no interest in kicking and a slight Pinterest addiction. She lives with her husband and children in the Pacific Northwest. When Maisey isn't writing, she can be found singing in the grocery store, shopping for shoes online and probably not doing dishes. Check out her website: www.maiseyyates.com.

UPSTAIRS DOWNSTAIRS BABY

CAT SCHIELD

CLAIM ME, COWBOY

MAISEY YATES

MIX
Paper from
responsible sources
FSC
FSC C007454

This book is produced from independently certified FSC™
paper to ensure responsible forest management.

For more information visit: www.harpercollins.co.uk/green

Printed and bound in Spain
by CPI, Barcelona

MILLS & BOON

First Published in Great Britain 2018
by Mills & Boon, an imprint of HarperCollinsPublishers,
1 London Bridge Street, London, SE1 9GF

Upstairs Downstairs Baby © 2018 Catherine Schield
Claim Me, Cowboy © 2018 Maisey Yates

ISBN: 978-0-263-93597-4

51-0418

UPSTAIRS DOWNSTAIRS BABY

CAT SCHIELD

Prologue

Everly Briggs made sure she gave every appearance of listening sympathetically as London McCaffrey imparted her romantic woes. They were attending the "Beautiful Women Taking Charge" networking event, featuring a keynote from Poppy Hart, a motivational speaker and owner of Hart Success Counseling.

"And he gave you no reason for breaking off your engagement?" Everly sounded aghast, though in truth, she already knew all about London's failed romance with professional baseball player Linc Thurston. It was the reason she'd contrived to meet her tonight.

London pressed her coral-tinted lips into a thin line as she shook her head. "He claims he isn't ready to get married, but we've been engaged for two years."

Everly tried not to wince at London's affected Southern accent. The beautiful woman, with her silky straight blond hair and expensive clothes, was originally from Connecticut and that made her an outsider here in Charleston.

"Do you think he was cheating on you?" Zoe Crosby

asked, her light brown eyes blazing with outrage from inside their frame of dark, lush lashes.

"Linc...cheat?" London toyed with her string of Mikimoto pearls as she considered this. "Yes, I suppose that's a possibility. He travels more than half the year with the team and lives in Texas during the season."

"And you know how women love professional sports players," Zoe added. "My former brother-in-law is a race car driver and has women after him all the time."

"These men have no right to treat us so badly," Everly said. Each of the three women had shared a tale of being wronged by a wealthy, powerful man. "We need to get back at all of them. Linc, Tristan and Ryan. They all need to be taught a lesson."

"As much as the idea appeals to me," London said, "I can't imagine taking revenge on Linc without it blowing up in my face."

"What good would it do any of us? Anything we try would only end up making us look bad," Zoe said, echoing London.

"Not if we go after each other's men." Everly restrained a smug smile as she took in her companions' curious expressions. "Think about it. We're strangers at a cocktail party. Who would ever connect us? I go after Linc. London goes after Tristan. And, Zoe, you go after Ryan."

"When you say 'go after,'" Zoe said, sounding hesitant even as her head bobbed eagerly, "what do you have in mind?"

"We're not going to do them bodily harm," Everly said with a silvery laugh. "But there's no reason why we couldn't ruin a business deal or mess with their current relationship. We've each been the victim of a ruthless man. And yet we're strong, empowered women. Don't you think it's time we acted like it?"

London started nodding right along with Zoe. "I like

the idea of striking back at Linc. He deserves to feel a little of the pain and humiliation I've endured since our engagement ended."

Zoe leaned forward. "Count me in, too."

"Marvelous. Now, here's what I think we should do…"

One

He needed to fire Claire.

Lincoln Thurston opened his mouth to do just that as she set his morning smoothie of kale, protein powder and blueberries on the breakfast bar near his gym bag. Then she gave him a smile of such sweetness that he was helpless to do anything but grin back.

Letting his housekeeper go was a matter of desperation. He was obsessed with the lovely young woman who cooked and cleaned for him. Over the twelve months since he'd hired her, it had become increasingly difficult to avoid thinking about her in a certain way. A certain carnal way. Which was why he absolutely, positively couldn't have her living in his house another day.

And yet he felt responsible for her welfare the way he did for his mother and sister. Claire was almost three thousand miles from her family and her husband had been killed in Afghanistan two years earlier. Besides, what excuse could he give? She cooked like a dream and kept his Charleston house in perfect order. And she was more than his housekeeper. She cared about him. Him. Linc Thurston, the regular guy. Not Linc Thurston, the ballplayer or the multimillionaire or the recently single and highly eligible bachelor.

Linc gave his head a brisk shake. He had to stop thinking about Claire as if she meant something to him. It had already proved detrimental to his love life, causing him to end his engagement.

Not that it was fair to blame Claire. She was the perfect employee. She never once encouraged him or acted as if she was even aware that he was an attractive, financially stable man who could take her away from the drudgery of her current occupation. It was refreshing that she wasn't working an angle, and yet part of him wished that seduction was her goal. He wouldn't have minded being at the heart of her sinister plot to trap him. At least then he could sleep with her and never for a second regret it.

As a shortstop with the Texas Barons, making fifteen million a year, Linc was accustomed to having women throw themselves at him. Not even his engagement had slowed them down. At twenty-six, when he was at the beginning of his eight-year, nine-figure contract, he'd basked in the attention. Now, at thirty-three, with only one year left to go, he wanted to settle down with a wife and kids. Or that had been the plan, until he'd reevaluated his feelings for London McCaffrey and realized he wasn't in love with her.

So, what was it about Claire that preoccupied him?

"Mama."

The reason Linc would be the biggest jerk of all time if he fired Claire ran into the kitchen buck naked.

"Where are your clothes?" Claire exclaimed as her daughter streaked past.

With her straight shoulder-length brown hair and a sprinkling of freckles over her nose, Claire had a fresh girl-next-door look that sometimes made her seem too young to be the mother of a toddler.

Two-year-old Honey Robbins made a beeline for Linc. He scooped her into his arms, whirling her around. She was a bright-eyed, enthusiastic charmer who'd wrapped him around her finger from their first meeting. Honey shrieked with laughter, and he smiled. Mother and daughter had burrowed beneath his skin to such an extent that not having them around would be so much worse than his constant battle with attraction.

He would just have to endure.

"I don't know what it is about this child that she can't manage to keep her clothes on," Claire said, her brown eyes fixed on the toddler's chubby cheeks.

"Maybe she takes after her mother?" Had he just said that? His careless words put bright spots of color in Claire's cheeks and inappropriate thoughts in his head. "I don't mean that you can't keep your clothes on," he hastened to add. "It's just something people say. I mean, about children taking after their parents."

"Well, that's a relief," Claire said. "I thought maybe the security cameras caught me skinny-dipping last week."

In truth, there were no security cameras and there was no way Claire would take her clothes off and slip naked into his pool. Which was why she could joke about it. Despite the provocative nature of the banter, Claire was a very proper and modest twenty-seven-year-old widow who still wore her wedding band. She obviously wasn't over her husband, a hero who'd died two years earlier when a suicide bomber attacked his military convoy.

"I guess I better go review the video," he said, filling his voice with lighthearted good humor. "What day might that have been?"

"I'm not gonna tell you." Her grin wasn't flirtatious, merely one of standard amusement. "It'll give you something to do while I'm vacuuming upstairs. You do get underfoot these days."

She was plainspoken and treated him like a cross between an older brother and the senile uncle everyone humored. It was his fault. When he hired her a year ago, he'd set the tone for their relationship, wanting—no, needing—someone in his life whom he could be himself around. That was part of why she'd crept beneath his skin. He didn't hold back around her. She was the one person who had heard all his darkest thoughts, his doubts, his secrets.

Except in one area: the way he'd come to feel about her.

And in turn, she'd talked to him about growing up in San Francisco and how she met her husband. Her eyes glowed when she talked about him and turned teary when she spoke of how Honey would grow up never knowing her father. Claire was not a woman who loved easily and then moved on.

How could he take advantage of someone like that? A single mother with no one to turn to if she lost both her job and the place she lived.

He might not be the best guy in the world—London could attest to that—but there were some lines he wouldn't cross. And seducing Claire was one of them.

Claire's heart ached as she watched Linc with Honey. The man was too ridiculously good-looking for her peace of mind. Since he broke off his engagement to London, it had become harder and harder to resist fantasizing about her and Honey being part of Linc's family. When the daydreams were at their strongest, she slid on her rubber gloves and cleaned his bathroom. Reminding herself that she was his housekeeper—not a beautiful, successful and pedigreed Charlestonian woman— grounded her flights of fancy. After all, Linc's mother, Bettina Thurston, had barely tolerated London, and the socialite had had it all: money, success and beauty.

Claire stared at Linc's bulging biceps as he lifted Honey

high into the air and whirled her around until she shrieked in excitement. It was nearly impossible to deny the man's appeal when he made her child happy. Nor did it help that his strong jaw, laughter-filled blue eyes and sensual lower lip made her blood run hot. Most days she wished he acted the part of a self-absorbed, successful jerk who thought all women were there to satisfy him. Then she wouldn't have had any tingly feelings for him.

"What are your plans for today?" he asked, settling Honey against his chest.

Her baby patted his cheek with a chubby palm and cooed at him. But Linc's bright blue eyes remained focused on Claire and the steadiness of his gaze made her temperature rise. She wanted to fan herself and drawl, *Oh, my*. She'd felt that way a lot since the baseball season ended and he'd returned from Texas. Too often. She couldn't let this go on. There had to be some way to stop or at least slow her ever-increasing attraction to him.

Claire pictured his mother's reaction to her predicament and that worked pretty well to cool her fever. Bettina was a true Southern belle from an old family line and rarely missed an opportunity to mention it. Having a pedigree in this town wasn't synonymous with having money. Even though Bettina's family had lost much of their fortune in the 1930s, her social standing hadn't been lowered, which made it unrealistic that she would accept Claire as a suitable match for her son.

"Claire?" Linc's deep voice roused her from her thoughts.

"I'm sorry. I was thinking about all the things I have to do today."

"What if I take Lil' Bit here off your hands, so you can get everything done faster and knock off early?" He tickled Honey, prompting a delighted giggle.

Claire shook her head. It wasn't professional to let her

boss play nanny, but in the months she'd worked for Linc, the line had grown ever more blurry between employer and friend.

"You don't have to do that," she said. "I can take care of everything."

Yet the way the pair got along, it was tempting to surrender Honey to Linc's care. And Claire had other concerns. With Jasper dead, Honey was going to grow up without a father. Claire wanted her daughter to know a good man, but she couldn't let that be Linc. Plus, she worried that Honey would get attached to him in ways she shouldn't. What happened when Linc got married and started to have babies of his own? How confused would Honey be when his children took his full attention and he had no more time for her?

"I could use the company," Linc continued.

Curse the man for being so persistent.

Claire opened her mouth to refuse yet again, but something in his manner stopped her. Since breaking off his engagement to the incredibly beautiful and successful London, his behavior had changed. It was as if he'd lost a bit of his cockiness, which was strange, since she knew he was the one who'd ended things. Maybe Linc had decided that had been a mistake.

London had already rebounded, making a splash in the society pages after being seen on the arm of millionaire playboy and race car driver Harrison Crosby. Claire wouldn't be surprised if Linc was a little jealous that London had bounced back so fast.

"You can't watch Honey," Claire said, plucking her daughter from his grasp.

Honey protested being taken away from Linc, but Claire struggled to maintain a severe expression while ignoring her daughter's scowl. It was like trying not to smile at a puppy growling fiercely as it plays. Honestly, the child was too adorable for her own good. She'd inherited her father's charisma. The man could charm fruit off trees. Or the pants off unsuspecting culinary school students, which was what she'd been when they first met.

"If I remember correctly," Claire continued, "you're supposed to have lunch with your mother today."

Linc made a face. "I haven't forgotten."

He grabbed his duffel bag and turned to leave the kitchen. Before he took more than two steps, Claire cleared her throat. When he pivoted back around, she was holding up the smoothie. Disgust twisted his handsome features, but he took the drink. She didn't know what sorts of things he put into his body when he was away from Charleston, but while he was within her care, she made sure he ate nutritious and delectable meals.

"I want to see you taste it before you leave," she said. "That way I know you won't throw it out."

"You seem pretty sure of yourself." He lifted the glass and took a doubtful sniff.

"Food can be healthy and delicious."

"In my experience, the two don't go hand in hand." He radiated suspicion as he took a small sip. "Hey!" His eyes widened. "This one actually tastes good."

Her heart did a happy little leap. To cover her reaction to his praise, she gave a satisfied nod. "I added a little agave syrup to satisfy your sweet tooth."

"You're the best."

Warmed by his words, Claire let her gaze linger on his departing figure. Then shaking herself free of his spell, she carried her daughter into the sunroom next to the kitchen, where Honey had stripped off her clothes earlier. The room was filled with books and toys to keep the toddler occupied while Claire worked in the kitchen.

Once Honey was dressed, Claire settled her into a booster chair at the kitchen table. Sunlight spilled across the two-year-old's light brown hair, awakening the gold highlights and making her hazel eyes twinkle. She had her father's coloring. Claire's espresso hair and brown eyes were not at all represented. The only mark she'd made on her daughter was her petite frame. Where Jasper had been six-three and broadly built, Honey was in the twenty-fifth percentile for height and weight.

With Linc off to the gym, the house settled back into its usual state of harmonious calm. It wasn't that his energy was all that chaotic, but his presence tended to stir up feelings Claire would have preferred not to think about. Plus, during the seven months of baseball season, she'd grown accustomed to having the four-bedroom, five-bathroom home in the prestigious South of Broad—or SOB—neighborhood to herself and Honey.

While the toddler ate bits of a homemade blueberry waffle and slices of banana, Claire made out a grocery list. Linc had decided to host a dinner party on Saturday. It was his first time entertaining formally since his engagement to London had ended. When they were together, the socialite had preferred to host all their events at her mansion. London had always made it clear she doubted Claire's experience and sophistication to pull off a Charleston-worthy event. On the surface, London had been right to judge Claire this way. Her upbringing in San Francisco was a pretty far cry from the pomp and circumstance that ruled Charleston society.

But Claire cooked like a dream. Everyone who'd tasted her food said so. In fact, it was on the strength of her culinary skills that she'd found her way to filling in for Bettina's housekeeper during a ladies' luncheon and eventually taking the job with Linc.

As soon as Honey finished her breakfast, Claire dressed her in an adorable outfit she'd found at a consignment shop and headed to the local gourmet grocery store with her list. The menu required several specialty ingredients and Claire knew she'd find everything she needed there.

While she shopped, she kept Honey occupied by practicing her colors.

"What color is this?" Claire asked, showing her a box of elbow macaroni.

"Green," Honey crowed and clapped her hands, obviously pleased with herself.

"That's right. It's green." She gave her daughter a smoochy kiss on her cheek, making her giggle.

"Well, isn't she a bright little girl."

Claire turned toward the speaker, a stunning woman in her early thirties with bright green eyes and dark blond hair subtly highlighted with gold. She had perfect skin and full lips, and her flawless makeup softened the angles of her face. In a yellow T-shirt and a flowered skirt, Claire felt dowdy and uninteresting beside her.

"Thank you. She picks up things so very quickly," she said, her wide smile broadcasting her pride. "She's already counting to fifty and knows her ABCs."

"My goodness. How old is she?"

"She just turned two last month."

The woman looked suitably impressed. "You must work with her a great deal."

"I'm home with her all day, so that really makes a difference."

The woman's gaze flicked to the plain gold band on Claire's left hand. Her first inclination was to cover the betraying lack of sparkle. A part of Claire winced at the impulse. In this part of town, status was everything, and she'd grown tired of how fast she was dismissed. Claire pushed her irritation aside. She was a housekeeper. She shouldn't be worrying about anyone's perception of her. Still, it smarted a little every time she glimpsed disdain in someone's eyes.

But there was nothing but kind interest in the woman's expression. "I bet you read to her all the time."

"I do. She loves books." Claire beamed at Honey, realizing how many memories of her own childhood involved her mother reading to her in the overstuffed armchair in their living room. "Do you have any children?"

"No. I'm not married." The woman sighed. "As much as I love children, I'm not really sure I'm cut out for motherhood."

"It's not always easy."

The woman acknowledged the remark with a faint smile. "I'm Everly Briggs."

"Nice to meet you, Everly. I'm Claire Robbins and this is my daughter, Honey."

"Well, Claire, that's an interesting collection of ingredients you have there," she said, letting her gaze travel over the contents of Claire's shopping cart. "What are you making?"

Smiling, Claire ticked off the menu she'd fretted over for the better part of a week. "Scallops with potato pancakes and caviar sauce. Braised lamb shanks with vegetable puree. And seared bitter greens with roasted beets and spiced pecans. And for dessert, a pomegranate-chocolate cake."

With each menu item she listed, the woman's eyes grew wider. "Well, that's quite impressive. What's the occasion?"

"My employer is hosting a dinner party."

"Who might that be? I'll have to wrangle an invitation. It all sounds delicious."

Everly fired off the question so blithely that Claire answered before considering whether she should. "Lincoln Thurston."

The woman's friendly manner underwent a slight transformation at the mention of Linc's name. She stopped making polite conversation and became riveted. "Oh." Her smile took on a keen edge. "Now I really want to come to the party. I heard he's single these days."

"Ah...yes."

Wishing she'd kept her mouth shut, Claire gathered breath to make a courteous exit, but the stranger latched on to the shopping cart, preventing Claire from going anywhere.

"I'm having some friends over next week and would love to hire you to cater my party."

"I'd love to, but I can't. When I said I worked for Linc..." Claire cursed her earlier lapse. For a moment, she'd seen the admiration in the woman's eyes and it had felt amazing. "I'm not his caterer. I'm his housekeeper."

"The one who lives-in?" Everly asked, a smooth drawl sugarcoating her avid curiosity.

Claire frowned. "Yes." *What was this woman after?*

"Oh." Everly shaded the word in all sorts of understanding. "Then you're the woman all Charleston is gossiping about."

Two

When Linc returned home from the gym, Claire's car wasn't in the driveway. She'd finalized the menu for his dinner party the night before and was likely shopping for ingredients. He was excited to have her cooking for his friends. Her culinary skills were fantastic. In fact, he was surprised she hadn't gone to work for a restaurant when she'd first moved to Charleston.

He'd asked her about it once and she'd explained about the long hours and how she'd struggled finding childcare. As he'd listened to her talk about her challenges being a single mom, he appreciated that she wanted to put her daughter's needs first. Still, he sensed there was more to the story. She seemed to lack confidence in her ability. Which made no sense. She cooked like a dream.

Maybe he'd put too much pressure on her. This was the first time he'd entertained since moving into the Battery Street house. While he and London had been together, she'd insisted on hosting all events. At first, he'd agreed because the house he'd purchased had gone through almost three years of renovations and wasn't the ideal place to entertain. But once the home had been restored to its former glory, his fiancée had been unable to relinquish control. Linc had begun to see their relationship wasn't the give-and-take partnership he craved. Too bad he hadn't realized this before proposing marriage.

Linc set his gym bag on a bar stool and rummaged in the refrigerator for something that would take the edge off his post-workout appetite. Claire always had snacks ready for him. Today was no exception. A quick glance at the clock confirmed that he had only an hour before his mother expected him for lunch. He was running late thanks to an impromptu shopping detour he'd made on the way to the gym. It had occurred to him as he was leaving the house that Claire had been working for him for a year. He'd neglected to mark the anniversary last week and decided to rectify the error. A few doors down from the gym was a boutique run by Theresa Owens, a friend of his sister Sawyer's from high school. He'd popped in to buy a small token.

After polishing off a turkey and Swiss cheese sandwich and a bowl of mixed berries, Linc rummaged for a pen to sign the card that would accompany the whimsical asymmetrical silver earrings embellished with turquoise, tourmaline and opal. He'd chosen earrings because aside from her plain wedding band, earrings were the only accessories he'd ever seen Claire wear.

Was it weird that he had bought Claire such a personal gift? He'd considered cash or a gift card but liked the idea of something he'd put thought into. Jewelry was a natural go-to purchase for him. His mother and sister both loved receiving sparkly earrings and necklaces. When he was a kid, there'd been little money available for such things. It made him feel good to be able to spoil the women in his life. And he knew they appreciated it.

Linc left the card and the jewelry box on the breakfast

bar where Claire was sure to find them and headed upstairs to shower and change. His mother expected him to arrive at her house promptly at noon, wearing pressed trousers, a crisp shirt and a blazer. Money might have been in short supply while his mother had been young, but her upbringing had been rich in Southern custom.

Linc's grandmother had clung to memories of wealth and power long after her husband had sold their South of Broad home to a wealthy gentleman from "off"—a man who had no history in the city. Keeping up with private school tuition and social pressures, as well as the increased expense of maintaining the large historic houses, had meant difficult choices for many old Charleston families.

Yet, despite the downturn in his financial circumstances, Linc's grandfather had retained enough status to keep his family afloat socially. Linc's mother had never given up her dream of returning her family to its former glory, not even when her husband proved no more financially astute than her father had been, and his embezzlement scheme caused the government to seize their property and bank accounts.

That was why as soon as he signed his first pro contract, Linc had made sure to set his mother up in the sort of Charleston house that would provide Bettina the level of comfort her mother had known growing up. The Mills-Forrest House was located on King Street, South of Broad. Built in 1790, it had been extensively restored and renovated by Knox Smith to provide Bettina with the best blend of historic charm and modern function.

Knox was Linc's best friend. A real estate developer, he'd worked hard on transforming the city of Charleston to its former glory. During their twenties, the two bachelors had spent a significant amount of time tearing up the town and breaking hearts. They'd been quite the dynamic duo.

Twenty minutes later, as he entered his mother's parlor, Linc was once again struck by a wave of gratitude that he could do this for her. She was in her element, holding court from a comfortable chintz armchair by the fireplace.

"Good afternoon, Mother. You look splendid today." Linc crossed the room and bent down to kiss Bettina's soft cheek.

He lingered a second and inhaled her rose perfume, smiling at the memory of snuggling on her lap when he was young. Even after his sister came along and monopolized their mother's time, Bettina always made sure she hugged her son before he went to bed.

"Of course I look splendid," his mother shot back tartly, her eyes twinkling. "I had a facial yesterday that took ten years off."

She squeezed his hand and then indicated the chair beside the sofa where she sat. On the side table was a silver bell. She picked it up and gave it a vigorous ring. A thin woman with gray-streaked blond hair appeared at the parlor door.

Dolly had been with his mother for ten years and the two women had developed a snarky, passive-aggressive relationship that worked for them. As outwardly hostile as his mother was toward the housekeeper, Linc was certain Bettina secretly enjoyed the ongoing battle. In turn, Dolly wasn't without a spine and often gave as good as she got. Linc didn't understand why she stayed. Dolly could have found less stressful employment in a dozen homes.

"Linc needs a martini," his mother proclaimed.

"No, thank you. Just some sparkling water with a lime." He bit down on the admonition that it was too early to start drinking, knowing his mother would simply ignore him.

"I'll have a bourbon with ice. Make sure you use the good stuff." Before Dolly was out of earshot, Bettina turned to Linc. "She's been giving me some swill she claims is from Grady's distillery. As if I haven't been drinking bourbon all my life and wouldn't know the difference."

Grady was Linc's cousin on his mother's side. Now that bourbon had been "rediscovered" by the masses, the trend seemed to be everyone with a little pocket change slapping a label on a barrel and calling it craft bourbon. Linc considered most of it swill. However, after attending one of Grady's tasting parties, Linc had been impressed enough to back his cousin's venture. So far, Grady hadn't gone bankrupt, so Linc figured his cousin must be doing something right.

"Tell me about your dinner party tomorrow night," Bettina said, turning her bright blue eyes on Linc. "Who all is invited?"

"The usual suspects. Knox, Sawyer, Austin, Roy, Grady and a few others. There will be twelve of us altogether."

His mother reeled back in dismay. "Did you invite any girls besides your sister?" Bettina had been unhappy when he started dating London and positively mortified when they got engaged. This time around he knew she intended to steer him toward a more appropriate choice, preferably a young woman whose Charlestonian roots went as deep as his own.

"She's promised to bring six friends so it'll be even numbers."

His mother had a knack for radiating displeasure without moving any of her facial muscles. "You can't let your love life be decided by your sister's random friends."

"I also can't let my love life be decided by my mother's social aspirations for me." He smiled to take any sting out of the words.

Bettina waved her hand as if she was shooing away a fly. "You have a duty to this family to marry well and have children who will carry on the Thurston name."

Seriously, Mother?

There was a time, after Linc's father was caught embezzling and went to jail for five years, that Bettina had cursed the Thurston name. Linc wisely chose not to point this out to her.

"If you don't ease up on my search parameters," Linc muttered, "I'm going to die childless and alone." He made it sound as if he was kidding, but in truth, he wasn't sure if he trusted himself to fall in love with the right woman.

Look at the mistake he'd made with London. He still wasn't clear if what he had felt for her was love, or if she'd simply won him over with her beauty, determined personality and competitive spirit.

They'd met when he was in his late twenties and starting to lose interest in the never-ending merry-go-round of women in and out of his life. He'd spotted her at a charity event she'd organized and been drawn to her beauty. That she'd also been blessed with brains and ambition had struck the right chord with him, and within a month, they'd become exclusive.

"Don't be ridiculous," his mother said. "I can name a dozen women who would be perfect for you. In fact, as soon as you leave, I'm going to make a list and invite them to a party here in a couple weeks. That girl of yours is a dream…"

While his mother prattled on, Linc grappled with his discomfort over being the main event at one of Bettina's gatherings. Part of him wanted to make his mother happy after everything she'd endured in her life, but he wasn't about to surrender his freedom unless the woman was nothing short of spectacular.

"…Claire?"

His heart gave a little jump as his mother mentioned the young widow. "What about Claire?" Had she guessed his ever-increasing preoccupation with the woman who worked for him?

"Can I borrow her to cater the party?"

His mother's request reminded Linc that his attraction to Claire needed to end. In any other town they could make it work, but in Charleston, where his mother was so entrenched in her family history, a Thurston and an outsider could never happen. Especially when that outsider was also his housekeeper.

"I'll ask her if she's willing," he said, his tone subdued.

"Wonderful. Send her by early next week so we can discuss the menu."

To Linc's relief, Dolly announced lunch a few minutes later. He could tell that the wheels were spinning in his mother's head. As the food was being served, Bettina demanded pen and paper so she could write down the list of appropriate women she intended to introduce to him.

Linc sipped tomato bisque soup and devoured curried shrimp and egg salad sandwiches in silence while his mother remarked over each woman she intended to include. Bettina made it sound as if they were candidates for him to choose from, but he knew the truth: the party would be one big husband hunt, with him, the unlucky prey.

The situation wasn't unfamiliar. Since high school, women had been throwing themselves at him. And once he'd started playing pro baseball, he couldn't turn around without a beautiful woman hitting on him. But those women weren't usually of a sort he took seriously. After a one-night stand or a brief hookup, they drifted out of his life.

This was different. His mother intended to toss him into a pit with a voracious group of marriage-minded females. He doubted he'd come out intact.

So Linc started making his own list of eligible guy friends whom he could persuade to attend to take some of the focus off him. He knew twenty who fit the bill, but the question remained: How many could he convince to attend? They had to realize what his mother was up to.

Over dessert, his mother turned her attention to gossiping about her neighbors and the antics of her former in-laws. There was little new or surprising in what she had to impart, and Linc let the white noise of her voice flow over him while he wondered if Claire had found the earrings and if she liked them.

The unique asymmetrical style wouldn't have suited most of the women he knew, but Claire would appreciate them. She had a quirky Bohemian style, a product of her growing up in California. He hoped she liked the interesting shapes and blue-green color of the stones. Would she guess that remembering turquoise was her favorite color had prompted him to choose this particular pair? Doubtful. He'd been doing a good job hiding his interest in her.

"I'm thinking about getting remarried." His mother's abrupt declaration jolted Linc out of his musings.

"Remarried?" he echoed dumbly, his thoughts scrambling to catch up. "I didn't realize you were seeing anyone."

"I'm not. At least, not exclusively."

Linc frowned. What did that mean? He narrowed his eyes and focused all his attention on his mother. "So you're seeing several men?"

He couldn't reconcile this with his mother's behavior after her husband went to jail, was released and then abruptly filed for divorce. After years of devoted support, Bettina had been blindsided, causing Linc to sever all contact with his father. Ever since, she'd kept a low profile and hadn't really dated, at least as far as Linc knew.

"Not in the way you're implying." His mother's tone sharpened. "I entertain gentlemen from time to time. They come by for lunch or cocktails. Sometimes dinner."

"Where do you meet these men?"

Bettina preened, obviously appreciating her son's alarm. "Is that concern I hear in your voice?"

"Of course it's concern. You can't just drop something like this on me." Linc shook his head. Today's lunch was certainly eventful. "Are you sure they're interested in you and not just—"

"I suggest you don't finish that statement," his mother said, eyes narrowing. "I'm an attractive woman."

"Yes, you are," he murmured.

Bettina rolled on as if he hadn't spoken. "With needs."

"Please, no more," he begged, cringing away from thoughts of his mother having any sort of sex life.

Bettina continued, either oblivious to or not concerned about her son's sensibilities. "You've been so busy with your life that you haven't paid all that much attention to what's going on with me or your sister." His mother paused for a beat. "Did you know she's been seeing someone?"

Linc shook his head, struck dumb by the twists and turns the conversation was taking. "Anyone I know?"

Bettina shook her head. "You know she doesn't tell me anything about her personal life."

Sawyer had learned that lesson watching their mother meddle in his life.

"Then how do you know?" he asked.

"A mother knows when her children are up to something, and Sawyer is definitely acting like she has a secret."

As the implication of Bettina's words hung in the air, Linc hoped that wasn't true, because the last thing he needed was for his mother to find out about his feelings for Claire.

Claire stood in the middle of The Market on Market and gaped at the woman who'd just issued such a provocative statement. With her brain short-circuited as the implications sank in, her entire body remained frozen. But as she watched Everly's gaze flick to Honey and narrow as if assessing the toddler from a fresh perspective, Claire regained her wits.

"Me?" she burst out, half laughing, half in irritation. "And Linc Thurston? That's absolutely ridiculous."

While Claire wasn't surprised the woman knew all about Linc's severed relationship with London, she was stunned to be thought of as the reason for the breakup.

Everly's perfectly arched eyebrows rose. "Is it?"

"You have it all wrong. I'm his housekeeper." Not to mention she was the furthest thing from Linc's type.

He was attracted to beautiful, elegant women with money and social graces. A man of his wealth and social position needed an accomplished hostess at his side, someone of equal standing in Charleston. His mother would demand nothing less.

"You think it's unusual for a man to have an affair with his hired help?" Everly asked, her voice sly and full of salacious undertones.

Claire considered all the scandals that had arisen surrounding famous men and their female staff. From nannies to assistants to housekeepers. She supposed it made sense for the woman to jump to the wrong conclusion about her.

"Linc is not like that," she said with mounting dismay.

Why was she bothering to defend herself and Linc when this woman was so far off track, not to mention completely out of line?

"You're female. And you're pretty. I'm sure you can understand how it looks."

The woman's insistence made Claire ponder her interactions with Linc. Sure, they had an occasional flirtatious exchange, such as the one this morning about her skinnydipping in his pool. Sudden heat flooded Claire's cheeks as she thought about how it could've been misinterpreted.

"He's never been anything but professional with me."

"Of course." But Everly didn't sound at all convinced.

Claire was on the verge of letting it go when she remembered that in Charleston's tight community even a whiff of scandal could be damaging. She sucked in a breath for one final clarification.

"Linc is surrounded by beautiful, interesting women all the time," Claire said evenly, keeping her features composed as she hit the woman with a final double-barreled shot. "I clean his toilets. There's nothing beautiful or interesting about that." Then, barely giving the woman a chance to let that sink in, she added, "Now, if you'll excuse me, I need to finish my shopping."

Claire pushed the cart forward. To her dismay, the woman wasn't giving up. Everly's heels clicked on the tile floor as she moved to intercept Claire once again. She snagged the shopping cart with one manicured hand and Claire noticed how she appeared contrite.

"I'm sorry. I was out of line to say what I did. Let me take you to lunch to apologize."

The urge to laugh almost overpowered Claire. She imagined how out of place she and Honey would be sitting down to a meal with Everly in one of the sophisticated restaurants that the elegant woman no doubt frequented.

"You don't need to do that."

"I feel terrible. Let me make it up to you."

The whiplash of the woman's abrupt turnaround left Claire feeling off balance. "I don't think so."

"Let me give you my card. You can call me when you have some free time."

With Everly's business card burning in her pocket, Claire finished her shopping. It had been easier to accept the card and agree to call the attractive blonde woman than to continue to put her off.

Anxiety had eased its grip on Claire once she got in line to pay for her groceries. Really, it was almost funny that anyone could imagine she was attractive enough to catch Linc's attention. The idea was absurd. By the time Claire exited the grocery store, with a small bag of items on one hip and her daughter on the other, she'd chalked up her encounter with Everly to one of the pitfalls of working for someone in the public eye.

Claire stored the groceries in her trunk before settling Honey into her safety seat in the back seat of her ten-year-old gray Saab. The car had taken her from California to Charleston when she fled with her daughter after Jasper's parents started threatening her with a custody suit. To obscure her trail and make it hard for them to know where she'd gone, Claire had sold her former car and paid cash for the Saab. A friend had helped by registering the car in his name. Claire probably should've ditched the Saab when she reached Charleston, but she felt unaccountably secure after she reached the city.

In an odd way, when she'd exited I-26 and driven south on Market Street all the way into historic downtown Charleston, she'd been overwhelmed by a sense of coming home. Which was ridiculous, because until a little over a year ago, the farthest east she'd ever been was Las Vegas.

During the short drive back to Linc's house, she shook off the eerie feeling from the odd encounter with Everly. In a town like Charleston, it made sense that most people would feel as if they had some connection to Linc and speculate on the reason behind his abrupt breakup with London.

He was a media darling. Not only was he a famous baseball player, handsome, wealthy and from one of Charleston's older families, but he was also an active philanthropist, offering his personal and financial support to numerous charities. His innate charisma dominated whatever room he walked into. In short, Linc was a colossal celebrity.

"People make up all sorts of absurd things," she remarked to her daughter as she unbuckled Honey from her seat and lifted her out.

As soon as Honey's sandal-covered feet touched the brick pavers of Linc's driveway, the toddler made a beeline for the kitchen door, leaving her mother to follow more slowly after collecting her bags. In addition to grocery shopping, Claire had purchased flowers and containers for centerpieces. She intended to make those up this afternoon because tomorrow would be reserved for cooking.

"Mama!" Honey's excited call pulled Claire away from the refrigerator, where she'd been putting food away.

"What, baby?"

Honey's bare feet slapped the kitchen's wood floor as she brought her mother a small flat box of a size perfect for earrings. "Blue."

"Yes, it is. Where did you find that?"

Honey pointed to the center island. Claire glanced over and spied a white envelope. She took the present from her daughter's hand and carried it back to where Honey had found it. She set the box on the envelope and her daughter immediately protested.

"No!"

"That's not ours to play with."

"Mama." Another thing Honey had inherited from her father was stubbornness. The toddler marched back to the island, climbed up on the nearest chair and once again reached for the present. "Mine."

As quick as her daughter could be, Claire had learned to be quicker. She scooped up the envelope and present, depositing them into the upper cupboard that held everyday dishes. Honey set her hands on her hips and scowled her displeasure.

Lips twitching, Claire turned her back to her daughter and began making her lunch. It was almost one and her errands had taken longer than she'd expected. Not until Honey sat at the kitchen table with turkey, cheese and apple slices did the two-year-old's sour expression ease. With her daughter occupied, Claire focused on the centerpiece arrangements. During the two-year period in her life when she'd been attending culinary school, to make ends meet Claire had gone to work for a florist, first as a delivery driver and then as an arranger.

"Nice flowers," she heard Linc say from the back door.

Claire looked up from her project and spied him entering the kitchen. Her heart gave a foolish little jump. He looked handsome in his navy blazer with the delphinium-blue pocket square that matched his eyes.

"Thank you, but the arrangement is far from done."

"I like the colors you picked out." He approached the center island where she was working and selected a stem of pale gold freesia. Setting the horn-shaped flowers to his nose, he inhaled. "This one smells good."

"I thought the color and shape would go nice with the Golden Forest china. What do you think?"

Although Claire doubted Linc cared which of his three sets of dishes she chose, talking—or babbling, in this case—kept her from doing something foolish, like blurting out the story of her encounter with Everly.

"And the Waterford, of course," she continued. "Your mother would approve. What do you think?"

She clamped her lips together to shut down the flow of words, all too aware that Linc was eyeing her. Damn that woman in the grocery store for filling her head with thoughts of being in a steamy affair with Linc.

"Sounds like you have everything in hand." He glanced at the spot where Honey had found the jewelry box and envelope and then surveyed the rest of the kitchen.

When his brows drew together, Claire realized what he must be looking for. "I put it in the cabinet," she explained, wiping her hands on a dish towel before crossing to where she'd secured the present. "Honey was all over it. We've been working on her colors and she noticed the box was blue."

"Blue," Honey chortled from the kitchen table, clapping her hands enthusiastically. "Mama. Down."

"Finish your lunch, baby." Claire retrieved the box and envelope and extended it to Linc.

"You didn't open it?" he asked in surprise.

"No." Claire gave her head a vigorous shake. She'd never step across the line like that. Was that what he'd made of her bout of awkward chattiness earlier? That she'd snooped and felt guilty about it? She placed the gift on the counter in front of him and returned to her flower arranging. "I'd never do something like that."

"Mama. Down."

A weird buzzing filled Claire's ears, distorting her daughter's voice, as a lazy smile played over Linc's lips. He set his hand on the counter and leaned in her direction.

"Did you even look at the envelope?"

A lock of blond hair fell across his forehead, lending a boyish charm to his already overwhelming handsomeness. She realized his effect on her had grown stronger lately.

What would it be like to have him close his arms around her and kiss her hard and deep? Just the thought of being crushed between his ripped body and the unyielding kitchen cabinets made her blood heat. She reflexively clamped down on the rose stem she was holding and winced as a thorn pricked her thumb.

"No," she said, sticking the injured thumb in her mouth. "Should I have?"

"Mama!" Honey was rocking in her booster seat, demanding that Claire release her.

"It's for you."

Her stomach dropped to her toes at his sly grin. He'd

bought her a gift? Why would he have done that? From his triumphant expression, he was obviously pleased with himself. Despite her lingering discomfort from Everly's scandalous assumptions, Claire found herself smiling back at Linc with no clear understanding why.

"For me?" In her bewilderment, she sounded like a complete chowderhead.

"Your name is on the envelope, isn't it?"

"It is?" Her pulse jerked in an erratic rhythm as she shifted her gaze to the small box and envelope.

He tapped the center of the paper where *Claire* was scrawled in Linc's familiar handwriting. "It is."

"I don't understand." The jewelry box felt heavy in her hand.

"You've been working for me for a year. I bought you something to celebrate your anniversary."

"You didn't have to do that." But she was thrilled that he had and more than a little relieved that was all there was to it.

She'd enjoyed working for him this past year. His house had become her sanctuary and she'd do anything to protect that. Feeling safe was a luxury she hadn't known since she'd become pregnant with Honey.

"I wanted to." His deep voice resonated through her. "Why don't you take a look at what I got you. I've been dying to see if you like it."

Something in his tone made her skin flush hot.

"Of course I'll like it." Telling herself it was silly to feel so breathless over an anniversary token didn't stop the flutters in her stomach. "You have wonderful taste."

Linc was always doing something nice for the women in his life. His mother loved to collect cloisonné pillboxes, so he was always on the lookout for them. And whenever he visited her house, he never showed up empty-handed. It might be a bouquet of flowers, sugar-glazed pecans or a bottle of craft bourbon—Linc was always thinking of what Bettina might enjoy.

He'd been the same way with London. In her case, his purchases had been expensive pieces of jewelry or designer handbags. His sister liked gadgets, so whenever Linc ran across something new and innovative, he made sure Sawyer got one.

Conscious of Linc's keen blue eyes on her, Claire started with the card. As she glanced at the cover, some of the tightness in her throat eased. He'd chosen something funny, a drawing of a dog wearing a big smile above the words *Thank You*. But when she flipped open the card and glanced at what he'd written, tears stung her eyes.

You've been a bright spot in my life for the last year. Thanks for all you've done. —Linc

"That's so nice," Claire croaked out, blinking rapidly to clear her vision. "Honey and I have really appreciated how kind and generous you've been. Not to mention patient." She indicated the kitchen table, where her daughter was throwing herself back and forth in the chair and chanting to get down.

"It's been great having you here." He went over to lift Honey into his arms. "Both of you."

Claire refused to give in to the warmth suffusing her at the sight of her daughter in Linc's arms. It wasn't an unusual occurrence. Linc always enjoyed Honey's company. So why today was Claire overwhelmed by sentiment? Because that woman at the grocery store had drawn a startling connection between her and Linc? Or was it the notion Everly had put in Claire's head that she was in a vulnerable position living and working in the same house as a man as attractive as her boss? Not that he would ever take advantage of her. But what if it wasn't a matter of him taking advantage?

For the first time since Jasper had left for his final overseas tour, Claire confronted the ache building in her body. She'd been doing a decent job of focusing on Honey's needs and ignoring her own—especially while Linc was engaged to London. He'd been completely off-limits while he'd belonged to another woman.

But now that Linc was single, parts of Claire felt reckless and uninhibited. She longed to wrap her arms around Linc's neck and plant hot kisses on his sensual lips. To feel his strong hands slide over her heated flesh.

She gulped as her body was battered by cravings she suspected Linc could satisfy only too well. Damn it. She was falling for her boss. This would not do.

Three

Silence reigned in the gourmet kitchen as Linc freed the toddler from her booster seat and set her on her feet. Giggling, Honey clung to his leg for a couple seconds before racing into the sunroom, where her toys were kept.

When he turned back to Claire, he saw that she was staring at the contents of the jewelry box. Her slight frown worried him.

"You don't like them?"

At his question, Claire took a couple breaths and seemed to gather herself. "It's too much."

Linc chuckled warmly. "I assure you it's not nearly enough."

"They're beautiful."

"You like turquoise, right?"

For a span of a few heartbeats, Claire seemed to stop breathing. Had it been too much that he'd not only remembered her favorite color, but also that he'd found her something quirky to match her style?

"I've never seen anything like these," she murmured.

"I got them at that boutique Sawyer's friend owns.

A local artist makes them. Each pair is one of a kind. I thought you'd appreciate that."

"I do." A smile accompanied her words, but it lacked something, making Linc frown.

"You're sure you like them? I have the receipt if you want to return them and choose something else." Hopefully she wouldn't. He wanted her to wear something he'd picked out for her.

"I'd never do that," she rushed to assure him. "They're beautiful and I'll treasure them." As if to indicate the conversation was at an end, she set the top back on the box and put it aside. "Thank you."

Linc wondered if the earrings were destined for a drawer, never to see the light of day again. His mood dipped. This wasn't at all the outcome he'd been hoping for. He wanted her to love the earrings and think of him every time she wore them. Each time they tickled her neck, he'd imagine the contact was his lips grazing across her soft, fragrant skin. If he couldn't touch her, he wanted something from him to caress her.

"You're not going to wear them?" He couldn't stop himself from asking the question.

She shook her head. "They're too fancy for every day."

"Then you'll wear them tonight when I take you and Honey out for dinner."

She looked appalled. "Dinner? Tonight?"

"Part two of your anniversary celebration."

"But I have so much to do to get ready for tomorrow night's dinner party." She gestured to the flowers. "Why don't I make something and we can eat here."

"I don't want you cooking or cleaning up." He assumed she'd appreciate eating a meal she hadn't prepared. "Let me give you a break from all that. A thank-you for all you've done for me."

Her mouth opened and closed as if she wanted to continue arguing. At last, she nodded. "May I pick the place?"

"Of course. Where would you like to go?"

"There's a seafood restaurant by Wappoo Creek I've been dying to try."

"If it's seafood you want, the yacht club has a fantastic restaurant."

When her eyes widened in dismay, Linc wondered what was wrong.

"I'd really rather not go there." Her chin lifted and her body language screamed determination. "And you said I could choose wherever I wanted." When he nodded, she relaxed. "Besides, I'd rather go somewhere more kid-friendly, since Honey is coming along."

"There are always families eating at the yacht club. You don't need to worry about Honey being out of place."

She shook her head. "How was lunch with your mother?"

Her change of subject reminded him of his mother's request. He grimaced.

"She wants to throw a party and asked if you could cater it."

"Of course." Even as she spoke, her gaze grew unfocused. The wheels were already turning as she sorted through what treats she might prepare. "When is the party?"

"Two weeks."

Another woman might have protested, but Claire merely nodded. "What's the occasion?"

"Nothing special." No need to explain that his mother intended to throw him to the wolves. "She just wants to invite some friends over."

"Did she mention how many people?"

"Not really." He sounded positively grim.

Claire gave him a curious once-over before saying, "I'll give her a call and discuss the particulars."

"If it gets to be too much, let me know. I don't want you feeling overwhelmed."

"Don't worry." She dismissed his concern with a flick of her hand. "Steve and Jenny will be here for your party tomorrow. I'll ask them if they're available. It's a little last-minute, but if they're busy, I'm sure they'll know some other people who could help serve." Claire glanced at the flowers on the counter. "Now, I'd better get back to these. I have lots to do before tomorrow night."

"Dinner at six?" Linc proposed, naming an earlier time than he usually ate so they could have a leisurely meal and still get home for Honey's bedtime.

"Sure. That will be fine."

Nodding, Linc headed for the stairs. With a packed schedule from February to October, he should have appreciated the downtime during off-season. Instead, he chafed at the inactivity. It gave him too much time to think.

Lately, he'd been preoccupied with life after baseball. He'd had a great run, but he was going to be thirty-four when his contract was up. Despite the fact that his performance hadn't slowed, at that age, there was no way he would get another big deal. Nor was he even sure he'd still be playing for the Barons. How much longer did he think his career in the major leagues was going to last?

So what was he planning to spend the rest of his life doing? It wasn't as if he needed the money. Even after taking care of his mother and sister, funding the charities he worked with, and buying and restoring his house, he'd spent only a small percentage of his millions. Most of the money went into investments that would sustain him long past his contract's end.

What he needed was to find something that inspired him. Because when baseball no longer consumed his life, he was going to go crazy. He envied Knox's passion for restoring Charleston's historic properties and his love of sailing, both locally and all over the world. Linc had joined Knox on several adventures but preferred a spacious suite on land to the claustrophobic quarters of a sailboat.

Knox's face appeared on the screen of Linc's phone, as if his thoughts had summoned his friend. He answered the call.

"What's up?"

"My afternoon appointment canceled," Knox said, sounding chipper. "Want to hit the batting cages so I can give you a few tips? Maybe you can bring your average up next season."

Linc grunted good-naturedly as he took the hit. He'd been in a slump for the last four weeks of the season. All the sports commentators pointed to his broken engagement as the reason, but that had been the cure, not the cause of his problem.

"Sure," he said. "I need to change. Meet you in thirty?"

"See you then."

An hour later, as he took his turn with the pitching machine, Linc felt some of his tension melt away. Playing baseball had always let him escape whatever troubled him. It had been a godsend when his father went to jail and then divorced Bettina, abandoning the three of them to start a new life. Sometimes Linc wondered if he would have been good enough to make it in the majors if he hadn't practiced so much back then.

He'd devoted every spare second to batting practice and perfecting his fielding techniques. Granted, he'd been endowed with a great deal of natural talent as well, but mostly he attributed his success to hard work and determination.

"Want to grab a beer after this?" Knox asked as they exchanged places.

"Can't."

Knox shot him a look. "Got plans?"

"I'm having dinner…" Linc paused, gripped by a sudden reluctance to tell his best friend about the anniversary dinner with Claire. He didn't want to hear Knox's opinion on taking the beautiful widowed housekeeper and her adorable toddler out to dinner.

"Anyone I know?" Knox quizzed, his tone sly.

"It's not like that," Linc countered. As much as he hated keeping Knox in the dark, Linc didn't want to get into a huge discussion about Claire. Deciding a subject change was in order, he steered his best friend on to the topic he loved best. "How's the King Street project coming along? Have you got the plans approved yet?"

Six months ago Knox had purchased a building in the heart of the business district and was in the process of getting the permits to turn it into a ten-unit luxury condo complex. He'd paid four million for the property, and at the moment it was occupied by college students.

Working with their friend Austin's architectural firm, he'd commissioned plans that would include two private roof decks, as well as amenity space that would hold up to forty-eight people in the rear. Built in 1947, the building wasn't a historic property, but the location offered an opportunity for people to buy in the downtown area and that was always a draw.

"Not yet. The BAR requested we tweak a couple things on the rooftop decks before they'd give the go-ahead." The Board of Architecture Review met only twice a month, so the approval process was never speedy. "We're slotted into the agenda for next week, so hopefully the third time's the charm."

Knox didn't sound particularly stressed about the delays. They were the norm when doing any construction or development in the old city and the historic district. In fact, as frustrating as the board could be as they scrutinized projects from a dozen different angles, Linc knew

Knox appreciated the board's dedication to preserving Charleston's past.

Of course, there was the other, less sentimental motivation for keeping the romance of Charleston's historic district alive: tourism. The city survived on its five million visitors each year who brought in nearly four billion dollars in revenue. And the number-one reason cited for visiting Charleston was the city's history and historic sites, followed by restaurants and local cuisine.

"I hope you get the approval this time around," Linc said.

Knox nodded. "Are you still planning on making the hunting trip?" Knox's family owned a large plantation a couple hours west of Charleston. Each fall, Knox brought a handful of his friends there for a weekend of deer hunting.

Linc cursed. Until now, he hadn't realized that the hunting trip and his mother's party were happening at the same time.

"I'm going to have to skip it this year. My mom's decided to host a party and wants me to attend."

"Can't you tell her you already have plans?"

"Not exactly." Linc was starting to understand how the deer must feel as Knox's buddies gathered for their weekend of sport. "I'm afraid the party is about finding someone for me to date."

"I'm not surprised," Knox said with a broad grin. "She wasn't too happy when you picked London. I'm sure she'll make sure every woman there will be perfect for you."

"Their pedigrees will be everything she could ever ask for," Linc replied. "As for whether they'll be perfect for me...that remains to be seen."

Claire noticed a slight tremble in her hands as she dressed Honey in a new outfit to go out to dinner with Linc. Excitement raced through her body, bringing a sparkle to her eyes and color to her cheeks. She'd noticed the betraying effect while applying eyeliner and sweeping brick-red gloss across her smiling lips. It was impossible to subdue her high spirits despite several reproachful warnings to herself.

This was just a casual dinner between a boss and employee to celebrate one year of employment. Common enough in a professional setting. Nothing to get giddy over. Yet scolding herself didn't settle her jittery nerves. Feeling this way would only bring her trouble. Plain and simple, she found her boss attractive, and instead of shutting her emotions down, she reveled in the thought that they were going to spend the evening together.

Fight it though she might, Claire had always been led by her emotions. If she'd done a better job listening to logic, she might have avoided getting involved with Jasper. On the other hand, whatever mistakes she'd made with him had given her Honey, and she wouldn't trade her daughter for anything. Still, in the past few years, she'd become more cautious when following her heart.

"There," she told her daughter, stepping back to admire the pale blue sundress covered in bright butterflies she'd recently bought. "You look so nice."

A quick glance at the clock showed they were running late. Claire twisted her daughter's hair into a loose topknot and fastened a bow. She felt a twinge at how adorable the two-year-old looked. Honey's hair had the perfect length and texture to do all sorts of fun braids and updos, and when Claire had time, she enjoyed experimenting with ideas she gleaned off the internet.

"Can you play with your toys for a couple minutes while Mama gets dressed?"

Honey nodded and headed toward the books that lined the lower shelf of the nightstand in her room.

Claire headed next door to slip into the dress she had

laid out. It was a simple short-sleeved dress, the color of wisteria. She fit her feet into a pair of beige sandals and snagged a white sweater out of her closet in case she needed it.

In less than five minutes, she returned to her daughter's room to collect Honey, and the two of them headed downstairs.

Linc awaited them in the kitchen. He wore khaki pants and a navy cotton sweater over a white button-down shirt. The look was perfect for the casual seafood restaurant near Wappoo Creek.

"Oh, good," he said, "you both have sweaters. I reserved a table outside. I thought you might enjoy the view."

"That sounds wonderful."

Linc escorted them out to his car. Earlier he'd borrowed her keys so he could transfer Honey's car seat from Claire's Saab into the back of his white BMW X6. As she slid into the passenger seat, Claire couldn't help but savor the thrill of being enfolded in the soft camel leather. The Saab was in good shape, but it couldn't compare to this sort of luxury.

"All set?" Linc asked, glancing at Claire.

She nodded. As they made their way west on Broad Street, her anxiety began to fade. She and Linc had dined together several times in the year she'd been working for him. Granted, all those times had been impromptu meals in the kitchen or out by the pool, but it wasn't like this was some momentous occasion. It was a work dinner.

"I've been thinking about the party my mom wants to have," he began, breaking the silence as they crossed the Ashley River. "I hope you don't feel obligated to do it."

"Of course not." While Linc was gone for the summer, Claire didn't have a lot to do and she had assisted Dolly with three of Bettina's dinner parties. "I'm always happy to help her out."

"It's extra work and, of course, you'll be compensated."

While she understood what he was getting at and appreciated his attempt to be fair, the conversation did serve to drive home that she worked for him. Maybe this was exactly what she needed to hear. A reminder of their relative positions. He was the boss. She, the employee. It cut the jubilant buzz about their evening nearly in half, so that by the time they reached the restaurant, she'd successfully tamed her wayward pulse.

Linc took charge of getting Honey out of her car seat and carrying her into the restaurant. Although the two-year-old was perfectly capable of walking, Linc always seemed to be in a hurry to get places and her short stubby legs were no match for his long ones.

The hostess led them to a table that overlooked the water. Although called a creek, the average width of the Wappoo was ninety feet. It connected the intracoastal waterways around Charleston. Beyond the weathered wooden railing extended a dock, where several small boats were tied.

Linc settled into his chair, looking completely at home in the casual atmosphere. "I didn't realize they had a dock," he said. "Next time we should come by boat." He noticed her looking at him and cocked an eyebrow. "What?"

"You look like you fit right in."

"Why shouldn't I?"

"This place is a little more casual than what I imagine you're used to."

"You forget I didn't always have money. In fact, I waited tables at a place very much like this the summer before my senior year of high school."

"I have a hard time picturing you waiting tables."

"Why?"

She was used to thinking about him as someone she took care of. It was hard to imagine him taking orders and schlepping food.

"You don't really seem the sort."

"The money was good." He paused and regarded her with a slight frown. "I know what it's like to struggle and worry about taking care of my family."

"I know." But she couldn't picture him as desperate or poor.

"I didn't go to private school. My mom worked hard to take care of Sawyer and me. When I got old enough to pitch in and help, I did." As he spoke, his gaze grew more piercing. "So you see, we're not so different. If I hadn't been good enough to make it in the majors, our paths might've crossed in a restaurant instead." He frowned thoughtfully.

While she wondered what had prompted his change in mood, a waiter approached to take their drink order. When she ordered a lemonade, Linc shook his head.

"What about a glass of wine?" he prompted. "We're celebrating, remember?"

She wasn't sure alcohol was a good idea but didn't want to disappoint him. "What are you having?"

"I'm going to have a beer."

"Make it two." She turned her attention to the menu. "This all looks delicious."

"Is there anything in particular you had in mind?"

"They're known for their steampots," she pointed out, noting there were six to choose from.

"Let's get the Battery Street Bucket."

Naturally, he'd pick the most expensive dish on the menu. Her mouth watered as she scanned what all was included. In addition to shrimp and sausage, the pot contained both Alaskan snow and king crab as well as lobster. It was something she'd never have been able to afford, but since Linc insisted they were celebrating, Claire nodded.

"And how about a dozen raw oysters to start?" he prompted.

"Why not."

When the waiter returned with their drinks, Linc placed their order and Claire selected macaroni and cheese for Honey. Linc insisted they needed a side of hush puppies as well. She laughed as she contemplated how they were going to get through so much food.

"You must be hungry."

"I worked up an appetite at the batting cages with Knox this afternoon." Linc took a long pull from his beer and set the bottle down. "He seems to think that I need the practice because of my end-of-season slump."

"He should be nicer to you. Doesn't he realize you were under a lot of pressure this year because of what was going on in your personal life?"

Linc snorted. "No one cares."

"That's not fair."

"They're not paying me all those millions so I can let a failed romance distract me," he pointed out.

"I suppose not." She pushed her glass around the weathered table. "But you didn't have a failed romance," she countered, unsure where the compulsion to stick up for him was coming from. "You decided things weren't working. It wasn't anyone's fault. Sometimes love dies."

His gaze sharpened. "Are you speaking from experience?"

"Sure." Claire pondered her relationship with Jasper.

"So you were in love with someone before you met your husband?"

Recognizing her mistake, Claire said, "I guess I thought I was."

She hated lying to Linc about being married to Jasper but couldn't change her story a year into her deception. If only she'd thought the whole thing through before deciding life would be less complicated if everyone thought she was still grieving her hero husband. And the truth was, she had moments when she missed Jasper. Or at least the Jasper she'd fallen in love with. The one who'd been a gentle lover and romantic boyfriend.

"You guess?" Linc echoed, his expression curious.

"Sure. I mean, how much does anyone know about being in love when they're still in their teens?"

"How old were you when you met your husband?"

"I'd just turned twenty. It was Mother's Day. He'd come into the florist where I started working after high school, looking for a gift for his mom." She'd thought it was sweet the way he'd considered her opinion on the perfect bouquet.

"Did he sweep you off your feet?"

"No. I was dating someone. And Jasper was almost eight years older than me. That, combined with his military experience, made him seem too mature." Plus, at the time, he'd just gone through a horrendous divorce and wasn't in a place where he was interested in dating. He was more interested in getting Stephanie out of his system with a string of hookups.

"So, what changed?"

"My boyfriend at the time was an immature idiot." She smiled faintly, remembering the day she'd woken up to the fact that she wanted to date someone whose idea of fun went beyond partying and playing video games. "I realized that a man who knew what he wanted and went after it was way more appealing."

"And Jasper wanted you?"

Claire nodded. "He'd made it pretty clear from the start."

"So you fell in love."

Linc made it sound so simple, but Claire couldn't look back on that time without remembering how Jasper had grown edgier each time he came back from an overseas tour. The way he behaved had made her a little afraid to tell him she was pregnant. But once he learned he was going to become a father, he'd gone back to the man she'd first met and had given her hope that he would be able to overcome his PTSD.

"I did." And she had. At least, she'd been in love in the beginning. "It happened pretty fast. Sometimes I think that was due to the fact that he was going to Fort Benning for training in a few months."

"Did you get married before he left?"

"No, we hadn't been together that long and I was in culinary school." Nor had Claire been convinced that she wanted to be a military wife, traveling to wherever her husband was posted, worrying whenever he was deployed.

Suddenly Claire didn't want to talk about Jasper or spin any more half-truths about their relationship. She was overcome by relief as the waiter brought their appetizers and she focused on breaking up a hush puppy so it would cool down enough for Honey to be able to eat it. Several minutes went by before Claire shifted her attention back to Linc.

"I'm sorry if I made you uncomfortable with my questions about your husband," he said, squeezing lemon onto several of the oysters.

"You didn't."

"I don't think that's true."

His ability to read her made Claire wary. At least he didn't know why she was uncomfortable. "It must seem like I can't move on…"

"I can't imagine what it's like to lose someone you love like that." Linc doctored one of the oysters with horseradish and cocktail sauce before lifting the shell to his lips and letting it slide into his mouth. When he set the empty shell down, his eyes glinted with pleasure.

Claire followed his example and sighed in delight as the sharp bite of horseradish mingling with the richness of the oyster lingered on her tongue. "This is exactly what

I imagined when I decided to move to Charleston. Dining on fresh seafood by the water."

"California has water and seafood. What brought you here?"

"Believe it or not, my great-great-grandfather is from Charleston. He left here ten years before the Civil War began and chased gold all the way to California."

"Did he have any luck?"

"A little. But there were nearly a hundred thousand people who descended on California in 1849 alone, and the chances of getting rich weren't all that high. In the end, he decided there was more money to be made in supporting the gold-seekers and married a widow nearly ten years his senior. Together, they ran her hotel business." Claire's lips twitched.

"What?" Linc prompted.

"It's been argued among my family that it might have been more of a gaming establishment or brothel than a hotel."

"You don't say."

"It's pretty scandalous, don't you think? Especially when the story goes that James Robbins came from an elite Charleston family." Claire laughed. "Of course, none of it's true about my great-great-grandfather's background. But it sure makes for a good story."

"What makes you think it's not true?"

"Did you miss the part where James was a scoundrel? He probably told people he was from a wealthy Charleston family so they'd take him seriously as a businessman. At the time, Charleston was one of the richest cities in the country."

"How do you know all this?"

"Grandma Sylvia kept diaries. She and her first husband traveled from Massachusetts in 1848. He died on the way, and when she got to California, she figured out that men coming out of the mountains with gold would want all the creature comforts they could afford."

"You know a lot about this."

"My great-aunt Libby was really into all this genealogy stuff. She was a women's studies professor at Berkeley."

"Did she ever look into James Robbins of Charleston?"

"I don't know. Libby died five years ago."

"You should talk to Sawyer about this. Her friend Ruby likes to dig into old records. Maybe she could find some mention of James."

As a member of the preservation society, Sawyer would be a good resource for such a quest. "I wouldn't want to bother her."

"Are you kidding? One thing about this town is they love their history. I'll bet Ruby would enjoy hearing your story."

Although Claire knew Sawyer wasn't prone to gossip, she didn't want anyone to start poking around her background and discover that she wasn't a widow. The best thing would be to let the whole matter drop, but she knew Linc wouldn't understand why she wanted to do that. Abruptly, Claire wished she'd never said anything about her family.

"I'll give Sawyer a call," she said and hoped her promise would pacify him, because the last thing she needed was for Jasper's parents to find her in Charleston.

Four

Dinner wasn't going quite the way Linc had hoped. Claire had become subdued and distracted after talking about her husband. He'd intended for the evening to be fun and entertaining. Instead, he'd dredged up her past and reminded her of all she'd lost.

How terrifying it must have been for her to lose the man she'd planned to spend the rest of her life with. What must it have been like for her to be widowed with a newborn? Claire didn't talk much about the family she'd left behind in California except to say that she didn't have a relationship with her mother—who'd left when Claire was seven—and that her father had his hands full with three kids from his second marriage.

"You know, it occurs to me that you haven't had any significant time off since you came to work for me," Linc said. "If you want to go visit your family over Christmas or Thanksgiving, I'm sure we could make that work."

Claire's eyes widened and she immediately started shaking her head. "That's really nice of you, but I remember how much you entertained last year, and now that you aren't seeing London, you'll be hosting all the parties."

"I don't have to be the host. My mother is always happy to show off the Mills-Forrest House."

"I wouldn't feel right about it," Claire said, smiling in a way that was both polite and firm. Arguing with her would get him nowhere.

"Fine, not the holidays, then. Maybe you could take some time off in January and go see them."

"I'll think about it."

"You know, Charleston is a great place to visit. You could invite them to come out here and see you."

She was shaking her head before he had even finished speaking. "With the kids in school and all their activities, it's just too hard for them to take time off during the winter. Plus, it's really expensive to fly everyone."

"What about your in-laws? How long has it been since they've seen their granddaughter?"

"Jasper didn't get along with his parents," Claire said in a breathless rush. "And didn't want them anywhere near his daughter. So it's really just Honey and me. She's all the family I need."

As close as Linc was to his mom and Sawyer, his father had been mostly absent during Linc's childhood, so he recognized Claire's reluctance to reach out. Had her family not been there for her after her husband's death? Was a lack of support the reason she came to Charleston in search of her ancestors?

Interesting about her great-great-grandfather's connection to Charleston. Linc didn't have a passion for the city's history like Sawyer and Knox, or his mother's obsession for improving the Thurston family's status in society, but he knew enough that the surname Robbins wasn't familiar. Likely, the entire story was little more than a family legend. Still, it wouldn't hurt to bring the matter to Sawyer's attention. Who knew what his sister might dig up?

As much as Linc wished they could linger over dessert and coffee, Honey was up past her bedtime and she was getting fussy. So he paid their bill and carried the sleepy toddler out to his car. As he buckled her into her safety seat, he considered what a contrast this evening had been to when he and London went out.

First of all, they'd rarely gone out alone. Even when they'd started the evening with a romantic dinner, inevitably the meal was merely a prelude for the main event, a gathering of friends at one of the local bars or the yacht club. Most of the time when they'd gone out, it was to attend a party or charity event. Sometimes it had seemed like the only time he and London were alone was when they were in bed.

While the low-key meal had given him an opportunity to get to know Claire better, he still sensed there was more to her that she didn't want to share. In the year since he'd hired her as his housekeeper, he'd held a picture of her in his head as sweet, earnest and haunted by her husband's death. Tonight's conversation had added dimensions to her personality and raised more questions than it had answered. She wasn't as uncomplicated as he'd thought.

"This was nice," Claire said as he eased the car out of the parking spot and headed for the exit. She sounded relaxed and a bit dreamy. "Thank you for dinner."

"I'm glad you enjoyed it." He had as well. So much, in fact, that he wanted to repeat it. "We should make a habit of it."

They were stopped, waiting for cars to pass so he could merge onto the main road. She turned her head so that she was no longer staring out the passenger window. Her eyes locked on him and he was besieged by the urge to slide his hand under her thick brown hair and draw her closer.

Imagining the softness of her full lips yielding beneath a passionate kiss sent a flare of heat through his body.

"I'm sure you'd much rather be spending your time with your friends," she said and then yawned.

Despite his heightened awareness of the curve of her breasts barely outlined beneath the thin cotton of her sundress, he forced a light laugh. "Am I boring you?"

She covered her mouth and said, "Of course not. I'm just so full. I don't remember when I've eaten so much."

"It was a lot of food."

He tightened his hands on the wheel and told himself to relax. At an opening in the traffic, he sent the car surging forward. When the car was settled into the flow, he glanced at her and noticed her eyes were closed.

"As for spending time with my friends," he continued, "I get more than enough of their company. They like to go out, hit the bars and pick up women. It gets old. One thing I realized about myself after being with London is that I'm looking to settle down and have a family."

In fact, the escalating desire to become a dad had been one of the reasons he'd ended things with London. She'd been very clear that with her event-planning business starting to pick up, she didn't want to disrupt the momentum by starting a family.

"I think that will make your mother very happy," Claire said.

She was right, but he refrained from adding that he had to choose the right woman. And if his relationship with London had taught him anything, it was that making everyone happy was impossible. Dating London had made his mother miserable. His mother's not-so-subtle digs at London's "off" status had irritated him. Having the women in his life at odds was the furthest thing from peaceful. The question he had yet to settle was could he succeed in being happy if he married someone his mother was dead set against?

That was why this attraction he felt for Claire was eating him up. If he pursued her and desire turned to lasting love, there was no way his mother could ever accept that he married not just an outsider, but a penniless one as well. Claire lacked London's confidence and sophistication. Charleston society would eat her alive.

"What my mother doesn't realize is that I'm not interested in any of the women she might choose for me," Linc said.

"Don't underestimate her."

"Charleston has a limited number of old families, and I know nearly all of their eligible daughters."

"Don't forget you've been off the market for several years. Isn't it possible that someone new may have come on the scene? Someone who was previously unavailable?"

"I suppose." Although he wasn't feeling particularly hopeful. "But it's a long shot, don't you think?"

"With that attitude, you're probably right."

"Is that criticism I hear?"

"Of course not. I wouldn't presume…" she trailed off and stared at him with worried eyes.

"Relax. I'm not going to take offense," he told her. "I like to think you and I have become friends. And as such, I hope you feel comfortable telling me the truth."

"Sometimes I don't know how to be around you," she grumbled. "We laugh and get along so well, but in the end, I am your live-in housekeeper. You pay my salary and I don't want to step across a line."

"I'd never fire you because you said something I needed to hear. I'm not like that."

"Well, then, I guess I get to be more blunt." She shot him a wry smile, but her eyes remained cautious. "Just out of curiosity, what would it take for you to fire me?"

"If you were stealing from me."

"I'd never do that."

"Disloyalty." He noticed her confusion and elaborated. "Like if you decided to write a tell-all."

"I'm not sure there'd be any money in it. I think you're an open book. That's one of the things I admire the most about you. Despite the fact that you're a huge celebrity, you don't have any skeletons or dirty laundry in your closet. And I should know, since I clean your house." Her self-deprecating smile faded. "Since we're on the subject of public awareness, I should probably mention something that happened to me earlier today."

"What?"

"I met a woman at the grocery store who thought I was the reason you broke up with London."

Claire's declaration slammed into him like a fastball to the temple. At first, the words bounced around his stunned brain, but then he started to consider the implications.

"Do you know who she was?"

"Everly…" Claire shook her head. "I can't remember her last name, but she gave me her card." She reached into her purse and pulled out a small white business card. "Everly Briggs."

He tried to recall if he'd ever heard of her before. "Why would she say something like that?"

"I don't know." Scarlet swept up Claire's throat and flooded her cheeks. "She stopped me in the grocery store and we were talking about Honey, and then she noticed what I had in my cart and I accidentally told her I worked for you, and then she thought we were having an affair."

Claire ejected the explanation in a rush, not pausing for breath. As she stumbled to a halt, he glimpsed mortification and horror in her eyes, but guilt as well. Suddenly he felt a little light-headed. Because she was so devoted to Honey, he'd always perceived her as a devoted mom, first and foremost. Plus, she was still in love with her dead husband.

So where was the guilt coming from? Did she secretly desire him? The notion delighted him and awakened a whole new realm of possibilities.

"What did you say?" he asked, curious how she'd handled the conversation.

Her lashes flickered. "I told her that was ridiculous. That's not the sort of man you are, and there's nothing going on between us."

"Have you ever considered you're wrong about the kind of man I am?"

"Of course not." She looked startled. "You would never have cheated on London."

"You're right about that. Although, my reputation hasn't always been stellar. Knox, Austin and I used to tear up this town. Drinking. Hooking up with random women."

"But all that was before London. That's not who you are now."

Claire's fierce defense of him made his chest tighten. He doubted she'd rush to champion him if she knew how she'd featured in his dreams in the days and weeks before he'd ended his engagement. Her husband had been a hero. He'd died while serving his country. That man deserved Claire's love. The purity of her heart made Linc want to deserve her.

"Did she believe you?" he asked.

"Not at first, but then I set her straight."

Linc wished he'd been there to hear it. "How did you do that?"

"I explained to her that I clean your toilets and that's far from being romantic." Claire's dry tone didn't quite match the bright color in her cheeks.

"So you didn't clue her in to the skinny-dipping incident?"

"There was no skinny-dipping incident. Whenever I take Honey into your pool, I wear a very conservative one-piece suit." Her eyebrows drew together as she regarded him sternly. "This isn't funny. What if that's what everyone is thinking?"

"So what if it is?" Linc was completely intrigued by what Claire's body language had revealed. He offered her a lazy grin. If the gossip was widespread, they were already perceived as being guilty of having an affair. Part of him wanted to just go ahead and prove everybody right. "I'm sure everyone will congratulate me on my excellent taste in women."

She huffed impatiently. "You should be worried that it will appear as if you took advantage of someone you employ."

"Anyone who knows me will realize I would never do that. If anything happened between us, it would be because you couldn't keep your hands off me." His outrageous words produced a squawk of outrage.

"I am not seeing the humor in this," she said, her annoyance making her look more beautiful than ever.

Seeing that his teasing had taken her past her comfort zone, Linc sobered. "Are you worried about your reputation?"

"I'm your housekeeper. Why would I care what anyone thinks of me?"

"But you do," he guessed and could see from her expression that he was right. "Don't worry. No one who knows you would believe we were engaged in an affair, illicit or otherwise."

"Why is that?" she asked, her voice giving nothing away.

"Because everyone who knows you is aware…" He hesitated to continue, conscious of stepping over a line they hadn't to this point approached.

"Aware of what?"

"Your husband. That he was very important to you."

It occurred to him as he glanced her way, watching emotions play across her features, that he wanted her to deny how she continued to cling to her dead husband's memory. And why was that? As much as he wanted to, pursuing her was a bad idea.

"There are a lot of people who don't know me and will be quick to believe the worst," Claire said.

"Why do you care what those people believe? They are nobody to you."

"I don't. But you should. Those are your friends and neighbors. People in this town who matter."

"You don't think you matter? I do. You and Honey both."

"Well, of course Honey matters to me. And you matter to me. I mean, as my employer," she rushed on. "And your reputation matters to me. It should matter to you as well. Think of what your mother would say if she caught wind of the gossip. The whole thing could blow up into a huge scandal."

"You matter to me, too," he said, ignoring the latter part of what she had said. When she gave a start, he wondered if his stronger feelings had leaked through. "You and Honey. And I don't give a damn about the gossip or what my mother thinks about it."

His phone began to ring and his sister's name flashed on the screen built into the car dashboard. As much as he wanted to ignore the interruption and continue this fascinating conversation with Claire, she'd wonder why he hadn't taken Sawyer's call.

"Hey," he said after keying in the call. "Claire and I are on our way back from dinner at a restaurant near Wappoo Creek."

After a brief pause, Sawyer asked, "You and Claire had dinner together?"

"It's our anniversary," he explained, wishing he didn't have to defend the act of taking Claire and Honey out for a simple meal. "She's been working for me for a year."

"Oh, sure. It's surprising how fast the time goes."

"You have that right. So, what's up?"

"We're finalizing the list of historic homes for our holiday tour and I want to make sure you're still willing to participate."

His sister was an active member of the Preservation Society of Charleston, working tirelessly to promote conservation of the city's historic homes and public buildings. In the fall, they offered several tours of historic homes and gardens. This year they were trying something new: a mid-December tour of homes decorated for Christmas.

"Do you have a date in mind?"

"It's probably going to be the second Saturday in December from two to five. We have six houses south of Broad participating at the moment."

"That should work out okay." Linc glanced at Claire. "Unless you can think of a conflict I've missed?"

Claire had been correct earlier when she'd mentioned how he liked to entertain around the holidays. He intended to host several events in December.

"That date should work," Claire said.

"Wonderful," Sawyer said. "Your house was so beautifully decorated for Christmas last year. I can't wait for people to see it."

When he'd purchased the Jonathan Elliot house several years earlier, the 1830s Greek Revival home from the antebellum period had been in rough shape, needing all new wiring and plumbing. Knox had spearheaded the project, coordinating the contractors, while Bettina had overseen the interior designer and given her opinion on all the finishes. The project had taken in excess of eighteen months and garnered him a Carolopolis Award from the Preservation Society of Charleston.

"You can thank Claire for the festive transformation," Linc said. "It was her vision."

"I'm sure she'll do just as wonderful a job this year," Sawyer said. "I have to run. See you tomorrow night."

"I'm looking forward to it."

Linc ended the call and shot Claire a glance. "No pressure," he said, amused by her scowl. "Just do what you did last year."

"Everyone will expect to be wowed again," she countered. "I have to come up with something even more spectacular."

"Whatever it is, I know it will be perfect."

"Why do you have such faith in me?" she demanded.

Linc shrugged. "You've never given me any reason to doubt you."

Something felt so right about donning her chef whites to prepare the dishes for Linc's dinner party. Claire was a little surprised how much she missed the hectic pace of a restaurant kitchen. Although she'd spent only a few years working alongside some really talented chefs in the San Francisco area, the experience she'd gained was immeasurable. And in moments like this, Claire wondered if she'd been a fool to give it up.

"Wow, it smells incredible in here." Linc's appreciative tones broke through Claire's musings.

Dressed in khaki pants and a pale blue button-down shirt with a white linen jacket and a bright blue pocket square that matched his eyes, Linc looked every inch the elegant Southern gentleman. During her time in Charleston, she'd noticed how the men of this town oozed charm and gracious manners that lulled a woman into thinking they weren't the least bit dangerous, while in fact they were heartbreakers one and all.

Claire doubted Linc had any idea just how devastating he could be to a woman's willpower through the simple act of sauntering into a room. His wavy blond hair was still damp and his elegant clothes couldn't camouflage the raw masculinity of his athletic body. She gulped in reaction to the sex appeal radiating from him.

"You smell pretty good yourself," she murmured, treating her nose to a deep pull of his scent as he came up beside her.

"Thanks, it's Armani's new cologne. They want me as their spokesmodel. My agent thinks I should do it."

"You'd be great." She had no trouble picturing his piercing blue eyes in magazine and television ads, inviting men and women alike to buy.

"I don't know. I've never considered myself a fashion guy."

"Well—" she cast her gaze over him and then zeroed in on his azure suede loafers "—you look pretty fashionable tonight."

He glanced down at himself. "You know my stylist does all my shopping. If it was left up to me, I'd be wearing jeans and a T-shirt."

And look amazingly hot in them. Honestly, the man could wear mud and look great. Sometimes just standing in the same room with all his gorgeous perfection made her ache.

"Is something wrong?"

Claire shook her head and turned her gaze away. "No." A flush crept up her cheeks and she hoped he would attribute it to the heat of the stove.

"Because the way you were staring at me just now…"

"Did you check the dining room to make sure everything looked okay?" It was a lame attempt to deflect his curiosity.

"I'm sure it's fine." Then he lowered his deep voice to a husky rumble that made her stomach drop and finished, "You look really professional in your chef whites."

"Thank you. I hope it's okay that I'm wearing them."

"Of course. You are a professional chef after all."

His nearness and the way his gaze lingered on the spot on her chest where her name was embroidered made Claire's heart bump like carriage wheels over cobblestones. Instinct warred with desire. Torn between stepping away and moving closer, her attention snagged on his lips and the tempting half smile that tugged one corner upward.

Handsome, powerful and forbidden. Any one of these qualities made him irresistible. Combined, they gave him an advantage that was entirely unfair.

"I noticed you're wearing your new earrings."

Linc touched the left one, sending it swinging. When it grazed the side of her neck, she shivered. There wasn't anything intimate in his manner, but her heart still raced with joy and longing.

"I really like them," she breathed, resisting the urge to rub at the goose bumps that had appeared on her arms.

"I'm glad." He dipped his head and peered more closely at the jewelry. "Yesterday, I wasn't sure if I'd chosen the right pair."

"I'm sorry if I seemed less than enthusiastic. I was a little overwhelmed by your generosity and the fact that you remembered my year anniversary." Not to mention there'd been that pesky longing to throw herself into his arms. "I can't believe how fast the time has gone."

"Claire."

Don't look at him. Don't look...

She might as well try to stop the sun from rising. His vivid blue eyes were mesmerizing. While it was true she'd shut down her sexuality, choosing instead to focus on being a mother, her body recognized the signs of sexual interest even as her brain denied it.

Linc, attracted to her?

Ridiculous.

Yet maybe not?

Living in such close proximity had enabled her and Linc to become friends of a sort. After all, Claire was the woman who took care of his house and fussed over him like a mother hen, making sure he ate well and providing a sounding board for him to share his thoughts. And in his vulnerable state after breaking off his engagement, he could feel safe around her because she was just his employee.

And that was all it should be between them.

Besides, she was wary of romantic entanglements after dealing with the way Jasper had changed over the course of their relationship. And Linc wouldn't repeat his mistake of falling for someone his mother didn't approve of. Claire put the brakes on her train of thought.

"I probably shouldn't say this…" He dragged his gaze over her lips.

Her dormant hormones flared to life. She swayed and placed her palm against the cool granite countertop to steady herself.

Falling for Linc was the height of stupidity, but how much harm could there be in tumbling into bed with him? Such an arrangement might benefit them both in the short-term. Besides, the gossip was already circulating about just such a thing. If she was already being blamed, why not actually be guilty.

"Say what?" she asked, losing her fight with temptation.

A knock sounded on the kitchen door. Regret filled her as she took a jerky half step away from Linc.

"That'll be tonight's waitstaff," she said in a breathless rush. "Your guests will be arriving shortly. You should…"

Claire found herself unable to finish the statement. Her thoughts darted and spun, refusing to form any recognizable pattern. "Be ready to greet them," she concluded at last.

Linc's wide grin left little doubt he recognized his ability to fluster her. "I'll go do that."

Claire's knees wobbled as she made her way toward the kitchen door. She'd met the two people working for her tonight when she'd first arrived in Charleston. She and Jenny Moore had become friends and often met for lunch. Steve Henning was Jenny's boyfriend, and on a couple occasions, Claire had agreed to be fixed up with one of Steve's friends so the four of them could double date. While the evenings had been fun, none of the men had appealed to her enough to keep seeing them.

"Thanks for helping me out tonight," Claire said as she invited them into the kitchen.

"We're glad to be here," Jenny replied. She was a bubbly brunette who often spoke for the pair. "I can't believe we're serving for Linc Thurston's dinner party. Is he as gorgeous in person as on TV?"

"You'll have to see for yourself." Claire glanced at Steve to see his reaction but glimpsed only fond amusement on his narrow face as he gazed at Jenny. They really were the cutest couple.

"Steve's nephew gave us Linc's rookie card," Jenny said, reaching into her purse and pulling out a card encased in plastic. "Do you think he'd sign it for him?"

"I'm sure he would." Claire glimpsed a bit of sparkle on Jenny's left hand and gasped. "You two are engaged? When did that happen?"

Jenny was glowing as she glanced up at Steve. "Last night."

"That's amazing." Claire wrapped her arms around her friend and squeezed, before turning to Steve. "I'm so happy for you both."

"We're pretty excited as well," Jenny said.

"Have you set a date?"

"We're thinking next April. Both of us have huge families, so the wedding is going to be big. We'll need lots of time to plan."

As much as Claire could've stood around and listened to Jenny describe her dream wedding, all three recognized they had a job to do. There would be plenty of time to talk after the meal was served and the guests left.

While Claire walked them through her menu and the wines she'd chosen, she noticed a trace of wistfulness threading through her emotions. Although she and Jasper had dated for several years, she'd never enjoyed the type of partnership Jenny and Steve had. Would she ever feel that with anyone? Should she settle for less? The thought didn't appeal to her. Yet she loved being a mom and wanted more children. And as much as she'd adapted to raising Honey on her own, she didn't want to slip up and get pregnant a second time without a solid commitment with the child's father.

The sound of the door chimes came from the front of the house. Linc's guests were starting to arrive. She needed to focus on the meal and push all unprofessional thoughts out of her mind. This proved easy once she heard all the laughter and jovial voices in the dining room. Claire was determined to make her first big dinner party for Linc memorable. She'd spent hours on the menu, deciding what flavor combinations might impress a group of people who were used to the finest.

"They're raving about your lamb," Jenny crowed as she entered the kitchen with an armload of empty plates. "I'd say Linc will be thanking you for making this dinner party memorable."

Claire smiled in pleasure as she assembled the final

course. "I'm really glad. I was nervous that the food wouldn't be up to their regular standards."

"Are you kidding?" Jenny peered over Claire's shoulder as she plated the decadent chocolate cake with pomegranate sauce. "Your food rivals anything these types could find along King Street."

Her friend's praise warmed Claire. "Thanks."

As Jenny departed with the first of the desserts, Steve returned to the kitchen with another empty wine bottle and a message from Linc.

"He asked if you'd come in and meet everyone." When she hesitated, Steve handed her one of the desserts and motioned toward the dining room. "Come on. Take your bow."

Caving to Steve's encouraging smile and her own need to see Linc's reaction for herself, Claire carried in the final dessert plate and placed it in front of Linc. She then stepped back to survey the group.

The assembled guests were dressed for a formal dinner party with the men in suits and ties, while the women donned expensive cocktail dresses and jewelry. They sparkled and glittered beneath the dining room's large chandelier and Claire couldn't help but wonder which of them would be on Linc's arm at the next charity event or at the yacht club, helping him cheer on Knox during the upcoming regatta.

"This is Claire Robbins," Linc said with a smile. His eyes connected with hers, sending a light shiver down her spine. "You can thank her for the delicious dinner."

Claire had paired each course with a separate wine; most of the guests had the relaxed appearance of the mildly intoxicated. Still, she hoped that her food—and not just the wine—had contributed to the convivial atmosphere.

The redhead seated to Linc's right took note of Claire's

chef whites. "Oh, you're a real chef. Where did you learn to cook like that?"

"I attended culinary school in San Francisco," she explained.

"And now you're Linc's housekeeper?" A blond man, his green eyes lazy as he sipped his wine, looked her over as if she was a piece of artwork he was evaluating. "Seems like your skills are wasted on him."

"Claire is a single mom," Linc jumped in before she could defend her choices. "Working for me is a lot less stressful than slaving away in a restaurant kitchen."

"Is that true, Claire?" A man with glasses and dark hair asked. "Is working for Linc as easy as he makes it sound?"

"He is gone over half the year." Claire masked her discomfort with a polite smile. "And I appreciate being able to spend so much time with my daughter."

"Honey is so sweet," Sawyer put in. "She just turned two a few weeks ago."

"I'll bet she's beautiful just like her mother," the blond man said.

"Actually, she takes after her father's side of the family," Claire responded with a polite smile. "Well, I'll leave you to your desserts. I'm glad you enjoyed the meal."

Returning to the kitchen, Claire regarded the dirty dishes piled on the countertops and sighed. She liked maintaining a neat, organized work space and this was far from it. Jenny was rinsing plates in the sink and piling them so they could be loaded into the dishwasher. Fortunately, all the china was dishwasher safe, so the only items Claire had to wash by hand were the antique crystal stemware.

"Thanks for getting this started," Claire said to Jenny.

"Are you kidding? You promised us leftovers. And I want you to know you can hire Steve and me to serve anytime. Linc Thurston is really nice. And most of his friends aren't too bad, either. You're really lucky to work for him."

"I am lucky."

Claire lifted her fingers to touch the earrings Linc had given her, remembering how his eyes had lit up earlier that evening when he noticed her wearing them. Just thinking about it sent her blood thundering through her veins. He'd almost looked...possessive. Which thrilled her even though she recognized the danger inherent in the feeling.

On the other hand, considering how well her food had gone over, perhaps he was a little concerned that one of his friends might try to poach her. The thought pleased her. Not that she'd ever consider leaving Linc. But it gave her ego a bump, thinking her skills might have garnered some interest.

While Steve kept an eye on things in the dining room, Jenny and Claire packed up the leftover food and chatted about Jenny's dream wedding. Claire could picture the low-country wedding on the grounds of an antebellum mansion. The ceremony would take place beneath oak trees dripping with moss, followed by an elegant reception beneath a tulle-draped tent.

"It's going to be beautiful," Claire said with a sigh. "Have you thought about colors yet?"

"I'm thinking a misty blue with accents of pale and bright pink."

"That sounds gorgeous."

"What colors did you have for your wedding?"

On the long trip from California, Claire had prepared for all sorts of questions about her wedding and marriage, so the lie came easily to her lips. "We eloped to Las Vegas and I carried a little bouquet of pink and white roses."

Jenny looked disappointed. "I couldn't imagine eloping. My family would be so disappointed. I'm the only girl, so my momma has been dreaming about my wedding for as long as I can remember."

"It wasn't like that for me," Claire said. "My mom left when I was seven."

And made limited attempts to stay in touch. This was what motivated Claire to devote her energy to Honey. She didn't want her daughter to know the slightest trace of neglect.

"I'm sorry," Jenny said, looking mortified. "I didn't realize that. You don't talk much about your family."

"There's not much to say. I don't speak with my mom and my dad has a wife and kids that keep him really busy." Hearing a trace of sadness in her tone, Claire forced a smile. "I have Honey, and she's all the family I need."

"But what about getting married again?"

"Maybe. I know it would be good for Honey to have a daddy, but I'm not sure I'm ready…" She trailed off and hoped Jenny wouldn't suggest another evening out with one of Steve's friends.

"I'm starting to get the picture."

Claire's gaze snapped to her friend. "What do you mean?"

"You have a thing for your boss. I don't blame you. He's hot. But don't let that get in the way of finding love."

"Linc?" Claire's voice broke a little as she said his name. "That's silly. Sure, he's charming and sweet, but he's way out of my league."

"He's out of nearly everyone's league. Unless you're a supermodel, sports star or a celebrity."

Jenny was right, and Claire considered how earlier she'd imagined Linc was attracted to her. What a ridiculous misconception that had been.

"Linc has nothing to do with my disinterest in hitting the dating scene," Claire said. "I'm just not ready."

"But you have a little crush on him."

Why deny it? "Well, of course. I'd have to be dead not to. But where he's concerned, I have my head on straight."

Five

The dinner party dissolved around ten o'clock with most of the guests departing for The Lucky Mojo, a rooftop bar featuring Cuban jazz music and salsa dancing. It was a favorite spot for their group of friends, who often ended the night there.

To Linc's surprise, Knox chose to stick around and join him poolside for a cigar and a glass of Glenmorangie Signet. Roses, hydrangea and freshly mowed grass scented the November evening. A cool breeze sifted through the crepe myrtle and palm fronds that provided shade for the private garden during the day.

"Nice party," Knox commented, nodding toward the lights still shining in the kitchen.

"Except for Austin and Roy," Linc countered. "Any idea why they were acting like complete assholes tonight?"

"Roy has a thing for Della Jefferson." Knox enjoyed dishing on their friends and could be called on for all the latest drama. "But Austin got there first."

Austin had the money, looks and social position to have any woman in Charleston and used the triple threat to

score as often as possible. Roy was an engineer from Sa-
vannah who'd gone to work with Boeing straight out of
grad school. He liked to party and had been introduced to
Austin, Knox and Linc after his attempt to pick up Sawyer at Burns Alley on King Street had met with devastating failure.

"Got to her as in slept with?" Linc rolled his eyes.
"Didn't he know Roy took her out to dinner last week?"

"You know how Austin is. A different girl every night."
Knox smirked. "He probably didn't even remember Della's
name the next morning."

Linc considered that and wondered when Austin would
stop acting like a frat boy. The guy was turning thirty. It
was time to slow down.

"Do you think Roy is really into her?" Linc quizzed.
"Or is he just pissed that Austin cut in on him again?"

Knox shrugged. "Between the two of them, Roy and
Austin have slept their way through most of the eligible
women in Charleston. I've never known either of them to
get territorial before."

"Then maybe Roy does like her." Linc pondered the
changes in their group dynamic as each of his friends
began to settle down. "Speaking of people hooking up
and/or dating, do you have any idea who Sawyer is seeing?"

Knox didn't miss a beat. "No. As far as I know, she
isn't seeing anyone."

"That surprises me." Linc puffed on his cigar and stared
at his friend. Had Knox's response been too carefully casual? "Usually you know everything that's going on with
our circle."

"She hasn't said anything to me."

Linc considered this. Would Sawyer confide in Knox?
She'd always viewed Linc's friends as a group of party
boys, despite the fact that they all had successful careers.

And she was right. Work hard and play hard. That was their motto.

"I thought maybe you'd heard something. You two cross paths all the time, know the same people. I can't imagine she could keep *everyone* from knowing."

Knox shook his head. "Have you asked her?"

"She told me to mind my own business."

"Shouldn't you do that?"

"I can't. She's seeing someone and doesn't want anybody to know. That piques my curiosity."

More than anything, Linc wanted Sawyer to be happy. It worried him that she was seeing someone and refused to come clean about the guy. What was wrong that she felt compelled to keep him a secret?

"Your sister is an intelligent, savvy woman. She doesn't need you playing interfering older brother."

"I didn't realize you were such a fan of my sister." Linc narrowed his eyes at his friend. "Are you seeing someone?"

"No."

"Have you ever considered dating Sawyer? You two have a lot in common, and I could think of worse brothers-in-law than you."

"Brother-in-law?" Knox looked shocked. "I'm not going to marry Sawyer. What is going on with you? Man, you need to get laid. Stop worrying about everyone else's love life and get one of your own."

Getting one of his own was what he was trying to avoid at the moment. Had he really almost kissed Claire earlier? The temptation to slide his fingers around the back of her neck and pull her close had almost overwhelmed him. The arrival of the waitstaff had happened about ten seconds too soon.

Linc shook free of the memory. "What's wrong with Sawyer?" he demanded, getting the topic back where he wanted it.

"Nothing. She's fantastic."

"But you wouldn't consider dating her?"

"I…" Knox trailed off, eyes wide as he contemplated Linc. "Why are you trying to fix me up with Sawyer?"

"I know you'd treat her well."

"What makes you assume that?"

"Because you know how protective I am of her and that would make you work damned hard to be sure she's the happiest woman on the planet."

"That is exactly why I'd never get involved with your sister. You are such a jerk to every guy she dates. No one is ever good enough. If she is seeing someone, it's no wonder she's keeping it a secret."

"I hate secrets," Linc said, thinking about how his father's unwillingness to come clean about his bad business deals had caused him to sink deeper and deeper into trouble. "Nothing good comes of keeping the truth hidden no matter how bad it is."

"You should talk," Knox said, his tone loading the words with significance.

"What do you mean?"

"Your housekeeper?"

The sharpness of Knox's tone penetrated Linc's good mood. "What are you talking about?"

"Tonight at dinner. I saw the way you looked at her."

"How was that?" he asked lightly as if he didn't want to grab his best friend by his lapels and shake the answer out of him.

"Like you couldn't wait for the rest of us to get the hell out of your house so you could be alone with her."

"That's ridiculous." Linc made a scoffing sound to throw Knox off but saw that his friend wasn't to be deterred. "Claire works for me. That's all there is to it."

"And if she didn't?"

"She's still hung up on her dead husband."

"Are you so sure about that?"

"Yeah." Linc doubted his drawl gave anything away. "Why would you think otherwise?"

"Because there's the way she gobbles you up with her eyes."

Although Linc's heart stopped at Knox's observation, he'd spent enough time in the public eye to keep his expression under control.

"She doesn't." Linc frowned. *Did she?* The thought appealed to him. "You're making stuff up to mess with me."

"Only partially. I wanted to see your reaction."

"And?"

"You might not be sleeping with Claire, but you want to."

"And what's so wrong with that? She's beautiful, sweet, and we get along great." Wait…where was he going with this? Linc was supposed to be coming up with reasons why he didn't want to sleep with Claire.

"She's also your housekeeper," Knox pointed out unnecessarily.

"Men have been known to fall for their secretaries and nannies. Why not a housekeeper?"

Knox's eyebrows shot up. "Fall for?"

"Figure of speech," Linc said with a careless shrug. "Sounds better than 'sleep with.'" He rubbed his face. "Damn. I'm back in Charleston only a few weeks and my Southern manners kick in."

Knox laughed the way Linc had hoped he would, and for a few minutes, they smoked in companionable silence. It couldn't last. Linc could feel his friend's curiosity pressing on him even as he kept his gaze fixed on the tranquil turquoise pool glowing softly a few feet away.

"Why did you really break up with London?" Knox asked.

"I've already told you. Because I wasn't in love with her. And I don't really think she was in love with me."

"What makes you think that?"

Linc shrugged. "She liked the idea of what I represented, an old Charleston family. Ever since her family moved here, they've been trying to crack the 'inner circles' of Charleston society. London wanted to be a debutante and that was never going to happen. But if she married me and we had a daughter, she could live vicariously through her."

"You're not interested in all that stuff."

"I don't really care one way or the other."

"Are you sure about all this? She's been seen out with Harrison Crosby and he's the furthest thing from old Charleston as you can get."

"Trust me. London was obsessed with the whole society thing. So much so that every woman who attended tonight's dinner party has pulled me aside at some point since my engagement ended and given me an earful about my ex-fiancée."

Knox chuckled. "I'm surprised they waited that long."

"What do you mean?"

"A year ago, Augusta and Ruby approached Austin, Roy and me. They wanted us to warn you that London was too focused on your social position. I think they spent quite a bit of time chatting with your mother about it as well."

It wasn't a stretch to imagine how some of those conversations must've gone. Bettina often entertained his friends and saw nothing wrong with cultivating relationships with women she perceived as being more suitable for Linc to marry.

"Did London know that so many of my friends were rallying against her?"

"How could she not?"

That explained a lot of things. As his relationship with London had deepened toward marriage, she'd made it so that he spent less and less time with his old circle of friends. How ironic that the very people she wanted to associate with had shut her out and she'd responded by cutting them off from Linc. It had become a vicious cycle.

"I guess it's better for all of us that we're no longer getting married," Linc said.

"It's certainly better for your housekeeper."

Linc frowned at his friend. "Leave it alone."

"So you're not going after her?"

"No." He stared at the pool. "Maybe if things were different…"

If Claire wasn't still in love with her dead husband.

"You mean if she didn't work for you?" Knox asked.

"Yeah."

"You could always fire her."

Linc gave his friend a rueful grin. "I actually thought about it a couple days ago. But that would probably just make her hate me."

"What if she quit?"

"Why would she do that? She has a swell setup here, and I'm a great boss."

Knox finished off his scotch. "Ever think that Claire might be interested in turning in her French maid costume for a set of chef whites?"

Linc hadn't considered this. In fact, although he'd hired her more for her cooking skills than her cleaning abilities, there hadn't been much opportunity for him to utilize the former in the past year.

"She's happy right where she is."

"Maybe. But Austin was right when he pointed out that her culinary talent is wasted on just you."

"So I'll entertain more."

"Didn't you say she's catering your mother's party in a couple weeks?"

"Yeah. What of it?"

"Augusta cornered Claire just before we left and asked if she could do the food for the function she's coordinating next month for that free medical clinic her cousin volunteers at."

"Did she agree?" It hadn't occurred to Linc that Claire might be interested in picking up some extra work here and there.

"She said she'd think about it and give her a call."

Linc didn't consider himself selfish, but the thought of sharing Claire irritated him.

"Have you considered that you're doing her a disservice by having her as your housekeeper?"

"I guess I haven't."

Until now, he hadn't given it much thought. She seemed happy enough keeping his forty-five-hundred-square-feet home neat and clean. Often she pointed out that his long periods of absence during the spring and summer months enabled her to devote time and attention to her daughter. But now that Honey was getting older, wouldn't she be going off to preschool? Maybe with more free time Claire would start to explore opportunities where she could use her culinary skills.

And if Claire decided to quit and pursue a career as a chef? Linc fought down a rising uneasiness. The idea that his house would no longer ring with Honey's silver giggles or be filled with Claire's beautiful smiles made his gut knot.

"She won't leave me."

"What if she does?"

Something in Knox's tone snagged Linc's attention. He turned from his contemplation of the pool and noted his friend wore a concerned expression.

"She won't."

* * *

With Linc's guests gone, Honey finally succumbed to sleep. Although the rooms Claire and Honey occupied were on the third floor, noise from the boisterous dinner party had filtered up the stairs and the unusual activity in the house meant her curious daughter had resisted settling down for the night. Even though Claire had been the one to finally get Honey to fall asleep, she'd given the babysitter a little extra for her trouble.

Confident Honey was down for the night, Claire descended to the quiet kitchen to survey what still needed to be done. Since they'd finished most of the cleanup, she probably could've left the balance for the morning, but with euphoria pumping through her body on the heels of the successful dinner party, there was no way she was going to be able to sleep.

So, instead of pacing around her room or lying in bed and staring at the ceiling, Claire decided to wash the table linens and put away the crystal and china in the butler's pantry off the kitchen. With Honey's ever-increasing climbing ability, the sooner Claire could secure the breakable items, the better.

Claire padded barefoot into the kitchen. She'd exchanged her chef whites for what served as pajamas for her: a pair of blue-and-green-striped drawstring pants and a light camisole. Because it was cooler downstairs, she'd also slipped on a thin hoodie.

Under-cabinet lighting softened the stark white cabinetry and marble countertops, giving the kitchen a cozy feel. When Linc wasn't home, Claire often put Honey to bed and then came back to the first floor to fix a cup of herbal tea or enjoy a rare glass of wine. As much as she loved spending time with her daughter, Honey's high energy level left her needing a little peace and quiet at the end of the day.

She set the linen napkins to soaking in the laundry room and then carefully dried and placed all the china and glassware back where it belonged. Deciding she deserved a glass of wine after all her hard work, Claire chose one of the crystal goblets and poured some of the crisp leftover Soave that she'd paired with the scallops. A dry white from northern Italy, this particular vintage had notes of peach and marjoram. Savoring the flavor, Claire wandered into the dark sunroom and sat in her favorite chair overlooking the pool.

Several windows were opened to allow the cool night air to filter in. Cigar smoke drifted toward her on the breeze. Obviously, Linc hadn't gone to the bar with the rest of the party. And from the sound of things, he wasn't alone. Claire recognized the second voice as belonging to Knox Smith.

"Tonight at dinner," Knox said. "I saw the way you looked at her."

"How was that?" Linc asked, his tone light and unconcerned.

Claire knew she shouldn't stick around to overhear her employer's conversation, but curiosity kept her in place. Which of tonight's guests had piqued Linc's interest? From her brief glimpse of the assembled women, if she had to bet, Claire's money was on Landry, the stunning brunette with the green eyes.

It would be another adorable *L* and *L* combination. Linc and Landry. Like it had once been Linc and London. Plus, her rich sable hair would make for a nice contrast with Linc's blond all-American looks. The media would eat them up.

"Like you couldn't wait for the rest of us to get the hell out of your house so you could be alone with her," Knox replied, his tone dry.

"That's ridiculous." Linc sounded calm, almost bored. "Claire works for me. That's all there is to it."

They were talking about her. Shock and panic swamped Claire's lighthearted mood. She nervously rubbed her arms.

"And if she didn't?"

"She's still hung up on her dead husband."

"Are you so sure about that?"

"Yeah. Why would you think otherwise?"

"Because there's the way she gobbles you up with her eyes."

Claire shook her head, rejecting everything Knox was saying. It had been bad enough indulging her fantasy about sleeping with her boss, but that her interest in Linc was so obvious…

The heat of humiliation threatened to turn her to ash. What could be worse than having Linc's best friend point out her secret crush on him? She scooted forward on the chair, perched on the edge of the floral cushion. But instead of fleeing the room, she stayed to hear what Linc had to say about her in reply.

"She doesn't." Linc sounded doubtful. "You're making stuff up to mess with me."

"Only partially. I wanted to see your reaction."

And in turn, Claire wanted to pummel Knox. How dare he put ideas like that in Linc's head. The last thing she needed was for Linc to start questioning her reactions to him.

"And?"

"You might not be sleeping with Claire, but you want to."

Claire's thoughts flashed once again to the moment they'd shared before dinner. By the time she'd put the finishing touches on the dessert course, she'd convinced herself that she'd completely misread his signals.

"And what's so surprising about that?" Linc asked. "She's beautiful, sweet, and we get along great."

"She's also your housekeeper."

"Men have been known to fall for their secretaries and nannies. Why not a housekeeper?"

"Fall for?" Knox sounded surprised, but no more so than Claire.

Had she stepped into some sort of alternate universe where she had a shot with someone as wealthy and socially connected as Linc Thurston? Claire didn't know whether to laugh or cry.

"Figure of speech. Sounds better than 'sleep with.'" A pause and then, "Damn. I'm back in Charleston only a few weeks and my Southern manners kick in."

Jolted by the realization that she'd heard too much, Claire got to her feet and moved like a ghost from the room. Heart pounding, she stood in the kitchen, an empty wine glass in her hand, her thoughts reeling. She poured herself a second glass and sat at the breakfast bar to ponder what she'd overheard.

You might not be sleeping with Claire, but you want to.

Was that true? It seemed impossible. Especially after she'd glimpsed the beautiful, socially connected women who'd come to his party. Surely he'd be more likely to settle on one of them. Each one was sophisticated and, if not wealthy, they sure dressed and shopped as if the words *on sale* and *discounted* were not in their vocabulary. They had grace and manners. Or if they didn't, at least they'd been raised knowing how to behave in Charleston society. Claire thought back over some of the conversations she'd heard Linc have with his sister and Knox.

One thing about being a housekeeper, she was often taken for granted. Like the furniture. People rarely guarded their conversations around her, speaking of anything and everything without fear of the information going anywhere. And why not? She was good at keeping secrets. Her own and those of others.

Besides, what did she have to gain by taking gossip to the media? Nothing. Why risk her job? And Linc had been good to her and Honey. She'd never do anything to harm him.

She's beautiful, sweet, and we get along great. What's not to like?

Like being the operative word. He liked her. She liked him. They'd become friends. To misinterpret something he said during a private conversation was foolish. Men talked about women and sex all the time. No need for her to go all stupid over it. She'd bet that every single one of Linc's friends had considered hitting on her at one point or another. Part of the reason she'd put on a wedding band and let everyone believe she was a widow was to avoid such awkwardness. If a man showed any interest in her, Claire merely whipped out her grief over her late husband and it shut down any advances.

Her status as a military widow had also lulled London's objections. Claire doubted that Linc would've been allowed to hire an attractive single mom as his live-in housekeeper, but a wife who was mourning the love of her life could be expected to keep her thoughts and hands off her employer.

When she heard the sound of a car door closing and an engine starting, Claire noticed the goblet was empty in her hand and was surprised how much time had passed. As the knob on the back door began to turn, she sat frozen at the breakfast bar, her cheeks heating as she realized she would have to face Linc after what he'd said about her. Why hadn't she gone upstairs?

"You're still up," Linc said, entering the kitchen.

"I came down to put everything away before morning." She gestured at the tidy, organized space with her glass. "And have some wine."

"You deserve to relax after such a long day."

"Just part of what I signed up for when I became your housekeeper." With her body moving of its own accord, leaning into the space between them, suddenly Claire recognized the importance of maintaining her distance. What better way than by bringing up her role in his house.

"Maybe, but you're more than just my housekeeper."

You might not be sleeping with Claire, but you want to.

Heat flared as Knox's words came back to haunt her. "You did hire me for my cooking skills."

"They are pretty spectacular."

Claire sneaked several glances in his direction and decided the conversation she'd overheard earlier hadn't meant anything. Nothing about his expression gave any indication that he was attracted to her. Was she doing as good a job concealing her own feelings? Claire hoped so.

The last thing she needed was for Linc to pick up on her impossible longing for him. The best she could hope for was that he'd be flattered by her interest. The worst thing that could happen would be they'd cross a line, and then everything would blow up in her face. She couldn't risk having that happen. What if he kicked Honey and her out and she had to scramble to find a new place to live and work?

"You could've left everything until morning." His gaze drifted from her eyes to her lips and then over her sleepwear. "Looks like you're ready for bed."

Claire cursed herself for trembling in reaction to his lazy smile. "I wouldn't be able to sleep, imagining the mess. You know how I am about the kitchen."

"Clutter is definitely your Achilles' heel." Linc set two crystal tumblers in the sink. "I challenge you to leave those unwashed until tomorrow."

"Ha ha. Very funny." But her fingers twitched as she regarded the dirty glasses.

"It's making you crazy, isn't it?"

"A little."

Bantering like this with Linc made it easier for her to ignore the drumbeat of her heart at his nearness. Did the man have any idea of the power of his sex appeal? How could he not with all the advertisers clamoring for him to represent their product, the Armani cologne being the latest?

He turned on the faucet and ran water into the glasses. "I'm happy to wash them. It's the least I can do after how hard you worked to make the dinner party a success." He gestured toward her empty crystal goblet. "If you're done with that, I can do it as well."

"I was just having a glass of wine," she replied, unsure why she felt compelled to explain herself. "Some of the leftover Soave."

"Which one was that?"

"The one I paired with the scallops."

Linc nodded. "That was nice. Dry with a note of peach." He arched an eyebrow at her. "What? You're surprised I remember it?"

"I did throw a lot of different wines at you."

"Showing off?"

"A little. I thought your first post-London dinner party should be memorable."

"You succeeded."

Claire immediately wished she hadn't mentioned London. "I'm sorry."

"For what?"

"I shouldn't have brought up London."

"I'm the one who ended the relationship," he reminded her. "The person who might be sensitive about discussing our breakup is London."

"I know, but you can't tell me that ending your engagement was easy on you."

"I feel guilty that I let it go on so long."

"You shouldn't. Sometimes falling out of love can sneak up on you in the same way falling in love does."

"What do you know about falling out of love?"

Although he didn't say Jasper's name, she suspected he was on Linc's mind.

"I'm not still hung up on my..." She couldn't call him her husband, couldn't speak the lie in this moment. "On Jasper." She delivered the statement with more heat than either of them had expected.

"Okay."

"You don't sound like you believe me." Now she was getting annoyed. "You know I've been out on several dates in the last year."

Linc's eyes widened at her fierceness. "Several dates," he mused. "Well, there you go. Sounds like you're ready to move on to the next stage in your life. Was there anyone special?"

His question flustered her. She opened her mouth to reply but had no idea what to say and set her hands on her hips in an imitation of Honey's terrible-twos willfulness.

"The point I'm trying to make is that I'm ready to move on. I just haven't found the right guy yet."

"You've always struck me as a woman who wants the right guy as opposed to a right-now guy."

"What does that mean?"

"That you aren't going to give someone a chance unless you can see yourself with him for the long-term."

"That just shows how little you understand me. Women have needs, too, you know. I have needs."

Linc nodded sagely, but the glint in his eye told Claire he wasn't done teasing her. "No doubt."

"I heard Knox teasing you about me." She cursed the husky note in her voice.

His expression turned to granite, all amusement gone.

Looking chastened, he raked his fingers through his hair. "Damn, I'm sorry."

While her sensible side screamed at her to drop it, reckless urges had been building in her since he'd come home from Texas. The conversation she'd overheard combined with the two glasses of wine she'd consumed were making it hard to ignore her longing to press against the hard muscular body that was so close to hers.

"Don't be. It was my fault. I shouldn't have been eavesdropping. And it doesn't bother me that you've thought about sleeping with me." She got the words out only by studying the decorative marble backsplash behind the six-burner stove. This let her detach from the intensity of the exchange. "With our proximity..." She shrugged. "It only makes sense that you'd consider it."

He was silent for what felt like minutes, but based on the rapid thump of her heart, it was more like seconds.

"I think you're discounting how important you are to me. You and Honey." His fingertips grazed her knuckles. The fleeting touch awakened a kaleidoscope of butterflies in her stomach. "Have I thought about you in that way, sure. But you know I'd never take advantage of our situation in that way."

"What if you weren't taking advantage?" She couldn't believe such bold words spilled from her lips. What was she saying? He was her boss. "And it's not as if the gossip hasn't already condemned us."

"Claire." He sounded half amused and half despairing.

"Do you want to?" She shuffled forward until the heat of his body made her light hoodie unnecessary. Suddenly far too warm, she slid the zipper down and let it fall off her shoulders.

"Claire." This time when he said her name, there was a warning in it. He gripped her bare shoulders, sending shock waves of longing searing through her. "You have no idea what you do to me."

Linc's palms skimmed down her arms and gathered the cotton of her hoodie, pulling it up over her shoulders once more. She stood frozen as he covered her bare skin. Embarrassment spilled through her as she wondered what the hell had gotten into her.

"I'm sorry." Humiliated, she took a step back, surprised how hard it was to move away from him.

"No, I'm the one who should apologize. Knox and I should never have been talking about you."

"He's worried about you."

Despite Linc's rejection, her body continued to rumble with hungry impulses. While her brain screamed, *What were you thinking?* her body shouted, *Why did you stop?*

"I think he's more worried about you," Linc countered, his deep voice reverberating with regret.

"Why? You're his friend. If anyone stands to be hurt, it's you."

Linc cocked his head. "How do you figure?"

"Your reputation."

"To hell with my reputation. That's important to my mother, not to me."

"But your mother is important to you. Imagine how something like you being discovered sleeping with your housekeeper would hinder her mission to find you a suitable Charlestonian woman to marry."

Linc expelled his breath on a derisive snort. "My mother has weathered bigger scandals just fine. Besides, what she wants for me is not necessarily what I want for myself."

"You mean you don't want to marry a girl from a good family and start having children?"

"I want to marry a woman I love. I don't care what sort of a family she comes from."

While his determination was sexy and thrilling, Claire

knew that his engagement to London had strained his relationship with Bettina.

"That's all well and good," she said, "but your mother does care, and in the end, you know that matters to you."

And there was no way Bettina Thurston was going to approve of her son getting into any sort of relationship with his housekeeper.

Six

Claire's words infuriated him because he knew she was right. But he didn't want it to matter that his choice of a fiancée had upset his mother when he and London were engaged.

"I like to think she'd eventually come around if she knew it would make me happy."

"Your mother is a strong matriarch who believes she knows what's best for you."

Linc couldn't argue with that. She'd certainly recognized that London wasn't the girl for him. He eyed Claire. No doubt his mother would have an even stronger aversion to his starting up with his housekeeper. He raked his fingers through his hair, utterly at war with himself over what he wanted and what he knew to be the best thing to do.

Before Linc could fall victim to his conscience, he reached out and curved his fingers around the back of Claire's neck. Her hand came up between them, the side of her fist resting lightly against his chest. He expected her to push him away and was surprised when her fingers wrapped around his lapel and tugged him toward her.

Dipping his head, he grazed his lips over hers, noting her soft murmur of pleasure. For a second, she leaned into him, her slight weight a sensual blow that knocked his thoughts askew. His heart pumped like he'd run a mile full-out.

"Claire." He went back for a second taste, lingering over her soft lips.

But before he could kiss her yet again, she set her fingertips against her mouth and ducked her head.

"I've been dying to do that since last night," he admitted, setting her free and taking a step back. His hands shook, so he shoved them into his pockets. What was this strange power she had over him that a single chaste kiss turned him inside out?

"I thought it was just me."

Thoughts flitted through his head, none lingering for more than a second.

Mistake. Again. She wants this. I want this. No. Yes.

But what it came down to, what kept him from reaching for her a second time, was the consequences for both of them. She had Honey to think about. He didn't want to jeopardize her future if he pushed forward with this attraction between them.

He needed to know if he was just reacting to something forbidden, or if she was as desirable as he imagined. In truth, he wasn't sure if he could answer any of these questions. In his younger days, he'd never had to pursue women. They had just fallen into his lap like overripe fruit. Nor had London given him a run for his money. Things between them had been easy and familiar right off the bat. In fact, he couldn't think of a single woman he'd ever chased. He was too busy putting all his energy into baseball.

"I'd better get the china and crystal put away," Claire said as she rinsed out her wine glass and set it in the sink.

"My offer to help still stands."

"Thanks, but it won't take me very long."

In a strange way, he felt dismissed. Clearly, she was trying to reestablish the nature of their relationship. Employer and housekeeper.

Instead of arguing, Linc headed upstairs to the large master bedroom on the second floor. As he trudged up the wide staircase, he stripped out of his blazer and unbuttoned his shirtsleeves. He'd scarcely entered his bedroom when his ears picked up the soft squeak of a pine board in the hallway behind him. Tossing his coat onto a nearby chair, he turned and spied Claire standing just outside his room.

"I'm sorry about what happened earlier," she said, uttering the last thing he wanted to hear. "I've put you in a bad position."

"You haven't." He watched as she covered one bare foot with the other and seemed to withdraw into herself as if trying to disappear.

She cleared her throat. "Can we chock it up to…"

"Moonlight?"

Her lips twitched in a familiar wry smile. "I was going to say curiosity."

"But that's not all it was." He stepped into the hallway, body coming alive as he drew within arm's length of her.

"I didn't realize until recently just how much I ignored my own needs."

"You've had Honey to think about."

He wasn't going to bring up her devotion to her deceased husband again. Obviously, she was ready to move on. Or she thought she was.

"She's been my priority, but I also think I've used her to isolate myself. The only way I've ever successfully conquered loneliness is to keep busy and stay focused."

"I'm familiar with the technique. How do you think I got so good at baseball? During the years that my father was in prison, I spent hours and hours at the batting cages or running catch-and-throw drills."

"I get that."

Linc reached out and set his fingers beneath her chin, tipping her head back so he could drown in her big brown eyes. "I'm here for you. Whenever you need me."

"Some uncomplicated sex?" Her tone was light and teasing, but her somber expression betrayed her nervousness.

"Whatever you need." He shaped his grin so she could either take his offer seriously or dismiss it as a joke. He hoped she chose the former.

She sighed. "You have no idea how much I want to take you up on that."

"Hopefully as much as I want you to."

"Oh, hell."

And then she was taking him by the hand and drawing him back into his bedroom. It was the sign he'd been waiting for. With a relieved sigh, Linc strode forward, scooped Claire into his arms and carried her purposefully toward his bed.

He set her down on the coverlet and stripped off his shirt. Eyes never leaving her, he made quick work of his shoes and watch. While he was thus occupied, she peeled her hoodie off and tossed all the decorative pillows aside.

"I make your bed every morning and never found all these things to be as annoying as I do right now." Her unsteady breath and wicked grin had a predictable effect on his arousal.

"Will it shock you to know how many times I've wanted to surprise you in the act of making the bed and tumble you into the sheets?"

"Would it shock you to know how many times I've pressed my face into your pillow and imagined what it would be like to be naked in this bed with you?"

He groaned. "You win."

"Tonight, I think we both win."

He unfastened his belt buckle and popped open the button on his pants, but when he noticed she was lifting her top over her head, he stopped to watch. Inch by gorgeous inch, her naked torso came into view. He stopped breathing as the pale blue fabric rode up over the lower curve of her breasts. And then suddenly her dusky nipples appeared and his mouth went dry.

As soon as she'd stripped the shirt off, he encircled her tiny waist with his hands and drew her toward him. She hummed joyously as his mouth came down over hers. Her fingers skimmed over his shoulders and sank into his hair, tugging fiercely as her lips parted beneath his to allow the thrust of his tongue.

Her hardened nipples raked his chest, her passion driving his desire even higher. He stroked his palms up her back, feeling her muscles shift beneath her silky skin. Leaving one hand to delve into the satin curtain of her hair, he sent his other down her spine to the small of her back. She shivered and moaned as he delicately caressed the indents on either side of her spine, before sliding his hand beneath the waistband of her pajama bottoms and cupping her bare butt.

"Linc." His name broke from her lips as he kissed his way down her neck to the sensitive hollow of her throat. "That feels incredible."

"I haven't begun to make you feel incredible yet," he replied, determined to rein in his lust so he could make this a night she'd never forget.

"Pretty much everything you do is wonderful."

"It feels like you set the bar too low."

"I don't want to put any pressure on you."

Her lopsided smile set him on fire, but it was the sudden flash of shyness he glimpsed that enabled him to calm down.

"How long has it been for you?" he asked, wanting to

take things slow and make it perfect for her. She deserved to be cherished and that was what he intended to do.

She bit her lip and thought about it. "Since the night Honey was conceived?"

Wondering if that was guilt flickering in her eyes, Linc did the math. Almost three years. Damn. The knowledge that he would be the first man to have her since her husband cooled his ardor somewhat. Instinctively, he knew he wasn't competing with the man, but how could she help but compare them?

Her palms framed his face, bringing him back to the moment. "Tonight, there's only you and me."

It didn't surprise Linc that she had a knack for reading his mind. From the beginning, she'd anticipated his needs. Sometimes it was disturbing, but mostly he enjoyed the hell out of it. Once, he'd seen a three-foot-tall tiger displayed in a toy store window and pictured her buying it for Honey, just to see if he and Claire were communicating telepathically. And two weeks later, she'd bought her daughter a stuffed cat. Granted, it wasn't the three-foot-tall tiger, but she definitely picked up on the vibe he'd been sending.

"I'm glad to hear that. I've never had a threesome."

She paused in the act of sliding her fingers along his abdomen and hit him with a dry look. "Never?"

Despite her doubting tone, Linc spied hope in her expression and promised never to do anything that would erase her faith in him.

"You say that as if you think I'm some sort of player."

"Not a player," she corrected. "But you are a sports star. Women must throw themselves at you all the time. I imagine you've had plenty of opportunities."

"Oh, I've been approached, but I like my women one at a time. It gives me an opportunity to focus all my attention on what gives them the most pleasure." He gave her butt a little squeeze and heard her light gasp. "You'll find I like to be very thorough."

She ran her finger down his fly. "No more of that until I get your pants off."

"Let me take care of that for you." He brushed her fingers aside and slid his zipper down.

As much as he'd enjoyed the glancing contact of her hands on his erection through two layers of clothing, more than anything he wanted to feel her skin sliding along his hardened length. But it was much too early for that. He slipped off his pants but kept on his boxer briefs.

"Three years is a long time," he murmured, sliding his fingertips beneath the waistband of her pajama bottoms and carefully easing them down her hips. "I'm going to take things slowly. We have no need to rush."

As the cool air touched more of her skin, Claire gasped and her trembling increased. Linc coaxed her onto her back and skimmed her cotton pants off her legs. He drank his fill of her naked body, gaze skimming over her small breasts and flat stomach. The indent of her waist and her long, slender legs. How had he not realized how beautifully put together she was?

"Is everything okay?" she asked, her voice sounding rusty from disuse.

"Just about perfect," he replied, settling onto the bed and moving between her thighs. "I want to kiss every inch of you, but right now I need to start here."

"Are...are you sure?" she stammered as he leaned forward and gave her one long lick. "Oh, yes," she moaned, answering her own question.

He went back for a second taste, liking the way her flavor filled his mouth and her sexy groans caressed his ears. She wasn't quiet, and her unsteady exclamations of pleasure drove him on. It didn't take him long to figure out exactly what she liked. He debated urging her into a fast orgasm or letting one build until she was out of her mind.

In the end, what decided him was the three years she'd gone without making love. As much as he wanted this moment embedded in her psyche forever, he knew how he'd feel if he'd been celibate that long. As it was, Claire was the first woman he'd slept with since ending his relationship with London. While all his friends had encouraged him to jump straight into the dating pond again, the reason why he'd broken off his engagement was the woman currently occupying his bed. He couldn't deny it any longer. Why settle for hamburger when what he craved was a Japanese Wagyu striploin.

Claire came for him with a startled cry as if she hadn't expected to climax. The sound stripped his soul bare, so he kept going, digging his fingertips into her hips to keep her tight against his mouth as he drove her harder.

"No. No. It's too much." Her body shuddered and quaked as she continued to orgasm. "Linc, I can't..."

But she could. And she did. Beautifully.

As she lay gasping for breath, he kissed his way back up her body and gathered her into his arms, ignoring the sharp bite of lust so he could soothe her with gentle kisses and soft murmurs. His emotions tangled as she murmured his name.

"Don't thank me yet," he replied. "We've only just gotten started."

She threaded her fingers through his hair and seized his lower lip between her teeth, growling playfully at him. "You're such an amazing man—"

He didn't want her praise, didn't want to think about her comparing him to the husband she'd lost. Instead, he kissed her deeply, until there was nothing but her heat and the softness of her skin beneath his hands and his lips.

"I have to have you," he murmured, his tongue swirling around her nipple.

"I'm all yours."

The steamy rasp of her voice only added to his excitement and Linc knew if he didn't get a condom rolled on in the next few minutes, there was going to be trouble. She watched him from beneath her lashes through the entire procedure, but when he shifted between her spread thighs and positioned himself at her entrance, he saw that her eyes had drifted closed.

"Open your eyes," he commanded. "I need to know you're with me."

She smiled languidly, lifting her hips so that he slipped a little ways inside her. "I'm here."

And when she did as he requested and met his gaze with her own, he plunged inside her in one smooth stroke. She whimpered and arched her back, accepting every inch of him. Gliding into her wetness proved to be mind-altering. Her long celibacy made her so tight that by the time he was seated deep in her heat, he was reeling.

Grinding his teeth together to keep himself from coming, he glanced down and saw her lips curve into the most glorious smile he'd ever seen. With his brain waging a fierce battle against his body, Linc began a steady, torturously slow rhythm, determined to give her everything he had and more.

"You are so tight," he groaned. "You're driving me crazy, Claire."

In answer, her snug, slick walls pulsed around him and he began pumping into her harder, going as deep as he could. She met each thrust with a little chant and sank her nails into his skin.

"More," she begged. "I want all of you."

So he gave her everything he had. His breath rasped against her neck as he filled her again and again. Reaching between their bodies, he cupped her, putting the perfect pressure on her clit.

"Come for me."

And then she was. With a long, searing cry, her body began to shake. Linc clamped his mouth over hers, drinking her pleasure as her body gripped him and started a chain reaction that sent him soaring off a cliff right after her.

Ten days before Bettina's party, Claire took her culinary expertise to the Mills-Forrest House and spent several hours preparing a selection for Linc's mom to choose from. Although Bettina had a reputation for being a tough cookie, Claire had always gotten along well with the Charleston matriarch.

And Claire wanted to keep it that way, which was why for the past couple days her focus had been on brainstorming dishes and assembling her menu. Not on daydreaming about the magical night she'd spent with Linc.

Today's plan was for her to serve her menu ideas to Bettina as a mid-afternoon snack. While she was occupied doing this, Linc had offered to take Honey to the Children's Museum of the Lowcountry so she wouldn't have to hire a babysitter.

It still perplexed her that he enjoyed spending time with the two-year-old. Honey could be challenging at times, although the toddler's sunny personality made up for the worst of it. But Linc was fond of Honey and, of course, she adored him. Watching them together made Claire's heart ache because it reminded her that Honey would never know her father. And despite how Jasper had begun changing as his many tours overseas took their toll on his psyche, from the expression on his face when he held Honey in his arms at the hospital, Claire knew he would've done anything for his little girl.

Dolly was ironing sheets in a small nook near the kitchen when Claire carried in several grocery bags of ingredients. The older woman scowled as she watched Claire unpack and arrange things on the enormous marble island.

"I told her I'm not helping with the cooking for the party," Dolly said with an imperious sniff she'd picked up from her longtime employer.

"You already do so much for Bettina," Claire said, her tone soothing. "I wouldn't want you to feel pressure to do more. So I hired waitstaff and an assistant to help me prepare all the food."

With a satisfied nod, Dolly returned to her task, and for the next two hours, the two women worked in companionable silence. For her part, Claire was happy to not have to chat.

As she was finishing up, she heard the distant sound of the doorbell ringing. Fortunately, Bettina had warned her that she was inviting some of her friends, so Claire had come prepared with enough food. While Dolly headed off to welcome the guests, Claire put the final touches on her plates, wondering whom she might encounter today.

Promptly at four o'clock, she carried the first two offerings out to the dining room and found five women sitting around the table. Besides Bettina, Sawyer and her friend Augusta, who'd approached Claire after Linc's dinner party about catering the food for a fund-raiser, there were two women in their early forties.

"Good afternoon, ladies," Claire said, setting her first menu items on the table. "Today, I have for you a mozzarella and grape tomato skewer with basil drizzled with a balsamic reduction, as well as a salmon and cream cheese bite."

While Dolly set about pouring glasses of white wine, Claire went back into the kitchen to fetch serving plates with spicy tuna wrapped in pickled cucumber, baked brie with walnuts and pistachios, and yellow tomato gazpacho shooters with basil crab salad crostini.

One of the first chefs Claire had worked for had been a stickler for presentation and had hammered into his employees that food needed to be visually pleasing as well as a festival of flavors. That was why she'd made certain that each selection she presented to Bettina was not only a treat for the palate, but interesting to the eye as well.

By the time she finished setting the last of her eight plates on the table, the women were exclaiming over the food. A warm sense of accomplishment flooded Claire. Cooking was her passion and it thrilled her when people enjoyed what she lovingly created.

"In addition to these," she said, making eye contact with Sawyer, who gave her an encouraging smile, "I thought we should have boiled shrimp and a cheese platter. And I have a friend who is an excellent pastry cook. For dessert, I could order up a selection."

"This is all quite nice," Bettina said, proving far less difficult to please than Claire had anticipated. "I approve of everything."

"Wonderful."

"I agree," Augusta spoke up. "This is all amazing."

Buoyed by all the positive feedback, Claire grinned. "I'm glad you like it."

Augusta indicated the two woman who'd accompanied her. "Let me introduce you to these ladies. This is Genevieve Brand and Portia Hillcrest. I brought them along today because they are in charge of organizing the charity polo match to support the local YMCA next Saturday, and they were hoping you could help them out of a jam."

Genevieve Brand was nodding as Augusta spoke. A thin woman with sleek blond hair and a smooth round face, Genevieve wore a beautiful pale pink suit and a triple-strand pearl necklace that looked like it cost more than Claire had paid for her Saab.

"Our caterer had a family emergency and canceled last minute," Genevieve said. "We are in a terrible predicament with the event coming up so soon and no food. Would you be able to help us out?"

Claire's first impulse was to say no. When Augusta had approached her after Linc's dinner party, asking if she would be interested in catering an event in the future, Claire hadn't dreamed anything would come up so soon. She didn't have the facilities or the staff to handle a large party.

"I'd have to talk to Linc." When Genevieve and Portia exchanged a confused look, Claire explained, "I'm his housekeeper."

"I'm sure he'll say yes." Augusta beamed as if everything was settled. "It's one of his favorite events, after all."

"Does he play polo?" The question slipped out of Claire's mouth before she could stop it.

Sawyer laughed. "No, but he's big on any charity that helps out kids, and he loves rooting for Austin."

"By rooting for," Bettina murmured wryly, "Sawyer means betting on."

"There's always a little friendly wagering that goes on during the match," Portia explained. "Those proceeds also go to the charity."

"Sounds like a worthwhile event," Claire said, a little overwhelmed by the weight of these women's expectations. "Still, I should run it by Linc."

"Of course."

"Run what by Linc?" came the question from the doorway.

Claire's eyes snapped to her employer and her heart skipped a beat. Nor was she the only one affected. A collective sigh went up from the room's occupants as each took in the charming picture of the gorgeous blond man with an armful of adorable toddler. It was hard for Claire to keep her expression neutral as she was suddenly besieged by the memories of his touch.

"Genevieve and Portia need Claire's help with the charity polo match next Saturday," Augusta said to him. "They lost their caterer at the last minute."

"What an adorable little girl," Portia exclaimed, looking perplexed.

"This is Honey," Linc said, his smiling blue eyes landing on Claire.

"She's Claire's daughter," Bettina clarified, her tone flat.

"How was the children's museum?" Claire asked. "Did she behave herself?"

"She was a perfect angel."

"I don't believe you," she replied, all too aware that their exchange was being closely observed.

"You know she always behaves for me," Linc said, shifting his attention to Honey. "Don't you?"

"Yes." The little girl patted his cheek with her palm and giggled.

"They had a fire truck exhibit. She was a huge fan."

"Whoooo, whooo." Honey sounded more like an alarm than a train.

"It was nice of you to take your housekeeper's daughter to the children's museum," Genevieve murmured, mild judgment in her tone.

When Claire stiffened at the remark, Linc shot the woman an uncompromising look.

"She's catering my mother's party as a favor. The least I could do was save her from having to hire a babysitter today."

While everyone nodded, Claire stood frozen with humiliation. Once again, it was pretty obvious in the eyes of many people that a clearly defined line existed between the haves and those who work for them.

"Why don't I take Honey now," Claire said, sliding around the outer perimeter of the room in Linc's direction. "You should sit down and visit with these ladies. I can bring you a plate if you'd like to taste the food."

"No, thanks. Honey and I are going to hang out in the kitchen with you while you finish up."

Curiosity was almost palpable in the dining room.

"Before you go, Linc," Genevieve said. "Can you give Claire permission to work our fund-raiser? She won't do it without your approval."

Linc shook his head. "She doesn't need my permission. She's free to do whatever she wants with her weekends."

All eyes turned in Claire's direction as he finished speaking, and she felt like a rabbit that had stumbled into a wolves' den.

"Then I guess my answer is yes," she said, eager to escape a situation that had suddenly become awkward and embarrassing. More than anything, she wished the scene with Linc and Honey hadn't played out in front of these women. Gossip around town already had it that there was something going on between her and Linc. Thanks to his arrival, it was pretty obvious that Claire and her employer were friends and possibly a little too comfortable with each other.

As she left, her gaze fell on Bettina. Linc's mother wore a slight frown. Claire returned to the kitchen, hoping Bettina wasn't concerned that Linc had babysat Honey.

"Thank you for watching Honey for me today so I could concentrate on getting everything ready," she said. "If you want to leave her with me and head out…"

"I don't have anything else to do this afternoon, so I'm happy to hang out with her until you're done here," Linc said, setting Honey on the ground and finding her a couple pots and a wooden spoon. He then demonstrated drumming on the cookware and the toddler set to work making noise.

"Thanks," Claire mumbled, rinsing the last of the plates and loading them into the dishwasher.

While she finished up, Linc leaned on the counter and surveyed the leftovers. "How did the tasting go?" He reached out and snagged one of the appetizers, popping it into his mouth. "This is fantastic. What is it?"

"Puffed pastry with caviar." Claire dodged around Linc and began packing up the leftovers. "Your mom liked everything."

"Terrific." He tried a tartlet with goat cheese and fig and moaned appreciatively. "Then why are you upset?"

"I'm not upset."

"Is it because they badgered you into catering the charity polo match next week?" He grinned at her over a shot glass of gazpacho. "Don't do it if you think it's going to be too much."

"It isn't that…" She trailed off, not wanting to get into her concerns right there in his mother's kitchen.

"Is it the reason my mother is having the party?" He lowered his voice until only she could hear him. "Are you worried that I'm going to meet someone? Because if that's it, you don't need to give it a second thought. I'm only going through the motions to satisfy my mother."

Claire stopped what she was doing and gave him her full attention. Was she acting like she was jealous? They'd slept together only once and she hoped she'd been clear about it not becoming a habit.

Yet, if she investigated her churning emotions, she suspected the fear in her heart had little to do with concern over whether his next serious relationship would want the live-in housekeeper fired. Claire suspected she was well on her way to falling for her handsome, charming employer.

"You need to take her matchmaking more seriously," Claire said, denying the truth staring her straight in the face. "She has only your best interest at heart."

"That doesn't sound like the sort of advice I'd expect from a woman who had her world rocked by me a few nights ago."

"My world rocked?" Claire repeated in a barely audible whisper while glancing toward the hall that led into the dining room. Embarrassment and desire warred inside her. "Can we not talk about this here?"

"Relax." His voice was a husky rasp across her senses. "No one can hear us."

"Nevertheless." She tried for crisp and professional but came across tremulous and disturbed. Her breath hitched as his fingers tugged at her chef jacket, making the fabric slide across her overly sensitive skin. "Linc."

"You know it's going to happen again. Tonight, I think." His eyes glittered, making it impossible for her to look away.

"I don't know that." But she wanted it to. So badly. Her entire body screamed for him to kiss her. Caution was quickly drowning beneath the flood of desire. "Linc," she almost pleaded. "It was supposed to be one and done. Just two people who turn to each other in a moment of weakness."

She managed to tear her gaze away and shot a glance toward the dining room. To her relief, no one was skulking in the butler's pantry, listening to them, but she really didn't want to talk about this anymore.

"Weakness?" He took his time tasting the word. "Yeah, I guess that sounds about right. When it comes to you, my willpower is shot to hell."

"Linc, please." She was begging now through clenched teeth.

"Those were your exact words that night."

"Oh, Linc…"

The heat scorching her cheeks wasn't caused by the temperature in the kitchen. She hungered to take hold of Linc's knit shirt and drag it over his head. To feel his hands slide beneath her chef whites and claim her breasts.

He set his palm on the kitchen island and leaned toward her, pitching his voice to a sexy murmur that made her muscles bunch in anticipation.

"'Oh, Linc…' I'm going to make you say them again," he vowed, his whole manner leaving no doubt that he wouldn't stop until she'd given him everything he wanted. "And again."

Pledge delivered, he stepped back, leaving her quaking and achy and oh, so ready to do anything he asked. From the satisfaction glinting in his eyes, he knew what his words had done to her. A second later, he scooped Honey into his arms and carried her out the kitchen door, and Claire watched after him, a trembling bundle of unsatisfied longing.

Seven

The opportunity to lure Claire back into his bed failed to materialize in the days that followed the tasting at his mother's house. Claire was completely engrossed in preparations for the party, and while he missed spending time with her, Linc appreciated her passion and wanted her to shine. At least that was what he told himself as his ache for her grew.

At eleven o'clock on a Saturday—far too early for him to be coming home from a night out with the guys—Linc eased his BMW into the driveway and parked beside Claire's ancient Saab. He shut off the engine and in the ensuing silence listened to the insects drone. His jaw ached from grinding his teeth. The whole evening had tested his patience as he watched his friends hit on a variety of women and compete to see who could take the prettiest one home.

Usually he found their antics amusing, but ever since he'd warned Claire he intended to make her moan for him again, he'd been distracted and edgy.

In fact, he hadn't planned to go out at all tonight. He'd intended to stay close to Claire in case she wanted to knock off early and hang out, but she had plans of her own. Since he hadn't been all that keen on staying home alone, he'd let Knox and Austin drag him out. He'd pretty quickly discovered that being by himself wasn't the problem—it was being away from Claire. She'd become like a drug in his system. No one but her appealed to him.

It hadn't helped that he'd caught a glimpse of London having dinner with Harrison Crosby as he headed toward The Lucky Mojo. She'd looked as elegant and unflappable as ever, but something about the way her date smiled at her kicked Linc in the gut. He recognized a man on the hunt. He'd seen the same expression reflected in his mirror over the past several days.

While he didn't begrudge London her happiness, Linc couldn't help but experience a small flash of envy that Harrison could wine and dine her to his heart's content, while Linc was left skulking around in secret with Claire.

Linc didn't give a damn who knew he was pursuing her, but Claire was sensitive about the situation and worried because she worked for him. Although he didn't want to add to her concern, Linc sensed that by keeping their budding relationship quiet and acting like being with her was something he was ashamed of, she would never believe their divergent social positions didn't matter.

As he stepped out of the BMW, the sound of splashing came from the direction of the pool. He headed for the source of the noise. The thick vegetation surrounding the concrete pool deck gave him cover as he lurked and watched Claire make her way from one end of the narrow pool to the other with slow, lazy strokes.

Tonight, she wore a utilitarian black one-piece that did nothing to enhance her slender curves. Even so, Linc found himself mesmerized by the flash of her slender arms and legs as she negotiated a flip turn and resumed her smooth rhythm. She was swimming for pleasure rather than fitness, but there was no missing the precision in her strokes. She moved like a trained swimmer and this showcased yet another example of how little he knew about her.

When she drew close to the end nearest him, Linc stepped out of the shadows and approached the turquoise water. "It's a little chilly for a night swim, isn't it?" He figured the air temperature was around sixty.

"You keep the pool at a comfortable eighty-two degrees, so it doesn't bother me until I get out." She frog kicked to the edge and looped her arms over the concrete.

The dark smudge of mascara beneath her eyes gave her an edgy look he appreciated. He imagined licking the water from her throat as her legs wrapped around his waist in the weightless environment.

"How long have you been out here?" he asked.

"Fifteen minutes or so."

"Were you waiting for me to come home?"

The corners of her mouth turned up in an enigmatic smile. "How come you're home so early? Did all your friends get lucky and ditch you?"

For once, he wasn't in the mood to flirt. "I couldn't stop thinking about you," he said in all seriousness.

She hummed as if considering how to take this. Linc found himself taking off his jacket and reaching for his shirt buttons before he realized his intent.

"What are you doing?" she demanded as he stripped off his shirt, stepped out of his shoes and got to work on his pants.

"Joining you."

Her eyes widened as his pants fell to his ankles and he kicked out of them.

"Don't you need a suit?"

In answer, he executed a shallow dive and surfaced ten feet beyond her. The shock of the cool water on his overheated skin diminished none of the desire pulsing through his veins. Three powerful strokes brought him within arm's reach of her and he wasted no time snagging her around the waist and dragging her flush against his body.

"Linc—" Her protest was cut off as he claimed her mouth in a hard kiss that let her know just how much he needed her.

She tasted like salt from the pool water and fresh peach pie with ice cream. He fed on her deliciousness with a ravenous appetite as she draped her thigh over his hip and gathered his wet hair between her fingers. She rocked her pelvis into him and moaned. Peeling one strap of her bathing suit off her shoulder, he coasted his lips over her silky skin, enjoying the way she trembled.

"We shouldn't be doing this out here," she warned, her voice a husky rasp. She pushed weakly against his chest. "What if we're seen?"

"Stop worrying about that." He skimmed her bathing suit lower, baring one small breast. "I don't care if the whole world knows."

"You should," she gasped unsteadily.

Dipping his head, he pulled her tight nipple into his mouth and smiled as she shivered. For a long, heady moment, she was all pliant eagerness and he took complete advantage. But then she began shaking her head.

"Damn it, Linc." Her voice was a breathless moan as he nipped at her neck. "I'm trying to be sensible."

"There's no need."

"There's every need."

Hearing the solid conviction in her tone, he released a heartfelt sigh before peeling her hand off his bicep and kissing her palm. "Fine. But you need to know that I'm not a huge fan of sensible when it comes to you."

"I don't believe that's true. You are the most prudent and mindful man I've ever met."

Linc winced at her description of him, even though he

knew it was true. His father had demonstrated what happens to a man who acts unwisely without considering the consequences to those around him. Linc would never do anything that would hurt his family or friends. He'd never expose Claire to what would surely be a scandal if they were caught.

"What if we skip all this sneaking around and just date? In public. Dinner. Dancing."

"Did you forget that I recently spent the day cooking so your mother could decide what to serve at the party she's throwing to introduce you to Charleston's most eligible females?"

"Fine," Linc grumbled. "I'll go to her party, and when I don't find anyone who suits me, will you be my date to the polo event next weekend?"

A breeze moved across the surface of the pool, agitating the illuminated water, casting shimmers of reflected light over Claire's damp skin. Shadows moved through her eyes as her hand came up and cupped his cheek.

"Take me upstairs and make love to me," she murmured, the words barely reaching his ears. "More than anything else, that's what I want."

Sensing it would do no good to push her further on the subject, Linc took her hand and drew her toward the stairs. She was giving him what she thought he needed. Physical companionship that made no demands on him. Well, that wasn't good enough, and it was about time he started convincing her that she deserved more and so did he.

Claire buried her face in a sweetly scented pillow and clung to a delicious dream. Linc's lips were moving along her neck while his fingers traced along her thigh toward her hip. This fantasy was familiar and reoccurred more frequently since he'd returned to Charleston after the baseball season. The more time she spent with Linc, the more treacherous her subconscious became. In the early morning hours before she slipped from her bed, he did incredible things to her body. She'd lost track of just how many times a climax had visited her with the dawn.

She moaned a little, trembling on the edge of wakefulness. Resisting the return to reality, she clung to the delicious sensations ranging across her sleep-warmed flesh. The contrast of his silky warm lips exploring her shoulder and the roughness of his beard aroused her, the light scrape of stubble against her skin awakening goose bumps all over her body.

For so long she'd immersed herself in scented lotions, sweet baby smells and gourmet meals for one. She hadn't wanted to acknowledge how much she'd missed the strength of a man's hands on her body, his wicked words whispered in her ears, telling her all the naughty things he wanted to do to her, the power of an orgasm she couldn't control.

"Now, this is a wonderful way to wake up," Linc murmured, his fingers lazily drifting over her abdomen before sliding lower.

Claire's eyes flashed opened. This wasn't a dream. She glanced around the dim room and spied the clock on the nightstand. It was shortly before six. Honey would still be sleeping. She could linger in this delicious fantasy a little while longer.

And yet it wasn't a dream. This was happening. The hand sliding between her legs to cup her belonged to a very real, very turned-on Linc. She clamped her eyes shut as a groan ripped from her throat. Panic smacked her hard in the chest, but that didn't stop her thighs from parting.

Her pulse began to race. All traces of sleepiness vanished beneath a rush of lust as his fingers traveled along her inner thigh, not quite making it to where she wanted him most.

"What are you doing to me?" She shifted her hips, rubbing against his morning erection, and was rewarded by his swift intake of breath followed by the bite of his fingers on her thigh, far from where she ached but near enough to cause her to groan.

"Yeah, that's the stuff." He kissed her ear, before taking the lobe between his teeth. The tiny flare of pain sent a rush of pleasure through her body.

"Linc." His name came out in a whimper, a plea for him to stop teasing her.

"What do you want?"

"Touch me."

"I am."

Her head thrashed on the pillow, hips gyrating as frustration built to a crescendo. "Not where I want you."

"And where is that?"

"Between my legs. I want to feel you inside me." She'd stopped feeling embarrassed about telling him what she needed. "Every part of me aches for you."

"That's my girl."

At last, his fingers glided into her core and she stopped breathing. She felt the lazy drift of his tongue against her neck as he circled her clit with an expert touch. The pressure was perfect and she surrendered to the building pleasure.

"You're so wet," he murmured, his low voice rumbling through her.

"You wake up hard," she teased breathlessly. "I wake up wet."

He paused. "All the time?"

From his tone, he was surprised. That made her smile. She reached back and hooked her arm around his neck, arching her body, offering him every part of her.

"When I'm dreaming about you." After last night, it

made no sense to be cagey. She'd already revealed too much about how she felt.

"Does that happen often?" His hands stroked her with possessive expertise, claiming and demanding her surrender.

"Almost every night."

"Moan for me like you did last night," he whispered against her skin while pushing a finger inside her.

A kiss landed in the sensitive spot where her shoulder and neck came together. Claire's lips parted and she moaned as his finger started to move in and out of her.

"You are so soft. So perfect," he growled as she rocked her hips. "Yes, that's it. Show me how much you love this."

"Linc," she moaned again, but this time in protest. The building pressure warned her she was close. She grabbed his hand and sank her fingernails into his skin to let him know she meant business. "Not like this. I need you inside me."

He cursed softly and rolled away from her. Claire shifted onto her back and watched him find one of the foil packets. She briefly remembered how they hadn't used a condom last night before her mind snapped back to the present moment. To her delight, his hands shook a little as he tore it open and rolled the condom onto his erection.

And then he was sliding between her thighs and into her open arms, driving into her body with a groan that made her heart sing.

Claire clenched her eyes shut as Linc moved inside her, the better to savor the fullness of his possession. She'd never been particularly vocal during sex, but last night and now this morning, the urge to chant encouragement couldn't be denied.

"Yes, yes, yes. Please." She had no idea what she was asking for, but the pleas rolled off her tongue. "More. That feels amazing."

Her declaration ended on a gasp as he shifted the angle of his hips and changed his thrusts, going deeper, taking her pleasure higher.

"That's it," he coaxed, his voice raspy and gruff. "Show me what you like."

Had she ever felt like this before? Was it merely the years she'd gone without or did Linc have some sort of magic that made her wild?

"Oh, Linc."

They were moving together in a frenzy of hands and hips. Her body tightened with ever-increasing need until Claire wondered if she might explode. His name poured from her lips again and again, and she heard him murmuring encouragement as he thrust into her smoothly but with surging power.

And then she was coming, her orgasm catching up with her so fast she wasn't ready for the blinding pleasure that blew her apart.

"You are perfect," he whispered. "I've never felt like this before."

With a final thrust, he let go and Claire watched his expression transform into something that both thrilled and terrified her. His lips claimed hers in a searing kiss that left her reeling. She clutched his hair and met the thrust of his tongue with desperation-fueled passion, recognizing that they couldn't keep doing this, yet she didn't want to stop. Being with Linc like this made her happier than she'd been in a long time. Maybe ever.

So what if it couldn't last. Nothing so perfect was meant to. She would simply have to take this time with him and appreciate every second. Being together, loving like this, wasn't hurting anyone. To hell with what the gossips said about them. Eventually their passion would run its course and Linc would find the woman he was meant to spend the rest of his life with.

As for what would happen to Claire…

She would just have to trust that he would treat her and Honey fairly.

"What are you thinking about?" Linc asked, his face buried in her neck.

"How nice it is to wake up with you."

He hummed. "I could get used to this."

She agreed. It would be so easy to lose herself in him. In this secret connection they shared. "You shouldn't."

His lips moved over her skin, and her breath quickened as dozens of nerve endings came to life.

How could she already want him again? Her body hadn't calmed from the last orgasm he'd given her and she craved more of his touch. An ache bloomed between her thighs and she resisted the urge to rub herself against him.

"You're not the boss of me," he teased, his lips coasting along the curve of her breast, tongue flicking over her nipple, making her suck in a sharp breath.

"Of course not." She arched her back, offering herself to him. "That's your mother's job."

He lifted his head and snagged her gaze. The blue of his eyes seemed to intensify. "I'm my own man. I make my own decisions."

"Of course you do."

Her teasing was distracting him from the romantic mood he'd been in a moment earlier. She breathed a little sigh of relief. Passionate Linc she could handle. Sex was a physical act. She might crave it, hunger for his lips on her and the heat of their lovemaking, but when things ended, her heart would still be intact. Affectionate Linc was trouble. She could come to depend on his smiles and ache for his company.

"You're patronizing me."

"I wouldn't dream of it." She tunneled her fingers in his

soft golden hair, enjoying its silky feel. "It's just that you don't really belong only to yourself. You're a star. A hero."

He shook his head. "I'm no one's hero."

Why didn't he see himself as everyone else did? Didn't he realize the impact he had on his friends and family?

"The decisions you make affect the people around you," she told him.

"What happens between us doesn't affect anyone outside this bed."

"Have you forgotten your mother?"

He blinked at her. "Please tell me you didn't just bring her into this."

"She wants you involved with the sort of quality woman you can eventually marry. Don't you want to make her happy?"

Linc flopped onto his back and stared at the ceiling. "This is without a doubt the strangest post-sex conversation I've ever had with a woman."

"I'm just looking out for you."

He shifted his gaze back to her. "Maybe you should stop worrying about me and consider what makes you happy."

Claire opened her mouth to say that she was doing just that but shook her head instead. Since finding out she was pregnant with Honey, she'd put her daughter first. Honey's security and happiness was all that mattered. This interlude with Linc had been selfish and reckless. Claire's throat closed as panic enveloped her.

"I shouldn't be here," she whispered, sitting up and looking around for her clothes. "I'm so sorry."

"Why are you apologizing?" Linc made a grab for her arm, but she'd already slipped out of the bed. "Claire, don't go."

"It's late. Honey will be getting up soon and I have to start your breakfast." She knew she was babbling, but she had to remind herself what was important. "You're supposed to be at the gym for your workout."

"I already had my morning workout."

His tone was so smoky she couldn't resist glancing at him. Her heart gave a start as he slipped off the bed and stood naked before her. The sheer perfection of his chiseled torso, powerful thighs and sleep-tossed hair made her knees weak and her blood started to pound in her ears. If he reached for her, she'd fall back into his arms without a moment's hesitation.

"That was cardio," she retorted, tearing her eyes from him. "You need to balance it with lifting and…"

The rest was lost as he grabbed her around the waist and hauled her up against him. He set his fingers beneath her chin and tilted her head to the perfect angle. She melted against his solid form as his lips claimed hers in a possessive kiss. Her tongue darted forward to tangle with his and she moaned as he palmed her butt cheek and lifted her against his growing erection. She dug her fingers into his shoulders and hung on as he feasted on her mouth. The rest of the world fell away, leaving her trapped in a whirlpool where only his hard muscles, strong hands and passionate mouth kept her grounded.

By the time he broke the kiss and gazed down at her dazed expression, she was weak with desire. Whatever he wanted to do to her, she would've gladly said yes. He surveyed her bruised lips and brushed his knuckles lightly against her tight nipples, satisfaction plain in his half smile.

"I'm going to take you and Honey out for breakfast," he announced. "You have half an hour to get ready."

Before she could protest that she wasn't recovered enough from their morning activity to be seen in public with him, he turned her toward the door and gave her a friendly pat on her rear end. She was in the hallway before her brain could form a coherent thought and by then he'd disappeared into his master bathroom.

After checking on Honey and finding her still sleeping, Claire decided she would take a cold shower and restore her equilibrium. If this was to work with Linc, she had to figure out how to give him everything in the bedroom while giving nothing away outside of it. It was a tricky path to walk, but if she wanted this time with him, she would just have to make it work.

Eight

The morning of his mother's party, Linc woke alone in his bed with a sense of foreboding. These past few nights with Claire had been some of the best he'd ever known. Her passion and openness drove him to want to take her pleasure higher each time they made love.

And she'd surprised him by being a curious and sensitive partner in bed, up for any number of adventurous activities. The shyness she often demonstrated vanished behind his closed bedroom door and this intrigued Linc all the more.

One thing she hadn't given him was any deeper insight into the hopes, fears and dreams that had shaped the woman she'd become. As much as he'd spoken of how things had been before and after his father's illegal dealings had surfaced, she'd glossed over her own childhood experiences growing up in San Francisco, leaving him with a vague picture of a little girl who'd been lonely and neglected by her father after her mother had left them.

Nor had he had any luck bringing their relationship into the light of day. As soon as the sun came up, she returned to her housekeeper role. He'd made no headway on breaching the walls she erected that kept him at a professional distance.

Which was why when he found her in his kitchen, going over her to-do lists for his mother's party, he decided to tackle what was bothering him.

"This upstairs-downstairs thing with you isn't working for me."

She regarded him blankly. "The what?"

"You and I have a connection. I want more than just a sexual relationship with you."

For a moment, she had the audacity to grin at him, but when he continued to regard her in all seriousness, she sobered. "I get what you're trying to say, but it's the way things have to be."

"I don't like it."

"Be realistic, Linc. You can't trot me out as the woman you're sleeping with—"

"Seeing."

She made a face and shook her head. "Because I will never fit in."

"That's not true. Not one of my friends gives a damn who I choose to date as long as I'm happy."

She cocked her head. "Really? So they supported you marrying London?"

He considered his conversation with Knox. "That's different. They were worried that she wasn't right for me."

Claire's expression said it all.

Linc snorted in disgust. "Not because she wasn't from an old Charleston family, but because they weren't sure she loved me."

"Has it occurred to you that they're going to be even more skeptical of my motives? London has a lot of money and she runs a successful business. She's a gorgeous trend-setter and well connected. I'm your *housekeeper*." Claire's expression twisted into disgust. "We're nothing but a cliché. They are going to see me as nothing more than an opportunist."

"Not once they get to know you."

She shook her head. "I won't fit in."

"You don't even want to try."

"You're right. I'm afraid." Color spilled into Claire's cheeks. "One of the things I'm terrible at is standing up for myself. I can't tell you how many times I've let people bully me." She paused and met his gaze with eyes as hard as granite. "This town is elitist, judgmental and cliquey. Why would you want to be with a woman who won't fit in?"

It was on the tip of his tongue to insist that he didn't care when he realized that didn't matter. Claire cared. For her own peace of mind as well as for his reputation and how this would affect his mother.

"I wish you could trust me," he said after a short pause. The throb in his voice made her flinch.

"It's not a matter of trusting you." But she didn't sound convincing.

From the little she'd shared about her past, he was pretty sure that every time she needed to rely on someone, that person had come up short. He thought of what had happened to his mother when Linc's dad had first gone to prison and then divorced her. What if Linc and Sawyer hadn't been there with their love and support, making a tough time a little easier?

Often Linc had thought it odd that Claire had moved to Charleston and put the entire width of the country between her and her family. Maybe she didn't have anyone who made her life easier or better.

"I'd never do anything to hurt you," he told her.

"I'm not worried about that." She sucked in a lungful of air and then expelled it on a harsh sigh. "It's not you I don't trust, it's me. Sometimes I don't protect myself well enough and get hurt because of it. I know you aren't going to hurt me. It's not in your nature. But you can't control everyone or everything."

He was starting to understand her concerns. "So it's okay for us to keep sleeping together as long as no one finds out."

"For now. It's working for both of us at the moment." She shrugged. "When that changes, it will mean a cleaner finish if we keep things in perspective."

Basically, what she was saying was that she didn't want to get emotionally entangled with him. He'd been right to think that she wasn't over her late husband. And wasn't he the perfect guy for her to take up with? In her mind, their relationship had a built-in countdown. A few weeks. Maybe a month. Some palate-cleansing sex for him. A bridge between London and the next woman he became seriously involved with.

Linc wanted to punch something. This wasn't what he'd signed up for when he pursued Claire, but it seemed that it was all she intended to offer.

"How very practical of you," he said. "I guess I'd better head to the gym and get my workout in before the party."

After waiting a heartbeat for her to say something more, Linc realized she'd emptied her conversational basket of all its goodies and he would get nothing else. Turning on his heel, he exited the kitchen.

By the time he returned home, Claire was gone and the house had the same empty feeling it always did when she and Honey were out. Funny how he didn't get the same vibe in his Fort Worth home. Maybe because his house-keeper there didn't live-in, so her presence in the house didn't have any impact one way or another. Or perhaps because during baseball season his head was filled with the game and he had little downtime to notice that he was lonely.

Knowing his mother would be on edge before the party, Linc made sure he was at her house half an hour early. She received him in her bedroom, where she was having her makeup done. Sawyer had also arrived and was sitting on the chaise in the corner, watching their mother's transformation. She winked at him as he entered.

Bettina waved her hand. "Come over here so I can get a look at you."

Linc did as he was asked. Tonight, he'd donned a navy suit with a white shirt and bright blue-striped tie. When he'd chosen the latter, he'd imagined Claire smiling up at him as she commented how the blue matched his eyes.

"Do I meet with your approval?" he teased, seeing his mother's fond smile.

"You make me proud." Her gaze flashed toward her daughter, who wore a figure-hugging black dress that bared her toned legs and arms. Bettina frowned. "There's still time before the party if you want to run home and change," she told Sawyer. "To put on something with a little more color maybe."

"I like what I'm wearing." In one smooth move, Sawyer got to her feet and headed for the door. "Besides, Linc is the one everyone is going to be focused on tonight. No one will even notice I'm here."

Before their mother could do more than snort her disapproval, Sawyer vanished through the door. Linc stared after her in amusement. At least until her words penetrated.

Everyone would be focused on him tonight. He was the main event.

Normally this would appeal to him, but the idea that most of the women attending the party had their sights set on becoming his wife meant he would be disappointing a lot of people over the course of the evening.

"I'm going to go grab a drink," he murmured, setting his hands on his mother's shoulders and meeting her gaze in the mirror. "You look beautiful."

"Don't drink too much. Remember, this party is a marathon, not a sprint."

"But I'm such a happy drunk," he teased.

In fact, he held his liquor very well and tended to quit earlier than most of his friends. The last thing he needed was to get caught in a compromising situation because he'd drunk to excess and have his exploits splashed all over social media.

His mother regarded him in mock sternness. "We're trying to make a good impression here."

"Everyone finds me charming and irresistible. I'll be fighting them off by the end of the evening."

"I hope so. Not everyone in this town is convinced you are a good catch."

Linc could see this bothered his mother and thought he understood why. "I don't care what people think and you'd be a lot happier if you didn't, either. There are a lot of small-minded people who believe their social position gives them the right to judge others. The same people who were happy standing on the shoulders of those less fortunate when Daddy roped them into his Ponzi scheme are the ones who think they're better than him. But they behaved just as badly."

"Your father made things hard for all of us."

"Which is why you should be so proud of everything you accomplished."

His mother's expression became uncharacteristically bleak. "What did I do besides keep a roof over your heads and put food on the table? Even that was a struggle until you started pitching in." Bettina shook her head. "And don't think for one second that I don't realize my blind desire for social prominence is what prompted me to marry your father. If I hadn't been so focused on the Thurston name, I might have chosen a man with integrity. Instead, I took someone without a lick of sense and made him think he had to take idiotic risks to further our social standing."

Linc hated hearing his mother take the blame for his father's bad judgment. "He chose to rely on shortcuts instead of hard work."

"He was never all that ambitious."

Which was why after getting out of prison, he'd divorced Bettina and married an outsider with a lot of money.

"You know, it was your belief in me that made me such a success. And what about Sawyer? She's a driving force for conservation in this city. Do you think she would have the passion for preserving Charleston's history if not for the stories you told us growing up?"

"You two are my joy. I want the best for you."

Linc gave his mother's shoulders a gentle squeeze. "I know."

"That's why I threw this party, so you could meet some suitable women."

His mother hadn't yet asked what was going on between him and Claire, but he suspected she would if he didn't go on a date with one or more of tonight's guests. "Go check on Claire and see how she's doing," his mother said. "I want everything to be perfect tonight."

"I'm sure she has everything in hand, but I'll see if she needs anything."

Downstairs, Linc poked his head into the kitchen and found a completely unflustered Claire giving instructions to her waitstaff. Determining she had everything under control, he went in search of Sawyer and found her chatting with the bartender setting up in the sunporch off the main living room.

"Hey," Linc said, eyeing the drink in Sawyer's hand. "Starting already?"

"Not that it's any of your business, but it's club soda." She sipped the drink and changed the subject. "Are you sure it was a good idea inviting all your friends tonight?"

"Absolutely." Linc had hoped to redistribute some of the pressure the female guests were sure to bring. All his friends were single and one perfect girl away from settling down. "Austin, Knox and Roy have been looking for some new meat."

Sawyer made a face. "Yuck."

"You say that, but I bet every one of them hooks up tonight."

"Challenge accepted," she said, an adversarial glint in her eye. "I will make it my solemn duty to warn everyone in here about your buddies."

The idea that Sawyer would be running around cock-blocking his friends amused Linc. "They're not all bad," he said, testing out a theory. "Knox, for example, is a great guy."

"He's no better than the rest."

Even though he watched his sister carefully, she gave no sign that corroborated his suspicions that she was into his best friend. Time to push a little harder. "That's not true. In fact, I think he's seriously interested in someone."

"Why do you say that?" Sawyer looked only mildly curious.

"Because from what I can tell, he hasn't taken a girl back to his place since I returned to Charleston and there are a lot of nights he doesn't come out with us at all."

Sawyer waved her hand, dismissing his theory. "That doesn't mean he's interested in someone. Maybe he's really busy or just sick of hanging out and drinking every night with a bunch of thirtysomething adolescents."

Linc shook his head. "There's more to it than that. I

know my friend. The only time he isn't looking to hook up is when he's already involved."

"You're imagining things."

"Sort of like you," he said, hoping this time he could trip her up and she'd admit she was seeing someone. Someone like Knox.

"Sort of like me what?"

"I think you're dating someone. I've put Knox on your trail. It's only a matter of time before he figures out who it is and tells me."

Sawyer frowned at him in puzzlement. "Why do you care?"

"I need to set the guy straight about you." Linc liked playing the part of the protective big brother. He'd assumed the role as soon as Sawyer started kindergarten. "It's important that he knows if he breaks your heart, I'm going to kick his ass."

"Nice," she scoffed, her voice dry. "You don't need to worry. No one is going to break my heart, and besides, what if he's bigger than you and kicks your ass instead?"

Linc snorted. At six feet two inches of solid muscle, he wasn't worried. "Yeah, that's not going to happen."

"It's not going to happen because it doesn't need to happen." Sawyer set her empty glass down and indicated she wanted a refill. "You don't need to watch out for me. I'm a big girl."

"But it's my job to take care of you and Mom."

Their dad sure as hell hadn't been around to do that, even before his financial schemes landed him in jail.

"That's sweet," Sawyer said. "Worry about Mom all you want, but I can take care of myself just fine."

"Okay, then answer me this. Are you dating anyone?"

"Shouldn't you be greeting your guests or something?"

"Nobody's here yet."

"Then why don't you go pester Claire? Or bug this

guy to make sure the bar is stocked with the right kind of bourbon."

"Why don't you answer my question?" Both her expression and her silence told Linc he would get nowhere. That didn't stop him from persisting. "Have you ever considered dating Knox?"

"I thought you said he was already interested in someone."

"What if that someone is you?"

Sawyer's eyes went wide and she gave her head a vigorous shake. "Me and your best friend? That's a recipe for disaster."

"I disagree. You two have a lot in common with your love of preserving Charleston's old buildings. I figure if he ever decides to settle down, you'd be good for him."

"What about him being good for me?"

"You're right." Linc knew his sister well enough to recognize when it was time to back off. While he believed she and Knox would be a perfect match, too much pushing from him and they'd never realize it. "Forget I said anything."

Sawyer was quiet for a long time, but Linc held his tongue and waited her out. In the end, his patience was rewarded.

"You're right that we do have a lot in common."

"Do you want me to have him ask you out?"

"Geez, Linc. No. Forget it. Don't you dare say anything to him."

"Too late. I've already put the idea in his head."

"Linc Thurston, how dare you meddle in my love life."

"To quote our mother, 'I just want you to be happy.'"

"Then you'll mind your own business and never speak of this again."

"You know I can't do that. I inherited our mother's meddling gene."

To his surprise, Sawyer wrapped her arms around his neck and gave him a fierce hug. "Everything is going to be all right with both of us," she murmured. "You'll see."

Linc put his arms around her and squeezed gently in return, basking in her affection. "I hope you're right."

But all he could think about was the endless party that stretched before him and how a certain brunette with soulful brown eyes was going to handle seeing dozens of women flirting with him all evening long. He only hoped she'd hate it as much as he was going to.

Carrying a stack of clean plates, Claire scanned Bettina's party guests and the waitstaff and the bartenders, making sure everything was running smoothly. In addition to sending Jenny and Steve around with trays of appetizers and glasses of wine, Claire had opted to set up hors d'oeuvres in a couple locations. Every fifteen minutes or so, she made a loop of the party.

It might have seemed like she was micromanaging things, but staying focused on the tasks at hand kept her from dwelling on all the beautiful women in attendance and wondering which of them would end up with Linc. Automatically, her gaze swept the room in search of him. Her chest ached when she spied him in a group composed of his friends and a familiar blonde woman. Everly Briggs looked comfortable and at home as she repeatedly touched Linc's arm as if to punctuate whatever she was saying.

Although Claire had seen a significant number of women vying for Linc's attention tonight, for some reason, seeing him with Everly made her feel slightly sick. Perhaps it was because the woman had been so forward at the grocery store. And even though she suspected it had been more curiosity than cruelty that had made the woman so blunt, Claire couldn't help but feel uneasy at her appearance here tonight. Would she be bold enough to repeat to Linc the gossip she'd shared with Claire?

"Claire, are you all right?" Jenny asked, pulling her attention away from Everly and Linc. The waitress stood beside her with a tray of dirty glasses and plates.

"I'm fine," Claire said as she surreptitiously indicated Everly. "I ran into that blonde woman standing next to Linc a few weeks ago at the grocery store and made the mistake of telling her I worked for him. Do you know anything about her?"

"Everly Briggs? She's big on the charity circuit."

"That makes sense. She wanted to hire me to do an event. What does she do?"

"She owns some sort of branding company." Jenny lowered her voice. "There was a huge scandal involving her sister last year. She went to jail after leaking a bunch of engineering documents or something to her employer's competitor. I heard they were worth over two million dollars."

"Why would she do that?"

"Apparently, she thought she was going to get fired and wanted to get back at the company before that happened. Plus, she thought it would help her get a job with the competitor."

That Jenny knew so much of the story didn't surprise Claire at all. She'd heard snatches of several tales tonight as she moved through the crowd. This group of people seemed to feed off drama and loved to share every juicy tidbit.

"Well, that's just crazy," Claire said. "Why would she think that was a good idea?"

"I don't know. Maybe crazy runs in the family."

"Should I warn Linc?" He didn't need someone like that in his life.

"Naw," Jenny said, sliding a sidelong glance in Claire's direction. "I don't think she's Linc's type."

Her friend's sly grin caught Claire off guard, but she quickly recovered. "I wasn't wondering that."

"Sure."

"I wasn't." Claire gave her head a little toss. "Although, I think he could do better."

"Well, he certainly has plenty to choose from at this party. I wonder if he enjoys all the attention or if he finds it irritating."

"Most men would love to be fawned over by all these women," Claire said. "On the other hand, Bettina has made it clear that she's hosting this party so he can meet some eligible women and possibly start a relationship with one of them. I imagine he has to feel a little bit like prey."

The two women went their own way, Jenny to deliver the dirty dishes to the kitchen and Claire to continue making sure the party was going smoothly. She greeted several of Linc's friends as she passed them. Apparently, Linc hadn't wanted to face the horde of marriage-minded women without backup. Claire spied Knox deep in conversation with Sawyer and wondered if those two had ever tried dating or if Linc didn't trust his baby sister with his best friend.

After checking on the inventory behind the portable bar set up in the parlor and finding satisfactory levels of alcohol and mix, she retreated into the kitchen to assess the situation there.

"How are we doing?" she asked Trudy, the woman she'd hired to assist her with the preparations. "Anything we're running low on?"

"Your crab puffs are a huge hit. Good thing we made more than you originally planned."

Claire nodded. "This is a town that likes its seafood."

With a large party like this, so many things could go wrong, but she'd been planning and organizing like a fiend. Over the next few hours, things went so smoothly it was almost anticlimactic. By ten o'clock, she estimated a third of the party guests had taken off. With the gathering winding down, all she had left to do was clean up and head out.

While she collected trays and chafing dishes from the buffet, Claire surreptitiously looked around for Linc, curious if he'd found someone he wanted to spend some quiet one-on-one time with. Throughout the evening, every time she'd ventured through the room, he'd been conversing with a different woman. His mother had to be thrilled that he was taking her matchmaking so seriously.

As if her thoughts had summoned him, Linc came up beside her. His long, warm fingers curved around her arm, and he gave her a brief heart-wrenching squeeze.

"Another successful event under your belt. Your food is fantastic and pretty soon everyone in Charleston is going to know who you are."

His praise and support made Claire light-headed. "I'm sure they already know I'm your housekeeper."

"I'm talking about the polo match that's coming up. You'll make a huge splash as the caterer and I'm sure my mother would be happy to talk you up to her friends."

"You know, it sounds like you're trying to get rid of me."

"Not at all. It's just that several people have mentioned to me lately that your talents are going to waste as my housekeeper. I thought maybe your loyalty to me might be stopping you from starting your own catering business." Though he smiled as he said it, his blue eyes were grave.

"I'd never do that." Her throat tightened at the thought of leaving him. "I don't have the money or the know-how to start my own company."

"But if you did?"

Although she was flattered that so many people had faith in her cuisine, the pressure to succeed overwhelmed her. "I also don't have the time or the desire. You know that Honey is my top priority. Also, there are so many well-established caterers in Charleston, I can't imagine being able to compete." She offered him a wry smile. "So it looks like you're stuck with me."

To her relief, the corner of his mouth kicked up in a matching grin. "That's good to hear, but I don't want to stand in your way if you think doing something else might be better for you and Honey."

"I know it must seem that I'm unambitious, but I'm happy right where I am." The position enabled her to stay below the radar and out of sight of Jasper's parents. "So, have you picked one yet?" she asked, deciding to change the subject.

"Picked one?" he echoed with a slight frown.

She used her chin to indicate the crowd. Hadn't he noticed the way all eyes had been following him tonight? Every single woman here, with the exception of Sawyer, had her sights set on becoming Mrs. Lincoln Thurston.

"Your mother and sister have delivered every eligible female in Charleston to your doorstep. All you need to do is choose."

"Truthfully, they all look the same to me. Not one of them stands out as someone I want to get to know." He sighed.

"You haven't given any of them a chance," Claire said, secretly hoping that it would take him a while to settle on just one. For the moment, she liked having him all to herself. "You should pick three tonight and invite each of them out for dinner."

Linc's blue eyes glinted with irritation. "I can't believe you're okay with this."

"I'm a realist." Claire hoped her voice didn't betray the lie. "It's what has to happen."

"It doesn't have to happen this way."

"You know that it does. You might have been okay

marrying a woman your mother didn't approve of, but I'll bet it was hard on London knowing Bettina would never fully welcome her."

Before she'd finished speaking, a lovely blonde appeared at Linc's side and wrapped her hand around his arm in a possessive gesture. From what Claire had observed, Charleston seemed to have an overabundance of slender, elegant blonde women with perfect teeth and fine manners. She almost pitied Linc having to choose one, because none had stood out for her and she couldn't imagine him settling for a woman who was interchangeable with a dozen others.

"There you are," the newcomer said, behaving as if Linc had been having a conversation with thin air. "I've been dying for a chance to catch up with you all night, but you've been surrounded."

Although Claire expected to be treated as if she didn't exist, Linc wasn't the sort to play along. Claire had noticed that he gave everyone his full attention, treating them like they mattered. From the gardener who maintained the meticulous landscaping around the Jonathan Elliot House to the mailman and his neighbor's dog walker.

"Phoebe Reed," he said, gesturing toward Claire, "this is Claire Robbins. She is responsible for all the delicious food."

Forced to be polite, the blonde tore her rapt gaze from Linc and glanced in Claire's direction, giving her a perfunctory nod. "I'm sure it's all quite yummy." Minor courtesy out of the way, she returned her full attention to Linc. "Your sister tells me you're going to be a part of the holiday home tour. I can't wait to see what you've done to the Jonathan Elliot House."

Rather than be an awkward third wheel, Claire murmured, "I have to get back to the kitchen." And before Linc could stop her, she faded into the dwindling crowd.

As much as she wanted to dwell on Phoebe and the dozen other beautiful, wealthy, socially connected women who'd been brought here with the purpose of getting acquainted with Linc, Claire had a job to do. Taking up one of the big trays she'd brought from the kitchen, she moved around the room, collecting empty dishes and glasses. The guests thinned out more still as she worked.

She was making her third round of the rooms when someone spoke from just behind her. "Hello." The cultured female voice sounded familiar. "It's Claire, right?"

Claire turn to face Everly Briggs and her stomach dropped.

"Yes," Claire said cautiously, with a polite smile fixed on her lips. "And you're Everly."

She was dying to ask how the woman knew Bettina, but she figured Everly fell into the same category as most of the women attending the party: Charleston social elite.

"I hear you were in charge of the food tonight. I just knew you were talented."

The woman's enthusiasm wasn't winning Claire over. Something about their encounter at the grocery store and the assumptions Everly had made, followed by her appearance tonight, left Claire feeling uneasy.

"Thank you." She glanced to the side, hoping Everly would take the hint and let Claire get about her task.

"I suppose you're a little surprised to see me here," Everly continued, relaxing into the conversation and missing Claire's subtle signal.

"A little." Claire told herself to let it go, but curiosity had a mind of its own. Maybe if she hadn't heard about Everly's sister from Jenny, she wouldn't have cared. After all, in certain circles, most everyone in Charleston was connected in one way or another. "From our last conversation, I got the impression you didn't know Linc."

"I don't. I tagged along with a friend of mine, Augusta Hobbs." Everly gave Claire a conspiratorial smile. "Although we've been at several of the same events, I've never actually met Linc. Turns out he's as wonderful as you said."

Had Claire described Linc as wonderful?

"I can see why you'd enjoy working for him," the woman continued. "He's very genuine. As well as handsome and wealthy. How have you managed to be around him all the time and not fall in love?"

Claire felt herself flushing beneath the woman's keen regard, but she kept her gaze and voice cool as she said, "He's my boss."

Everly smirked. "Yes, I know, but haven't you fantasized about him even a little?"

"No." Once again, their conversation was straying to inappropriate topics. Cheeks hot, Claire regarded the woman with a flat stare before she found her voice again. "If you'll excuse me, I still have a lot to do."

"Of course, but before you go, I was wondering if we could meet for lunch early next week to discuss the food for the charity polo match."

The request seemed to come from out of the blue. "Are you involved with the event?"

"Yes. I wasn't able to make the meeting last week with Genevieve and Portia when they asked you to cater the event. I'm in charge of the food and wanted to discuss the menu with you."

Claire wished Everly had led with that instead of talking about Linc. She relaxed a little. "Of course. When would you like to do that?"

"Could you meet on Monday or Tuesday?"

"How about Tuesday. Would one o'clock work?"

"One o'clock would be perfect. Why don't I meet you at Magnolias."

"That would be fine. Now, I really need to get back to

the kitchen," Claire said, pretending she'd seen something that needed her attention. Instinct urged her to get away from this woman.

"Looking forward to our meeting on Tuesday." Everly's drawl pursued Claire as she fled.

Nine

The morning following his mother's party, Linc was summoned to her house for a debriefing. She wanted his opinion of the women he'd met and some indication that he intended to date one or two of them.

When he arrived, Bettina was at her dining room table, eating a poached egg with toast and fresh fruit. She liked her coffee dark and rich with liberal splashes of cream and instructed Dolly to pour him a cup before he sat down.

"I thought last night's party went quite well," his mother said without preamble. "Lyla Madison's daughter is quite accomplished and has the sort of beauty that ages well."

"Which one was she?" he asked, thanking Dolly with a smile as he accepted a delicate china cup.

"The brunette in pink. She's a CPA at the accounting firm I use." Bettina frowned as Linc continued to regard her blankly. "You spoke with her for half an hour."

"Sorry. There were so many women there. I lost track of names."

"Linc, I need you to take this seriously." Bettina let her

gaze rest on him for a long moment before speaking again. "You simply must marry someone from our social circles."

As much as Linc hated to disappoint his mother, he needed to get something off his chest. "What if I fall in love with someone who isn't from an old Charleston family?"

"Have you?"

Confronted by his mother's demand, Linc found himself hesitating.

"Is this about Claire?" Bettina continued. "I've seen how you are with her. But she's your housekeeper."

"I don't care."

His mother huffed. "You're acting like your father, doing something without considering the consequences."

"I'm nothing like my father," he retorted through gritted teeth.

"I'll admit you haven't behaved like him before this." Bettina tossed her napkin onto her half-finished breakfast. "Honestly, Linc. Have you thought any of this through? You have a social position—"

"You've never accepted that I don't care about that." He'd come here today expecting resistance, but he wasn't prepared to defend his future with Claire, because he hadn't figured out what he wanted.

"Then what do you care about?"

"I care about Claire."

"That's all well and good…" His mother regarded him in exasperation. "And I've always said my children's happiness is my top priority, but—"

"She makes me happy." Linc was firm on that. "She's an amazing woman and a terrific mother. We have this amazing chemistry, and I'm happier spending time with her and Honey than with anyone else on the planet." His voice grew stronger with each sentence.

"So what are you planning to do? Marry Claire and become Honey's father?" Bettina demanded, her tone skeptical. "Is that what she wants?"

Linc would be lying if he said he had everything figured out, but now that the question had been asked, the answer was clear. "I think that's where we're headed. And if anyone has anything negative to say about that or her, they will have me to contend with."

His mother narrowed her eyes and regarded him for several seconds before nodding. "When you put it that way, of course I'll accept Claire."

"Just like that?" Linc couldn't help being suspicious of his mother's abrupt capitulation. "After everything you said about London's lack of a social pedigree, you're suddenly okay with me being in a relationship with my housekeeper?"

"You never fought for London." It was less a statement of fact and more of an accusation.

Leave it to Bettina to twist things around until Linc didn't know if he was coming or going.

"I shouldn't have had to."

"Regardless." Disapproval tightened his mother's mouth. "You never championed her."

Linc couldn't understand where she was coming from. "What does that matter? London was strong and could take care of herself."

"Are you saying Claire isn't as strong?"

"She may not always defend herself, but she will do whatever it takes to keep Honey safe."

"I agree about Claire, but I think you're wrong about London. She needed you to be there, but you weren't. I kept waiting for you to stand up for her, and when you never did, I knew she wasn't the woman for you."

Linc studied his mother while he processed her statement. "Are you telling me London's outsider status didn't bother you? You were just using it to test if I was willing to fight for our love?"

"Exactly."

"So you wanted me to convince you I was madly in love with her?"

"And you never did," his mother said. "I never believed London was the most important woman in your life and neither did she. That's what kept her from feeling secure in your relationship. What made her so needy and controlling."

Was that true? Had he let London down? What his mother said made sense. He and London had been engaged for two years without committing to a wedding date. She'd tried pinning him down several times and each time he came up with an excuse for why he wasn't ready. Was it because with each passing month, he'd grown less and less confident that she was the right woman for him?

Would he eventually feel that way about Claire?

Linc couldn't imagine a time that he wouldn't want to be with her. In fact, with each hour they spent apart, he grew more impatient to have her all to himself. Was that love? He'd certainly never felt like this with London.

And what if Claire didn't feel the same way about him? She'd made it pretty clear all she was interested in was a casual physical relationship. Was that what she'd told him because she didn't believe he could ever want more? Or because she hadn't stopped grieving for her late husband?

One thing he was certain of, after the polo match event, they were going to have a serious discussion about taking their relationship public. His conversation with his mother today had made it clear that the only way Claire was going to believe they had a future was if he demonstrated he was going to fight for one.

After spending a fun morning with Honey and Linc at the aquarium, Claire was not in the mood for a business lunch with Everly Briggs. But she'd committed to doing the food for the polo event and Everly was the one in charge.

Claire dressed for the meeting in a blue-and-white seersucker shirtdress with short sleeves and a belt. She'd bought the dress at a consignment shop she'd found near Meeting and George Street and liked how the style was both professional and feminine.

When she arrived at the restaurant, Everly wasn't yet there. The hostess showed Claire to a table beneath an enormous painting of a magnolia blossom. While the exposed ceiling beams and pine floors gave the space an industrial feel, the white tablecloths and metal vines corkscrewing up the iron support posts added sophistication. Claire was pondering the squat crystal vase with sprigs of tiny white flowers in the middle of the table when her lunch companion arrived.

"You're early," Everly said as she sat down opposite Claire. "I can't tell you how much that impresses me. So many people don't value another person's time. Where is your daughter? I was looking forward to seeing her again."

"I left her home. We went to the aquarium this morning and she's pretty tired out." Claire wondered why Everly thought she'd bring Honey. "And this is a business lunch, after all. It didn't seem appropriate to bring her."

"Of course. Is she with Linc Thurston? I heard he took her to the children's museum a week ago." Everly looked delighted. "How nice for you to have a built-in babysitter."

Claire fought against rising panic. "He was just helping me out the one time because I was catering his mother's party." Although in truth, it had happened several times. Linc was someone who needed to keep busy, and for him, spending time with a toddler was anything but boring. Plus, not having to keep an eye on Honey freed Claire to tackle some projects that were challenging with a toddler around.

"Don't worry," Everly said with a toothy smile that didn't quite reach her eyes. "I wouldn't dream of saying anything."

"The food here looks so good. Do you have anything you recommend?"

Everly languidly waved her hand. "It's all good."

As soon as the women ordered lunch, Claire got down to business. She didn't like this woman and refused to linger over the meal any longer than absolutely necessary. But Everly had a different agenda.

"With your accent, you obviously aren't from the South," the blonde woman began, her bright green eyes fixed on Claire as if she was the most fascinating person in the room. "Where is your family from?"

Although the last thing Claire wanted to do was talk about herself, she imagined that parting with a few details would be okay.

"I grew up in California, the Bay Area. San Francisco." Claire added this last detail because she'd found some people in Charleston acted as if little beyond South Carolina was worth knowing about.

"I've never been to San Francisco, but I understand there's a lot of fine dining there. Is that why you became a chef?"

No need to explain that her father hadn't been the sort to take her out for fancy dinners. Or that she'd waitressed all through high school and became fascinated by everything that went on in the kitchen.

"I grew up watching cooking shows and started experimenting with recipes when I was nine."

"I imagine your mother appreciated the help in the kitchen. Are you looking forward to sharing your love of food with your daughter?"

Actually, her mother had left shortly after Claire turned seven and her father hadn't been all that good in the kitchen. So if she wanted something more than canned spaghetti and hot dogs, she'd realized she needed to learn how to cook.

"Honey is already showing signs of being an excellent chef," Claire said.

"Is your husband a chef as well?"

Claire kept her smile in place, but her irritation was growing. "No, actually he was in the military."

"I see." Everly's nod seemed to indicate that explained something. "Is he stationed nearby?"

"No." Claire stared at her water glass to avoid meeting Everly's gaze. She hated how everyone reacted when she spoke of what had happened to Jasper. "He was killed in action several years ago."

"Oh, that's just terrible. I'm so sorry. What a shame that Honey will never get to know her father."

"Yes. Well…" Claire trailed off into uncomfortable silence. She was used to people's condolences, but this conversation was more of an interview than idle lunch chatter. "Unfortunately, she wasn't the only child who lost her father that day."

"So you moved all the way across the country to Charleston. That's a big step. Don't you miss your family?"

"I wanted to start fresh," Claire said, keeping her answer vague. "Charleston has an interesting history and it's quite lovely."

She had no intention of sharing the story of her family connection to one of the state's founding families. Chances were it was just some bit of nonsense made up by one of her ancestors. Back in the 1800s, with travel being so arduous and a Civil War brewing between the North and the South, it would've been virtually impossible to prove someone's claim of being the second son of a wealthy well-connected family.

And even if the story was true, Claire couldn't imagine

some long lost relatives opening their arms to welcome a stranger into their exclusive group, especially one who'd grown up in California.

Deciding to take control of the conversation, Claire cleared her throat and said, "Can you tell me a little bit about the food you arranged with the former caterer for your polo event? Is it a buffet or a sit-down lunch?"

Everly hesitated before answering, looking like she was reluctant to get down to business. At last, she gave a little flutter of her fingers and began. "The way we bring in revenue at this event is by selling tickets to the match and also offering special baskets for lunch. We've had a hundred baskets preordered. Each one costs three hundred dollars and will feed two people."

Claire nodded as she jotted notes on a small pad of paper. She'd done a little research on the sorts of food served at a polo match. She intended to propose a sampler of sandwiches made with beef, ham, perhaps salmon, definitely one of vegetables. An artisanal meat and cheese tray with a delectable kale salad or perhaps a cold soup, maybe both. And seasonal fruit. For drinks, she'd recommend a bottle of Txakoli and her homemade *aguas frescas*.

As she spelled out her plans, Everly nodded her agreement and Claire relaxed with each minute that went by. While she was confident in her ability to cook, satisfying a crowd of people accustomed to the best was daunting. Plus, what she might have fixed for a San Francisco crowd wouldn't necessarily cut it in Charleston.

"Another thought would be to offer wines made by someone who plays polo." Claire went on to list a couple brands that she'd researched.

"Well, aren't you thorough," Everly said, looking surprised.

The waitress brought their food, interrupting the flow of the conversation, and Claire picked up her fork, eager to taste what she'd chosen. Magnolias was known for their refined take on Southern cuisine. The menu had offered several dishes featuring fried green tomatoes, creamy grits and, of course, shellfish. But one dish in particular had caught her eye: a bourbon fried catfish with pickled hot peppers, okra and sweet corn fricassee, and Tabasco rémoulade.

Everly ignored her own plate of delicious-looking scallops. "After Bettina's party, I knew that you were a fantastic chef, but your suggestions today are so much better than I expected. What made you think of the wine made by polo players?"

"I remember reading an article about the Argentinian wineries building polo fields because the pairing made so much sense."

"It's brilliant. Have you ever considered opening your own catering company? Someone with your talent could be a big hit in Charleston. I have a lot of connections in town and could help you get started."

"That's really nice of you," Claire said, appreciating Everly's enthusiasm but wishing everyone would stop trying to push her into something she wasn't ready for. "But I'm not interested in catering full-time."

"I don't see why not. I recognize talent when I see it."

"Thank you, but I like working for Linc and don't intend to stop."

"But your talent is wasted." At last, Everly picked up her fork and turned her attention to her meal. "You could be doing so much more than just cleaning Linc Thurston's house."

"To be honest, I don't know where to begin when it comes to launching a business. I'm only catering these few events because Bettina is Linc's mother and your committee members seemed in a desperate situation."

"I understand that starting a business must seem daunting. But here's how I can help you. I belong to an organization of women entrepreneurs and we make it our mission to support and encourage people like you."

"That sounds like a worthwhile mission," Claire said, "but I don't have the time or money to start my own catering company." *Why wouldn't this woman stop pushing?*

"I understand your concerns, but I'm sure you can work something out. You don't have to do it all at once. Why don't we get together after the polo match and I can walk you through some of the options. Your food is so good. I just know you'd be a huge success."

Sensing the woman wouldn't drop it, Claire managed a vague smile and a half-hearted nod. This encounter with Everly reinforced for Claire why she had no interest in starting a catering business. Too often, she struggled to assert herself. As a kid, she'd never learned to stand and fight. It was always easier to run away.

Fortunately for Claire, as the two women ate, she was able to turn the tables on Everly and persuade her to talk about her own background. Claire wasn't surprised that, although Everly spoke about growing up in Charleston, she never mentioned her sister who'd been imprisoned for stealing.

When lunch was over, Everly snagged the check as soon as the waitress set it down and slid her credit card into the holder, ignoring Claire's protest.

"My treat," the blonde said. "You are saving us from a disaster. The least I could do is buy you lunch. Besides, I suggested eating here and I know it's a little expensive."

"Thank you," Claire replied, deciding against letting the subtle jab get to her.

Still, no matter how much Everly complimented her talents as a chef, the Charlestonian would always view Claire as "the help." It was this prejudicial view that Linc couldn't seem to understand or refused to acknowledge despite growing up in this town.

No matter how successful or rich she became, as far as everyone who mattered was concerned, Claire would never be good enough for Linc. Although it put an ache in her heart, she'd accepted it. If only he would as well. Because if he didn't, his faith in them as a couple was going to tear them apart sooner rather than later.

Claire stood beside Linc and marveled as the mass of horses and riders charged from one end of the field to the other in pursuit of a small white ball. The thunder of the hooves on the grass made her heart pound. She hadn't been prepared for the adrenaline rush of watching the nonstop action of a polo match.

It was the second match of the day. She'd been occupied getting the luncheon baskets ready and missed the first. For some reason, she'd assumed polo was like other sports where it would take hours to play the game. Today, she'd discovered that the match was composed of six chukkers—or periods—lasting seven and a half minutes each, with a ten-minute halftime during which the spectators went out onto the field for the traditional divot stomp.

"What do you think?" Linc asked.

Flushed with enthusiasm, she glanced away from the field, noting that several of the ladies dressed in party frocks with adorable hats festooned with ribbons and flowers were paying more attention to her and Linc than the match.

"The spectators appear so civilized," she said, grinning up at him. "While the polo riders are intense and a little crazy."

The sport wasn't for the fainthearted. Four horses from each team galloped down the field, bumping and jockey-

ing for position while their riders swung four-foot mallets.
It was a wonder no one was seriously hurt.

A cry went up from the crowd as Sawyer's friend Ruby
scored yet again for the women. This particular match was
a battle of the sexes, and at the moment, the women were
kicking butt.

"How come you don't play?" Claire asked Linc. She'd
noticed that several of his friends were on teams today.

Linc shook his head. "I like to keep both my feet on the
ground when I'm chasing little white balls."

"Have you tried it?"

"Once. It didn't go well." Linc's grin was rueful. "Do
you ride? I'm sure Ruby would be happy to give you some
lessons in how to play."

Although Claire had never been on a horse, she could
imagine how empowering it would feel to charge down
the field in pursuit of the ball at speeds of thirty to forty
miles an hour. "I don't think so."

"Why not?"

"It must take years to learn to ride well enough to do
this."

"You wouldn't play at this level to start off. I'm sure
there are plenty of people who are beginners that you could
team up with."

Though intrigued, Claire shook her head. She didn't
have the time or the money to spend on something like
polo.

"Linc, there you are." It was Landry Beaumont, yet another stunning woman with her sights set on Linc. "Where
did you disappear to after lunch? It's nearly halftime. Come
meet my brother. He's on Austin's team. We can harass
them about losing to a bunch of girls."

While Linc was distracted by Landry, Claire faded from
his side, fighting the dismay swelling in her chest. What

had she expected? She'd known from the first that anything between her and Linc was temporary at best.

And from what she'd gleaned after Bettina's party, it sounded like everyone was rooting for a relationship to develop between Linc and Landry. With her family connections, beauty and interests, she was being touted as the perfect girl for him.

Done with her work, Claire headed for the exit, her foolish heart aching. Unfortunately, her escape was thwarted by Everly Briggs.

"There you are," Everly said. Today, she wore a filmy floral dress in various warm pastel shades, a broad-brimmed hat festooned with poppies, and dark glasses. "You're not leaving already, are you?"

Feeling shabby beside the socialite, Claire nodded. "It's been a long day and I should be getting back to my daughter."

"Well, then, I'm so glad I caught you. You did a terrific job for us today. Do you have all the receipts so I can get our treasurer to write a check for you?"

The last thing Claire wanted was to be delayed, but she'd paid for the food out of her own pocket and needed to be reimbursed. "I have everything in my car."

"Can you get it and bring it back here? I'll go find Deirdre."

"Of course."

Claire made her way through the parking lot to her Saab and retrieved the folder that held all her receipts, as well as the paperwork the committee had requested she fill out so they could reimburse her.

When she arrived at the spot where she and Everly had parted, the other woman hadn't yet returned. While she waited, Claire's gaze roved the crowd in search of Linc's tall form. She spotted him with Austin and a blond man she assumed was Landry's brother, since the group also included her and Ruby.

"Well, look who's here," said a familiar female voice from just behind her shoulder.

Claire's head snapped around and there stood Jasper's mother and father. The malicious satisfaction in their expressions caused Claire to step back from them.

"Doug. Sharon." Claire couldn't believe what she was seeing. "What are you doing here?"

"You look surprised." Doug Patmore sneered. "Didn't think we would find you?"

Of average height with tanned skin and a fleshy face, Jasper's father used the force of his personality rather than his physical presence to intimidate. Claire had never cared for the way he invaded her space. She suspected he enjoyed her discomfort.

The incongruity of seeing these two in Charleston, at a polo match, a party she was catering, left her dumbfounded and mute.

"Where's our granddaughter?" Sharon demanded. "You had no right to take her away from us and we insist on seeing her at once to make sure she's okay."

The accusation made Claire want to shriek. Their outrageous claims were the reason why she'd packed up and fled California not long after Jasper's death. She was terrified she might lose Honey once his parents started challenging her for custody of their granddaughter.

Logically, she knew that they might not have enough against her to convince a judge that Honey wasn't safe in her care, but she wasn't confident that the system would work for her this time after it had failed her seven years earlier when a lie had branded Claire as dangerous to children.

And with Jasper dead, who would believe his parents were poor guardians? It would be her word against both of theirs if she claimed that as soon as he graduated high school, Jasper had gone into the military and cut all ties with his parents.

"Honey is perfectly fine." It was an effort to keep her voice calm and steady when her whole body trembled with fear and fury. "And I haven't changed my mind about you seeing her."

Their distress at being kept from their granddaughter spun Claire's emotions into a chaotic mess. On one hand, Jasper was their only son, and even though they'd driven him away over fifteen years earlier, Claire recognized that they might want to try to do better with his daughter.

Unfortunately, they'd shown themselves to be toxic people and had resisted Claire's attempts to deal fairly with them. From the moment they reached out to her after Jasper's death, they hadn't had a single nice thing to say and had even gone so far as to accuse her of deliberately getting pregnant to force Jasper to take care of her.

"You will let us see her now," Jasper's father stated, his voice rising. "Or we will call the authorities."

Although Claire never took her eyes off the pair, she became aware that heads were turning in their direction. The last thing she needed was for the stir to reach Linc. He'd feel compelled to come see if she was okay. Then he'd meet Jasper's parents and find out that she'd been lying to him for over a year.

"Honey is our granddaughter," Sharon said, picking up the argument. "We need to make sure she's safe. You had no right to take her away from us."

Claire ground her teeth. She had every right to move across the country and away from these people. Jasper had told her numerous stories of his childhood and how he'd been verbally abused if he got a couple answers wrong on a test or didn't get his chores done fast enough. She couldn't imagine entrusting her sweet-natured baby to these unhappy, abrasive people.

Claire tried again. "Let's go somewhere and talk. We don't want to disturb this lovely function."

"I don't give a damn about this party," Jasper's mother said. "I just want my grandbaby."

"Is everything okay?" To Claire's dismay, Linc was approaching with Knox and Sawyer trailing after him.

"Everything is fine," she answered.

"Everything is not fine," Jasper's mother declared. "This girl has stolen our granddaughter from us."

"That's not true," Claire said. She couldn't look at Linc. This sort of outrageous scene was the height of disrespect. What he must think of her.

"Are you Claire's family?" he asked, his deep voice ringing with authority and bringing a much-needed calm to the situation.

"Her family?" Doug Patmore gave a caustic laugh. "Hardly. She wanted to marry our son, but we wouldn't have her."

That wasn't true. At least the part about her wanting to marry Jasper. No doubt Jasper's parents blamed her for their estrangement from their son, even though it had begun years before she and Jasper had ever met.

Linc was frowning at Jasper's parents. "I'm sorry, but I'm confused. Claire was married to your son."

"Well, that's a pack of lies," Jasper's father said, his eyes narrowing as he regarded Claire. "I guess we shouldn't be surprised, considering the way you duped my son into thinking you gave a damn about him and got pregnant so he'd have to take care of you."

Horror kept Claire pinned in place even as the desire to crawl under a shrub and die flooded her. She told herself not to glance Linc's way for his reaction, but she simply had to know if he believed the lies Jasper's father was spouting.

Linc's face was an impenetrable mask. Only his eyes expressed the deep sadness and crushing disappointment he was feeling.

"You were never married?" he asked her, his voice low and husky.

Her gaze flickered to Jasper's parents. It was all over. She might as well come clean. There'd been no future for her and Linc anyway. But watching his faith in her crumble was a blow she hadn't seen coming.

"No."

Ten

Scarcely able to believe that Claire had been lying to him this whole time, Linc tried to get his head around what was going on. She wasn't a military widow, or any sort of widow. Had any of what she'd said been true? Or had she simply been playing him all along?

"Why did you tell everyone you were?" he demanded.

Instead of rushing into an explanation of her actions, she crossed her arms over her chest and glanced at the older couple who'd been harassing her as he walked up.

She ducked her head and spoke in a low voice. "Can we please talk about this later?"

"Why can't you just tell me?" Linc growled, staring at the woman he'd started thinking in terms of spending the rest of his life with, willing her to say something—anything—that would make the churning in his gut go away. "Claire, what the hell is going on? Who are these people?"

"Jasper's parents. Doug and Sharon Patmore."

"What are they doing here?"

Claire shook her head. "Can we please talk about this later?"

Knox set his hand on Linc's arm. "The media is going to be all over this if we don't step away right now."

A portion of his mind registered that Sawyer was also standing beside him. Their support meant everything in that moment. Unfortunately, they weren't the only ones there. Linc glanced around, noticing several people clicking away on their phones. The curiosity of the crowd surrounding them was palpable. No doubt, dozens of social media posts were being uploaded that very second.

"Knox is right," Claire said, her eyes wide and pleading. "You don't want to get dragged into any sort of a scene."

And before he could say another word, she darted away, headed in the opposite direction from the older couple she'd been speaking with. They started off after her and Linc's gut twisted as he watched them all disappear into the crowd. Letting her go taxed his willpower.

Despite knowing she'd lied, his instincts told him to follow and fight at her side. It was pretty obvious that the older couple were up to no good. He'd never seen Claire look so miserable.

"Any idea what that was about?" Knox asked. "They accused Claire of stealing their granddaughter."

"That's ridiculous." Linc might not know Claire as well as he'd assumed, but he doubted she'd do anything like that. "There's something strange going on here and I'd like to get to the bottom of it."

"So you didn't know she was never married?"

Linc shook his head. "She's been lying to all of us."

"Why would she do that?" Sawyer murmured, sliding her hand around his arm and giving a gentle squeeze.

Linc glanced at Sawyer and nodded his appreciation of her comforting gesture. "I don't know, but there's something wrong with those people claiming to be Honey's grandparents. Claire once told me her... Jasper didn't have any sort of relationship with his parents and didn't want them near Honey. If that's the case, I wonder what they're doing here."

"Claire sure didn't look happy to see them," Sawyer added.

He knew better than to feel sympathy for Claire, but he couldn't help it.

"So if she didn't invite them, how did they know to find her here?" Knox asked.

"That's a good question," Linc said. "Maybe we need to find out how they got in."

"I can check with Portia and see if they were on the list of people who bought tickets," Knox offered.

When Linc nodded, Knox headed off, leaving brother and sister by themselves.

"Are you going to be okay?" Sawyer asked.

"I'm perfectly fine," Linc said. "Just surprised, that's all."

But from his sister's expression, Linc realized he'd given away that he felt more for Claire than what a boss feels for an employee. And if he didn't take himself in hand right now, the entire world would know he'd been behaving like a complete idiot.

"Are you and Claire..." Sawyer paused and glanced around, but they were out of earshot. "Have you been sleeping together?"

"Only just recently."

"Linc." She packed a world of concern into the single syllable.

"You don't need to tell me I screwed up."

And yet, until a moment ago, he'd been convinced that he'd had it all figured out. When he imagined the rest of his life, he pictured every day with Claire and Honey in it. Not as his housekeeper, but as something more permanent. Wife. The word didn't trigger any sort of alarm. It should have. Given what he'd learned just now.

The kicker was he still wanted her in his life. Knowing she'd lied to him and that he had no true idea of who she was, he still couldn't imagine anyone who made him as happy as she did.

"I don't think you screwed up," Sawyer said.

Hadn't he? Linc reminded himself he'd done all the pursuing. If he hadn't let his feelings for her be known, would she have slept with him? In fact, she'd resisted all his attempts to move their relationship forward. But if he took her at her word and believed she never intended their relationship to be public, then why had she created a fictitious husband?

"We need to get more information before we judge her," Sawyer continued. "Claire isn't malicious and I can't imagine her setting out to hurt you. In fact, when she was talking to those people, I thought she looked afraid."

He nodded. "I thought so, too." And suddenly, he couldn't believe he'd let worry about bad publicity keep him from helping her. "I have to go find her and figure out what's going on."

Claire picked up speed as she broke away from Jasper's parents and Linc. Uppermost in her mind was escaping the polo grounds and getting to her daughter. The decisions she needed to make could wait until she held Honey in her arms once more.

"Claire!" Everly Briggs was bearing down on her. "Where are you going? I thought we were going to meet up so I could get you the money we owe you."

"I have the receipts here. Can you mail me the check? I need to leave."

As she extended the folder to Everly, Claire glanced

over her shoulder, looking for the Patmores. But she didn't see Jasper's parents. Maybe she'd given them the slip. She sure hoped so. The thought of them following her to Linc's house alarmed her.

"Is something wrong?" Everly made no attempt to take the folder from Claire. "You seem upset. Has something happened?"

"My address is on the paperwork." She'd secured a PO Box when she'd first arrived in Charleston and had all her mail sent there.

"Did you and Linc have a fight?"

"What?"

"I saw him a few seconds ago and noticed that he looked angry. Did you fight about how much time he spent with Landry Beaumont today?" Everly's green eyes gleamed with interest. "Jealousy doesn't suit you."

Claire stared at the woman in dumbfounded silence. "I'm not jealous."

"Because you think he's going to pick you over her?" Everly laughed, and it wasn't a nice sound. "That's never going to happen. You're not in her league."

"You don't think I know that?"

It was hard always being treated like she wasn't good enough. First, her mother had walked out on Claire. Then her father chose his new family over her. Maybe there was something wrong with her, because she'd become embroiled in a relationship with Linc knowing she was even less suitable than his former fiancée.

"And it doesn't matter," Claire continued. "Linc and I aren't involved."

"Who do you think you're kidding?" Everly leaned in and pinned Claire with a malicious stare. "I watched the two of you together and saw exactly what's going on. You're sleeping with him."

Claire recoiled, wondering how such a fun day had

gone to hell so fast. She was opening her mouth to deny Everly's claim when they were interrupted by a familiar voice.

"There you are," Jasper's mother said. "Don't think you can get away so easily."

"Who are these people?" Everly demanded, assessing the Patmores with a frown. "Did you invite them?"

"No."

"How did you get in here?" Everly continued.

"Not that it's any of your business," Doug Patmore said, "but we had tickets."

Seeing this answer wasn't going to satisfy Everly, Claire decided the sooner she got Jasper's parents out of there, the better. Rather than argue with them any further near witnesses, Claire once again broke off and headed in the direction of the parking lot. As she expected, the Patmores were hot on her heels.

"Where do you think you're going?" Doug demanded, panting a little as he caught up with her.

"Away from you." But as they reached the parking lot, Claire slowed down so she could ask the question uppermost in her thoughts. "How did you find me in Charleston and how did you know where I would be today?"

"A woman called us and said you'd moved here," Sharon said.

Doug nodded. "She said you'd taken up with some ballplayer and were living with him."

"What woman?" Claire demanded, gripping her car keys as her blood ran cold. Who would go to all the trouble to do something like this?

"She didn't give us her name, but she said she was from Charleston and had met you at a party." Jasper's father looked disgusted. "Is that what you've been doing since you've been here? Neglecting our granddaughter while you go out carousing at night?"

"The only party I've attended was one I catered recently. I was working, not carousing."

Claire thought back to Bettina's party. Was it possible that one of the guests had suspected something was going on between her and Linc and decided that she needed to be out of the picture? That was crazy. No one in their right mind would consider Claire competition. But what other explanation could there be? And how would anyone have known how to find Jasper's parents? She hadn't told anyone his last name. Would someone have gone so far as to have her investigated? If so, it was a despicable thing to do.

"What about the baseball player you're shacked up with?" Doug asked. "Is he doing drugs and partying? What sort of environment is that for our granddaughter?"

If she wasn't used to their harassment, these sorts of accusations might've shocked Claire. But it wasn't much different from what they'd thrown at her in San Francisco and reinforced why she'd left. Even though she'd told herself that it was difficult for grandparents to take custody of a child away from its mother, she didn't trust that the system always worked the way it was supposed to. Nor did she have the means to fight a lengthy battle against Jasper's parents.

"He doesn't party," Claire said. "And where I'm living is none of your business."

"I'll bet he has money," Jasper's father said, his eyes narrowing to slits.

She shook her head. "What does that have to do with anything?"

"Maybe you don't want to lose your meal ticket."

"My meal ticket?" Until Jasper's death, Claire hadn't had any contact with his parents and everything since then had been negative, but this was beyond anything she'd expected. "What are you talking about?"

"Seems to us that you have a sweet situation here."

What was he trying to get at? Claire looked from Doug to Sharon and back again. The disgust on their faces set something off. Shame flooded her. She wasn't the horrible person they imagined, but there was no question that she'd been sleeping with Linc and behaving recklessly.

"Give us our sweet baby," Sharon said, "and we'll leave you be."

"She's not your sweet baby." Fury burned away Claire's confusion. The idea of running again filled her with dread, but the last thing she was going to do was let Jasper's parents take her daughter. "Jasper didn't want you in his life and he certainly didn't want you in his daughter's life, either."

"Better us than you. We're going to get her one way or another."

Claire shook her head and tried to look confident, even as she cringed inside. "You have no grounds to take Honey away from me."

"I'm sure there is a judge in California that would disagree with you."

"But we're not in California." It was all a huge bluff on her part. Claire wasn't sure if what had happened when she was twenty would have any bearing on a court case here in South Carolina.

"You might think you're safe here, but we could make things pretty uncomfortable for you," Jasper's mother said.

"You and that Linc Thurston fellow," Doug Patmore agreed.

When Jasper's dad spoke Linc's name, Claire went cold all over. The last thing she wanted to do was drag Linc into a scandal, and it looked like Jasper's father was eager to make trouble.

"I'm not going to give you my daughter," Claire growled, feeling very much like a cornered mama bear. The more time she spent with Jasper's parents, the more convinced she became that she would do whatever it took to keep Honey away from them.

"Then give us the hundred thousand dollars she got."

"What hundred thousand dollars?"

"Don't play dumb with us. She's the beneficiary of his death benefit for being killed in active duty. That's a hundred thousand tax-free."

With those words, the whole reason for their interest in their granddaughter became crystal clear. As Honey's guardians, they would be able to control that death benefit. A hundred thousand dollars was a lot of money.

"I don't have it." In truth, it had never occurred to her that there might be something Honey would receive after Jasper's death.

"You are a terrible liar," Doug said. "Of course you have it."

Claire shook her head. "I never applied for any money."

"Well, then, you're an even bigger idiot than we thought." Doug exchanged a look with his wife. "You need to get us that money."

"But it belongs to Honey." A second earlier, Claire had been willing to do whatever it took to protect her daughter. That money would go a long way toward securing Honey's future. "And I know Jasper would want her to have it."

"He's our son. We raised him. If anyone should get the money, it's us, not some mistake he made with you."

Claire sucked in a deep breath to bolster her courage and set her chin at a defiant angle. For her daughter's sake, she would not let these people bully her.

"You're wasting your breath," Claire said, no longer afraid that they could take Honey from her now that she had their measure. "You aren't getting my daughter and you aren't getting any money. Go back to San Francisco and leave us alone."

And with that, Claire turned her back on Jasper's parents and strode away. But she wasn't moving fast enough to escape Doug Patmore's final words.

"Give us that money or we'll make sure everyone knows what you've been up to with your boss. You might not care what people say about you, but I'll bet he and that family of his will."

Eleven

Even though Linc knew he should stay at the charity event until all the polo matches were done, he couldn't focus on anything but the expression on Claire's face when she'd admitted that she'd been lying to him for a year. As it was, he stuck around long enough only for Knox to report that no one by the name of Patmore had bought tickets to the event.

But someone had gotten tickets for them. Someone who'd hoped Jasper's parents would make a scene at a public event to embarrass Claire. But why? Linc knew he couldn't wait much longer to find out.

To his relief, Claire's car was parked in the driveway when he arrived home. But upon entering the house, Linc spied two suitcases sitting in the kitchen near the back door and stopped dead while his brain tried to wrap itself around the reason they were there.

Claire was leaving him.

Just as he arrived at that conclusion, she entered the kitchen carrying Honey. As soon as the toddler spied him, she lifted both her arms, opening and closing her fists in a double wave that put a lump in his throat. It hit him then that no matter what Claire had done or how angry he was with her, he couldn't bear to let her go.

"Where are you going?" he demanded, more pain than accusation in his voice.

She gazed at him in wide-eyed dismay. "Why are you here? You're supposed to be at the polo match."

"I left early because I needed to talk to you." He gestured at the luggage. "Are you running out on me?"

Before she could answer, he plucked Honey from her arms. The toddler cooed with delight and wrapped her arms around his neck. She smelled faintly of her mother's perfume mixed with baby lotion. He breathed in the familiar scent, relieved that he'd been in time to stop these two from vanishing from his life.

"I'm not running out on you. I'm leaving before I embroil you in a huge scandal."

"As if I care what people say about me," he said, keeping his tone calm, not wanting to upset Honey.

"You should. Your family and friends do."

"Are you ready to tell me what the hell is going on?" He asked the question without any heat, just needing to understand. "Why did you tell everyone you were married?"

Claire stared at the floor without answering for so long he wasn't sure if she would speak without further prodding. But then after a long-suffering sigh, she walked to the sunroom and pulled out Honey's toys.

"Bring her in here. She can play while we talk."

Once Honey was occupied with a sorting game, Claire went into the kitchen and began emptying the dishwasher. The mundane task seemed to soothe her, and as she put plates and cups away, she began to explain.

"I discovered when I first moved to Charleston that being a military widow with a child made people more likely to give me a chance. Was it wrong?" She nodded emphatically. "Absolutely. But I don't think I'd change what I did."

"But why didn't you come clean with me? I wouldn't have judged you."

"I wanted to." Claire didn't meet his eyes. "I should have."

"I don't understand what stopped you."

"At first, it was because I needed the job as your house-keeper. Living here meant I could stay under the radar. Jasper's parents would have a harder time finding me."

"Why were you trying to avoid them?"

"Before Jasper went overseas the last time, he made me promise that I would keep our child away from his parents. Their relationship was strained and he was afraid they would treat his child the way they behaved toward him."

"But you're her mother, and you don't have to give them access to her."

"They made things very uncomfortable for me. Plus…"

She looked incredibly uncomfortable. What was she so reluctant to say? He couldn't reconcile the woman he had come to care for this past year with this secretive individual who'd spun one lie after another.

"At the party, they said you'd stolen their granddaughter. What aren't you telling me?"

"They were the reason I left California."

"You moved all the way across the country to keep Honey away from her grandparents?"

Claire nodded. "They threatened to take her away from me."

"You're her mother," Linc said. "There's no way that could happen."

"Unfortunately, if they decided to push the issue, there was a possibility that I could've been deemed an unfit mother and lost her."

"An unfit mother?" *Was this another lie?* It seemed impossible that she could believe something so far-fetched. "You're the furthest thing from it."

"There was an incident back when I'd just turned twenty." Her eyes darted in his direction and then away. She was obviously grappling with something. "I told you my father got remarried. It was pretty obvious from the start that Aubrey wanted my father to focus on her and their new family, and she got it into her head that I resented her."

"Did you?" Linc recalled Claire telling him that her stepmother was only eight years older than her. "It seemed like your dad was all the family you had for most of your life."

"I will admit that at sixteen I wasn't thrilled when Aubrey moved in. She and my dad had been dating for about six months and she'd gotten pregnant. I never knew if they got married because he loved her or if he just felt responsible for the baby. Either way, once she came to live with us, everything changed. She had really strong opinions about everything and wasn't shy about asserting herself."

Linc recalled how Sawyer had been at sixteen and remembered epic battles with their mother over nothing. It wasn't hard to imagine Claire and her stepmother locked in a power struggle. After all, Claire had been the only woman in her father's life for nine years after her mother had left. No doubt, she'd taken care of him as much as she'd been taken care of. Giving that up couldn't have been easy.

"I understand, but what does this have to do with your concern that Honey's grandparents could interfere with your custody of her?"

"By the time I turned twenty, Aubrey had given birth to my half brother, Shane, and half sister, Grace. Shane was a total momma's boy and a terror. I moved out right after high school because of how bad things were between

Aubrey and me. She made sure I wasn't welcome and I stopped visiting."

Linc remembered how it had hurt when his father had left them after serving his five-year sentence. The betrayal Linc had felt after he, Sawyer and their mother had stuck by him during the trial and scandal, and made regular trips to visit him in prison.

At least he'd had his sister and mother. Who had supported Claire?

She lied to you.

While it was important to remind himself of that fact, Linc was starting to soften his stance toward Claire. Especially when what she'd done hadn't actively hurt anyone. Could he really blame her for doing whatever it took to survive?

"My dad didn't understand what was going on between us," Claire continued, "and I knew it hurt him that I never came around anymore. So, on Grace's second birthday, I went to her party. Shane was acting out worse than usual because his sister was getting all the attention."

Linc had little trouble picturing the scene. Claire's discomfort as she recounted the story was palpable. Obviously, whatever had happened continued to bother her.

"When it was time for cake and opening presents, Shane was nowhere to be found. Aubrey was making a big deal out of wanting him to be there when Grace blew out her candles, so I went to find him. He'd gone up into this little tree house my dad had built for him."

With each sentence, Claire tensed. Her fingers tightened and straightened. Linc's gut became a solid knot of discomfort as he suspected where the tale might lead.

"Was it high?"

"Not more than six feet off the ground, but high enough that a child falling out of it could get hurt."

"And is that what happened?"

Claire nodded. She let loose a shaky breath and kept going. "I started out at the bottom, trying to coax him to come down, but he didn't like me very much. I think he'd picked up on the antagonism between his mother and me. Anyway, I ended up climbing up into the tree house, hoping to talk some sense into him. But he started screaming at me and told me to go away, acting like I was scaring him half to death." A mirthless smile twisted her lips. "The little brat was good at making scenes and knew exactly how to manipulate his mother. Anyway, I was on the verge of leaving him be when he decided to go out the window and try to climb across to a nearby branch."

"Did he make it?"

"Yes, but once he got there, he lost his balance. I tried to grab him, but he was just out of reach and he fell." Claire closed her eyes for a long second. "Because he was making such a fuss, a bunch of the guests were looking our way, and from their angle, they said it looked like I'd pushed him."

"You can't be serious."

Even before she answered, Claire's grim expression told him just how bad things had been. "Needless to say, Aubrey's family already disliked me and I think one of them called child protective services, claiming I was a danger to the kids."

"Surely no one could possibly have believed that."

"Those sorts of agencies get things wrong all the time. It didn't help that Shane also claimed I'd pushed him. He ended up with a broken arm and devoured all the attention he got that day." As the story wound down, Claire trailed off with a sigh.

Linc remembered how he'd encouraged her to take some time off and go home to visit her family. He understood now why she hadn't looked all that excited about it.

"When the findings came back from the social worker

that I posed a potential danger to my half siblings, I realized that maintaining a relationship with my father was going to be tough."

"I can't believe your father believed you could hurt them. What is your relationship with him like now?"

"I think he feels bad, but he's married to Aubrey and has a responsibility to their children. We talk when she's not around and he came to visit me in the hospital after Honey was born. When I told him what Jasper's parents were trying to do, he gave me some money to help me get out of San Francisco and start over somewhere new. I know he'd like to do more, but…" She trailed off.

Linc ached, seeing her pain. "That's not fair to you."

"And it's made me wary of trusting people." She cast a burning look his way from beneath her lashes. "Even those I want to."

He caught her meaning and gave a small nod. "So this business with Shane and child protective services stepping in is what Jasper's parents have against you?"

"Yes. I'm not sure how they found out about it, but when they started threatening me for custody of Honey, I left town."

"You could've fought it. All you needed was a good lawyer."

"I couldn't afford one. With the high cost of living in California, it was all I could do to keep my head above water. And I was too afraid if I'd stayed to fight them that I might lose Honey." Tears glinted at the corners of her eyes. "I bought a car and a friend of mine registered it in his name. Then I drove across country, stopping in small towns and picking up odd jobs here and there. It took me nearly six months to get to Charleston. I wasn't sure how long I was going to stick around, but then I met your mother and she thought I'd be a good fit for your housekeeper. It's been great working for you and living here. It's the first time since learning Jasper was dead that I've felt safe. I should've known it wouldn't last."

"How did the Patmores find you?"

"I don't have a clue. I've been careful to stay under the radar. I suppose they could've hired someone. But even if they'd located me in Charleston, to show up at the party like that is so odd. Because there was no doubt they were there specifically to find me."

"Someone in Charleston must have tipped them off," Linc said thoughtfully. "But for what purpose?"

Claire's brown eyes looked huge in her pale face. "Because they figured out we're involved and want me out of the picture."

"What? Don't be ridiculous."

"Jasper's parents knew all about you and threatened to go public with a bunch of lies unless I paid them off."

"How much do they want?"

"A hundred thousand dollars. It's the amount Honey would receive from the military because her father died in the line of duty." Claire's chin went up and her eyes grew cold. "But I'm not going to pay it to them."

"Of course not." But Linc would have no qualms about parting with the sum if it gave Claire some peace of mind. He was busy calculating the wisdom of paying off blackmailers when Claire made her stunning announcement.

"Honey and I are going to leave Charleston instead."

Linc was shaking his head before Claire finished speaking. "Absolutely not. You've lost your mind if you think I'm going to let you leave Charleston." From the tone of his voice, he meant every word. "Whatever it takes to keep you here is what we'll do."

"But this isn't your problem," she protested. "It's mine, and I refuse to let you be dragged into my mess."

"But it's not your mess. You didn't cause the problem.

Vile people are trying to take advantage of you. Let me help you stop them."

"Don't you understand?" Her heart hammered in her chest at the fierce determination on his face. "This isn't your fight."

As much as she longed to surrender to his will and accept his protection, her doubts were stronger. No one had ever had her back before. She also couldn't forget his anger at the polo grounds.

"I'm making it my fight."

"But the scandal..."

"There won't be any scandal—" he grasped her chin and brought her gaze to his "—if you marry me."

"What?" She jerked free and took a half step back, her senses reeling as if he'd slapped her. "Your mother will never accept me. London was beautiful, wealthy and sophisticated and she wasn't good enough. I'll always be the woman who cleaned your house. Think of how it will look. I can't do that to you."

"My mother knows how I feel about you. All she wants is for me to be happy."

Claire covered her eyes with her hands, blocking out his earnest expression. Immediately, her other senses took over. She inhaled his familiar cologne and listened to the rough cadence of his breathing.

"You were happy with London," she reminded him, "and that didn't improve Bettina's opinion of her."

"I never should've proposed to London." Linc tugged her hands down so he could meet her gaze. "She wasn't the love of my life. You are."

Her chest tightened at his words. "We haven't known each other long enough for you to believe that." What would it take for him to realize this was crazy? How could he possibly love her? She'd made so many mistakes. "And I lied to you."

"All that is true, but it doesn't change that I love you."

Claire hunched her shoulders. With her head and her heart locked in a fierce battle, all she could do was keep trying to make him see reason.

"It won't work," she said. "You'll see."

"It can and it will. All you need to do is trust me."

She shook her head. "I do trust you, but there are greater forces at work in your life than how we feel about each other."

"How do we feel about each other?" he asked, taking her by the shoulders. The pressure of his warm fingers brought her close to tears. "I love you. I want to marry you and for us to be a family."

"Damn it, Linc. Be reasonable."

He ignored her objection. "How do you feel about me?"

A sob bloomed in her chest, making her breath erratic. While the words she'd longed to speak stuck in her throat, Claire grappled with fear. If she opened her heart and told him the truth—that she couldn't bear the thought of living without him—he would never let her go. And then what if all his friends and family opposed their relationship? How could she hope to make Linc happy?

"I love you," she confessed, her strong emotions refusing to remain bottled up any longer.

"That's my girl." He cupped her face in his palms and leaned down to graze her lips with his. "It feels like I've been waiting forever to hear those words from you."

"But, Linc, we can't—"

He stopped her words with another kiss, this one longer and deeper. She was light-headed and giddy by the time he lifted his head.

"Let's just focus on you, me and Honey. No one else matters."

"But they do. Maybe in a thousand other cities things

would be different. But in Charleston, everyone's opinion matters."

"So we'll live in Texas or California or wherever you
want. What matters is that we're together."

She couldn't believe what he was saying. "But your
family and friends are here. And say what you want, but
the fact is they are important to you."

"So what will it take?"

"For what?"

"For you to marry me in a huge ceremony in front of
all our friends and family? I want to shout my love for you
from the rooftops."

His question overwhelmed her, but she recognized that
running was impossible now. Even if it was the smartest
thing for everyone, hope had seized control. What if she
and Linc could make a go of things? She loved him. Could
she really turn her back on a chance for happiness?

"I can't honestly say what would change my mind," she
said, but in fact, she knew. If by some miracle the family
origin legend was true and she was descended from an old
Charleston family...

"You underestimate how persuasive I can be." A wicked
grin lit up his expression.

"Well, there's a welcome sight."

Claire glanced toward the back door and spied Sawyer
standing just inside the kitchen.

"What are you doing here?" Linc demanded.

"Interrupting something, obviously." Wearing an un-
repentant grin, Sawyer strode toward them and snagged
Claire by the arm, tugging her away from Linc. "Excuse
us, brother dear. I need to speak with Claire."

"What's going on?"

"Give Mom a call. She wants to know if you're interested in coming by for dinner. Claire and I will be right
back."

Claire bit her lip as Sawyer led her toward the front of the house. Her stomach, still unsettled by the day's events, began churning in earnest as Sawyer directed her into the living room and onto the tufted cobalt sofa.

"What's going on?" she asked, echoing Linc's earlier question. "Did something happen after I left the polo event today? Does everyone know what's been going on between Linc and me? Is that why your mother wants him to come over for dinner? So she can tell him to send me packing?"

And yet, wasn't that what she'd been all ready to do mere minutes earlier? To disappear out of Linc's life? What was so different now that he'd told her he loved her and wanted to marry her?

"Nothing like that," Sawyer assured her. "As for Mother, she's delighted that Linc has found someone who makes him as happy as you do."

"She knows about me? About us? How did she find out?" Claire sagged back against the sofa and closed her eyes. "I'm so embarrassed."

"Linc told her the day after the party. I don't think he went into any great detail about what you two have been up to, but she knows he loves you."

Claire sat up and stared at Sawyer. "Then what is it you needed to tell me?"

"What I found out from my friend at the historical society about your ancestor James Robbins."

"What you found out?" Claire regarded Sawyer in confusion. "I don't understand. How did you know about him?"

"Linc told me your story, so I went to the historical society and did some digging to find out about the Robbins family."

Claire couldn't believe Sawyer's excitement over what she'd found and noticed her own pulse picking up speed.

Although her great-aunt had believed the stories of James Robbins leaving behind his Charleston family to chase his fortune in the California gold rush, part of Claire hadn't quite believed that there was anything more to the tales than family legend.

"So there's a Robbins family in Charleston?"

Sawyer shook her head. "Not anymore. They died out when their first son was killed during the Civil War."

"Oh." Claire struggled to contain her rising disappointment. What a fool she was to think maybe she had a connection to a family that might impress Bettina. "Well, thanks for looking."

"Not so fast. Just because the Robbins name died out doesn't mean they weren't an important Charleston family. There was a daughter. Penelope. She married well and had lots of descendants."

It hadn't occurred to Claire that after all this time she might actually have family living in Charleston. She'd been focused on the members of her great-great-grandfather's generation and determining if James Robbins had been telling the truth. "What would they be? My distant cousins?"

"It will take a while to sort out all the genealogies and how everyone connects to you, but I know for sure that you're related to the Haskells. As in my friend Shelby Haskell." Sawyer beamed at Claire.

"Really?"

Claire recalled a brief exchange she'd had with Shelby at Bettina's party and something clicked in her heart. A missing fragment of her identity slipped into place and made her feel whole for the first time in what felt like forever. She belonged here in Charleston in a way that had nothing to do with Linc.

"Yes, really," Sawyer exclaimed. "Isn't that exciting?"

"You have no idea." All at once, Claire burst into tears. For a long moment, she couldn't breathe and her throat hurt too much to get out a word, but she managed to find her voice again. "I can't believe this is real."

"It sure is. Even before you two figured out that you loved each other, I could see that you were special to him. He told me how important this was to you and I'm so glad I was able to help."

"Have you told Linc?" Claire wondered if this was what had caused him to propose. Maybe he'd decided she was suitable after all.

Sawyer shook her head. "I just found out myself not more than half an hour ago. I thought maybe you'd like to be the one to share your news."

"And your mother?"

"Stop worrying about things that don't matter," Sawyer counseled, clearly recognizing what Claire feared. "Linc loves you and that's all there is to it. Neither he nor my mother care where you came from."

Since when?

Claire repressed the thought. If she had any chance of making things work with Linc, she simply had to stop using the gap in their social stations as an excuse to guard herself from getting hurt.

"I know," she said, expelling her breath in a long sigh. "It's just that it's been so long since anyone has made me feel safe and I'm a little skittish."

"Linc is the best guy around."

"You should listen to her," Linc said from the wide arch that led to the hall. He'd followed Honey, who now raced into the room in Claire's direction. "Are you ready to go tell my mother that I've chosen my future bride?" he asked as she scooped her daughter onto her lap and hugged her.

"Are you sure that's what you want?"

"Do you really need to ask?"

Claire glanced down at her jeans and cotton sweater. "I should change my clothes."

"You are beautiful no matter what you're wearing." He took her hand and grazed his lips across her palm, making Claire shiver. "I'll give you ten minutes to change."

While Sawyer entertained Honey, Claire rummaged through her suitcase. She'd bought a beautiful floral dress a week earlier. It wasn't an expensive designer original, but the soft pastel tones brought out the gold highlights in her hair and the wrap style flattered her slim figure.

Claire slipped into the first-floor bathroom and, within the allotted ten minutes, transformed herself from a fearful runaway to a woman ready to face the upcoming challenges and grab the brass ring.

"You look beautiful," Linc said as she reentered the kitchen.

Sawyer had left moments earlier, leaving Claire and Honey alone with Linc once again. Claire smoothed her palms down the skirt as he approached, keenly aware as he scrutinized every inch of her appearance.

"Do you think your mother will approve?" In truth, she already knew the answer, but her confidence grew beneath Linc's possessive regard.

"Yes."

"Then I guess we'd better go."

"One thing before we do," he said, reaching into his coat pocket. "I have something for you." He displayed a ring box and popped the top. Framed in black velvet was a huge oval-cut diamond set on a thin rose gold band of micropave-set diamonds. "Claire Robbins, will you marry me?"

This time she didn't have to think about the answer. "Linc Thurston, I love you with all my heart and want to be your wife."

She took his face in her hands as he leaned down to kiss her. Distantly, she heard Honey's sweet giggle. Then she was swept into the heat and wonder of the connection she always felt with him and all her fears melted away.

Both of them were breathing a little unsteadily when they broke off the kiss. Honey was growing impatient, her calls penetrating the fog of passion that had enveloped them. Claire watched while Linc slid the diamond ring onto her left hand, her heart stopping at the joy glinting in his eyes.

How had she gotten so lucky to win this man's heart?

On the way to his mother's house, Claire sat paralyzed, fearing that if she moved a single muscle, the whole thing would vanish like a beautiful dream.

Yet with each block they traversed, alarm zinged with ever-increasing speed along Claire's nerves until by the time they pulled into his mother's driveway she was buzzing with tension.

"Relax," Linc murmured as he turned off the car. "No one is going to eat you alive."

"That's easy for you to say," she retorted more sharply than she intended. "You're wealthy and socially prominent. I'm a nobody who cleans your house."

His eyebrows rose at her vehemence, but then he nodded. "Thanks for reminding me. There's something I forgot to do." He flashed her a mischievous grin. "You're fired."

Taking his dismissal in the manner he intended, she smiled in return. "I've never been fired from a job before."

"Never?"

"I'm an exceptional employee. Every boss I've ever worked for has given me glowing performance reviews."

"Of course they have," he murmured in a fond tone.

Linc opened his car door and started to get out but then noticed that she hadn't moved. He reached out and caught her hand, giving her fingers a gentle squeeze. "Come on."

She slipped from the car and went to stand on the brick walkway that stretched from the driveway to the front door while Linc got Honey from her car seat. He moved with confidence and care, having done this dozens of times.

Claire then realized how long this moment had been coming. She just hadn't seen it. Linc had never been just her employer. He'd been her friend. Someone who cared about her and Honey, who'd invited himself into her life.

This flash of insight bolstered her courage. She would face his mother with her head high, confident in the knowledge that she was the woman he loved and intended to marry.

"It's about time you arrived," Bettina called from the living room. "Sawyer tells me you two are engaged."

Claire glanced at Linc as the three of them crossed the threshold and entered the room. The next ten minutes would tell her how the rest of her life would play out. Linc gave her a reassuring smile before answering his mother.

"We are, indeed," Linc said, his satisfaction bolstering Claire.

If this amazing man loved her, she could face whatever the future held.

"Wonderful." Bettina got to her feet as they neared and her gaze met Claire's. She held out her arms and Claire hesitated only a second before stepping into the older woman's embrace. "I just know you and Linc will be so very happy together," she whispered, giving Claire a hard hug before letting her go.

"Thank you," Claire murmured, overwhelmed by a flood of emotions.

Bettina sat down as Dolly appeared with a bottle of champagne and crystal flutes.

"We are going to plan the most lavish wedding this town has seen in years," Linc's mother stated. "Claire will have a dozen bridesmaids and the most expensive gown we can find."

While Bettina began mulling over ideas for the venue and potential wedding planners, Claire sipped her champagne and held Linc's hand. A surge of fondness and belonging flooded her as she realized the acceptance and family she'd craved for so long were going to be hers.

"Thank you," she murmured, resting her head on his arm.

"For what?"

"Making me a part of your family. I love you so much." She tilted her head back and met his gaze. "I never thought I could be as happy as I am right now."

"I'm the lucky one. We belong together. You and Honey make my life complete." He leaned down and placed a soft kiss on her lips.

"I like belonging with you," she agreed, thinking how the Robbins family had come full circle now that she'd returned to Charleston.

She couldn't wait until she and Linc were alone so she could share with him what Sawyer had found out. Yet as excited as she was by the news that she had a connection to the Charleston elite, it no longer determined who she was. For that, all she needed to do was gaze into Linc's blue eyes to see her true self reflected there. His love was all she needed to accept that she was exactly where she should be.

* * * * *

CLAIM ME,
COWBOY

MAISEY YATES

For Jackie Ashenden,
my conflict guru and dear friend.
Without you my books would take a heck
of a lot longer to write, and my life
would be a heck of a lot more boring.
Thank you for everything. Always.

November 1, 2017
LOOKING FOR A WIFE—

Wealthy bachelor, 34, looking for a wife. Never married, no children. Needs a partner who can attend business and social events around the world. Must be willing to move to Copper Ridge, Oregon. Perks include: travel, an allowance, residence in several multimillion-dollar homes.

November 5, 2017
LOOKING FOR AN UNSUITABLE WIFE—

Wealthy bachelor, 34, irritated, looking for a woman to pretend to be my fiancée in order to teach my meddling father a lesson. Need a partner who is rough around the edges. Must be willing to come to Copper Ridge, Oregon, for at least thirty days. Generous compensation provided.

One

"No. You do not need to *send pics*."

Joshua Grayson looked out the window of his office and did not feel the kind of calm he ought to feel.

He'd moved back to Copper Ridge six months ago from Seattle, happily trading in a man-made, rectangular skyline for the natural curve of the mountains.

Not the best thing for an architect to feel, perhaps. But he spent his working hours dealing in design, in business. Numbers. Black, white and the bottom line. There was something about looking out at the mountains that restarted him.

That, and getting on the back of a horse. Riding from one end of the property to the other. The wind blocking out every other sound except hoofbeats on the earth.

Right now, he doubted anything would decrease

the tension he was feeling from dealing with the fall-out of his father's ridiculous ad. Another attempt by the old man to make Joshua live the life his father wanted him to.

The only kind of life his father considered success-ful: a wife, children.

He couldn't understand why Joshua didn't want the same.

No. That kind of life was for another man, one with another past and another future. It was not for Joshua. And that was why he was going to teach his father a lesson.

But not with Brindy, who wanted to send him self-ies with "no filter."

The sound she made in response to his refusal was so petulant he almost laughed.

"But your ad said…"

"That," he said, "was not my ad. Goodbye."

He wasn't responsible for the ad in a national paper asking for a wife, till death do them part. But an unsuitable, temporary wife? Yes. That had been his ad.

He was done with his father's machinations. No matter how well-meaning they were. He was tired of tripping over daughters of "old friends" at family gatherings. Tired of dodging women who had been set on him like hounds at a fox hunt.

He was going to win the game. Once and for all. And the woman he hoped would be his trump card was on her way.

His first respondent to his counter ad—Danielle Kelly—was twenty-two, which suited his purposes nicely. His dad would think she was too young, and

frankly, Joshua also thought she was too young. He
didn't get off on that kind of thing.

He understood why some men did. A tight body
was hot. But in his experience, the younger the
woman, the less in touch with her sensuality she was
and he didn't have the patience for that.

He didn't have the patience for this either, but here
he was. The sooner he got this farce over with, the
sooner he could go back to his real life.

The doorbell rang and he stood up behind his desk.
She was here. And she was—he checked his watch—
late.

A half smile curved his lips.

Perfect.

He took the stairs two at a time. He was impatient
to meet his temporary bride. Impatient to get this plan
started so it could end.

He strode across the entryway and jerked the door
open. And froze.

The woman standing on his porch was small.
And young, just as he'd expected, but... She wore no
makeup, which made her look like a damned teenager. Her features were fine and pointed; her dark
brown hair hung lank beneath a ragged beanie that
looked like it was in the process of unraveling while
it sat on her head.

He didn't bother to linger over the rest of the details—her threadbare sweater with too-long sleeves,
her tragic skinny jeans—because he was stopped,
immobilized really, by the tiny bundle in her arms.

A baby.

His prospective bride had come with a baby.

Well, hell.

* * *

She really hoped he wasn't a serial killer. Well, *hoped* was an anemic word for what she was feeling. Particularly considering the possibility was a valid concern.

What idiot put an ad in the paper looking for a temporary wife?

Though, she supposed the bigger question was: What idiot responded to an ad in the paper looking for a temporary wife?

This idiot, apparently.

It took Danielle a moment to realize she was staring directly at the center of a broad, muscular male chest. She had to raise her head slightly to see his face. He was just so…tall. And handsome.

And she was confused.

She hadn't imagined that a man who put an ad in the paper for a fake fiancée might be attractive. Another anemic word. *Attractive.* This man wasn't simply *attractive*…

He was… Well, he was unreal.

Broad shouldered, muscular, with stubble on his square jaw adding a roughness to features that might have otherwise been considered pretty.

"Please don't tell me you're Danielle Kelly," he said, crossing his arms over that previously noted broad chest.

"I am. Were you expecting someone else? Of course, I suppose you could be. I bet I'm not the only person who responded to your ad, strange though it was. The mention of compensation was pretty tempting. Although, I might point out that in the future maybe you should space your appointments further apart."

"You have a baby," he said, stating the obvious.

Danielle looked down at the bundle in her arms. "Yes."

"You didn't mention that in our email correspondence."

"Of course not. I thought it would make it too easy for you to turn me away."

He laughed, somewhat reluctantly, a muscle in his jaw twitching. "Well, you're right about that."

"But now I'm here. And I don't have the gas money to get back home. Also, you said you wanted unsuitable." She spread one arm wide, keeping Riley clutched firmly in her other arm. "I would say that I'm pretty unsuitable."

She could imagine the picture she made. Her hideous, patchwork car parked in the background. Maroon with lighter patches of red and a door that was green, since it had been replaced after some accident that had happened before the car had come into her possession. Then there was her. In all her faded glory. She was hungry, and she knew she'd lost a lot of weight over the past few weeks, which had taken her frame from slim to downright pointy. The circles under her eyes were so dark she almost looked like she'd been punched.

She considered the baby a perfect accessory. She had that new baby sallowness they never told you about when they talked about the miracle of life.

She curled her toes inside her boots, one of them going through a hole at the end of her sock. She frowned. "Anyway, I figured I presented a pretty poor picture of a fiancée for a businessman such as yourself. Don't you agree?"

The corners of his lips tightened further. "The baby."

"Yes?"

"You expect it to live here?"

She made an exasperated noise. "No. I expect him to live in the car while I party it up in your fancy-pants house."

"A baby wasn't part of the deal."

"What do you care? Your email said it's only through Christmas. Can you imagine telling your father that you've elected to marry Portland hipster trash and she comes with a baby? I mean, it's going to be incredibly awkward, but ultimately kind of funny."

"Come in," he said, his expression no less taciturn as he stood to the side and allowed her entry into his magnificent home.

She clutched Riley even more tightly to her chest as she wandered inside, looking up at the high ceiling, the incredible floor-to-ceiling windows that offered an unparalleled mountain view. As cities went, Portland was all right. The air was pretty clean, and once you got away from the high-rise buildings, you could see past the iron and steel to the nature beyond.

But this view... This was something else entirely.

She looked down at the floor, taking a surprised step to the side when she realized she was standing on glass. And that underneath the glass was a small, slow-moving stream. Startlingly clear, rocks visible beneath the surface of the water. Also, fish.

She looked up to see him staring at her. "My sister's work," he said. "She's the hottest new architect on the scene. Incredible, considering she's only in her early twenties. And a woman, breaking serious barriers in the industry."

"That sounds like an excerpt from a magazine article."

He laughed. "It might be. Since I write the press releases about Faith. That's what I do. PR for our firm, which has expanded recently. Not just design, but construction. And as you can see, Faith's work is highly specialized, and it's extremely coveted."

A small prickle of…something worked its way under her skin. She couldn't imagine being so successful at such a young age. Of course, Joshua and his sister must have come from money. You couldn't build something like this if you hadn't.

Danielle was in her early twenties and didn't even have a checking account, much less a successful business.

All of that had to change. It had to change for Riley.

He was why she was here, after all.

Truly, nothing else could have spurred her to answer the ad. She had lived in poverty all of her life. But Riley deserved better. He deserved stability. And he certainly didn't deserve to wind up in foster care just because she couldn't get herself together.

"So," she said, cautiously stepping off the glass tile. "Tell me more about this situation. And exactly what you expect."

She wanted him to lay it all out. Wanted to hear the terms and conditions he hadn't shared over email. She was prepared to walk away if it was something she couldn't handle. And if he wasn't willing to take no for an answer? Well, she had a knife in her boot.

"My father placed an ad in a national paper saying I was looking for a wife. You can imagine my surprise when I began getting responses before I had ever seen the ad. My father is well-meaning, Ms. Kelly, and he's willing to do anything to make his children's lives better. However, what he perceives as perfection can only come one way. He doesn't think all of this can possibly make me happy." Joshua looked up, seeming to indicate the beautiful house and view around them. "He's wrong. However, he won't take no for an answer, and I want to teach him a lesson."

"By making him think he won?"

"Kind of. That's where you come in. As I said, he can only see things from his perspective. From his point of view, a wife will stay at home and massage my feet while I work to bring in income. He wants someone traditional. Someone soft and biddable." He looked her over. "I imagine you are none of those things."

"Yeah. Not so much." The life she had lived didn't leave room for that kind of softness.

"And you are right. He isn't going to love that you come with a baby. In fact, he'll probably think you're a gold digger."

"I am a gold digger," she said. "If you weren't offering money, I wouldn't be here. I need money, Mr. Grayson, not a fiancé."

"Call me Joshua," he said. "Come with me."

She followed him as he walked through the entryway, through the living area—which looked like something out of a magazine that she had flipped through at the doctor's office once—and into the kitchen.

The kitchen made her jaw drop. Everything was so shiny. Stainless steel surrounded by touches of wood. A strange clash of modern and rustic that seemed to work.

Danielle had never been in a place where so much work had gone into the details. Before Riley, when she had still been living with her mother, the home decor had included plastic flowers shoved into some kind of strange green Styrofoam and a rug in the kitchen that was actually a towel laid across a spot in the linoleum that had been worn through.

"You will live here for the duration of our arrangement. You will attend family gatherings and work events with me."

"Aren't you worried about me being unsuitable for your work arrangements too?"

"Not really. People who do business with us are fascinated by the nontraditional. As I mentioned earlier, my sister, Faith, is something of a pioneer in her field."

"Great," Danielle said, giving him a thumbs-up. "I'm glad to be a nontraditional asset to you."

"Whether or not you're happy with it isn't really my concern. I mean, I'm paying you, so you don't need to be happy."

She frowned. "Well, I don't want to be unhappy. That's the other thing. We have to discuss…terms and stuff. I don't know what all you think you're going to get out of me, but I'm not here to have sex with you. I'm just here to pose as your fiancée. Like the ad said."

The expression on his face was so disdainful it was almost funny. Almost. It didn't quite ascend to funny because it punched her in the ego. "I think I can control myself, Ms. Kelly."

"If I can call you Joshua, then you can call me Danielle," she said.

"Noted."

The way he said it made her think he wasn't necessarily going to comply with her wishes just because she had made them known. He was difficult. No wonder he didn't have an actual woman hanging around willing to marry him. She should have known there was something wrong with him. Because he was rich and kind of disgustingly handsome. His father shouldn't have had to put an ad in the paper to find Joshua a woman.

He should be able to snap his fingers and have them come running.

That sent another shiver of disquiet over her. Yeah, maybe she should listen to those shivers… But the compensation. She needed the compensation.

"What am I going to do…with the rest of my time?"

"Stay here," he said, as though that were the most obvious thing in the world. As though the idea of her rotting away up here in his mansion wasn't weird at all. "And you have that baby. I assume it takes up a lot of your time?"

"He. Riley. And yes, he does take up a lot of time. He's a baby. That's kind of their thing." He didn't respond to that. "You know. Helpless, requiring every single one of their physical and emotional needs to be met by another person. Clearly you don't know."

Something in his face hardened. "No."

"Well, this place is big enough you shouldn't have to ever find out."

"I keep strange hours," he said. "I have to work with offices overseas, and I need to be available to speak to them on the phone, which means I only sleep for a couple of hours at a time. I also spend a lot of time outdoors."

Looking at him, that last statement actually made sense. Yes, he had the bearing of an uptight business-man, but he was wearing a T-shirt and jeans. He was also the kind of physically fit that didn't look like it had come from a gym, not that she was an expert on men or their physiques.

"What's the catch?" she asked.

Nothing in life came this easy—she knew that for certain. She was waiting for the other shoe to drop. Waiting for him to lead her down to the dungeon and show her where he kept his torture pit.

"There is no catch. This is what happens when a man with a perverse sense of humor and too much money decides to teach his father a lesson."

"So basically I live in this beautiful house, I wear your ring, I meet your family, I behave abominably and then I get paid?"

"That is the agreement, Ms. Kelly."

"What if I steal your silverware?"

He chuckled. "Then I still win. If you take off in the dead of night, you don't get your money, and I have the benefit of saying to my father that because of his ad I ended up with a con woman and then got my heart broken."

He really had thought of everything. She supposed there was a reason he was successful.

"So do we… Is this happening?"

"There will be papers for you to sign, but yes. It

is." Any uncertainty he'd seemed to feel because of Riley was gone now.

He reached into the pocket of his jeans and pulled out a small, velvet box. He opened it, revealing a diamond ring so beautiful, so big, it bordered on obscene.

This was the moment. This was the moment when he would say he actually needed her to spend the day wandering around dressed as a teddy bear or something.

But that moment didn't come either. Instead, he took the ring out of the box and held it out to her. "Give me your hand."

She complied. She complied before she gave her body permission to. She didn't know what she expected. For him to get down on one knee? For him to slide the ring onto her fourth finger? He did neither. Instead, he dropped the gem into her palm.

She curled her fingers around it, an electric shock moving through her system as she realized she was probably holding more money in her hand right now than she could ever hope to earn over the course of her lifetime.

Well, no, that wasn't true. Because she was about to earn enough money over the next month to take care of herself and Riley forever. To make sure she got permanent custody of him.

Her life had been so hard, a constant series of moves and increasingly unsavory *uncles* her mother brought in and out of their lives. Hunger, cold, fear, uncertainty…

She wasn't going to let Riley suffer the same fate. No, she was going to make sure her half brother was

protected. This agreement, even if Joshua did ultimately want her to walk around dressed like a sexy
teddy bear, was a small price to pay for Riley's future.

"Yes," she said, testing the weight of the ring. "It
is."

Two

As Joshua followed Danielle down the hall, he regretted not having a live-in housekeeper. An elderly British woman would come in handy at a time like this. She would probably find Danielle and her baby to be absolutely delightful. He, on the other hand, did not.

No, on the contrary, he felt invaded. Which was stupid. Because he had signed on for this. Though, he had signed on for it only after he had seen his father's ad. After he had decided the old man needed to be taught a lesson once and for all about meddling in Joshua's life.

It didn't matter that his father had a soft heart or that he was coming from a good place. No, what mattered was the fact that Joshua was tired of being hounded every holiday, every time he went to dinner

with his parents, about the possibility of him starting a family.

It wasn't going to happen.

At one time, he'd thought that would be his future.
Had been looking forward to it. But the people who
said it was better to have loved and lost than never to
have loved at all clearly hadn't *caused* the loss.

He was happy enough now to be alone. And when
he didn't want to be alone, he called a woman, had
her come spend a few hours in his bed—or in the
back of his truck, he wasn't particular. Love was not
on his agenda.

"This is a big house," she said.

Danielle sounded vaguely judgmental, which
seemed wrong, all things considered. Sure, he was
the guy who had paid a woman to pose as his temporary fiancée. And sure, he was the man who lived in
a house that had more square footage than he generally walked through in a day, but she was the one who
had responded to an ad placed by a complete stranger
looking for a temporary fiancée. So, all things considered, he didn't feel like she had a lot of room to judge.

"Yes, it is."

"Why? I mean, you live here alone, right?"

"Because size matters," he said, ignoring the shifting, whimpering sound of the baby in her arms.

"Right," she said, her tone dry. "I've lived in apartment buildings that were smaller than this."

He stopped walking, then he turned to face her.
"Am I supposed to feel something about that? Feel
sorry for you? Feel bad about the fact that I live in
a big house? Because trust me, I started humbly

enough. I choose to live differently than my parents. Because I can. Because I earned it."

"Oh, I see. In that case, I suppose I earned my dire straits."

"I don't know your life, Danielle. More important, I don't want to know it." He realized that was the first time he had used her first name. He didn't much care.

"Great. Same goes. Except I'm going to be living in your house, so I'm going to definitely…infer some things about your life. And that might give rise to conversations like this one. And if you're going to be assuming things about me, then you should be prepared for me to respond in kind."

"I don't have to do any such thing. As far as I'm concerned, I'm the employer, you're the employee. That means if I want to talk to you about the emotional scars of my childhood, you had better lie back on my couch and listen. Conversely, if I do not want to hear about any of the scars of yours, I don't have to. All I have to do is throw money at you until you stop talking."

"Wow. It's seriously the job offer I've been waiting for my entire life. Talking I'm pretty good at. And I don't do a great job of shutting up. That means I would be getting money thrown at me for a long, long time."

"Don't test me, Ms. Kelly," he said, reverting back to her last name, because he really didn't want to know about her childhood or what brought her here. Didn't want to wonder about her past. Didn't want to wonder about her adulthood either. Who the father of her baby was. What kind of situation she was in. It wasn't his business, and he didn't care.

"Don't test me, Ms. Kelly," she said, in what he assumed was supposed to be a facsimile of his voice.

"Really?" he asked.

"What? You can't honestly expect to operate at this level of extreme douchiness and not get called to the carpet on it."

"I expect that I can do whatever I want, since I'm paying you to be here."

"You don't want me to dress up as a teddy bear and vacuum, do you?"

"What?"

She shifted her weight, moving the baby over to one hip and spreading the other arm wide. "Hey, man, some people are into that. They like stuffed animals. Or rather, they like people dressed as stuffed animals."

"I don't."

"That's a relief."

"I like women," he said. "Dressed as women. Or rather, undressed, generally."

"I'm not judging. Your dad put an ad in the paper for some reason. Clearly he really wants you to be married."

"Yes. Well, he doesn't understand that not everybody needs to live the life that he does. He was happy with a family and a farmhouse. But none of the rest of us feel that way, and there's nothing wrong with that."

"So none of you are married?"

"One of us is. The only brother that actually wanted a farmhouse too." He paused in front of the door at the end of the hall. He was glad he had decided to set this room aside for the woman who answered the ad. He hadn't known she would come with a baby in tow, but the fact that she had meant he really, really wanted her out of earshot.

"Is this it?" she asked.

"Yes," he said, pushing the door open.

When she looked inside the bedroom, her jaw dropped, and Joshua couldn't deny that he took a small amount of satisfaction in her reaction. She looked… Well, she looked amazed. Like somebody standing in front of a great work of art. Except it was just a bedroom. Rather a grand one, he had to admit, down to the details.

There was a large bed fashioned out of natural, twisted pieces of wood with polished support beams that ran from floor to ceiling and retained the natural shape they'd had in the woods but glowed from the stain that had been applied to them. The bed made the whole room look like a magical forest. A little bit fanciful for him. His own bedroom had been left more Spartan. But, clearly, Danielle was enchanted.

And he shouldn't care.

"I've definitely lived in apartments that were smaller than this room," she said, wrapping both arms around the baby and turning in a circle. "This is… Is that a loft? Like a reading loft?" She was gazing up at the mezzanine designed to look as though it was nestled in the tree branches.

"I don't know." He figured it was probably more of a sex loft. But then, if he slept in a room with a loft, obviously he would have sex in it. That was what creative surfaces were for, in his opinion.

"It reminds me of something we had when I was in first grade." A crease appeared between her eyebrows. "I mean, not me as in at our house, but in my first-grade classroom at school. The teacher really loved books. And she liked for us all to read. So we were able to lie around the classroom anywhere we wanted with a book and—" She abruptly stopped talking, as though she realized exactly what she was doing. "Never mind. You think it's boring. Anyway, I'm going to use it for a reading loft."

"Dress like a teddy bear in it, for all I care," he responded.

"That's your thing, not mine."

"Do you have any bags in the car that I can get for you?"

She looked genuinely stunned. "You don't have to get anything for me."

It struck him that she thought he was being nice. He didn't consider the offer particularly nice. It was just what his father had drilled into him from the time he was a boy. If there was a woman and she had a heavy thing to transport, you were no kind of man if you didn't offer to do the transporting.

"I don't mind."

"It's just one bag," she said.

That shocked him. She was a woman. A woman with a baby. He was pretty sure most mothers traveled with enough luggage to fill a caravan. "Just one bag." He had to confirm that.

"Yes," she returned. "Baggage is another thing entirely. But in terms of bags, yeah, we travel light."

"Let me get it." He turned and walked out of the room, frustrated when he heard her footsteps behind him. "I said I would get it."

"You don't need to," she said, following him persistently down the stairs and out toward the front door.

"My car is locked," she added, and he ignored her as he continued to walk across the driveway to the maroon monstrosity parked there.

He shot her a sideways glance, then looked down at the car door. It hung a little bit crooked, and he lifted up on it hard enough to push it straight, then he jerked it open. "Not well."

"You're the worst," she said, scowling.

He reached into the back seat and saw one thread-bare duffel bag, which had to be the bag she was talking about. The fabric strap was dingy, and he had a feeling it used to be powder blue. The zipper was broken and there were four safety pins holding the end of the bulging bag together. All in all, it looked completely impractical.

"Empty all the contents out of this tonight. In the morning, I'm going to use it to fuel a bonfire."

"It's the only bag I have."

"I'll buy you a new one."

"It better be in addition to the fee that I'm getting," she said, her expression stubborn. "I mean it. If I incur a loss because of you, you better cover it."

"You have my word that if anything needs to be purchased in order for you to fit in with your sur-roundings, or in order for me to avoid contracting scabies, it will be bankrolled by me."

"I don't have scabies," she said, looking fierce.

"I didn't say you did. I implied that your gym bag might."

"Well," she said, her cheeks turning red, "it doesn't. It's clean. I'm clean."

He heaved the bag over his shoulder and led the way back to the house, Danielle trailing behind him like an angry wood nymph. That was what she reminded him of, he decided. All pointed angles and spiky intensity. And a supernaturally wicked glare that he could feel boring into the center of his back. Right between his shoulder blades.

This was not a woman who intimidated easily, if at all.

He supposed that was signal enough that he should make an attempt to handle her with care. Not because she needed it, but because clearly nobody had ever made the attempt before. But he didn't know how. And he was paying her an awful lot to put up with him as he was.

And she had brought a baby into his house.

"You're going to need some supplies," he said, frowning. Because he abruptly realized what it meant that she had brought a baby into his house. The bedroom he had installed her in was only meant for one. And there was no way—barring the unlikely reality that she was related to Mary Poppins in some way—that her ratty old bag contained the supplies required to keep both a baby and herself in the kind of comfort that normal human beings expected.

"What kind of supplies?"

He moved quickly through the house, and she scurried behind him, attempting to match his steps. They walked back into the bedroom and he flung the bag on the ground.

"A bed for the baby. Beyond that, I don't know what they require."

She shot him a deadly glare, then bent down and unzipped the bag, pulling out a bottle and a can of formula. She tossed both onto the bed, then reached back into the bag and grabbed a blanket. She spread it out on the floor, then set the baby in the center of it.

Then she straightened, spreading her arms wide and slapping her hands back down on her thighs. "Well, this is more than we've had for a long time. And yeah, I guess it would be nice to have nursery stuff. But I've never had it. Riley and I have been doing just fine on our own." She looked down, picking at some dirt beneath her fingernail. "Or I guess we haven't been *fine*. If we had, I wouldn't have responded to your ad. But I don't need more than what I have. Not now. Once you pay me? Well, I'm going to buy a house. I'm going to change things for us. But until then, it doesn't matter."

He frowned. "What about Riley's father? Surely he should be paying you some kind of support."

"Right. Like I have any idea who he is." He must have made some kind of facial expression that seemed judgmental, because her face colored and her eyebrows lowered. "I mean, I don't know how to get in touch with him. It's not like he left contact details. And I sincerely doubt he left his real name."

"I'll call our office assistant, Poppy. She'll probably know what you need." Technically, Poppy was his brother Isaiah's assistant, but she often handled whatever Joshua or Faith needed, as well. Poppy would arrange it so that various supplies were overnighted to the house.

"Seriously. Don't do anything... You don't need to do anything."

"I'm supposed to convince my parents that I'm marrying you," he said, his tone hard. "I don't think they're going to believe I'm allowing my fiancée to live out of one duffel bag. No. Everything will have to be outfitted so that it looks legitimate. Consider it a bonus to your salary."

She tilted her chin upward, her eyes glittering. "Okay, I will."

He had halfway expected her to argue, but he wasn't sure why. She was here for her own material gain. Why would she reduce it? "Good." He nodded once. "You probably won't see much of me. I'll be working a lot. We are going to have dinner with my parents in a couple of days. Until then, the house and the property are yours to explore. This is your house too. For the time being."

He wasn't being particularly generous. It was just that he didn't want to answer questions, or deal with her being tentative about where she might and might not be allowed to go. He just wanted to install her and the baby in this room and forget about them until he needed them as convenient props.

"Really?" Her natural suspicion was shining through again.

"I'm a very busy man, Ms. Kelly," he said. "I'm not going to be babysitting. Either the child or you."

And with that, he turned and left her alone.

Three

Danielle had slept fitfully last night. And, of course, she hadn't actually left her room once she had been put there. But early the next morning there had been a delivery. And the signature they had asked for was hers. And then the packages had started to come in, like a Christmas parade without the wrapping.

Teams of men carried the boxes up the stairs. They had assembled a crib, a chair, and then unpacked various baby accoutrements that Danielle hadn't even known existed. How could she? She certainly hadn't expected to end up caring for a baby.

When her mother had breezed back into her life alone and pregnant—after Danielle had experienced just two carefree years where she had her own space and wasn't caring for anyone—Danielle had put all of her focus into caring for the other woman. Into arranging state health insurance so the prenatal care and hospital bill for the delivery wouldn't deter her mother from actually taking care of herself and the baby.

And then, when her mother had abandoned Danielle and Riley...that was when Danielle had realized her brother was likely going to be her responsibility. She had involved Child Services not long after that.

There had been two choices. Either Riley could go into foster care or Danielle could take some appropriate parenting classes and become a temporary guardian.

So she had.

But she had been struggling to keep their heads above water, and it was too close to the way she had grown up. She wanted more than that for Riley. Wanted more than that for both of them. Now it wasn't just her. It was him. And a part-time job as a cashier had never been all that lucrative. But with Riley to take care of, and her mother completely out of the picture, staying afloat on a cashier's pay was impossible.

She had done her best trading babysitting time with a woman in her building who also had a baby and nobody else to depend on. But inevitably there were schedule clashes, and after missing a few too many shifts, Danielle had lost her job.

Which was when she had gotten her first warning from Child Services.

Well, she had a job now.

And, apparently, a full nursery.

Joshua was refreshingly nowhere to be seen, which made dealing with her new circumstances much easier. Without him looming over her, being in his house felt a lot like being in the world's fanciest vacation rental. At least, the fanciest vacation rental she could imagine.

She had a baby monitor in her pocket, one that would allow her to hear when Riley woke up. A baby monitor that provided her with more freedom than she'd had since Riley had been born. But, she supposed, in her old apartment a monitor would have been a moot point considering there wasn't anywhere she could go and not hear the baby cry.

But in this massive house, having Riley take his nap in the bedroom—in the new crib, his first crib—would have meant she couldn't have also run down to the kitchen to grab snacks. But she had the baby monitor. A baby monitor that vibrated. Which meant she could also listen to music.

She had the same ancient MP3 player her mother had given her for her sixteenth birthday years ago, but Danielle had learned early to hold on to everything she had, because she didn't know when something else would come along. And in the case of frills like her MP3 player, nothing else had ever come along.

Of course, that meant her music was as old as her technology. But really, music hadn't been as good since she was sixteen anyway.

She shook her hips slightly, walking through the kitchen, singing about how what didn't kill her would only make her stronger. Digging through cabinets, she came up with a package of Pop-Tarts. *Pop-Tarts!*

Her mother had never bought those. They were too expensive. And while Danielle had definitely indulged herself when she had moved out, that hadn't lasted. Because they were too expensive.

Joshua had strawberry. And some kind of mixed

berry with bright blue frosting. She decided she would eat one of each to ascertain which was best.

Then she decided to eat one more of each. She hadn't realized how hungry she was. She had a feeling the hunger wasn't a new development. She had a feeling she had been hungry for days. Weeks even.

Suddenly, sitting on the plush couch in his living area, shoving toaster pastries into her mouth, she felt a whole lot like crying in relief. Because she and Riley were warm; they were safe. And there was hope. Finally, an end point in sight to the long, slow grind of poverty she had existed in for her entire life.

It seemed too good to be true, really. That she had managed to jump ahead in her life like this. That she was really managing to get herself out of that hole without prostituting herself.

Okay, so some people might argue this agreement with Joshua *was* prostituting herself, a little bit. But it wasn't like she was going to have sex with him.

She nearly choked on her Pop-Tart at the thought. And she lingered a little too long on what it might be like to get close to a man like Joshua. To any man, really. The way her mother had behaved all of her life had put Danielle off men. Or, more specifically, she supposed it was the way men had behaved toward Danielle's mother that had put her off.

As far as Danielle could tell, relationships were a whole lot of exposing yourself to pain, deciding you were going to depend on somebody and then having that person leave you high and dry.

No, thank you.

But she supposed she could see how somebody might lose their mind enough to take that risk. Especially when the person responsible for the mind loss had eyes that were blue like Joshua's. She leaned back against the couch, her hand falling slack, the Pop-Tart dangling from her fingertips.

Yesterday there had been the faint shadow of golden stubble across that strong face and jaw, his eyes glittering with irritation. Which she supposed shouldn't be a bonus, shouldn't be appealing. Except his irritation made her want to rise to the unspoken challenge. To try to turn that spark into something else. Turn that irritation into something more...

"Are you eating my Pop-Tarts?"

The voice cut through the music and she jumped, flinging the toaster pastry into the air. She ripped her headphones out of her ears and turned around to see Joshua, his arms crossed over his broad chest, his eyebrows flat on his forehead, his expression unreadable.

"You said whatever was in your house was mine to use," she squeaked. "And a warning would've been good. You just about made me jump out of my skin. Which was maybe your plan all along. If you wanted to make me into a skin suit."

"That's ridiculous. I would not fit into your skin."

She swallowed hard, her throat dry. "Well, it's a figure of speech, isn't it?"

"Is it?" he asked.

"Yes. Everybody knows what that means. It means that I think you might be a serial killer."

"You don't really think I'm a serial killer, or you wouldn't be here."

"I am pretty desperate." She lifted her hand and licked off a remnant of jam. "I mean, obviously."

"There are no Pop-Tarts left," he said, his tone filled with annoyance.

"You said I could have whatever I wanted. I wanted Pop-Tarts."

"You ate all of them."

"Why do you even have Pop-Tarts?" She stood up, crossing her arms, mimicking his stance. "You don't look like a man who eats Pop-Tarts."

"I like them. I like to eat them after I work outside."

"You work outside?"

"Yes," he said. "I have horses."

Suddenly, all of her annoyance fell away. Like it had been melted by magic. *Equine* magic. "You have horses?" She tried to keep the awe out of her voice, but it was nearly impossible.

"Yes," he said.

"Can I… Can I see them?"

"If you want to."

She had checked the range on the baby monitor, so depending on how far away from the house the horses were, she could go while Riley was napping.

"Could we see the house from the barn? Or wherever you keep them?"

"Yeah," he said, "it's just right across the driveway."

"Can I see them *now*?"

"I don't know. You ate my Pop-Tarts. Actually, more egregious than eating my Pop-Tarts, you threw the last half of one on the ground."

"Sorry about your Pop-Tarts. But I'm sure that a man who can have an entire nursery outfitted in less than twenty-four hours can certainly acquire Pop-Tarts at a moment's notice."

"Or I could just go to the store."

She had a hard time picturing a man like Joshua Grayson walking through the grocery store. In fact, the image almost made her laugh. He was way too commanding to do something as mundane as pick up a head of lettuce and try to figure out how fresh it was. Far too...masculine to go around squeezing avocados.

"What?" he asked, his eyebrows drawing together.

"I just can't imagine you going to the grocery store. That's all."

"Well, I do. Because I like food. Food like Pop-Tarts."

"My mom would never buy those for me," she said. "They were too expensive."

He huffed out a laugh. "My mom would never buy them for me."

"This is why being an adult is cool, even when it sucks."

"Pop-Tarts whenever you want?"

She nodded. "Yep."

"That seems like a low bar."

She lifted a shoulder. "Maybe it is, but it's a tasty one."

He nodded. "Fair enough. Now, why don't we go look at the horses."

Joshua didn't know what to expect by taking Danielle outside to see the horses. He had been irritated that she had eaten his preferred afternoon snack, and then, perversely, even more irritated that she had questioned the fact that it was his preferred afternoon snack. Irritated that he was put in the position of explaining to someone what he did with his time and what he put into his body.

He didn't like explaining himself.

But then she saw the horses. And all his irritation faded as he took in the look on her face. She was filled with...wonder. Absolute wonder over this thing he took for granted.

The fact that he owned horses at all, that he had felt compelled to acquire some once he had moved into this place, was a source of consternation. He had hated doing farm chores when he was a kid. Hadn't been able to get away from home and to the city fast enough. But in recent years, those feelings had started to change. And he'd found himself seeking out roots. Seeking out home.

For better or worse, this was home. Not just the misty Oregon coast, not just the town of Copper Ridge. But a ranch. Horses. A morning spent riding until the sun rose over the mountains, washing everything in a pale gold.

Yeah, that was home.

He could tell this ranch he loved was something beyond a temporary home for Danielle, who was looking at the horses and the barn like they were magical things.

She wasn't wearing her beanie today. Her dark brown hair hung limply around her face. She was pale, her chin pointed, her nose slightly pointed, as well. She was elfin, and he wasn't tempted to call her beautiful, but there was something captivating about her. Something fascinating. Watching her with the large animals was somehow just as entertaining as watching football and he couldn't quite figure out why.

"You didn't grow up around horses?"

"No," she said, taking a timid step toward the paddock. "I grew up in Portland."

He nodded. "Right."

"Always in apartments," she said. Then she frowned. "I think one time we had a house. I can't really remember it. We moved a lot. But sometimes when we lived with my mom's boyfriends, we had nicer places. It had its perks."

"What did?"

"My mom being a codependent hussy," she said, her voice toneless so it was impossible to say whether or not she was teasing.

"Right." He had grown up in one house. His family had never moved. His parents were still in that same farmhouse, the one his family had owned for a couple of generations. He had moved away to go to college and then to start the business, but that was different. He had always known he could come back here. He'd always had roots.

"Will you go back to Portland when you're finished here?" he asked.

"I don't know," she said, blinking rapidly. "I've never really had a choice before. Of where I wanted to live."

It struck him then that she was awfully young. And that he didn't know quite *how* young. "You're twenty-two?"

"Yes," she said, sounding almost defensive. "So I haven't really had a chance to think about what all I want to do and, like, be. When I grow up and stuff."

"Right," he said.

He'd been aimless for a while, but before he'd graduated high school, he'd decided he couldn't deal with a life of ranching in Copper Ridge. He had decided to get out of town. He had wanted more. He had wanted bigger. He'd gone to school for marketing because he was good at selling ideas. Products. He wasn't necessarily the one who created them, or the one who dreamed them up, but he was the one who made sure a consumer would see them and realize that product was what their life had been missing up until that point.

He was the one who took the straw and made it into gold.

He had always enjoyed his job, but it would have been especially satisfying if he'd been able to start his career by building a business with his brother and sister. To be able to market Faith's extraordinary talent to the world, as he did now. But he wasn't sure that he'd started out with a passion for what he did so much as a passion for wealth and success, and that had meant leaving behind his sister and brother too, at first. But his career had certainly grown into a passion. And he'd learned that he was the practical piece. The part that everybody needed.

A lot of people had ideas, but less than half of them had the follow-through to complete what they started. And less than half of *those* people knew how to get to the consumer. That was where he came in.

He'd had his first corporate internship at the age of twenty. He couldn't imagine being aimless at twenty-two.

But then, Danielle had a baby and he couldn't imagine having a baby at that age either.

A hollow pang struck him in the chest.

He didn't like thinking of babies at all.

"You're judging me," she said, taking a step back from the paddock.

"No, I'm not. Also, you can get closer. You can pet them."

Her head whipped around to look at the horses, then back to him, her eyes round and almost comically hopeful. "I can?"

"Of course you can. They don't bite. Well, they *might* bite, just don't stick your fingers in their mouths."

"I don't know," she said, stuffing her hands in her pockets. Except he could tell she really wanted to. She was just afraid.

"Danielle," he said, earning himself a shocked look when he used her name. "Pet the horses."

She tugged her hand out of her pocket again, then took a tentative step forward, reaching out, then drawing her hand back just as quickly.

He couldn't stand it. Between her not knowing what she wanted to be when she grew up and watching her struggle with touching a horse, he just couldn't deal with it. He stepped forward, wrapped his fingers around her wrist and drew her closer to the paddock. "It's fine," he said.

A moment after he said the words, his body registered what he had done. More than that, it registered the fact that she was very warm. That her skin was smooth.

And that she was way, way too thin.

A strange combination of feelings tightened his whole body. Compassion tightened his heart; lust tightened his groin.

He gritted his teeth. "Come on," he said.

He noticed the color rise in her face, and he wondered if she was angry, or if she was feeling the same flash of awareness rocking through him. He supposed it didn't matter either way. "Come on," he said, drawing her hand closer to the opening of the paddock. "There you go, hold your hand flat like that."

She complied, and he released his hold on her, taking a step back. He did his best to ignore the fact that he could still feel the impression of her skin against his palm.

One of his horses—a gray mare named Blue— walked up to the bars and pressed her nose against Danielle's outstretched hand. Danielle made a sharp, shocked sound, drew her hand back, then giggled. "Her whiskers are soft."

"Yeah," he said, a smile tugging at his lips. "And she is about as gentle as they come, so you don't have to be afraid of her."

"I'm not afraid of anything," Danielle said, sticking her hand back in, letting the horse sniff her.

He didn't believe that she wasn't afraid of anything. She was definitely tough. But she was brittle. Like one of those people who might withstand a beating, but if something ever hit a fragile spot, she would shatter entirely.

"Would you like to go riding sometime?" he asked.

She drew her hand back again, her expression… Well, he couldn't quite read it. There was a softness to it, but also an edge of fear and suspicion.

"I don't know. Why?"

"You seem to like the horses."

"I do. But I don't know how to ride."

"I can teach you."

"I don't know. I have to watch Riley." She began to withdraw, both from him and from the paddock.

"I'm going to hire somebody to help watch Riley," he said, making that decision right as the words exited his mouth.

There was that look again. Suspicion. "Why?"

"In case I need you for something that isn't baby friendly. Which will probably happen. We have over a month ahead of us with you living with me, and one never knows what kinds of situations we might run into. I wasn't expecting you to come with a baby, and while I agree that it will definitely help make the case that you're not suitable for me, I also think we'll need to be able to go out without him."

She looked very hesitant about that idea. And he could understand why. She clung to that baby like he was a life preserver. Like if she let go of him, she might sink and be in over her head completely.

"And I would get to ride the horses?" she asked, her eyes narrowed, full of suspicion still.

"I said so."

"Sure. But that doesn't mean a lot to me, Mr. Grayson," she said. "I don't accept people at their word. I like legal documents."

"Well, I'm not going to draw up a legal document about giving you horse-riding lessons. So you're going to have to trust me."

"You want me to trust the sketchy rich dude who put an ad in the paper looking for a fake wife?"

"He's the devil you made the deal with, Ms. Kelly. I would say it's in your best interest to trust him."

"We shake on it at least."

She stuck her hand out, and he could see she was

completely sincere. So he stuck his out in kind, wrapping his fingers around hers, marveling at her delicate bone structure. Feeling guilty now about getting angry over her eating his Pop-Tarts. The woman needed him to hire a gourmet chef too. Needed him to make sure she was getting three meals a day. He wondered how long it had been since she'd eaten regularly. She certainly didn't have the look of a woman who had recently given birth. There was no extra weight on her to speak of. He wondered how she had survived something so taxing as labor and delivery. But those were questions he was not going to ask. They weren't his business.

And he shouldn't even be curious about them.

"All right," she said. "You can hire somebody. And I'll learn to ride horses."

"You're a tough negotiator," he said, releasing his hold on her hand.

"Maybe I should go into business."

He tried to imagine this fragile, spiky creature in a boardroom, and it nearly made him laugh. "If you want to," he said, instead of laughing. Because he had a feeling she might attack him if he made fun of her. And another feeling that if Danielle attacked, she would likely go straight for the eyes. Or the balls.

He was attached to both of those things, and he liked them attached to him.

"I should go back to the house. Riley might wake up soon. Plus, I'm not entirely sure if I trust the new baby monitor. I mean, it's probably fine. But I'm going to have to get used to it before I really depend on it."

"I understand," he said, even though he didn't.

He turned and walked with her back toward the

house. He kept his eyes on her small, determined frame. On the way, she stuffed her hands in her pockets and hunched her shoulders forward. As though she were trying to look intimidating. Trying to keep from looking at her surroundings in case her surroundings looked back.

And then he reminded himself that none of this mattered. She was just a means to an end, even if she was a slightly more multifaceted means than he had thought she might be.

It didn't matter how many facets she had. Danielle Kelly needed to fulfill only one objective. She had to be introduced to his parents and be found completely wanting.

He looked back at her, at her determined walk and her posture that seemed to radiate with *I'll cut you.*

Yeah. He had a feeling she would fulfill that objective just fine.

Four

Danielle was still feeling wobbly after her interaction with Joshua down at the barn. She had touched a horse. And she had touched *him*. She hadn't counted on doing either of those things today. And he had told her they were going to have dinner together tonight and he was going to give her a crash course on the Grayson family. She wasn't entirely sure she felt ready for that either.

She had gone through all her clothes, looking for something suitable for having dinner with a billionaire. She didn't have anything. Obviously.

She snorted, feeling like an idiot for thinking she could find something relatively appropriate in that bag of hers. A bag he thought had scabies.

She turned her snort into a growl.

Then, rebelliously, she pulled out the same pair of faded pants she had been wearing yesterday.

He had probably never dealt with a woman who wore the same thing twice. Let alone the same thing two days in a row. Perversely, she kind of enjoyed that. Hey, she was here to be unsuitable. Might as well start now.

She looked in the mirror, grabbed one stringy end of her hair and blew out a disgusted breath. She shouldn't care how her hair looked.

But he was just so good-looking. It made her feel like a small, brown mouse standing next to him. It wasn't fair, really. That he had the resources to buy himself nice clothes and that he just naturally looked great.

She sighed, picking Riley up from his crib and sticking him in the little carrier she would put him in for dinner. He was awake and looking around, so she wanted to be in his vicinity, rather than leaving him upstairs alone. He wasn't a fussy baby. Really, he hardly ever cried.

But considering how often his mother had left him alone in those early days of his life, before Danielle had realized she couldn't count on her mother to take good care of him, she was reluctant to leave him by himself unless he was sleeping.

Then she paused, going back over to her bag to get the little red, dog-eared dictionary inside. She bent down, still holding on to Riley, and retrieved it. Then she quickly looked up scabies.

"I knew it," she said derisively, throwing the dictionary back into her bag.

She walked down the stairs and into the dining room, setting Riley in his seat on the chair next to hers. Joshua was already sitting at the table, looking as though he had been waiting for them. Which, she had a feeling, he was doing just to be annoying and superior.

"My bag can't have scabies," she said by way of greeting.

"Oh really?"

"Yes. I looked it up. Scabies are mites that burrow into your skin. Not into a duffel bag."

"They have to come from somewhere."

"Well, they're not coming from my bag. They're more likely to come from your horses, or something."

"You like my horses," he said, his tone dry. "Anyway, we're about to have dinner. So maybe we shouldn't be discussing skin mites?"

"You're the one who brought up scabies. The first time."

"I had pretty much dropped the subject."

"Easy enough for you to do, since it wasn't your hygiene being maligned."

"Sure." He stood up from his position at the table. "I'm just going to go get dinner, since you're here. I had it warming."

"Did you cook?"

He left the room without answering and returned a moment later holding two plates full of hot food. Her stomach growled intensely. She didn't even care what was on the plates. As far as she was concerned, it was gourmet. It was warm and obviously not from a can or a frozen pizza box. Plus, she was sitting at a real dining table and not on a patio set that had been shoved into her tiny living room.

The meal looked surprisingly healthy, considering she had discovered his affinity for Pop-Tarts earlier.

And it was accompanied by a particularly nice-looking rice. "What is this?"

"Chicken and risotto," he said.

"What's risotto?"

"Creamy rice," he said. "At least, that's the simple explanation."

Thankfully, he wasn't looking at her like she was an alien for not knowing about risotto. But then she remembered he had spoken of having simple roots. So maybe he was used to dealing with people who didn't have as sophisticated a palate as he had.

She wrinkled her nose, then picked up her fork and took a tentative bite. It was good. So good. And before she knew it, she had cleared out her portion. Her cheeks heated when she realized he had barely taken two bites.

"There's plenty more in the kitchen," he said. Then he took her plate from in front of her and went back into the kitchen. She was stunned, and all she could do was sit there and wait until he returned a moment later with the entire pot of risotto, another portion already on her plate.

"Eat as much as you want," he said, setting everything in front of her.

Well, she wasn't going to argue with that suggestion. She polished off the chicken, then went back for thirds of the risotto. Eventually, she got around to eating the salad.

"I thought we were going to talk about my responsibilities for being your fiancée and stuff," she said after she realized he had been sitting there staring at her for the past ten minutes.

"I thought you should have a chance to eat a meal first."

"Well," she said, taking another bite, "that's unexpectedly kind of you."

"You seem…hungry."

That was the most loaded statement of the century. She was so hungry. For so many things. Food was kind of the least of it. "It's just been a really crazy few months."

"How old is the baby? Riley. How old is Riley?"

For the first time, because of that correction, she became aware of the fact that he seemed reluctant to call Riley by name. Actually, Joshua seemed pretty reluctant to deal with Riley in general.

Riley was unperturbed. Sitting in that reclined seat, his muddy blue eyes staring up at the ceiling. He lifted his fist, putting it in his mouth and gumming it idly.

That was one good thing she could say about their whole situation. Riley was so young that he was largely unperturbed by all of it. He had gone along more or less unaffected by their mother's mistakes. At least, Danielle hoped so. She really did.

"He's almost four months old," she said. She felt a soft smile touch her lips. Yes, taking care of her half brother was hard. None of it was easy. But he had given her a new kind of purpose. Had given her a kind of the drive she'd been missing before.

Before Riley, she had been somewhat content to just enjoy living life on her own terms. To enjoy not cleaning up her mother's messes. Instead, working at the grocery store, going out with friends after work for coffee or burritos at the twenty-four-hour Mexican restaurant.

Her life had been simple, and it had been carefree. Something she hadn't been afforded all the years she'd lived with her mother, dealing with her mother's various heartbreaks, schemes to try to better their circumstances and intense emotional lows.

So many years when Danielle should have been a child but instead was expected to be the parent. If her mother passed out in the bathroom after having too much to drink, it was up to Danielle to take care of her. To put a pillow underneath her mother's head, then make herself a piece of toast for dinner and get her homework done.

In contrast, taking care of only herself had seemed simple. And in truth, she had resented Riley at first, resented the idea that she would have to take care of another person again. But taking care of a baby was different. He wasn't a victim of his own bad choices. No, he was a victim of circumstances. He hadn't had a chance to make a single choice for himself yet.

To Danielle, Riley was the child she'd once been.

Except she hadn't had anyone to step in and take care of her when her mother failed. But Riley did. That realization had filled Danielle with passion. Drive.

And along with that dedication came a fierce, unexpected love like she had never felt before toward another human being. She would do anything for him. Give anything for him.

"And you've been alone with him all this time?"

She didn't know why she was so reluctant to let Joshua know that Riley wasn't her son. She supposed it was partly because, for all intents and purposes, he was her son. She intended to adopt him officially as soon as she had the means to do so. As soon as everything in her life was in order enough that Child Services would respond to her favorably.

The other part was that as long as people thought Riley was hers, they would be less likely to suggest she make a different decision about his welfare. Joshua Grayson had a coldness to him. He seemed to have a family who loved and supported him, but instead of finding it endearing, he got angry about it. He was using her to get back at his dad for doing something that, in her opinion, seemed mostly innocuous. And yes, she was benefiting from his pettiness, so she couldn't exactly judge.

Still, she had a feeling that if he knew Riley wasn't her son, he would suggest she do the "responsible" thing and allow him to be raised by a two-parent family, or whatever. She just didn't even want to have that discussion with him. Or with anybody. She had too many things against her already.

She didn't want to fight about this too.

"Mostly," she said carefully, treading the line between the truth and a lie. "Since he was about three weeks old. And I thought... I thought I could do it. I'd been self-sufficient for a long time. But then I realized there are a lot of logistical problems when you can't just leave your apartment whenever you want. It's harder to get to work. And I couldn't afford childcare. There wasn't any space at the places that had subsidized rates. So I was trading childcare with a neighbor, but sometimes our schedules conflicted. Anyway, it was just difficult. You can imagine why responding to your ad seemed like the best possible solution."

"I already told you, I'm not judging you for taking me up on an offer I made."

"I guess I'm just explaining that under other circumstances I probably wouldn't have sought you out. But things have been hard. I lost my job because I wasn't flexible enough and I had missed too many shifts because babysitting for Riley fell through."

"Well," he said, a strange expression crossing his face, "your problems should be minimized soon. You should be independently wealthy enough to at least afford childcare."

Not only that, she would actually be able to make decisions about her life. About what she wanted. When Joshua had asked her earlier today about whether or not she would go back to Portland, it had been the first time she had truly realized she could make decisions about where she wanted to live, rather than just parking herself somewhere because she happened to be there already.

It would be the first time in her life she could make proactive decisions rather than just reacting to her situation.

"Right. So I guess we should talk about your family," she said, determined to move the conversation back in the right direction. She didn't need to talk about herself. They didn't need to get to know each other. She just needed to do this thing, to trick his family, lie…whatever he needed her to do. So she and Riley could start their new life.

"I already told you my younger sister is an architectural genius. My older brother Isaiah is the financial brain. And I do the public relations and marketing. We have another brother named Devlin, and he runs a small ranching operation in town. He's married, no kids. Then there are my parents."

"The reason we find ourselves in this situation," she said, folding her hands and leaning forward. Then she cast a glance at the pot of risotto and decided to grab the spoon and serve herself another helping while they were talking.

"Yes. Well, not my mother so much. Sure, she wrings her hands and looks at me sadly and says she wishes I would get married. My father is the one who…actively meddles."

"That surprises me. I mean, given what I know about fathers. Which is entirely based on TV. I don't have one."

He lifted a brow.

"Well," she continued, "sure, I guess I do. But I never met him. I mean, I don't even know his name."

She realized that her history was shockingly close to the story she had given about Riley. Which was a true one. It just wasn't about Danielle. It was about her mother. And the fact that her mother repeated the same cycle over and over again. The fact that she never seemed to change. And never would.

"That must've been hard," he said. "I'm sorry."

"Don't apologize. I bet he was an ass. I mean, circumstances would lead you to believe that he must be, right?"

"Yeah, it's probably a pretty safe assumption."

"Well, anyway, this isn't about my lack of a paternal figure. This is about the overbearing presence of yours."

He laughed. "My mother is old-fashioned—so is my father. My brother Devlin is a little bit too, but he's also something of a rebel. He has tattoos and things. He's a likely ally for you, especially since he got married a few months ago and is feeling soft about love and all of that. My brother Isaiah isn't going to like you. My sister, Faith, will try. Basically, if you cuss, chew with your mouth open, put your elbows on the table and in general act like a feral cat, my family will likely find you unsuitable. Also, if you could maybe repeatedly bring up the fact that you're really looking forward to spending my money, and that you had another man's baby four months ago, that would be great."

She squinted. "I think the fact that I have a four-month-old baby in tow will be reminder enough."

The idea of going into his family's farmhouse and behaving like a nightmare didn't sit as well with her as it had when the plan had been fully abstract. But now he had given names to the family members. Now she had been here for a while. And now it was all starting to feel a little bit real.

"It won't hurt. Though, he's pretty quiet. It might help if he screamed."

She laughed. "Oh, I don't know about that. I have a feeling your mom and sister might just want to hold him. That will be the real problem. Not having everyone hate me. That'll be easy enough. It'll be keeping everyone from loving him."

That comment struck her square in the chest, made her realize just what they were playing at here. She was going to be lying to these people. And yes, the idea was to alienate them, but they were going to think she might be their daughter-in-law, sister-in-law…that Riley would be their grandson or nephew.

But it would be a lie.

That's the point, you moron. And who cares? They're strangers. Riley is your life. He's your responsibility. And you'll never see these people again.

"We won't let them hold the baby," he said, his expression hard, as if he'd suddenly realized she wasn't completely wrong about his mother and sister and it bothered him.

She wished she could understand why he felt so strongly about putting a stop to his father playing matchmaker. As someone whose parents were ambivalent about her existence, his disregard for his family's well wishes was hard to comprehend.

"Okay," she said. "Fine by me. And you just want me to…be my charming self?"

"Obviously we'll have to come up with a story about our relationship. We don't have to make up how we met. We can say we met through the ad."

"The ad your father placed, not the ad you placed."

"Naturally."

She looked at Joshua then, at the broad expanse of table between them. Two people who looked less like a couple probably didn't exist on the face of the planet. Honestly, two strangers standing across the street from each other probably looked more like a happily engaged unit than they did.

She frowned. "This is very unconvincing."

"What is? Be specific."

She rolled her eyes at his impatience. "Us."

She stood up and walked toward him, sitting down in the chair right next to him. She looked at him for a moment, at the sharp curve of his jaw, the enticing shape of his lips. He was an attractive man. That was an understatement. He was also so uptight she was pretty sure he had a stick up his ass.

"Look, you want your family to think you've lost your mind, to think you have hooked up with a totally unsuitable woman, right?"

"That is the game."

"Then you have to look like you've lost your mind over me. Unfortunately, Joshua, you look very much in your right mind. In fact, a man of sounder mind may not exist. You are…responsible. You literally look like The Man."

"Which man?"

"Like, The Man. Like, fight the power. *You're* the power. Nobody's going to believe you're with me. At least, not if you don't seem a little bit…looser."

A slight smile tipped up those lips she had been thinking about only a moment before. His blue eyes warmed, and she felt an answering warmth spread low in her belly. "So what you're saying is we need to look like we have more of a connection?"

Her throat went dry. "It's just a suggestion."

He leaned forward, his gaze intent on hers. "An essential one, I think." Then he reached up and she jerked backward, nearly toppling off the side of her chair. "It looks like I'm not the only one who's wound a bit tight."

"I'm not," she said, taking a deep breath, trying to get her jittery body to calm itself down.

She wasn't used to men. She wasn't used to men touching her. Yes, intermittently she and her mother had lived with some of her mother's boyfriends, but none of them had ever been inappropriate with her. And she had never been close enough to even give any of them hugs.

And she really, really wasn't used to men who were so beautiful it was almost physically painful to look directly at them.

"You're right. We have to do a better job of looking like a couple. And that would include you not scampering under the furniture when I get close to you."

She sat up straight and folded her hands in her lap. "I did not scamper," she muttered.

"You were perilously close to a scamper."

"Was not," she grumbled, and then her breath caught in her throat as his warm palm made contact with her cheek.

He slid his thumb down the curve of her face to that dent just beneath her lips, his eyes never leaving hers. She felt...stunned and warm. No, hot. So very hot. Like there was a furnace inside that had been turned up the moment his hand touched her bare skin.

She supposed she was meant to be flirtatious. To play the part of the moneygrubbing tart with loose morals he needed her to be, that his family would expect her to be. But right now, she was shocked into immobility.

She took a deep breath, fighting for composure. But his thumb migrated from the somewhat reasonable point just below her mouth to her lip and her composure dissolved completely. His touch felt... shockingly intimate and filthy somehow. Not in a bad way, just in a way she'd never experienced before.

For some reason she would never be able to articulate—not even to herself—she darted her tongue out and touched the tip to his thumb. She tasted salt, skin and a promise that arrowed downward to the most private part of her body, leaving her feeling breathless. Leaving her feeling new somehow.

As if a wholly unexpected and previously unknown part of herself had been uncovered, awoken. She wanted to do exactly what he had accused her of doing earlier. She wanted to turn away. Wanted to scurry beneath the furniture or off into the night. Somewhere safe. Somewhere less confrontational.

But he was still looking at her. And those blue eyes were like chains, lashing her to the seat, holding her in place. And his thumb, pressed against her lip, felt heavy. Much too heavy for her to push against. For her to fight.

And when it came right down to it, she didn't even want to.

Something expanded in her chest, spreading low, opening up a yawning chasm in her stomach. Deepening her need, her want. Her desire for things she hadn't known she could desire until now.

Until he had made a promise with his touch that she hadn't known she wanted fulfilled.

She was just about to come back to herself, to pull away. And then he closed the distance between them.

His lips were warm and firm. The kiss was nothing like she had imagined it might be. She had always thought a kiss must reach inside and steal your brain. Transform you. She had always imagined a kiss to be powerful, considering the way her mother acted.

When her mother was under the influence of love—at least, that was what her mother had called it; Danielle had always known it was lust—she acted like someone entirely apart from herself.

Yes, Danielle had always known a kiss could be powerful. But what she hadn't counted on was that she might feel wholly like *herself* when a man fused his lips to hers. That she would be so perfectly aware of where she was, of what she was doing.

Of the pressure of his lips against hers, the warmth of his hand as he cradled her face, the hard, tightening knot of desire in her stomach that told her how insufficient the kiss was.

The desire that told her just how much more she wanted. Just how much more there could be.

He was kissing her well, this near stranger, and she never wanted it to end.

Instinctively, she angled her head slightly, parting her lips, allowing him to slide his tongue against hers. It was unexpectedly slick, unexpectedly arousing. Unexpectedly everything she wanted.

That was the other thing that surprised her. Because not only had she imagined a woman might lose herself entirely when a man kissed her, she had also imagined she would be immune. Because she knew better. She knew the cost. But she was sitting here, allowing him to kiss her and kiss her and kiss her. She was Danielle Kelly, and she was submitting herself to this sensual assault with almost shocking abandon.

Her hands were still folded in her lap, almost primly, but her mouth was parted wide, gratefully receiving every stroke of his tongue, slow and languorous against her own. Sexy. Deliciously affecting.

He moved his hands then, sliding them around the

back of her neck, down between her shoulder blades, along the line of her spine until his hands spanned her waist. She arched, wishing she could press her body against his. Wishing she could do something to close the distance between them. Because he was still sitting in his chair and she in hers.

He pulled away, and she followed him, leaning into him with an almost humiliating desperation, wanting to taste him again. To be kissed again. By Joshua Grayson, the man she was committing an insane kind of fraud with. The man who had hired her to play the part of his pretend fiancée.

"That will do," he said, lifting his hand and squeezing her chin gently, those blue eyes glinting with a sharpness that cut straight to her soul. "Yes, Ms. Kelly, that will do quite nicely."

Then he released his hold on her completely, settling back in his seat, his attention returning to his dinner plate.

A slash of heat bled across Danielle's cheekbones. He hadn't felt anything at all. He had been proving a point. Just practicing the ruse they would be performing for his family tomorrow night. The kiss hadn't changed anything for him at all. Hadn't been more than the simple meeting of mouths.

It had been her first kiss. It had been everything.

And right then she got her first taste of just how badly a man could make a woman feel. Of how—when wounded—feminine pride could be a treacherous and testy thing.

She rose from her seat and rounded to stand behind his. Then, without fully pausing to think about what she might be doing, she placed her hands on his shoulders, leaned forward and slid her hands beneath the collar of his shirt and down his chest.

Her palms made contact with his hot skin, with hard muscle, and she had to bite her lip to keep from groaning out loud. She had to plant her feet firmly on the wood floor to keep herself from running away, from jerking her hands back like a child burned on a hot oven.

She'd never touched a man like this before. It was shocking just how arousing she found it, this little form of revenge, this little rebellion against his blasé response to the earthquake he had caused in her body.

She leaned her head forward, nearly pressing her lips against his ear. Then her teeth scraped his earlobe.

"Yes," she whispered. "I think it's quite convincing."

She straightened again, slowly running her fingernails over his skin as she did. She didn't know where this confidence had come from. Where the know-how and seemingly deep, feminine instinct had come from that allowed her to toy with him. But there it was.

She was officially playing the part of a saucy minx. Considering that was what he had hired her for, her flirtation was a good thing. But her heart thundered harder than a drum as she walked back to Riley, picked up his carrier and flipped her hair as she turned to face Joshua.

"I think I'm going to bed. I had best prepare myself to meet your family."

"You'll be wearing something different tomorrow," he said, his tone firm.

"Why?" She looked down at her ragged sweatshirt and skinny jeans. "That doesn't make any sense. You wanted me to look unsuitable. I might as well go in this."

"No, you brought up a very good point. You have to look unsuitable, but this situation also has to be believable. Plus, I think a gold digger would demand a new wardrobe, don't you?" One corner of his lips quirked upward, and she had a feeling he was punishing her for her little display a moment ago.

If only she could work out quite where the trap was.

"I don't know," she said, her voice stiff.

"But, Ms. Kelly, you told me yourself that you *are* a gold digger. That's why you're here, after all. For my gold."

"I suppose so," she said, keeping her words deliberately hard. "But I want actual gold, not clothes. So this is another thing that's going to be on you."

Those blue eyes glinted, and right then she got an idea of just how dangerous he was to her. "Consider it done."

And if there was one thing she had learned so far about Joshua Grayson, it was that if he said something would be done, it would be.

Five

Joshua wasn't going to try to turn Danielle into a sophisticate overnight. He was also avoiding thinking about the way it had felt to kiss her soft lips. Was avoiding remembering the way her hands had felt sliding down his chest.

He needed to make sure the two of them looked like a couple, that much was true. But he wouldn't allow himself to be distracted by her. There were a million reasons not to touch Danielle Kelly—unless they were playing a couple. Yes, there would have to be some touching, but he was not going to take advantage of her.

First of all, she was at his financial mercy. Second of all, she was the kind of woman who came with entanglements. And he didn't want any entanglements.

He wasn't the type to have trouble with self-control. If it wasn't a good time to seek out a physical relationship, he didn't. It wasn't a good time now, which meant he would defer any kind of sexual gratification until the end of his association with Danielle.

That should be fine.

He should be able to consider any number of women who he had on-again, off-again associations with, choose one and get in touch with her after Danielle left. His mind and body should be set on that.

Sadly, all he could think of was last night's kiss and the shocking heat that had come with it.

And then Danielle came down the stairs wearing the simple black dress he'd had delivered for her.

His thoughts about not transforming her into a sophisticated woman overnight held true. Her long, straight brown hair still hung limp down to her waist, and she had no makeup on to speak of except pale pink gloss on her lips.

But the simple cut of the dress suited her slender figure and displayed small, perky breasts that had been hidden beneath her baggy, threadbare sweaters.

She was holding on to the handle of the baby's car seat with both hands, lugging it down the stairs. For one moment, he was afraid she might topple over. He moved forward quickly, grabbing the handle and taking the seat from her.

When he looked down at the sleeping child, a strange tightness invaded his chest. "It wouldn't be good for you or for Riley if you fell and broke your neck trying to carry something that's too heavy for you," he said, his tone harder than he'd intended it to be.

Danielle scowled. "Well, offer assistance earlier next time. I had to get down the stairs somehow. Anyway, I've been navigating stairs like this with the baby since he was born. I lived in an apartment. On the third floor."

"I imagine he's heavier now than he used to be."

"An expert on child development?" She arched one dark brow as she posed the question.

He gritted his teeth. "Hardly."

She stepped away from the stairs, and the two of them walked toward the door. Just because he wanted to make it clear that he was in charge of the evening, he placed his hand low on her back, right at the dip where her spine curved, right above what the dress revealed to be a magnificent ass.

He had touched her there to get to her, but he had not anticipated the touch getting to him.

He ushered her out quickly, then handed the car seat to her, allowing her to snap it into the base—the one he'd had installed in his car when all of the nursery accoutrements had been delivered—then sat waiting for her to get in.

As they started to pull out of the driveway, she wrapped her arms around herself, rubbing her hands over her bare skin. "Do you think you could turn the heater on?"

He frowned. "Why didn't you bring a jacket?"

"I don't have one? All I have are my sweaters. And I don't think either of them would go with the dress. Would kind of ruin the effect."

He put the brakes on, slipped out of his own jacket and handed it to her. She just looked at him like he was offering her a live gopher. "Take it," he said.

She frowned but reached out, taking the jacket and

slipping it on. "Thank you," she said, her voice sounding hollow.

They drove to his parents' house in silence, the
only sounds coming from the baby sitting in the back
seat. A sobering reminder of the evening that was
about to unfold. He was going to present a surprise
fiancée and a surprise baby to his parents, and suddenly, he didn't look at this plan in quite the same
way as he had before.

He was throwing Danielle into the deep end.
Throwing Riley into the deep end.

Joshua gritted his teeth, tightening his hold on
the steering wheel. Finally, the interminable drive
through town was over. He turned left off a winding
road and onto a dirt drive that led back to the familiar, humble farmhouse his parents still called home.

That some part of his heart still called home too.

He looked over at Danielle, who had gone pale.
"It's fine," he said.

Danielle looked down at the ring on her finger,
then back up at him. "I guess it's showtime."

Danielle felt warm all over, no longer in need of
Joshua's jacket, and conflicted down to the brand-new
shoes Joshua had ordered for her.

But it wasn't the dress, or the shoes, that had her
feeling warm. It was the jacket. Well, obviously a
jacket was supposed to make her warm, but this was
different. Joshua had realized she was cold. And it
had mattered to him.

He had given her his own jacket so she could keep
warm.

It was too big, the sleeves went well past the edges

of her fingertips, and it smelled like him. From the moment she had slipped it on, she had been fighting the urge to bury her nose in the fabric and lose herself in the sharp, masculine smell that reminded her of his skin. Skin she had tasted last night.

Standing on the front step of this modest farmhouse that she could hardly believe Joshua had ever lived in, wearing his coat, with him holding Riley's car seat, it was too easy to believe this actually was some kind of "meet the parents" date.

In effect, she supposed it was. She was even wearing his jacket. His jacket that was still warm from his body and smelled—

Danielle was still ruminating about the scent of Joshua's jacket when the door opened. A blonde woman with graying hair and blue eyes that looked remarkably like her son's gave them a warm smile.

"Joshua," she said, glancing sideways at Danielle and clearly doing her best not to look completely shocked, "I didn't expect you so early. And I didn't know you were bringing a guest." Her eyes fell to the carrier in Joshua's hand. "Two guests."

"I thought it would be a good surprise."

"What would be?"

A man who could only be Joshua's father came to the door behind the woman. He was tall, with dark hair and eyes. He looked nice too. They both did. There was a warmth to them, a kindness, that didn't seem to be present in their son.

But then Danielle felt the warmth of the jacket again, and she had to revise that thought. Joshua might not exude kindness, but it was definitely there, buried. And for the life of her, she couldn't figure out why he hid it.

She was prickly and difficult, but at least she had an excuse. Her family was the worst. As far as she could tell, his family was guilty of caring too much. And she just couldn't feel that sorry for a rich dude whose parents loved him and were involved in his life more than he wanted them to be.

"Who is this?" Joshua's father asked.

"Danielle, this is my mom and dad, Todd and Nancy Grayson. Mom, Dad, this is Danielle Kelly," Joshua said smoothly. "And I have you to thank for meeting her, Dad."

His father's eyebrows shot upward. "Do you?"

"Yes," Joshua said. "She responded to your ad. Mom, Dad, Danielle is my fiancée."

They were ushered into the house quickly after that announcement, and there were a lot of exclamations. The house was already full. A young woman sat in the corner holding hands with a large, tattooed man who was built like a brick house and was clearly related to Joshua somehow. There was another man, as tall as Joshua, with slightly darker hair and the same blue eyes but who didn't carry himself quite as stiffly. His build was somewhere in between Joshua and the tattooed man, muscular but not a beast.

"My brother Devlin," Joshua said, indicating the tattooed man before putting his arm around Danielle's waist as they moved deeper into the room, "and his wife, Mia. And this is my brother Isaiah. I'm surprised his capable assistant, Poppy, isn't somewhere nearby."

"Isaiah, did you want a beer or whiskey?" A petite woman appeared from the kitchen area, her curly, dark hair swept back into a bun, a few stray pieces bouncing around her pretty face. She was impeccable. From that elegant updo down to the soles of her tiny, high-heeled feet. She was wearing a high-waisted skirt that flared out at the hips and fell down past her knees, along with a plain, fitted top.

"Is that his…girlfriend?" Danielle asked.

Poppy laughed. "Absolutely not," she said, her tone clipped. "I'm his assistant."

Danielle thought it strange that an assistant would be at a family gathering but didn't say anything.

"She's more than an assistant," Nancy Grayson said. "She's part of the family. She's been with them since they started the business."

Danielle had not been filled in on the details of his family's relationships because she only needed to know how to alienate them, not how to endear herself to them.

The front door opened again and this time it was a younger blonde woman whose eyes also matched Joshua's who walked in. "Sorry I'm late," she said, "I got caught up working on a project."

This had to be his sister, Faith. The architect he talked about with such pride and fondness. A woman who was Danielle's age and yet so much more successful they might be completely different species.

"This is Joshua's fiancée," Todd Grayson said. "He's engaged."

"Shut the front door," Faith said. "Are you really?"

"Yes," Joshua said, the lie rolling easily off his tongue.

Danielle bit back a comment about his PR skills. She

was supposed to be hard to deal with, but they weren't supposed to call attention to the fact this was a ruse.

"That's great?" Faith took a step forward and hugged her brother, then leaned in to grab hold of Danielle, as well.

"Is nobody going to ask about the baby?" Isaiah asked.

"Obviously *you* are," Devlin said.

"Well, it's kind of the eight-hundred-pound gorilla in the room. Or the ten-pound infant."

"It's my baby," Danielle said, feeling color mount in her cheeks.

She noticed a slight shift in Joshua's father's expression. Which was the general idea. To make him suspicious of her. To make him think he had gone and caught his son a gold digger.

"Well, that's…" She could see Joshua's mother searching for words. "It's definitely unexpected." She looked apologetically at Danielle the moment the words left her mouth. "It's just that Joshua hasn't shown much interest in marriage or family."

Danielle had a feeling that was an understatement. If Joshua was willing to go to such lengths to get his father out of his business, then he must be about as anti-marriage as you could get.

"Well," Joshua said, "Danielle and I met because of Dad."

His mother's blue gaze sharpened. "How?"

His father looked guilty. "Well, I thought he could use a little help," he said finally.

"What kind of help?"

"It's not good for a man to be alone, especially not our boys," he said insistently.

"Some of us like to be alone," Isaiah pointed out.

"You wouldn't feel that way if you didn't have a woman who cooked for you and ran your errands," his father responded, looking pointedly at Poppy.

"She's an employee," Isaiah said.

Poppy looked more irritated and distressed by Isaiah's comment than she did by the Grayson family patriarch's statement. But she didn't say anything.

"You were right," Joshua said. "I just needed to find the right woman. You placed that ad, listing all of my assets, and the right woman responded."

This was so ridiculous. Danielle felt her face heating. The assets Joshua's father had listed were his bank account, and there was no way in the world that wasn't exactly what everyone in his family was thinking.

She knew this was her chance to confirm her gold-digging motives. But right then, Riley started to cry.

"Oh," she said, feeling flustered. "Just let me… I need to…"

She fumbled around with the new diaper bag, digging around for a bottle, and then went over to the car seat, taking the baby out of it.

"Let me help," Joshua's mother said.

She was being so kind. Danielle felt terrible.

But before Danielle could protest, the other woman was taking Riley from her arms. Riley wiggled and fussed, but then she efficiently plucked the bottle from Danielle's hand and stuck it right in his mouth. He quieted immediately.

"What a good baby," she said. "Does he usually go to strangers?"

Danielle honestly didn't know. "Other than a neighbor whose known him since he was born, I'm the only one who takes care of him," she said.

"Don't you have any family?"

Danielle shook her head, feeling every inch the curiosity she undoubtedly was. Every single eye in the room was trained on her, and she knew they were all waiting for her to make a mistake. She was *supposed* to make a mistake, dammit. That was what Joshua was paying her to do.

"I don't have any family," she said decisively. "It's just been me and Riley from the beginning."

"It must be nice to have some help now," Faith said, not unkindly, but definitely probing.

"It is," Danielle said. "I mean, it's really hard taking care of a baby by yourself. And I didn't make enough money to…well, anything. So meeting Joshua has been great. Because he's so…helpful."

A timer went off in the other room and Joshua's mother blinked. "Oh, I have to get dinner." She turned to her son. "Since you're so helpful, Joshua." And before Danielle could protest, before Joshua could protest, Nancy dumped Riley right into his arms.

He looked like he'd been handed a bomb. And frankly, Danielle felt a little bit like a bomb might detonate at any moment. It had not escaped her notice that Joshua had never touched Riley. Yes, he had carried his car seat, but he had never voluntarily touched the baby. Which, now that she thought about it, must have been purposeful. But then, not everybody liked babies. She had never been particularly drawn to them before Riley. Maybe Joshua felt the same way.

She could tell by his awkward posture, and the way

Riley's small frame was engulfed by Joshua's large, muscular one, that any contact with babies was not something he was used to.

She imagined Joshua's reaction would go a long way in proving how unsuitable she was. Maybe not in the way he had hoped, but it definitely made his point.

He took a seat on the couch, still holding on to Riley, still clearly committed to the farce.

"So you met through an ad," Isaiah said, his voice full of disbelief. "An ad that Dad put in the paper."

Everyone's head swiveled, and they looked at Todd. "I did what any concerned father would do for his son."

Devlin snorted. "Thank God I found a wife on my own."

"You found a wife by pilfering from my friendship pool," Faith said, her tone disapproving. "Isaiah and Joshua have too much class to go picking out women that young."

"Actually," Danielle said, deciding this was the perfect opportunity to highlight another of the many ways in which she was unsuitable, "I'm only twenty-two."

Joshua's father looked at him, his gaze sharp. "Really?"

"Really," Danielle said.

"That's unexpected," Todd said to his son.

"That's what's so great about how we met," Joshua said. "Had I looked for a life partner on my own, I probably would have chosen somebody with a completely different set of circumstances. Had you asked me only a few short weeks ago, I would have said I didn't want children. And now look at me."

Everybody *was* looking at him, and it was clear he was extremely uncomfortable. Danielle wasn't entirely sure he was making the point he hoped to make, but he did make a pretty amusing picture. "I also would have chosen somebody closer to my age. But the great thing about Danielle is that she is so mature. I think it's because she's a mother. And yes, it happened for her in non-ideal circumstances, but her ability to rise above her situation and solve her problems—namely by responding to the ad—is one of the many things I find attractive about her."

She wanted to kick him in the shin. He was being an asshole, and he was making her sound like a total flake... But that was the whole idea. And, honestly, given the information Joshua had about her life...he undoubtedly thought she *was* a flake. It was stupid, and it wasn't fair. One of the many things she had learned about people since becoming the sole caregiver for Riley was that even though everyone had sex, a woman was an immediate pariah the minute she bore the evidence of that sex.

All that mattered to the hypocrites was that Danielle appeared to be a scarlet woman, therefore she was one.

Never mind that in reality she was a virgin.

Which was not a word she needed to be thinking while sitting in the Grayson family living room.

Her cheeks felt hot, like they were being stung by bees.

"Fate is a funny thing," Danielle said, edging closer to Joshua. She took Riley out of his arms, and from the way Joshua surrendered the baby, she could tell he was more than ready to hand him over.

The rest of the evening passed in a blur of awkward moments and stilted conversation. It was clear to her that his family was wonderful and warm, but that they were also seriously questioning Joshua's decision making. Todd Grayson looked as if he was going to be physically assaulted by his wife.

Basically, everything was going according to Joshua's plan.

But Danielle couldn't feel happy about it. She couldn't feel triumphant. It just felt awful.

Finally, it was time to go, and Danielle was ready to scurry out the door and keep on scurrying away from the entire Grayson family—Joshua included.

She was gathering her things, and Joshua was talking to one of his brothers, when Faith approached.

"We haven't gotten a chance to talk yet," she said.

"I guess not," Danielle said, feeling instantly wary. She had a feeling that being approached by Joshua's younger sister like this wouldn't end well.

"I'm sure he's told you all about me," Faith said, and Danielle had a feeling that statement was a test.

"Of course he has." She sounded defensive, even though there was no reason for her to feel defensive, except that she kind of did anyway.

"Great. So here's the thing. I don't know exactly what's going on here, but my brother is not a 'marriage and babies' kind of guy. My brother dates a seemingly endless stream of models, all of whom are about half a foot taller than you without their ridiculous high heels on. Also, he likes blondes."

Danielle felt her face heating again as the other woman appraised her and found her lacking. "Right. Well. Maybe I'm a really great conversationalist. Although, it could be the fact that I don't have a gag reflex."

She watched the other woman's cheeks turn bright pink and felt somewhat satisfied. Unsophisticated, virginal Danielle had made the clearly much more sophisticated Faith Grayson blush.

"Right. Well, if you're leading him around by his... *you know*...so you can get into his wallet, I'm not going to allow that. There's a reason he's avoided commitment all this time. And I'm not going to let you hurt him. He's been hurt enough," she said.

Danielle could only wonder what that meant, because Joshua seemed bulletproof.

"I'm not going to break up with him," Danielle said. "Why would I do that? I'd rather stay in his house than in a homeless shelter."

She wanted to punch her own face. And she was warring with the fact that Faith had rightly guessed that she was using Joshua for his money—though not in the way his sister assumed. And Danielle needed Faith to think the worst. But it also hurt to have her assume something so negative based on Danielle's circumstances. Based on her appearance.

People had been looking at Danielle and judging her as low-class white trash for so long—not exactly incorrectly—that it was a sore spot.

"We're a close family," Faith said. "And we look out for each other. Just remember that."

"Well, your brother loves me."

"If that's true," Faith said, "then I hope you're very happy together. I actually do hope it's true. But the problem is, I'm not sure I believe it."

"Why?" Danielle was bristling, and there was no

reason on earth why she should be. She shouldn't be upset about this. She shouldn't be taking it personally. But she was.

Faith Grayson had taken one look at Danielle and judged her. Pegged her for exactly the kind of person she was, really—a low-class nobody who needed the kind of money and security a man like Joshua could provide. Danielle had burned her pride to the ground to take part in this charade. Poking at the embers of that pride was stupid. But she felt compelled to do it anyway.

"Is it because I'm some kind of skank he would never normally sully himself with?"

"Mostly, it's because I know my brother. And I know he never intended to be in any kind of serious relationship again."

Again.

That word rattled around inside of Danielle. It implied he had been in a serious relationship before. He hadn't mentioned that. He'd just said he didn't want his father meddling. Didn't want marriage. He hadn't said it was because he'd tried before.

She blinked.

Faith took that momentary hesitation and ran with it. "So you don't know that much about him. You don't actually know anything about him, do you? You just know he's rich."

"And he's hot," Danielle said.

She wasn't going to back down. Not now. But she would have a few very grumpy words with Joshua once they left.

He hadn't prepared her for this. She looked like an idiot. As she gathered her things, she realized looking like an idiot was his objective. She could look bad in a great many ways, after all. The fact that they might be an unsuitable couple because she didn't know anything about him would be one way to accomplish that.

When she and Joshua finally stepped outside, heading back to the car amid a thunderous farewell from the family, Danielle felt like she could breathe for the first time in at least two hours. She hadn't realized it, but being inside that house—all warm and cozy and filled with the kind of love she had only ever seen in movies—had made her throat and lungs and chest, and even her fingers, feel tight.

They got into the car, and Danielle folded her arms tightly, leaning her head against the cold passenger-side window, her breath fanning out across the glass, leaving mist behind. She didn't bother fighting the urge to trace a heart in it.

"Feeling that in character?" Joshua asked, his tone dry, as he put the car in Reverse and began to pull out of the driveway.

She stuck her tongue out and scribbled over the heart. "Not particularly. I don't understand. Now that I've met them, I understand even less. Your sister grilled me the minute she got a chance to talk to me alone. Your father is worried about the situation. Your mother is trying to be supportive in spite of the fact that we are clearly the worst couple of all time. And you're doing this why, Joshua? I don't understand."

She hadn't meant to call him out in quite that way. After all, what did she care about his motivations? He was paying her. The fact that he was a rich, eccentric idiot kind of worked in her favor. But tonight had felt wrong. And while she was more into survival than into the nuances of right and wrong, the ruse was getting to her.

"I explained to you already," he said, his tone so hard it elicited a small, plaintive cry from Riley in the back.

"Don't wake up the baby," she snapped.

"We really are a convincing couple," he responded.

"Not to your sister. Who told me we didn't make any sense together because you had never shown any interest in falling in love *again*."

It was dark in the car, so she felt rather than saw the tension creep up his spine. It was in the way he shifted in his seat, how his fists rolled forward as he twisted his hands on the steering wheel.

"Well," he said, "that's the thing. They all know. Because family like mine doesn't leave well enough alone. They want to know about all your injuries, all your scars, and then they obsess over the idea that they might be able to heal them. And they don't listen when you tell them healing is not necessary."

"Right," she said, blowing out an exasperated breath. "Here's the thing. I'm just a dumb bimbo you picked up through a newspaper ad who needed your money. So I don't understand all this coded nonsense. Just tell me what's going on. Especially if I'm going to spend more nights trying to alienate your family—who are basically a childhood sitcom fantasy of what a family should be."

"I've done it before, Danielle. Love. It's not worth it. Not considering how badly it hurts when it ends. But even more, it's not worth it when you consider how badly you can hurt the other person."

His words fell flat in the car, and she didn't know how to respond to them. "I don't…"

"Details aren't important. You've been hurt before, haven't you?"

He turned the car off the main road and headed up the long drive to his house. She took a deep breath. "Yes."

"By Riley's father?"

She shifted uncomfortably. "Not exactly."

"You didn't love him?"

"No," she said. "I didn't love him. But my mother kind of did a number on me. I do understand that love hurts. I also understand that a supportive family is not necessarily guaranteed."

"Yeah," Joshua said, "supportive family is great." He put the car in Park and killed the engine before getting out and stalking toward the house.

Danielle frowned, then unbuckled quickly, getting out of the car and pushing the sleeves of Joshua's jacket back so she could get Riley's car seat out of the base. Then she headed up the stairs and into the house after him.

"And yet you are trying to hurt yours. So excuse me if I'm not making all the connections."

"I'm not trying to hurt my family," he said, turning around, pushing his hand through his blond hair. His blue eyes glittered, his jaw suddenly looking sharper, his cheekbones more hollow. "What I want is for them to leave well enough alone. My father doesn't understand. He thinks all I need is to find somebody to love again and I'm going to be fixed. But there is no fixing this. There's no fixing me. I don't want it. And yeah, maybe this scheme is over the top, but don't you think putting an ad in the paper looking for a wife for your son is over the top too? I'm not giving him back anything he didn't dish out."

"Maybe you could talk to him."

"You think I haven't talked to him? You think this was my first resort? You're wrong about that. I tried reasonable discourse, but you can't reason with an unreasonable man."

"Yeah," Danielle said, picking at the edge of her thumbnail. "He seemed like a real monster. What with the clear devotion to your mother, the fact that he raised all of you, that he supported you well enough that you could live in that house all your life and then go off to become more successful than he was."

She set the car seat down on the couch and unbuckled it, lifting Riley into her arms and heading toward the stairs.

"We didn't have anything when I was growing up," he said, his tone flat and strange.

Danielle swallowed hard, lifting her hand to cradle Riley's soft head. "I'm sorry. But unless you were homeless or were left alone while one of your parents went to work all day—and I mean *alone*, not with siblings—then we might have different definitions of nothing."

"Fine," he said. "We weren't that poor. But we didn't have anything extra, and there was definitely nothing to do around here but get into trouble when you didn't have money."

She blinked. "What kind of trouble?"

"The usual kind. Go out to the woods, get messed up, have sex."

"Last I checked, condoms and drugs cost money."

She held on to Riley a little bit tighter. "Pretty sure you could have bought a movie ticket."

He lifted his shoulder. "Look, we pooled our money. We did what we did. Didn't worry about the future, didn't worry about anything."

"What changed?" Because obviously something had. He hadn't stayed here. He hadn't stayed aimless.

"One day I looked up and realized this was all I would ever have unless I changed something. Let me tell you, that's pretty sobering. A future of farming, barely making it, barely scraping by? That's what my dad had. And I hated it. I drank in the woods every night with my friends to avoid that reality. I didn't want to have my dad's life. So I made some changes. Not really soon enough to improve my grades or get myself a full scholarship, but I ended up moving to Seattle and getting myself an entry-level job with a PR firm."

"You just moved? You didn't know anybody?"

"No. I didn't know anyone. But I met people. And, it turned out, I was good at meeting people. Which was interesting because you don't meet very many new people in a small town that you've lived in your entire life. But in Seattle, no one knew me. No one knew who my father was, and no one had expectations for me. I was judged entirely on my own merit, and I could completely rewrite who I was. Not just some small-town deadbeat, but a young, bright kid who had a future in front of him."

The way he told that story, the very idea of it, was tantalizing to Danielle. The idea of starting over. Having a clean slate. Of course, with a baby in tow, a change like that would be much more difficult. But her association with Joshua would allow her to make it happen.

It was…shocking to realize he'd had to start over once. Incredibly encouraging, even though she was feeling annoyed with him at the moment.

She leaned forward and absently pressed a kiss to Riley's head. "That must've been incredible. And scary."

"The only scary thing was the idea of going back to where I came from without changing anything. So I didn't allow that to happen. I worked harder than everybody else. I set goals and I met them. And then I met Shannon."

Something ugly twisted inside of Danielle's stomach the moment he said the other woman's name. For the life of her she couldn't figure out why. She felt… curious. But in a desperate way. Like she needed to know everything about this other person. This person who had once shared Joshua's life. This person who had undoubtedly made him the man standing in front of her. If she didn't know about this woman, then she would never understand him.

"What, then? Who was Shannon?" Her desperation was evident in her words, and she didn't bother hiding it.

"She was my girlfriend. For four years, while I was getting established in Seattle. We lived together. I was going to ask her to marry me."

He looked away from her then, something in his blue eyes turning distant. "Then she found out she was pregnant, and I figured I could skip the elaborate proposal and move straight to the wedding."

She knew him well enough to know this story

wasn't headed toward a happy ending. He didn't have a wife. He didn't have a child. In fact, she was willing to bet he'd never had a child. Based on the way he interacted with Riley. Or rather, the very practiced way he avoided interacting with Riley.

"That didn't happen," she said, because she didn't know what else to say, and part of her wanted to spare him having to tell the rest of the story. But, also, part of her needed to know.

"She wanted to plan the wedding. She wanted to wait until after the baby was born. You know, wedding dress sizes and stuff like that. So I agreed. She miscarried late, Danielle. Almost five months. It was…the most physically harrowing thing I've ever watched anyone go through. But the recovery was worse. And I didn't know what to do. So I went back to work. We had a nice apartment, we had a view of the city, and if I worked, she didn't have to. I could support her, I could buy her things. I could do my best to make her happy, keep her focused on the wedding."

He had moved so quickly through the devastating, painful revelation of his lost baby that she barely had time to process it. But she also realized he had to tell the story this way. There was no point lingering on the details. It was simple fact. He had been with a woman he loved very much. He had intended to marry her, had been expecting a child with her. And they had lost the baby.

She held on a little bit more tightly to Riley.

"She kept getting worse. Emotionally. She moved into a different bedroom, then she didn't get out of bed. She had a lot of pain. At first, I didn't question it, because it seemed reasonable that she'd need pain medication after what she went through. But then she kept taking it. And I wondered if that was okay. We had a fight about it. She said it wasn't right for me to question her pain—physical or otherwise—when all I did was work. And you know… I thought she was probably right. So I let it go. For a year, I let it go. And then I found out the situation with the prescription drugs was worse than I realized. But when I confronted Shannon, she just got angry."

It was so strange for Danielle to imagine what he was telling her. This whole other life he'd had. In a city where he had lived with a woman and loved her. Where he had dreamed of having a family. Of having a child. Where he had buried himself in work to avoid dealing with the pain of loss, while the woman he loved lost herself in a different way.

The tale seemed so far removed from the man he was now. From this place, from that hard set to his jaw, that sharp glitter in his eye, the way he held his shoulders straight. She couldn't imagine this man feeling at a loss. Feeling helpless.

"She got involved with another man, someone I worked with. Maybe it started before she left me, but I'm not entirely sure. All I know is she wasn't sleeping with me at the time, so even if she was with him before she moved out, it hardly felt like cheating. And anyway, the affair wasn't really the important part. That guy was into recreational drug use. It's how he functioned. And he made it all available to her."

"That's…that's awful, Joshua. I know how bad that stuff can be. I've seen it."

He shook his head. "Do you have any idea what it's like? To have somebody come into your life who's beautiful, happy, and to watch her leave your life as something else entirely. Broken, an addict. I ruined her."

Danielle took a step back, feeling as though she had been struck by the impact of his words. "No, you didn't. It was drugs. It was…"

"I wasn't there for her. I didn't know how to be. I didn't like hard things, Danielle. I never did. I didn't want to stay in Copper Ridge and work the land—I didn't want to deal with a lifetime of scraping by, because it was too hard."

"Right. You're so lazy that you moved to Seattle and started from scratch and worked your way to the highest ranks of the company? I don't buy that."

"There's reward in that kind of work, though. And you don't have to deal with your life when it gets bad. You just go work more. And you can tell yourself it's fine because you're making more money. Because you're making your life easier, life for the other person easier, even while you let them sit on the couch slowly dying, waiting for you to help them. I convinced myself that what I was doing was important. It was the worst kind of narcissism, Danielle, and I'm not going to excuse it."

"But that was… It was a unique circumstance. And you're different. And…it's not like every future relationship…"

"And here's the problem. You don't know me. You don't even like me and yet you're trying to fix this. You're trying to convince me I should give relationships another try. It's your first instinct, and you don't even actually care. My father can't stop any more than you could stop yourself just now. So I did this." He gestured between the two of them. "I did this because he escalated it all the way to putting an ad in the paper. Because he won't listen to me. Because he knows my ex is a junkie somewhere living on the damned street, and that I feel responsible for that, and still he wants me to live his life. This life here, where he's never made a single mistake or let anyone down."

Danielle had no idea what to say to that. She imagined that his dad had made mistakes. But what did she know? She only knew about absentee fathers and mothers who treated their children like afterthoughts.

Her arms were starting to ache. Her chest ached too. All of her ached.

"I'm going to take Riley up to bed," she said, turning and heading up the stairs.

She didn't look back, but she could hear the heavy footfalls behind her, and she knew he was following her. Even if she didn't quite understand why.

She walked into her bedroom, and she left the door open. She crossed the space and set Riley down in the crib. He shifted for a moment, stretching his arms up above his head and kicking his feet out. But he didn't wake up. She was sweaty from having his warm little body pressed against her chest, but she was grateful for that feeling now. Thinking about Joshua and his loss made her feel especially grateful.

Joshua was standing in the doorway, looking at her. "Did you still want to argue with me?"

She shook her head. "I never wanted to argue with you."

She went to walk past him, but his big body blocked her path. She took a step toward him, and he refused to move, his blue eyes looking straight into hers.

"You seemed like you wanted to argue," he responded.

"No," she said, reaching up to press her hand against him, to push him out of the way. "I just wanted an explanation."

The moment her hand made contact with his shoulder, something raced through her. Something electric. Thrilling. Something that reached back to that feeling, that tightening low in her stomach when he'd first mentioned Shannon.

The two feelings were connected.

Jealousy. That was what she felt. Attraction. That was what this was.

She looked up, his chin in her line of sight. She saw a dusting of golden whiskers, and they looked prickly. His chin looked strong. The two things in combination—the strength and the prickliness—made her want to reach out and touch him, to test both of those hypotheses and see if either was true.

Touching him was craziness. She knew it was. So she curled her fingers into a fist and lowered her hand back down to her side.

"Tell me," he said, his voice rough. "After going through what you did, being pregnant. Being abandoned… You don't want to jump right back into relationships, do you?"

He didn't know the situation. And he didn't know it because she had purposefully kept it from him. Still, because of the circumstances surrounding Riley's birth, because of the way her mother had always conducted relationships with men, because of the way they had always ended, Danielle wanted to avoid romantic entanglements.

So she could find an honest answer in there somewhere.

"I don't want to jump into anything," she said, keeping her voice even. "But there's a difference between being cautious and saying never."

"Is there?"

He had dipped his head slightly, and he seemed to loom over her, to fill her vision, to fill her senses. When she breathed in, the air was scented with him. When she felt warm, the warmth was from his body.

Her lips suddenly felt dry, and she licked them. Then became more aware of them than she'd ever been in her entire life. They felt...obvious. Needy.

She was afraid she knew exactly what they were needy for.

His mouth. His kiss.

The taste of him. The feel of him.

She wondered if he was thinking of their kiss too. Of course, for him, a kiss was probably a commonplace event.

For her, it had been singular.

"You can't honestly say you want to spend the rest of your life alone?"

"I'm only alone when I want to be," he said, his voice husky. "There's a big difference between wanting to share your life with somebody and wanting to share your bed sometimes." He tilted his head to the side. "Tell me. Have you shared your bed with anyone since you were with him?"

She shook her head, words, explanations, getting stuck in her throat. But before she knew it, she couldn't speak anyway, because he had closed the distance between them and claimed her mouth with his.

Six

He was hell bound, that much was certain. After everything that had happened tonight with his family, after Shannon, his fate had been set in stone. But if it hadn't been, then this kiss would have sealed that fate, padlocked it and flung it right down into the fire.

Danielle was young, she was vulnerable and contractually she was at his mercy to a certain degree. Kissing her, wanting to do more with her, was taking being an asshole to extremes.

Right now, he didn't care.

If this was hell, he was happy to hang out for a while. If only he could keep kissing her, if only he could keep tasting her.

She held still against his body for a moment before angling her head, wrapping her arms around his neck, sliding her fingers through his hair and cupping the back of his head as if she was intent on holding him against her mouth.

As if she was concerned he might break the kiss. As if he was capable of that.

Sanity and reasonable decision making had exited the building the moment he had closed the distance between them. It wasn't coming back anytime soon. Not as long as she continued to make those sweet, kittenish noises. Not as long as she continued to stroke her tongue against his—tentatively at first and then with much more boldness.

He gripped the edge of the doorjamb, backing her against the frame, pressing his body against hers. He was hard, and he knew she would feel just how much he wanted her.

He slipped his hands around her waist, then down her ass to the hem of her dress. He shoved it upward, completely void of any sort of finesse. Void of anything beyond the need and desperation screaming inside of him to be inside her. To be buried so deep he wouldn't remember anything.

Not why he knew her. Why she was here. Not what had happened at his parents' house tonight. Not the horrific, unending sadness that had happened in his beautiful high-rise apartment overlooking the city he'd thought of as his. The penthouse that should have kept him above the struggle and insulated him from hardship.

Yeah, he didn't want to think about any of it.

He didn't want to think of anything but the way Danielle tasted. How soft her skin was to the touch.

Why the hell some skinny, bedraggled urchin had

suddenly managed to light a fire inside of him was beyond him.

He didn't really care about the rationale right now. No. He just wanted to be burned.

He moved his hands around, then dipped one between her legs, rubbing his thumb against the silken fabric of her panties. She gasped, arching against him, wrenching her mouth away from his and letting her head fall back against the door frame.

That was an invitation to go further. He shifted his stance, drawing his hand upward and then down beneath the waistband of her underwear. He made contact with slick, damp skin that spoke of her desire for him. He had to clench his teeth to keep from embarrassing himself then and there.

He couldn't remember the last time a woman had affected him like this, if ever. When a simple touch, the promise of release, had pushed him so close to the edge.

When so little had felt like so much.

He stroked her, centering his attention on her clit. Her eyes flew open wide as if he had discovered something completely new. As if she was discovering something completely new. And that did things to him. Things it shouldn't do. Mattered in ways it shouldn't.

Because this shouldn't matter and neither should she.

He pressed his thumb against her chin, leaned forward and captured her open mouth with his.

"I have to have you," he said, the words rough, unpracticed, definitely not the way he usually propositioned a woman.

His words seemed to shock her. Like she had made contact with a naked wire. She went stiff in his arms, and then she pulled away, her eyes wide. "What are we doing?"

She was being utterly sincere, the words unsteady, her expression one of complete surprise and even... fear.

"I'm pretty sure we were about to make love," he said, using a more gentle terminology than he normally would have because of that strange vulnerability lurking in her eyes.

She shook her head, wiggling out of his hold and moving away from the door, backing toward the crib. "We can't do that. We can't." She pressed her hand against her cheek, and she looked so much like a stereotypical distressed female from some 1950s comic that he would have laughed if she hadn't successfully made him feel like he would be the villain in that piece. "It would be... It would be wrong."

"Why exactly?"

"Because. You're paying me to be here. You're paying me to play the part of your fiancée, and if things get physical between us, then I don't understand exactly what separates me from a prostitute."

"I'm not paying you for sex," he said. "I'm paying you to pretend to be my fiancée. I want you. And that's entirely separate from what we're doing here."

She shook her head, her eyes glistening. "Not to me. I already feel horrible. Like the worst person ever, after what I did to your family. After the way we tricked them tonight. After the way we will continue to trick them. I can't add sex to this situation. I have to walk away from this, Joshua. I have to walk away and not feel like I lost myself. I can't face the idea that I might finally sort out the money, where I'm going to live, how I'll survive…and lose the only thing I've always had. Myself. I just can't."

He had never begged a woman in his life, but he realized right then that he was on the verge of begging her to agree that it would feel good enough for whatever consequences to be damned. But as he looked behind her at the crib—the crib with the woman's baby in it, for heaven's sake—he realized the argument wasn't going to work with her.

She had been badly used, and though she had never really given him details, the evidence was obvious. She was alone. She had been abandoned at her most vulnerable. For her, the deepest consequences of sex were not hypothetical.

Though, they weren't for him either. And he was a stickler for safe sex, so there was that. Still, he couldn't blame her for not trusting him. And he should want nothing more than to find a woman who was less complicated. One who didn't have all the baggage that Danielle carried.

Still, he wanted to beg.

But he didn't.

"Sex isn't that big of a deal for me," he said. "If you're not into it, that's fine."

She nodded, the gesture jerky. "Good. That's probably another reason we shouldn't."

"I'm going to start interviewing nannies tomorrow," he said, abruptly changing the subject, because if he didn't, he would haul her back into his arms and finish what he had started.

"Okay," she said, looking shell-shocked.

"You'll have a little bit more freedom then. And we can go out riding."

She blinked. "Why? I just turned you down. Why do you want to do anything for me?"

"I already told you. None of this is a trade for sex. You turning me down doesn't change my intentions."

She frowned. "I don't understand." She looked down, picking at her thumbnail. "Everything has a price. There's no reason for you to do something for me when you're not looking for something in return."

"Not everything in life is a transaction, Danielle."

"I suppose it's not when you care about somebody." She tilted her head to the side. "But nobody's ever really cared about me."

If he hadn't already felt like an ass, then her words would have done it. Because his family did care about him. His life had been filled with people doing things for him just because they wanted to give him something. They'd had no expectation of receiving anything in return.

But after Shannon, something had changed inside of him. He wanted to hold everybody at arm's length. Explaining himself felt impossible.

He hadn't wanted to give to anyone, connect with anyone, in a long time. But for some reason, he wanted to connect with Danielle. Wanted to give to that fragile, sweet girl.

It wasn't altruistic. Not really. She had so little that it was easy to step in and do something life altering. She didn't understand the smallest gesture of kindness, which meant the smallest gesture was enough.

"Tomorrow the interview process starts. I assume you want input?"

"Do I want input over who is going to be watching my baby? Yeah. That would be good."

She reached up, absently touching her lips, then lowered her hand quickly, wiggling her fingers slightly. "Good night," she said, the words coming out in a rush.

"Good night," he said, his voice hard. He turned, closing the door resolutely behind him, because if he didn't, he couldn't be responsible for what he might do.

He was going to leave her alone. He was going to do something nice for her. As if that would do something for his tarnished soul.

Well, maybe it wouldn't. But maybe it would do something for her. And for some reason, that mattered.

Maybe that meant he wasn't too far gone after all.

Danielle had never interviewed anyone who was going to work for her. She had interviewed for several jobs herself, but she had never been on the reverse side. It was strange and infused her with an inordinate sense of power.

Which was nice, considering she rarely felt powerful.

Certainly not the other night when Joshua had kissed her. Then she had felt weak as a kitten. Ready to lie down and give him whatever he wanted.

Except she hadn't. She had said no. She was proud of herself for that, even while she mourned the loss of whatever pleasure she might have found with him.

It wasn't about pleasure. It was about pride.

Pride and self-preservation. What she had said to

him had been true. If she walked away from this situation completely broken, unable to extricate herself from him, from his life, because she had allowed herself to get tangled up in ways she hadn't anticipated, then she would never forgive herself. If she had finally made her life easier in all the ways she'd always dreamed of, only to snare herself in a trap she knew would end in pain...

She would judge herself harshly for that.

Whatever she wanted to tell herself about Joshua—he was a tool, he didn't deserve the wonderful family he had—she was starting to feel things for him. Things she really couldn't afford to feel.

That story about his girlfriend had hit her hard and deep. Hit her in a place she normally kept well protected.

Dammit.

She took a deep breath and looked over at the new nanny, Janine, who had just started today, and who was going to watch Riley while Joshua and Danielle went for a ride.

She was nervous. Unsteady about leaving Riley for the first time in a while. Necessity had meant she'd had to leave him when she was working at the grocery store. Still, this felt different. Because it wasn't necessary. It made her feel guilty. Because she was leaving him to do something for herself.

She shook her head. Her reaction was ridiculous. But she supposed it was preferable to how her mother had operated. Which was to never think about her children at all. Her neglect of Danielle hadn't come close to her disinterest in her youngest child. Danielle supposed that by the time Riley was born, her mother had been fully burned-out. Had exhausted whatever maternal instinct she'd possessed.

Danielle shook her head. Then took a deep breath and turned to face Janine. "He should nap most of the time we're gone. And even if he wakes up, he's usually really happy."

Janine smiled. "He's just a baby. I've watched a lot of babies. Not that he isn't special," she said, as though she were trying to cover up some faux pas. "I just mean, I'm confident that I can handle him."

Danielle took a deep breath and nodded. Then Joshua came into the room and the breath she had just drawn into her lungs rushed out.

He was wearing a dark blue button-down shirt and jeans, paired with a white cowboy hat that made him look like the hero in an old Western movie.

Do not get that stupid. He might be a hero, but he's not your hero.

No. Girls like her didn't get heroes. They had to be their own heroes. And that was fine. Honestly, it was.

If only she could tell her heart that. Her stupid heart, which was beating out of control.

It was far too easy to remember what it had been like to kiss him. To remember what it had felt like when his stubble-covered cheek scraped against hers. How sexy it had felt. How intoxicating it had been to touch a man like that. To experience the differences between men and women for the first time.

It was dangerous, was what it was. She had opened a door she had never intended to open, and now it was hard to close.

She shook her hands out, then balled them into

fists, trying to banish the jitters that were racing through her veins.

"Are you ready?" he asked.

His eyes met hers and all she could think was how incredible it was that his eyes matched his shirt. They were a deep, perfect shade of navy.

There was something wrong with her. She had never been this stupid around a man before.

"Yes," she said, the answer coming out more as a squeak than an actual word. "I'm ready."

The corner of his mouth lifted into a lopsided grin. "You don't have to be nervous. I'll be gentle with you."

She nearly choked. "Good to know. But I'm more worried about the horse being gentle with me."

"She will be. Promise. I've never taught a girl how to ride before, but I'm pretty confident I can teach you."

His words ricocheted around inside of her, reaching the level of double entendre. Which wasn't fair. That wasn't how he'd meant it.

Or maybe it was.

He hadn't been shy about letting her know exactly what he wanted from her that night. He had put his hand between her legs. Touched her where no other man ever had. He'd made her see stars, tracked sparks over her skin.

It was understandable for her to be affected by the experience. But like he'd said, sex didn't really matter to him. It wasn't a big deal. So why he would be thinking of it now was beyond her. He had probably forgotten already. Probably that kiss had become an indistinct blur in his mind, mixed with all his other sexual encounters.

There were no other encounters for her. So there

he was in her mind, and in front of her, far too sharp and far too clear.

"I'm ready," she said, the words rushed. "Totally ready."

"Great," he said. "Let's go."

Taking Danielle out riding was submitting himself to a particular kind of torture, that was for sure. But he was kind of into punishing himself…so he figured it fit his MO.

He hadn't stopped thinking about her since they had kissed—and more—in her bedroom the other night. He had done his best to throw himself into work, to avoid her, but still, he kept waking up with sweat slicked over his skin, his cock hard and dreams of…her lips, her tongue, her scent…lingering in his thoughts.

Normally, the outdoors cleared his mind. Riding his horse along the length of the property was his therapy. Maneuvering her over the rolling hills, along the ridge line of the mountain, the evergreen trees rising behind them in a stately backdrop that left him feeling small within the greater context of the world. Which was something a man like him found refreshing some days.

But not today.

Today, he was obsessing. He was watching Danielle's ass as she rode her horse in front of him, the motion of the horse's gait making him think of what it would look like if the woman was riding him instead of his mare.

He couldn't understand this. Couldn't understand this obsession with her.

She wasn't the kind of sophisticated woman he

tended to favor. In a lot of ways, she reminded him of the kind of girl he used to go for here in town, back when he had been a good-for-nothing teenager spending his free time drinking and getting laid out in the woods.

Back then he had liked hometown girls who wanted the same things he did. A few hours to escape, a little bit of fun.

The problem was, he already knew Danielle didn't want that. She didn't find casual hookups fun. And he didn't have anything to offer beyond a casual hookup.

The other problem was that the feelings he had for her were not casual. If they were, then he wouldn't be obsessing. But he was.

In the couple of weeks since she had come to live with him, she had started to fill out a bit. He could get a sense of her figure, of how she would look if she were thriving rather than simply surviving. She was naturally thin, but there was something elegant about her curves.

But even more appealing than the baser things, like the perky curve of her high breasts and the subtle slope of her hips, was the stubborn set of her jaw. The straight, brittle weight of her shoulders spoke of both strength and fragility.

While there was something unbreakable about her, he worried that if a man ever were to find her weakness, she would do more than just break. She would shatter.

He shook his head. And then he forced himself to look away from her, forced himself to look at the scenery. At the mountain spread out before them, and the ocean gray and fierce behind it.

"Am I doing okay?"

Danielle's question made it impossible to ignore her, and he found himself looking at her ass again. "You haven't fallen off yet," he said, perhaps a bit unkindly.

She snorted, then looked over her shoulder, a challenging light glittering in her brown eyes. "Yet? I'm not going to fall off, Joshua Grayson. It would take a hell of a lot to unseat me."

"Says the woman who was shaking when I helped her mount up earlier."

She surprised him by releasing her hold on the reins with one hand and waving it in the air. "Well, I'm getting the hang of it."

"You're a regular cowgirl," he said.

Suddenly, he wanted that to be true. It was the strangest thing. He wanted her to have this outlet, this freedom. Something more than a small apartment. Something more than struggle.

You're giving her that. That's what this entire bargain is for. Like she said, she's a gold digger, and you're giving her your gold.

Yes, but he wanted to give her more than that.

Just like he had told her the other day, what he wanted to give her wasn't about an exchange. He wanted her to have something for herself. Something for Riley.

Maybe it was a misguided attempt to atone for what he hadn't managed to give Shannon. What he hadn't ever been able to give the child he lost.

He swallowed hard, taking in a deep breath of the sharp pine and salt air, trying to ease the pressure in his chest.

She looked at him again, this time a dazzling smile on her lips. It took all that pressure in his chest and punched a hole right through it. He felt his lungs expand, all of him begin to expand.

He clenched his teeth, grinding them together so hard he was pretty sure his jaw was going to break. "Are you about ready to head back?"

"No. But I'm not sure I'm ever going to be ready to head back. This was... Thank you." She didn't look at him this time. But he had a feeling it was because she was a lot less comfortable with sincere connection than she was with sarcasm.

Well, that made two of them.

"You're welcome," he said, fixing his gaze on the line of trees beside them.

He maneuvered his horse around in front of hers so he could lead the way back down to the barn. They rode on in silence, but he could feel her staring holes into his back.

"Are you looking at my butt, Danielle?"

He heard a sputtering noise behind him. "No."

They rode up to the front of the barn and he dismounted, then walked over to her horse. "Liar. Do you need help?"

She frowned, her brows lowering. "Not from you. You called me a liar."

"Because you were looking at my ass and we both know it." He raised his hand up, extending it to her. "Now let me help you so you don't fall on your pretty face."

"Bah," she said, reaching out to him, her fingers brushing against his, sending an electrical current arcing between them. He chose to ignore it. Because there was no way in the whole damn world that the brush of a woman's fingertips against his should get him hot and bothered.

He grabbed hold of her and helped get her down from the horse, drawing her against him when her feet connected with the ground. And then it was over.

Pretending that this wasn't a long prelude to him kissing her again. Pretending that the last few days hadn't been foreplay. Pretending that every time either of them had thought about the kiss hadn't been easing them closer and closer to the inevitable.

She wanted him, he knew that. It was clear in the way she responded to him. She might have reservations about acting on it, and he had his own. But need was bigger than any of that right now, building between them, impossible to ignore.

He was a breath away from claiming her mouth with his when she shocked him by curving her fingers around his neck and stretching up on her toes.

Her kiss was soft, tentative. A question where his kiss would have been a command. But that made it all the sweeter. The fact that she had come to him. The fact that even though she was still conflicted about all of it, she couldn't resist any longer.

He cupped her cheek, calling on all his restraint—what little there was—to allow her to lead this, to allow her to guide the exploration. There was something so unpracticed about that pretty mouth of hers, something untutored about the way her lips skimmed over his. About the almost sweet, soft way her tongue tested his.

What he wanted to do was take it deep. Take it hard. What he wanted to do was grab hold of her hips and press her back against the barn. Push her jeans down her thighs and get his hand back between her gorgeous legs so he could feel all that soft, slick flesh.

What he wanted was to press his cock against her entrance and slide in slowly, savoring the feel of her desire as it washed over him.

But he didn't.

And it was the damned hardest thing he had ever done. To wait. To let her lead. To let her believe she had the control here. Whatever she needed to do so she wouldn't get scared again. If he had to be patient, if he had to take it slow, he could. He would.

If it meant having her.

He had to have her. Had to exorcise the intense demon that had taken residence inside of him, that demanded he take her. Demanded he make her his own.

His horse snickered behind them, shifting her bulk, drawing Danielle's focus back to the present and away from him. Dammit all.

"Let me get them put away," he said.

He was going to do it quickly. And then he was going to get right back to tasting her. He half expected her to run to the house as he removed the tack from the animals and got them brushed down, but she didn't. Instead, she just stood there watching him, her eyes large, her expression one of absolute indecision.

Because she knew.

She knew that if she stayed down here, he wasn't going to leave it at a kiss. He wasn't going to leave it at all.

But he went about his tasks, slowing his movements, forcing himself not to rush. Forcing himself to draw it out. For her torture as well as his. He wanted her to need it, the way that he did.

And yes, he could see she wanted to run. He could also tell she wanted him, she wanted this. She was unbearably curious, even if she was also afraid.

And he was counting on that curiosity to win out.

Finally, she cleared her throat, shifting impatiently. "Are you going to take all day to do that?"

"You have to take good care of your horses, Danielle. I know a city girl like you doesn't understand how that works."

She squinted, then took a step forward, pulling his hat off his head and depositing it on her own. "Bullshit. You're playing with me."

He couldn't hold back the smile. "Not yet. But I plan to."

After that, he hurried a bit. He put the horses back in their paddock, then took hold of Danielle's hand, leading her deeper into the barn, to a ladder that went up to the loft.

"Can I show you something?"

She bit her lip, hesitating. "Why do I have a feeling that it isn't the loft you're going to show me?"

"I'm going to show you the loft. It's just not all I'm going to show you."

She took a step back, worrying her lip with her teeth. He reached out, cupping the back of her head and bringing his mouth down on hers, kissing her the way he had wanted to when she initiated the kiss outside. He didn't have patience anymore. And he wasn't going to let her lead. Not now.

He cupped her face, stroking her cheeks with his thumbs. "This has nothing to do with our agreement.

It has nothing to do with the contract. Nothing to do with the ad or my father or anything other than the fact that I want you. Do you understand?"

She nodded slowly. "Yes," she said, the word coming out a whisper.

Adrenaline shot through him, a strange kind of triumph that came with a kick to the gut right behind it. He wanted her. He knew he didn't deserve her. But he wasn't going to stop himself from having her in spite of that.

Then he took her hand and led her up the ladder.

Seven

Danielle's heart was pounding in her ears. It was all she could hear. The sound of her own heart beating as she climbed the rungs that led up to the loft.

It was different than she had imagined. It was clean. There was a haystack in one corner, but beyond that the floor was immaculate, every item stored and organized with precision. Which, knowing Joshua like she now did, wasn't too much of a surprise.

That made her smile, just a little. She did know him. In some ways, she felt like she knew him better than she knew anyone.

She wasn't sure what that said about her other relationships. For a while, she'd had friends, but they'd disappeared when she'd become consumed with caring for her pregnant mother and working as much as possible at the grocery store. And then no one had come back when Danielle ended up with full care of Riley.

In some ways, she didn't blame them. Life was hard enough without dealing with a friend who was juggling all of that. But just because she understood didn't mean she wasn't lonely.

She looked at Joshua, their eyes connecting. He had shared his past with her. But she was keeping something big from him. Even while she was prepared to give him her body, she was holding back secrets.

She took a breath, opening her mouth to speak, but something in his blue gaze stopped the words before they could form. Something sharp, predatory. Something that made her feel like she was the center of the world, or at least the center of his world.

It was intoxicating. She'd never experienced it before.

She wanted more, all of it. Wherever it would lead.

And that was scary. Scarier than agreeing to do something she had never done before. Because she finally understood. Understood why her mother had traded her sanity, and her self-worth, for that moment when a man looked at you like you were his everything.

Danielle had spent so long being nothing to anyone. Nothing but a burden. Now, feeling like the solution rather than the problem was powerful, heady. She knew she couldn't turn back now no matter what.

Even if sanity tried to prevail, she would shove it aside. Because she needed this. Needed this balm for all the wounds that ran so deep inside of her.

Joshua walked across the immaculate space and opened up a cabinet. There were blankets inside, thick, woolen ones with geometric designs on them. He pulled out two and spread one on the ground.

She bit her lip, fighting a rising tide of hysteria, fighting a giggle that was climbing its way up her throat.

"I know this isn't exactly a fancy hotel suite."

She forced a smile. "It works for me."

He set the other blanket down on the end of the first one, still folded, then he reached out and took her hand, drawing her to him. He curved his fingers around her wrist, lifting her arm up, then shifted his hold, lacing his fingers through hers and dipping his head, pressing his lips to her own.

Her heart was still pounding that same, steady beat, and she was certain he must be able to hear it. Must be aware of just how he was affecting her.

There were all sorts of things she should tell him. About Riley's mother. About this being her first time.

But she didn't have the words.

She had her heartbeat. The way her limbs trembled. She could let him see that her eyes were filling with tears, and no matter how fiercely she blinked, they never quite went away.

She was good at manipulating conversation. At giving answers that walked the line between fact and fiction.

Her body could only tell the truth.

She hoped he could see it. That he understood. Later, they would talk. Later, there would be honesty between them. Because he would have questions. God knew. But for now, she would let the way her finger-tips trailed down his back—uncertain and tentative—

the way she peppered kisses along his jaw—clumsy and broken—say everything she couldn't.

"It doesn't need to be fancy," she said, her voice sounding thick even to her own ears.

"Maybe it should be," he said, his voice rough. "But if I was going to take you back to my bedroom, I expect I would have to wait until tonight. And I don't want to wait."

She shook her head. "It doesn't have to be fancy. It just has to be now. And it has to be you."

He drew his head back, inhaling sharply. And then he cupped her cheek and consumed her. His kiss was heat and fire, sparking against the dry, neglected things inside her and raging out of control.

She slid her hands up his arms, hanging on to his strong shoulders, using his steadiness to hold her fast even as her legs turned weak.

He lifted her up against him, then swept his arm beneath her legs, cradling her against his chest like she was a child. Then he set her down gently on the blanket, continuing to kiss her as he did so.

She was overwhelmed. Overwhelmed by the intensity of his gaze, by his focus. Overwhelmed by his closeness, his scent.

He was everywhere. His hands on her body, his face filling her vision.

She had spent the past few months caring for her half brother, pouring everything she had onto one little person she loved more than anything in the entire world. But in doing so, she had left herself empty. She had been giving continually, opening a vein and bleeding whenever necessary, and taking nothing in to refill herself.

But this… This was more than she had ever had. More than she'd ever thought she could have. Being the focus of a man's attention. Of his need.

This was a different kind of need than that of a child. Because it wasn't entirely selfish. Joshua's need gave her something in return; it compelled him to be close. Compelled him to kiss her, to skim his hands over her body, teasing and tormenting her with the promise of a pleasure she had never experienced.

Before she could think her actions through, she was pushing her fingertips beneath the hem of his shirt, his hard, flat stomach hot to the touch. And then it didn't matter what she had done before or what she hadn't done. Didn't matter that she was a virgin and this was an entirely new experience.

Need replaced everything except being skin to skin with him. Having nothing between them.

Suddenly, the years of feeling isolated, alone, cold and separate were simply too much. She needed his body over hers, his body inside hers. Whatever happened after that, whatever happened in the end, right now she couldn't care.

Because her desire outweighed the consequences. A wild, desperate thing starving to be fed. With his touch. With his possession.

She pushed his shirt up, and he helped her shrug it over his head. Her throat dried, her mouth opening slightly as she looked at him. His shoulders were broad, his chest well-defined and muscular, pale hair spreading over those glorious muscles, down his ridged abdomen, disappearing in a thin trail beneath the waistband of his low-slung jeans.

She had never seen a man who looked like him

before, not in person. And she had never been this close to a man ever. She pressed her palm against his chest, relishing his heat and his hardness beneath her touch. His heart raging out of control, matching the beat of her own.

She parted her thighs and he settled between them. She could feel the hard ridge of his arousal pressing against that place where she was wet and needy for him. She was shocked at how hard he was, even through layers of clothing.

And she lost herself in his kiss, in the way he rocked his hips against hers. This moment, this experience was like everything she had missed growing up. Misspent teenage years when she should have been making out with boys in barns and hoping she didn't get caught. In reality, her mother wouldn't have cared.

This was a reclamation. More than that, it was something completely new. Something she had never even known she could want.

Joshua was something she had never known she could want.

It shouldn't make sense, the two of them. This brilliant businessman in his thirties who owned a ranch and seemed to shun most emotional connections. And her. Poor. In her twenties. Desperately clinging to any connection she could forge because each one was so rare and special.

But somehow they seemed to make sense. Kissing each other. Touching each other. For some reason, he was the only man that made sense.

Maybe it was because he had taught her to ride a horse. Maybe it was because he was giving her and

Riley a ticket out of poverty. Maybe it was because he was handsome. She had a feeling this connection transcended all those things.

As his tongue traced a trail down her neck to the collar of her T-shirt, she was okay with not knowing. She didn't need to give this connection a name. She didn't even want to.

Her breath caught as he pushed her shirt up and over her head, then quickly dispensed with her bra using a skill not even she possessed. Her nipples tightened, and she was painfully aware of them and of the fact that she was a little lackluster in size.

If Joshua noticed, he didn't seem to mind.

Instead, he dipped his head, sucking one tightened bud between his lips. The move was so sudden, so shocking and so damned unexpected that she couldn't stop herself from arching into him, a cry on her lips.

He looked up, the smile on his face so damned cocky she should probably have been irritated. But she wasn't. She just allowed herself to get lost. In his heat. In the fire that flared between them. In the way he used his lips, his teeth and his tongue to draw a map of pleasure over her skin. All the way down to the waistband of her pants. He licked her. Just above the snap on her jeans. Another sensation so deliciously shocking she couldn't hold back the sound of pleasure on her lips.

She pressed her fist against her mouth, trying to keep herself from getting too vocal. From embarrassing herself. From revealing just how inexperienced she was. The noises she was making definitely announced the fact that these sensations were revelatory to her. And that made her feel a touch too vulnerable.

She was so used to holding people at a distance. So used to benign neglect and general apathy creating a shield around her feelings. Her secrets.

But there was no distance here.

And certainly none as he undid the button of her jeans and drew the zipper down slowly. As he pushed the rough denim down her legs, taking her panties with them.

If she had felt vulnerable a moment before, that was nothing compared to now. She felt so fragile. So exposed. And then he reached up, pressing his hand against her leg at the inside of her knee, spreading her wide so he could look his fill.

She wanted to snap her legs together. Wanted to cover up. But she was immobilized. Completely captive to whatever might happen next. She was so desperate to find out, and at the same time desperate to escape it.

Rough fingertips drifted down the tender skin on her inner thigh, brushing perilously close to her damp, needy flesh. And then he was there. His touch in no way gentle or tentative as he pressed his hand against her, the heel of his palm putting firm pressure on her clit before he pressed his fingers down and spread her wide.

He made his intentions clear as he lowered his head, tasting her deeply. She lifted her hips, a sharp sound on her lips, one she didn't even bother to hold back. He shifted his hold, gripping her hips, holding her just wide enough for his broad shoulders to fit right there, his sensual assault merciless.

Tension knotted her stomach like a fist, tighter and tighter with each pass of his tongue. Then he pressed his thumb against her clit at the same time as he flicked his tongue against that sensitive bundle of nerves. She grabbed hold of him, her fingernails digging into his back.

He drew his thumb down her crease, teasing the entrance of her body. She rocked her hips with the motion, desperate for something. Feeling suddenly empty and achy and needy in ways she never had before.

He rotated his hand, pressing his middle finger deep inside of her, and she gasped at the foreign invasion. But any discomfort passed quickly as her body grew wetter beneath the ministrations of his tongue. By the time he added a second finger, it slipped in easily.

He quickened his pace, and it felt like there was an earthquake starting inside her. A low, slow pull at her core that spread outward, her limbs trembling as the pressure at her center continued to mount.

His thumb joined with his tongue as he continued to pump his fingers inside her, and it was that added pressure that finally broke her. She was shaken. Rattled completely. The magnitude of measurable aftershocks rocking her long after the primary force had passed.

He moved into a sitting position, undoing his belt and the button on his jeans. Then he stood for a moment, drawing the zipper down slowly and pushing the denim down his muscular thighs.

She had never seen a naked man in person before, and the stark, thick evidence of his arousal standing out from his body was a clear reminder that they weren't finished, no matter how wrung out and replete she felt.

Except, even though she felt satisfied, limp from the intensity of her release, she did want more. Because there was more to have. Because she wanted to be close to him. Because she wanted to give him even an ounce of the satisfaction that she had just experienced.

He knelt back down, pulling his jeans closer and taking his wallet out of his back pocket. He produced a condom packet and she gave thanks for his presence of mind. She knew better than to have unprotected sex with someone. For myriad reasons. But still, she wondered if she would have remembered if he had not.

Thank God one of them was thinking. She was too overwhelmed. Too swamped by the release that had overtaken her, and by the enormity of what was about to happen. When he positioned himself at the entrance of her body and pressed the thick head of his cock against her, she gasped in shock.

It *hurt*. Dear God it hurt. His fingers hadn't prepared her for the rest of him.

He noticed her hesitation and slowed his movements, pressing inside her inch by excruciating inch. She held on to his shoulders, closing her eyes and burying her face in his neck as he jerked his hips forward, fully seating himself inside her.

She did her best to breathe through it. But she was in a daze. Joshua was inside her, and she wasn't a virgin anymore. It felt… Well, it didn't feel like losing anything. It felt like gaining something. Gaining a whole lot.

The pain began to recede and she looked up, at his face, at the extreme concentration there, at the set of his jaw, the veins in his neck standing out.

"Are you okay?" he asked, his voice strangled.

She nodded wordlessly, then flexed her hips experimentally.

He groaned, lowering his head, pressing his forehead against hers, before kissing her. Then he began to move.

Soon, that same sweet tension began to build again in her stomach, need replacing the bone-deep satisfaction that she had only just experienced. She didn't know how it was possible to be back in that needy place only moments after feeling fulfilled.

But she was. And then she was lost in the rhythm, lost in the feeling of his thick length stroking in and out of her, all of the pain gone now, only pleasure remaining. It was so foreign, so singular and unlike anything she had ever experienced. And she loved it. Reveled in it.

But even more than her own pleasure, she reveled in watching his unraveling.

Because he had pulled her apart in a million astounding ways, and she didn't know if she could ever be reassembled. So it was only fair that he lost himself too. Only fair that she be his undoing in some way.

Sweat beaded on his brow, trickled down his back. She reveled in the feel of it beneath her fingertips. In the obvious evidence of what this did to him.

His breathing became more labored, his muscles shaking as each thrust became less gentle. As he began to pound into her. And just as he needed to go harder, go faster, so did she.

Her own pleasure wound around his, inextricably linked.

On a harsh growl he buried his face in her neck,

his arms shaking as he thrust into her one last time, slamming into her clit, breaking a wave of pleasure over her body as he found his own release.

He tried to pull away, but she wrapped her arms around him, holding him close. Because the sooner he separated from her body, the sooner they would have to talk. And she wasn't exactly sure she wanted to talk.

But when he lifted his head, his blue eyes glinting in the dim light, she could tell that whether or not she wanted to talk, they were going to.

He rolled away from her, pushing into a sitting position. "Are you going to explain all of this to me? Or are you going to make me guess?"

"What?" She sounded overly innocent, her eyes wider than necessary.

"Danielle, I'm going to ask you a question, and I need you to answer me honestly. Were you a virgin?"

Joshua's blood was still running hot through his veins, arousal still burning beneath the surface of his skin. And he knew the question he had just asked her was probably insane. He could explain her discomfort as pain because she hadn't taken a man to her bed since she'd given birth.

But that wasn't it. It wasn't.

The more credence he gave to his virgin theory, the more everything about her started to make sense. The way she responded to his kiss, the way she acted when he touched her.

Her reaction had been about more than simple attraction, more than pleasure. There had been wonder there. A sense of discovery.

But that meant Riley wasn't her son. And it meant she had been fucking lying to him.

"Well, Joshua, given that this is not a New Testament kind of situation…"

He reached out, grabbing hold of her wrist and tugging her upward, drawing her toward him. "Don't lie to me."

"Why would you think that?" she asked, her words small. Admission enough as far as he was concerned.

"A lot of reasons. But I have had sex with a virgin before. More accurately, Sadie Miller and I took each other's virginity in the woods some eighteen years ago. You don't forget that. And, I grant you, there could be other reasons for the fact that it hurt you, for the fact that you were tight." A flush spread over her skin, her cheeks turning beet red. "But I don't think any of those reasons are the truth. So what's going on? Who is Riley's mother?"

A tear slid down her cheek, her expression mutinous and angry. "I am," she said, her voice trembling. "At least, I might as well be. I should be."

"You didn't give birth to Riley."

She sniffed loudly, another tear sliding down her cheek. "No. I didn't."

"Are you running from somebody? Is there something I need to know?"

"It's not like that. I'm not hiding. I didn't steal him. I have legal custody of Riley. But my situation was problematic. At least, as far as Child Services was concerned. I lost my job because of the babysitting situation and I needed money."

She suddenly looked so incredibly young, so vulnerable… And he felt like the biggest prick on planet Earth.

She had lied to him. She had most definitely led him to believe she was in an entirely different circumstance than she was, and still, he was mostly angry at himself.

Because the picture she was painting was even more desperate than the one he had been led to believe. Because she had been a virgin and he had just roughly dispensed with that.

She had been desperate. Utterly desperate. And had taken this post with him because she hadn't seen another option. Whatever he'd thought of her before, he was forced to revise it, and there was no way that revision didn't include recasting himself as the villain.

"Whose baby is he?"

She swallowed hard, drawing her knees up to her chest, covering her nudity. "Riley is my half brother. My mother showed up at my place about a year ago pregnant and desperate. She needed someone to help her out. When she came to me, she sounded pretty determined to take care of him. She even named him. She told me she would do better for him than she had for me, because she was done with men now and all of that. But she broke her promises. She had the baby, she met somebody else. I didn't know it at first. I didn't realize she was leaving Riley in the apartment alone sometimes while I was at work."

She took a deep, shuddering breath, then continued. "I didn't mess around when I found out. I didn't wait for her to decide to abandon him. I called Child Services. And I got temporary guardianship. My mother left. But then things started to fall apart with the work, and I didn't know how I was going to pay for the apartment... Then I saw your ad."

He swore. "You should have told me."

"Maybe. But I needed the money, Joshua. And I didn't want to do anything to jeopardize your offer. I could tell you were uncomfortable that I brought a baby with me, and now I know why. But, regardless, at the time, I didn't want to do anything that might compromise our arrangement."

He felt like the ass he undoubtedly was. The worst part was, it shone a light on all the bullshit he'd put her through. Regardless of Riley's parentage, she'd been desperate and he'd taken advantage of that. Less so when he'd been keeping his hands to himself. At least then it had been feasible to pretend it was an even exchange.

But now?

Now he'd slept with her and it was impossible to keep pretending.

And frankly, he didn't want to.

He'd been wrestling with this feeling from the moment they'd gone out riding today, or maybe since they'd left his parents' house last week.

But today...when he'd looked at her, seen her smile...noticed the way she'd gained weight after being in a place where she felt secure...

He'd wanted to give her more of that.

He'd wanted to do more good than harm. Had wanted to fix something instead of break it.

It was too late for Shannon. But he could help Danielle. He could make sure she always felt safe. That she and Riley were always protected.

The realization would have made him want to laugh if it didn't all feel too damned grim. Somehow his father's ad had brought him to this place when he'd been determined to teach the old man a lesson.

But Joshua hadn't counted on Danielle.

Hadn't counted on how she would make him feel. That she'd wake something inside him he'd thought had been asleep for good.

It wasn't just chemistry. Wasn't just sex. It was the desire to make her happy. To give her things.

To fix what was broken.

He knew the solution wouldn't come from him personally, but his money could sure as hell fix her problems. And they did have chemistry. The kind that wasn't common. It sure as hell went beyond anything he'd ever experienced before.

"The truth doesn't change anything," she said, lowering her face into her arms, her words muffled. "It doesn't."

He reached out, taking her chin between his thumb and forefinger, tilting her face back up. "It does. Even if it shouldn't. Though, maybe it's not Riley that changes it. Maybe it's just the two of us."

She shook her head. "It doesn't have to change anything."

"Danielle… I can't…"

She lurched forward, grabbing his arm, her eyes wide, her expression wild. "Joshua, please. I need this money. I can't go back to where we were. I'm being held to a harsher standard than his biological mother would be and I can't lose him."

He grabbed her chin again, steadying her face, looking into those glistening brown eyes. "Danielle,

I would never let you lose him. I want to protect you. Both of you."

She tilted her head to the side, her expression growing suspicious. "You...do?"

"I've been thinking. I was thinking this earlier when we were riding, but now, knowing your whole story... I want you and Riley to stay with me."

She blinked. "What?"

"Danielle, I want you to marry me."

Eight

Danielle couldn't process any of this.

She had expected him to be angry. Had expected him to get mad because she'd lied to him.

She hadn't expected a marriage proposal.

At least, she was pretty sure that was what had just happened. "You want to…marry me? For real marry me?"

"Yes," he said, his tone hard, decisive. "You don't feel good about fooling my family—neither do I. You need money and security and, hell, I have both. We have chemistry. I want… I don't want to send you back into the world alone. You don't even know where you're going."

He wasn't wrong. And dammit his offer was tempting. They were both naked, and he was so beautiful, and she wanted to kiss him again. Touch him again.

But more than that, she wanted him to hold her in his arms again.

She wanted to be close to him. Bonded to him.

She wanted—so desperately—to not be alone.

But there had to be a catch.

There was always a catch. He could say whatever he wanted about how all of this wasn't a transaction, how he had taken her riding just to take her riding. But then they'd had sex. And he'd had a condom in his wallet.

So he'd been prepared.

That made her stomach sour.

"Did you plan this?" she asked. "The horse-riding seduction?"

"No, I didn't plan it. I carry a condom because I like to be prepared to have sex. You never know. You can get mad at me for that if you want, but then, we did need one, so it seems a little hypocritical."

"Are you tricking me?" she asked, feeling desperate and panicky. "Is this a trick? Because I don't understand how it benefits you to marry me. To keep Riley and me here. You don't even like Riley, Joshua. You can't stand to be in the same room with him."

"I broke Shannon," he said, his voice hard. "I ruined her. I did that. But I won't break you. I want to fix this."

"You can't slap duct tape and a wedding band on me and call it done," she said, her voice trembling. "I'm not a leaky faucet."

"I didn't say you were. But you need something I have and I… Danielle, I need you." His voice was rough, intense. "I'm not offering you love, but I can be faithful. I was ready to be a husband years ago, that part doesn't faze me. I can take care of you. I can keep you safe. And if I send you out into the world with nothing more than money and something happens to you or Riley, I won't forgive myself. So stay with me. Marry me."

It was crazy. He was crazy.

And she was crazy for sitting there fully considering everything he was offering.

But she was imagining a life here. For her, for Riley. On Joshua's ranch, in his beautiful house.

And she knew—she absolutely knew—that what she had felt physically with him, what had just happened, was a huge reason why they were having this conversation at all.

More than the pleasure, the closeness drew her in. Actually, that was the most dangerous part of his offer. The idea that she could go through life with somebody by her side. To raise Riley with this strong man backing her up.

Something clenched tight in her chest, working its way down to her stomach. Riley. He could have a father figure. She didn't know exactly what function Joshua would play in his life. Joshua had trouble with the baby right now. But she knew Joshua was a good man, and that he would never freeze Riley out intentionally. Not when he was offering them a life together.

"What about Riley?" she asked, her throat dry. She swallowed hard. She had to know what he was thinking.

"What about him?"

"This offer extends to him too. And I mean…not

just protection and support. But would you... Would you teach him things? Would your father be a grandfather to him? Would your brothers be uncles and your sister be an aunt? I understand that having a child around might be hard for you, after you lost your chance at being a father. And I understand you want to fix me, my situation. And it's tempting, Joshua, it's very tempting. But I need to know if that support, if all of that, extends to Riley."

Joshua's face looked as though it had been cast in stone. "I'm not sure if I would be a good father, Danielle. I was going to be a father, and so I was going to figure it out—how to do that, how to be that. I suppose I can apply that same intent here. I can't guarantee that I'll be the best, but I'll try. And you're right. I have my family to back me up. And he has you."

That was it.

That was the reason she couldn't say no. Because if she walked away from Joshua now, Riley would have her. Only her. She loved him, but she was just one person. If she stayed here with Joshua, Riley would have grandparents. Aunts and uncles. Family. People who knew how to be a family. She was doing the very best she could, but her idea of family was somewhere between cold neglectful nightmare and a TV sitcom.

The Grayson family knew—Joshua knew—what it meant to be a family. If she said yes, she could give that to Riley.

She swallowed again, trying to alleviate the scratchy feeling in her throat.

"I guess... I guess I can't really say no to that."

She straightened, still naked, and not even a little bit embarrassed. There were bigger things going on here than the fact that he could see her breasts. "Okay, Joshua. I'll marry you."

Nine

The biggest problem with this sudden change in plan was the fact that Joshua had deliberately set out to make his family dislike Danielle. And now he was marrying her for real.

Of course, the flaw in his original plan was that Danielle *hadn't* been roundly hated by his family. They'd distrusted the whole situation, certainly, but his family was simply too fair, too nice to hate her.

Still, guilt clutched at him, and he knew he was going to have to do something to fix this. Which was why he found himself down at the Gray Bear Construction office rather than working from home. Because he knew Faith and Isaiah would be in, and he needed to have a talk with his siblings.

The office was a newly constructed building fashioned to look like a log cabin. It was down at the edge of town, by where Rona's diner used to be, a former greasy spoon that had been transformed into a series of smaller, hipper shops that were more in line with the interests of Copper Ridge's tourists.

It was a great office space with a prime view of the ocean, but still, Joshua typically preferred to work in the privacy of his own home, secluded in the mountains.

Isaiah did too, which was why it was notable that his brother was in the office today, but he'd had a meeting of some kind, so he'd put on a decent shirt and a pair of nice jeans and gotten his ass out of his hermitage.

Faith, being the bright, sharp creature she was, always came into the office, always dressed in some variation of her personal uniform. Black pants and a black top—a sweater today because of the chilly weather.

"What are you doing here?" Faith asked, her expression scrutinizing.

"I came here to talk to you," he said.

"I'll make coffee." Joshua turned and saw Poppy standing there. Strange, he hadn't noticed. But then, Poppy usually stayed in the background. He couldn't remember running the business without her, but like useful office supplies, you really only noticed them when they didn't work. And Poppy always worked.

"Thanks, Poppy," Faith said.

Isaiah folded his arms over his chest and leaned back in his chair. "What's up?"

"I'm getting married in two weeks."

Faith made a scoffing sound. "To that child you're dating?"

"She's your age," he said. "And yes. Just like I said I was."

"Which begs the question," Isaiah said. "Why are you telling us again?"

"Because. The first time I was lying. Dad put that ad in the paper trying to find a wife for me, and I selected Danielle in order to teach him a lesson. The joke's on me it turns out." Damn was it ever.

"Good God, Joshua. You're such an ass," Faith said, leaning against the wall, her arms folded, mirroring Isaiah's stance. "I knew something was up, but of all the things I suspected, you tricking our mother and father was not one of them."

"What did you suspect?"

"That you were thinking with your... Well. And now I'm back to that conclusion. Because why are you marrying her?"

"I care about her. And believe me when I say she's had it rough."

"You've slept with her?" This question came from Isaiah, and there was absolutely no tact in it. But then, Isaiah himself possessed absolutely no tact. Which was why he handled money and not people.

"Yes," Joshua said.

"She must be good. But I'm not sure that's going to convince either of us you're thinking with your big brain." His brother stood up, not unfolding his arms.

"Well, you're an asshole," Joshua returned. "The sex has nothing to do with it. I can get sex whenever I want."

Faith made a hissing sound. He tossed his younger sister a glance. "You can stop hissing and settle down," he said to her. "You were the one who brought sex into it, I'm just clarifying. You know what I went through with Shannon, what I put Shannon through. If I send Danielle and her baby back out into the world and something happens to them, I'll never forgive myself."

"Well, Joshua, that kind of implies you aren't already living in a perpetual state of self-flagellation," Faith said.

"Do you want to see if it can get worse?"

She shook her head. "No, but marrying some random woman you found through an ad seems like an extreme way to go about searching for atonement. Can't you do some Hail Marys or something?"

"If it were that simple, I would have done it a long time ago." He took a deep breath. "I'm not going to tell Mom and Dad the whole story. But I'm telling you because I need you to be nice about Danielle. However it looked when I brought her by to introduce her to the family... I threw her under the bus, and now I want to drag her back out from under it."

Isaiah shook his head. "You're a contrary son of a bitch."

"Well, usually that's your function. I figured it was my turn."

The door to the office opened and in walked their business partner, Jonathan Bear, who ran the construction side of the firm. He looked around the room, clearly confused by the fact that they were all in residence. "Is there a meeting I didn't know about?"

"Joshua is getting married," Faith said, looking sullen.

"Congratulations," Jonathan said, smiling, which was unusual for the other man, who was typically pretty taciturn. "I can highly recommend it."

Jonathan had married the pastor's daughter, Hayley Thompson, in a small ceremony recently.

In the past, Jonathan had walked around like he had his own personal storm cloud overhead, and since meeting Hayley, he had most definitely changed. Maybe there was something to that whole marriage thing. Maybe Joshua's idea of atonement wasn't as outrageous as it might have initially seemed.

"There," Joshua said. "Jonathan recommends it. So you two can stop looking at me suspiciously."

Jonathan shrugged and walked through the main area and into the back, toward his office, leaving Joshua alone with his siblings.

Faith tucked her hair behind her ear. "Honestly, whatever you need, whatever you want, I'll help. But I don't want you to get hurt."

"And I appreciate that," he said. "But the thing is, you can only get hurt if there's love involved. I don't love her."

Faith looked wounded by that. "Then what's the point? I'm not trying to argue. I just don't understand."

"Love is not the be-all and end-all, Faith. Sometimes just committing to taking care of somebody else is enough. I loved Shannon, but I still didn't do the right thing for her. I'm older now. And I know what's important. I'm going to keep Danielle safe. I'm going to keep Riley safe. What's more important than that?" He shook his head. "I'm sure Shannon would have rather had that than any expression of love."

"Fine," she said. "I support you. I'm in."

"So you aren't going to be a persnickety brat?"

A small smile quirked her lips upward. "I didn't

say that. I said I would support you. But as a younger sister, I feel the need to remind you that being a persnickety brat is sometimes part of my support."

He shot Isaiah a baleful look. "I suppose you're still going to be an asshole?"

"Obviously."

Joshua smiled then. Because that was the best he was going to get from his siblings. But it was a step toward making sure Danielle felt like she had a place in the family, rather than feeling like an outsider.

And if he wanted that with an intensity that wasn't strictly normal or healthy, he would ignore that. He had never pretended to be normal or healthy. He wasn't going to start now.

Danielle was getting fluttery waiting for Joshua to come home. The anticipation was a strange feeling. It had been a long time since she'd looked forward to someone coming home. She remembered being young, when it was hard to be alone. But she hadn't exactly wished for her mother to come home, because she knew that when her mother arrived, she would be drunk. And Danielle would be tasked with managing her in some way.

That was the story of her life. Not being alone meant taking care of somebody. Being alone meant isolation, but at least she had time to herself.

But Joshua wasn't like that. Being with him didn't mean she had to manage him.

She thought of their time together in the barn, and the memory made her shiver. She had gone to bed in her own room last night, and he hadn't made any move toward her since his proposal. She had a feeling his hesitation had something to do with her inexperience.

But she was ready for him again. Ready for more.

She shook her hands out, feeling jittery. And a little scared.

It was so easy to want him. To dream about him coming home, how she would embrace him, kiss him. And maybe even learn to cook, so she could make him dinner. Learn to do something other than warm up Pop-Tarts.

Although, he liked Pop-Tarts, and so did she.

Maybe they should have Pop-Tarts at their wedding. That was the kind of thing couples did. Incorporate the cute foundations of their relationships into their wedding ceremonies.

She made a small sound that was halfway between a whimper and a growl. She was getting loopy about him. About a guy. Which she had promised herself she would never do. But it was hard *not* to get loopy. He had offered her support, a family for Riley, a house to live in. He had become her lover, and then he had asked to become her husband.

And in those few short moments, her entire vision for the rest of her life had changed. It had become something so much warmer, so much more secure than she had ever imagined it could be. She just wasn't strong enough to reject that vision.

Honestly, she didn't know a woman who would be strong enough. Joshua was hot. And he was nice. Well, sometimes he was kind of a jerk, but mostly, at his core, he was nice and he had wonderful taste in breakfast food.

That seemed like as good a foundation for a marriage as any.

She heard the front door open and shut, and as it slammed, her heart lurched against her breastbone.

Joshua walked in looking so intensely handsome in a light blue button-up shirt, the sleeves pushed up his arms, that she wanted to swoon for the first time in her entire life.

"Do you think they can make a wedding cake out of Pop-Tarts?" She didn't know why that was the first thing that came out of her mouth. Probably, it would have been better if she had said something about how she couldn't wait to tear his clothes off.

But no. She had led with toaster pastry.

"I don't know. But we're getting married in two weeks, so if you can stack Pop-Tarts and call them a cake, I suppose it might save time and money."

"I could probably do that. I promise that's not all I thought about today, but for some reason it's what came out of my mouth."

"How about I keep your mouth busy for a while," he said, his blue gaze getting sharp. He crossed the space between them, wrapping his arm around her waist and drawing her against him. And then he kissed her.

It was so deep, so warm, and she felt so...sheltered. Enveloped completely in his arms, in his strength. Who cared if she was lost in a fantasy right now? It would be the first time. She had never had the luxury of dreaming about men like him, or passion this intense.

It seemed right, only fair, that she have the fantasy. If only for a while. To have a moment where she actually dreamed about a wedding with cake. Where she fantasized about a man walking in the door and kissing her like this, wanting her like this.

"Is Janine here?" he asked, breaking the kiss just long enough to pose the question.

"No," she said, barely managing to answer before he slammed his lips back down on hers.

Then she found herself being lifted and carried from the entryway into the living room, deposited on the couch. And somehow, as he set her down, he managed to raise her shirt up over her head.

She stared at him, dazed, while he divested himself of his own shirt. "You're very good at this," she said. "I assume you've had a lot of practice?"

He lifted an eyebrow, his hands going to his belt buckle. "Is this a conversation you want to have?"

She felt…bemused rather than jealous. "I don't know. I'm just curious."

"I got into a lot of trouble when I was a teenager. I think I mentioned the incident with my virginity in the woods."

She nodded. "You did. And since I lost my virginity in a barn, I suppose I have to reserve judgment."

"Probably. Then I moved to Seattle. And I was even worse, because suddenly I was surrounded by women I hadn't known my whole life."

Danielle nodded gravely. "I can see how that would be an issue."

He smiled. Then finished undoing his belt, button and zipper before shoving his pants down to the floor. He stood in front of her naked, aroused and beautiful.

"Then I got myself into a long-term relationship,

and it turns out I'm good at that. Well, at the being faithful part."

"That's a relief."

"In terms of promiscuity, though, my behavior has been somewhat appalling for the past five years. I have picked up a particular set of skills."

She wrinkled her nose. "I suppose that's something."

"You asked."

She straightened. "And I wanted to know."

He reached behind her back, undoing her bra, pulling it off and throwing it somewhere behind him. "Well, now you do." He pressed his hands against the back of the couch, bracketing her in. "You still want to marry me?"

"I had a very tempting proposal from the UPS man today. He asked me to sign for a package. So I guess you could say it's getting kind of serious."

"I don't think the UPS man makes you feel like this." He captured her mouth with his, and she found herself being pressed into the cushions, sliding to the side, until he'd maneuvered her so they were both lying flat on the couch.

He wrapped his fingers around her wrists, lifting them up over her head as he bent to kiss her neck, her collarbone, to draw one nipple inside his mouth.

She bucked against him, and he shifted, pushing his hand beneath her jeans, under the fabric of her panties, discovering just how wet and ready she was for him.

She rolled her hips upward, moving in time with the rhythm of his strokes, lights beginning to flash behind her eyelids, orgasm barreling down on her at an embarrassingly quick rate.

Danielle sucked in a deep breath, trying her best to hold her climax at bay. Because how embarrassing would it be to come from a kiss? A brief bit of attention to her breast and a quick stroke between the legs?

But then she opened her eyes and met his gaze. His lips curved into a wicked smile as he turned his wrist, sliding one finger deep inside her as he flicked his thumb over her clit.

All she could do then was hold on tight and ride out the explosion. He never looked away from her, and as much as she wanted to, she couldn't look away from him.

It felt too intense, too raw and much too intimate.

But she was trapped in it, drowning in it, and there was nothing she could do to stop it. She just had to surrender.

While she was still recovering from her orgasm, Joshua made quick work of her jeans, flinging them in the same direction her bra had gone.

Then, still looking right at her, he stroked her, over the thin fabric of her panties, the tease against her overly sensitized skin almost too much to handle.

Then he traced the edge of the fabric at the crease of her thigh, dipping one finger beneath her underwear, touching slick flesh.

He hooked his finger around the fabric, pulling her panties off and casting them aside. And here she was, just as she'd been the first time, completely open and vulnerable to him. At his mercy.

It wasn't as though she didn't want that. There was something wonderful about it. Something incredible about the way he lavished attention on her, about being his sole focus.

But she wanted more. She wanted to be... She wanted to be equal to him in some way.

He was practiced. And he had skill. He'd had a lot of lovers. Realistically, she imagined he didn't even know exactly how many.

She didn't have skill. She hadn't been tutored in the art of love by anyone. But she *wanted*.

If desire could equal skill, then she could rival any woman he'd ever been with. Because the depth of her need, the depth of her passion, reached places inside her she hadn't known existed.

She pressed her hands down on the couch cushions, launching herself into a sitting position. His eyes widened, and she reveled in the fact that she had surprised him. She reached out, resting one palm against his chest, luxuriating in the feel of all that heat, that muscle, that masculine hair that tickled her sensitive skin.

"Danielle," he said, his tone filled with warning.

She didn't care about his warnings.

She was going to marry this man. He was going to be her husband. That thought filled her with such a strange sense of elation.

He had all the power. He had the money. He had the beautiful house. What he was giving her...it bordered on charity. If she was ever going to feel like she belonged—like this place was really hers—they needed to be equals in some regard.

She had to give him something too.

And if it started here, then it started here.

She leaned in, cautiously tasting his neck, tracing a line down to his nipple. He jerked beneath her touch, his reaction satisfying her in a way that went well beyond the physical.

He was beautiful, and she reveled in the chance to explore him. To run her fingertips over each well-defined muscle. Over his abs and the hard cut inward just below his hip bone.

But she didn't stop there. No, she wasn't even remotely finished with him.

He had made her shake. He had made her tremble. He had made her lose her mind.

And she was going to return the favor.

She took a deep breath and kissed his stomach. Just one easy thing before she moved on to what she wanted, even though it scared her.

She lifted her head, meeting his gaze as she wrapped her fingers around his cock and squeezed. His eyes glittered like ice on fire, and he said nothing. He just sat there, his jaw held tight, his expression one of absolute concentration.

Then she looked away from his face, bringing her attention to that most masculine part of him. She was hungry for him. There was no other word for it.

She was starving for a taste.

And that hunger overtook everything else.

She flicked her tongue out and tasted him, his skin salty and hot. But the true eroticism was in his response. His head fell back, his breath hissing sharply through his teeth. And he reached out, pressing his hand to her back, spreading his fingers wide at the center of her shoulder blades.

Maybe she didn't have skill. Maybe she didn't know what she was doing. But he liked it. And that made her feel powerful. It made her feel needed.

She slid her hand down his shaft, gripping the base before taking him more deeply into her mouth. His groan sounded torn from him, wild and untamed, and she loved it.

Because Joshua was all about control. Had been from the moment she'd first met him.

That was what all this was, after all. From the ad in the paper to his marriage proposal—all of it was him trying to bend the situation to his will. To bend those around him to his will, to make them see he was right, that his way was the best way.

But right now he was losing control. He was at her mercy. Shaking. Because of her.

And even though she was the one pleasuring him, she felt an immense sense of satisfaction flood her as she continued to taste him. As she continued to make him tremble.

He needed her. He wanted her. After a lifetime of feeling like nobody wanted her at all, this was the most brilliant and beautiful thing she could ever imagine.

She'd heard her friends talk about giving guys blow jobs before. They laughed about it. Or said it was gross. Or said it was a great way to control their boyfriends.

They hadn't said what an incredible thing it was to make a big, strong alpha male sweat and shake. They hadn't said it could make you feel so desired, so beloved. Or that giving someone else pleasure was even better—in some ways—than being on the receiving end of the attention.

She swallowed more of him, and his hand jerked up to her hair, tugging her head back. "Careful," he said, his tone hard and thin.

"Why?"

"You keep doing that and I'm going to come," he said, not bothering to sugarcoat it.

"So what? When you did it for me, that's what I did."

"Yes. But you're a woman. And you can have as many orgasms as I can give you without time off in between. I don't want it to end like this."

She was about to protest, but then he pulled her forward, kissing her hard and deep, stealing not just her ability to speak, but her ability to think of words.

He left her for a moment, retrieving his wallet and the protection in it, making quick work of putting the condom on before he laid her back down on the couch.

"Wait," she said, the word husky, rough. "I want... Can I be on top?"

He drew back, arching one brow. "Since you asked so nicely."

He gripped her hips, reversing their position, bringing her to sit astride him. He was hard beneath her, and she shifted back and forth experimentally, rubbing her slick folds over him before positioning him at the entrance of her body.

She bit her lip, lowering herself onto him, taking it slow, relishing that moment of him filling her so utterly and completely.

"I don't know what I'm doing," she whispered when he was buried fully inside of her.

He reached up, brushing his fingertips over her cheek before lowering his hand to grip both her hips tightly, lift her, then impale her on his hard length again.

"Just do what feels good," he ground out, the words strained.

She rocked her hips, then lifted herself slightly before taking him inside again. She repeated the motion. Again and again. Finding the speed and rhythm that made him gasp and made her moan. Finding just the right angle, just the right pressure, to please them both.

Pleasure began to ripple through her, the now somewhat familiar pressure of impending orgasm building inside her. She rolled her hips, making contact right where she needed it. He grabbed her chin, drawing her head down to kiss her. Deep, wet.

And that was it. She was done.

Pleasure burst behind her eyes, her internal muscles gripping him tight as her orgasm rocked her.

She found herself being rolled onto her back and Joshua began to pound into her, chasing his own release with a raw ferocity that made her whole body feel like it was on fire with passion.

He was undone. Completely. Because of her.

He growled, reaching beneath her to cup her ass, drawing her hard against him, forcing her to meet his every thrust. And that was when he proved himself right. She really could come as many times as he could make her.

She lost it then, shaking and shivering as her second orgasm overtook her already sensitized body.

He lowered his head, his teeth scraping against her collarbone as he froze against her, finding his own release.

He lay against her for a moment, his face buried in her neck, and she sifted her fingers through his hair, a small smile touching her lips as ripples of lingering pleasure continued to fan out through her body.

He looked at her, then brushed his lips gently over hers. She found herself being lifted up, cradled against his chest as he carried her from the couch to the stairs.

"Time for bed," he said, the words husky and rough.

She reached up and touched his face. "Okay."

He carried her to his room, laid her down on the expansive mattress, the blanket decadent and soft beneath her bare skin.

This would be their room. A room they would share.

For some reason, that thought made tears sting her eyes. She had spent so long being alone that the idea of so much closeness was almost overwhelming. But no matter what, she wanted it.

Wanted it so badly it was like a physical hunger.

Joshua joined her on the bed and she was overwhelmed by the urge to simply fold herself into his embrace. To enjoy the closeness.

But then he was naked. And so was she. So the desire for closeness fought with her desire to play with him a little more.

He pressed his hand against her lower back, then slid it down to her butt, squeezing tight. And he smiled.

Something intense and sharp filled her chest. It was almost painful.

Happiness, she realized. She was happy.

She knew in that moment that she never really had been happy before. At least, not without an equally weighty worry to balance it. To warn her that on the other side of the happiness could easily lie tragedy.

But she wasn't thinking of tragedy now. She couldn't.

Joshua filled her vision, and he filled her brain, and for now—just for now—everything in her world felt right.

For a while, she wanted that to be the whole story.

So she blocked out every other thought, every single what-if, and she kissed him again.

When Joshua woke up, the bedroom was dark. There was a woman wrapped around him. And he wasn't entirely sure what had pulled him out of his deep slumber.

Danielle was sleeping peacefully. Her dark hair was wrapped around her face like a spiderweb, and he reached down to push it back. She flinched, pursing her lips and shifting against him, tightening her arms around his waist.

She was exhausted. Probably because he was an animal who had taken her three, maybe four times before they'd finally both fallen asleep.

He looked at her, and the hunger was immediate. Visceral. And he wondered if he was fooling himself pretending, even for a moment, that any of this was for her.

That he had any kind of higher purpose.

He wondered if he had any purpose at all beyond trying to satisfy himself with her.

And then he realized what had woken him up.

He heard a high, keening cry that barely filtered through the open bedroom door. Riley.

He looked down at Danielle, who was still fast asleep, and who would no doubt be upset that they had forgotten to bring the baby monitor into the room.

Joshua had barely been able to remember his own name, much less a baby monitor.

He extricated himself from her hold, scrubbing his hand over his face. Then he walked over to his closet, grabbing a pair of jeans and pulling them on with nothing underneath.

He had no idea what in the hell to do with the baby. But Danielle was exhausted, because of him, and he didn't want to wake her up.

The cries got louder as he made his way down the hall, and he walked into the room to see flailing movement coming from the crib. The baby was very unhappy, whatever the reason.

Joshua walked across the room and stood above the crib, looking down. If he was going to marry Danielle, then that meant Riley was his responsibility too.

Riley would be his son.

Something prickled at the back of his throat, making it tight. So much had happened after Shannon lost the baby that he didn't tend to think too much about what might have been. But it was impossible not to think about it right now.

His son would have been five.

He swallowed hard, trying to combat the rising tide of emotion in his chest. That emotion was why he avoided contact with Riley. Joshua wasn't so out of touch with his feelings that he didn't know that.

But his son wasn't here. He'd never had the chance to be born.

Riley was here.

And Joshua could be there for him.

He reached down, placing his hand on the baby's chest. His little body started, but he stopped crying.

Joshua didn't know the first thing about babies. He'd never had to learn. He'd never had the chance to hold his son. Never gone through a sleepless night because of crying.

He reached down, picking up the small boy from his crib, holding the baby close to his chest and supporting Riley's downy head.

There weren't very many situations in life that caused Joshua to doubt himself. Mostly because he took great care to ensure he was only ever in situations where he had the utmost control.

But holding this tiny creature in his arms made him feel at a loss. Made him feel like his strength might be a liability rather than an asset. Because at the moment, he felt like this little boy could be far too easily broken. Like he might crush the baby somehow.

Either with his hands or with his inadequacy.

Though, he supposed that was the good thing about babies. Right now, Riley didn't seem to need him to be perfect. He just needed Joshua to be there. Being there he could handle.

He made his way to the rocking chair in the corner and sat down, pressing Riley to his chest as he rocked back and forth.

"You might be hungry," Joshua said, keeping his voice soft. "I didn't ask."

Riley turned his head back and forth, leaving a small trail of drool behind on Joshua's skin. He had a feeling if his brother could see him now, he would mock him mercilessly. But then, he couldn't imagine Isaiah with a baby at all. Devlin, yes. But only since he had married Mia. She had changed Devlin completely. Made him more relaxed. Made him a better man.

Joshua thought of Danielle, sleeping soundly back in his room. Of just how insatiable he'd been for her earlier. Of how utterly trapped she was, and more or less at his mercy.

He had to wonder if there was any way she could make him a better man, all things considered.

Though, he supposed he'd kind of started to become a better man already. Since he had taken her on. And Riley.

He had to be the man who could take care of them, if he was so intent on fixing things.

Maybe they can fix you too.

Even though there was no one in the room but the baby, Joshua shook his head. That wasn't a fair thing to put on either of them.

"Joshua?"

He looked up and saw Danielle standing in the doorway. She was wearing one of his T-shirts, the hem falling to the top of her thighs. He couldn't see her expression in the darkened room.

"Over here."

"Are you holding Riley?" She moved deeper into the room and stopped in front of him, the moonlight streaming through the window shadowing one side of her face. With her long, dark hair hanging loose around her shoulders, and that silver light casting her in a glow, she looked ethereal. He wondered how he had ever thought she was pitiful. How he had ever imagined she wasn't beautiful.

"He was crying," he responded.

"I can take him."

He shook his head, for some reason reluctant to give him up. "That's okay."

A smile curved her lips. "Okay. I can make him a bottle."

He nodded, moving his hand up and down on the baby's back. "Okay."

Danielle rummaged around for a moment and then went across the room to the changing station, where he assumed she kept the bottle-making supplies. Warmers and filtered water and all of that. He didn't know much about it, only that he had arranged to have it all delivered to the house to make things easier for her.

She returned a moment later, bottle in hand. She tilted it upside down and tested it on the inside of her wrist. "It's all good. Do you want to give it to him?"

He nodded slowly and reached up. "Sure."

He shifted his hold on Riley, repositioning him in the crook of his arm so he could offer him the bottle.

"Do you have a lot of experience with babies?"

"None," he said.

"You could have fooled me. Although, I didn't really have any experience with babies until Riley was born. I didn't figure I would ever have experience with them."

"No?"

She shook her head. "No. I was never going to get married, Joshua. I knew all about men, you see. My mother got pregnant with me when she was fourteen. Needless to say, things didn't get off to the best start. I never knew my father. My upbringing was…unstable. My mother just wasn't ready to have a baby, and honestly, I don't know how she could have been. She didn't have a good home life, and she was so young. I think she wanted to keep me, wanted to do the right thing—it was just hard. She was always looking for something else. Looking for love."

"Not in the right places, I assume."

She bit her lip. "No. To say the least. She had a lot of boyfriends, and we lived with some of them. Sometimes that was better. Sometimes they were more established than us and had better homes. The older I got, the less like a mom my mom seemed. I started to really understand how young she was. When she would get her heart broken, I comforted her more like a friend than like a daughter. When she would go out and get drunk, I would put her to bed like I was the parent." Danielle took a deep breath. "I just didn't want that for myself. I didn't want to depend on anybody, or have anyone depend on me. I didn't want to pin my hopes on someone else. And I never saw a relationship that looked like anything else when I was growing up."

"But here you are," he said, his chest feeling tight. "And you're marrying me."

"I don't know if you can possibly understand what this is like," she said, laughing, a kind of shaky nervous sound. "Having this idea of what your life will be and just…changing that. I was so certain about what I would have, and what I wouldn't have. I would never get married. I would never have children. I would never have…a beautiful house or a yard." Her words got thick, her throat sounding tight. "Then there was Riley. And then there was your ad. And then there was you. And suddenly everything I want is different, everything I expect is different. I actually hope for things. It's kind of a miracle."

He wanted to tell her that he wasn't a miracle. That whatever she expected from him, he was sure to disappoint her in some way. But what she was describing was too close to his own truth.

He had written off having a wife. He had written off having children. That was the whole part of being human he'd decided wasn't for him. And yet here he was, feeding a baby at three in the morning staring at a woman who had just come from his bed. A woman who was wearing his ring.

The way Joshua needed it, the way he wanted to cling to his new reality, to make sure that it was real and that it would last, shocked him with its ferocity.

A moment later, he heard a strange sucking sound and realized the bottle was empty.

"Am I supposed to burp him?"

Danielle laughed. "Yes. But I'll do that."

"I'm not helpless."

"He's probably going to spit up on your hot and sexy chest. Better to have him do it on your T-shirt." She reached out. "I got this."

She took Riley from him and he sat back and admired the expert way she handled the little boy. She rocked him over her shoulder, patting his back lightly until he made a sound that most definitely suggested he had spit up on the T-shirt she was wearing.

Joshua had found her to be such a strange creature when he had first seen her. Brittle and pointed. Fragile.

But she was made of iron. He could see that now. No one had been there to raise her, not really.

And then she had stepped in to make sure that her half brother was taken care of. Had upended every plan she'd made for her life and decided to become a mother at twenty-two.

"What?" she asked, and he realized he had been sitting there staring at her.

"You're an amazing woman, Danielle Kelly. And if no one's ever told you that, it's about time someone did."

She was so bright, so beautiful, so fearless.

All this time she had been a burning flame no one had taken the time to look at. But she had come to him, answered his ad and started a wildfire in his life.

It didn't seem fair, the way the world saw each of them. He was a celebrated businessman, and she... Well, hadn't he chosen her because he knew his family would simply see her as a poor, unwed mother?

She was worth ten of him.

She blinked rapidly and wasn't quite able to stop a tear from tracking down her cheek. "Why...why do you think that?"

"Not very many people would have done what you did. Taking your brother. Not after everything your mother already put you through. Not after spending your whole life taking care of the one person who should have been taking care of you. And then you came here and answered my ad."

"Some people might argue that the last part was taking the easy way out."

"Right. Except that I could have been a serial killer."

"Or made me dress like a teddy bear," she said,

keeping her tone completely serious. "I actually feel like that last one is more likely."

"Do you?"

"There are more furries than there are serial killers, thank God."

"I guess, lucky for you, I'm neither one." He wasn't sure he was the great hope she seemed to think he was. But right now, he wanted to be.

"Very lucky for me," she said. "Oh... Joshua, imagine if someone were both."

"I'd rather not."

She went to the changing table and quickly set about getting Riley a new diaper before placing him back in the crib. Then she straightened and hesitated. "I guess I could... I can just stay in here. Or..."

"Get the baby monitor," he said. "You're coming back to my bed."

She smiled, and she did just that.

The next day there were wedding dresses in Danielle's room. Not just a couple of wedding dresses. At least ten, all in her size.

She turned in a circle, looking at all of the garment bags with heavy white satin, beads and chiffon showing through.

Joshua walked into the room behind her, his arms folded over his chest. She raised her eyebrows, gesturing wildly at the dresses. "What is this?"

"We are getting married in less than two weeks. You need a dress."

"A fancy dress to eat my Pop-Tart cake in," she said, moving to a joke because if she didn't she might cry. Because the man had ordered wedding dresses and brought them into the house.

And because if she were normal, she might have friends to share this occasion with her. Or her mother. Instead, she was standing in her bedroom, where her baby was napping, and her fiancé was the only potential spectator.

"You aren't supposed to see the dresses, though," she said.

"I promise you I cannot make any sense out of them based on how they look stuffed into those bags. I called the bridal store in town and described your figure and had her send dresses accordingly."

Her eyes flew wide, her mouth dropping open. "You described my figure?"

"To give her an idea of what would suit you."

"I'm going to need a play-by-play of this description. How did you describe my figure, Joshua? This is very important."

"Elfin," he said, surprising her because he didn't seem to be joking. And that was a downright fanciful description coming from him.

"Elfin?"

A smile tipped his lips upward. "Yes. You're like an elf. Or a nymph."

"Nympho, maybe. And I blame you for that."

He reached out then, hooking his arm around her waist and drawing her toward him. "Danielle, I am serious."

She swallowed hard. "Okay," she said, because she didn't really know what else to say.

"You're beautiful."

Hearing him say that made her throat feel all dry

and scratchy, made her eyes feel like they were burn-ing. "You don't have to do that," she said.

"You think I'm lying? Why would I lie about that? Also, men can't fake this." He grabbed her hand and pressed it up against the front of his jeans, against the hardness there.

"You're asking me to believe your penis? Because penises are notoriously indiscriminate."

"You have a point. Plus, mine is pretty damn fa-mously indiscriminate. By my own admission. But the one good thing about that is you can trust I know the difference between generalized lust and when a woman has reached down inside of me and grabbed hold of something I didn't even know was there. I told you, I like it easy. I told you... I don't deal with difficult situations or difficult people. That was my past failing. A huge failing, and I don't know if I'm ever going to forgive myself for it. But what we have here makes me feel like maybe I can make up for it."

There were a lot of nice words in there. A lot of beautiful sentiments tangled up in something that made her feel, well, kind of gross.

But he was looking at her with all that intensity, and there were wedding dresses hung up all around her, his ring glittering on her finger. And she just didn't want to examine the bad feelings. She was so tired of bad feelings.

Joshua—all of this—was like a fantasy. She wanted to live in the fantasy for as long as she could.

Was that wrong? After everything she had been through, she couldn't believe that it was.

"Well, get your penis out of here. The rest of you too. I'm going to try on dresses."

"I don't get to watch?"

"I grant you nothing about our relationship has been typical so far, but I would like to surprise you with my dress choice."

"That's fair. Why don't you let me take Riley for a while?"

"Janine is going to be here soon."

He shrugged. "I'll take him until then." He strode across the room and picked Riley up, and Riley flashed a small, gummy smile that might have been nothing more than a facial twitch but still made Danielle's heart do something fluttery and funny.

Joshua's confidence with Riley was increasing, and he made a massive effort to be proactive when it came to taking care of the baby.

Watching Joshua stand there with Riley banished any lingering gross feelings about being considered difficult, and when Joshua left the room and Danielle turned to face the array of gowns, she pushed every last one of her doubts to the side.

Maybe Joshua wasn't perfect. Maybe there were some issues. But all of this, with him, was a damn sight better than anything she'd had before.

And a girl like her couldn't afford to be too picky.

She took a deep breath and unzipped the first dress.

Ten

The day of the wedding was drawing closer and Danielle was drawing closer to a potential nervous breakdown. She was happy, in a way. When Joshua kissed her, when he took her to bed, when he spent the whole night holding her in his strong arms, everything felt great.

It was the in-between hours. The quiet moments she spent with herself, rocking Riley in that gray time before dawn. That was when she pulled those bad feelings out and began to examine them.

She had two days until the wedding, and her dress had been professionally altered to fit her—a glorious, heavy satin gown with a deep V in the back and buttons that ran down the full skirt—and if for no other reason than that, she couldn't back out.

The thought of backing out sent a burst of pain blooming through her chest. Unfurling, spreading, expanding. No. She didn't want to leave Joshua. No matter the strange, imbalanced feelings between them, she wanted to be with him. She felt almost desperate to be with him.

She looked over at him now, sitting in the driver's seat of what was still the nicest car she had ever touched, much less ridden in, as they pulled up to the front of his parents' house.

Sometimes looking at him hurt. And sometimes looking away from him hurt. Sometimes everything hurt. The need to be near him, the need for distance.

Maybe she really had lost her mind.

It took her a moment to realize she was still sitting motionless in the passenger seat, and Joshua had already put the car in Park and retrieved Riley from the back seat. He didn't bother to bring the car seat inside this time. Instead, he wrapped the baby in a blanket and cradled him in his arms.

Oh, that hurt her in a whole different way.

Joshua was sexy. All the time. There was no question about that. But the way he was with Riley… Well, she was surprised that any woman who walked by him when he was holding Riley didn't fall immediately at his feet.

She nearly did. Every damned time.

She followed him to the front door, looking down to focus on the way the gravel crunched beneath her boots—new boots courtesy of Joshua that didn't have holes in them, and didn't need three pairs of socks to keep her toes from turning into icicles—because otherwise she was going to get swallowed up by the nerves that were riding through her.

His mother had insisted on making a prewedding dinner for them, and this was Danielle's second chance to make a first impression. Now it was real and she felt an immense amount of pressure to be better than she was, rather than simply sliding into the lowest expectation people like his family had of someone like her, as she'd done before.

She looked over at him when she realized he was staring at her. "You're going to be fine," he said.

Then he bent down and kissed her. She closed her eyes, her breath rushing from her lungs as she gave herself over to his kiss.

That, of course, was when the front door opened.

"You're here!"

Nancy Grayson actually looked happy to see them both, and even happier that she had caught them making out on the front porch.

Danielle tucked a stray lock of hair behind her ear. "Thank you for doing this," she said, jarred by the change in her role, but desperate to do a good job.

"Of course," the older woman said. "Now, let me hold my grandbaby."

Those words made Danielle pause, made her freeze up. Made her want to cry. Actually, she *was* crying. Tears were rolling down her cheeks without even giving her a chance to hold them back.

Joshua's mother frowned. "What's wrong, honey?"

Danielle swallowed hard. "I didn't ever expect that he would have grandparents. That he would have a family." She took a deep breath. "I mean like this. It means a lot to me."

Nancy took Riley from Joshua's arms. But then she reached out and put her hand on Danielle's shoulder. "He's not the only one who has a family. You do too."

Throughout the evening Danielle was stunned by the warm acceptance of Joshua's entire family. By the way his sister-in-law, Mia, made an effort to get to know her, and by the complete absence of antagonism coming from his younger sister, Faith.

But what really surprised her was when Joshua's father came and sat next to her on the couch during dessert. Joshua was engaged in conversation with his brothers across the room while Mia, Faith and Joshua's mother were busy playing with Riley.

"I knew you would be good for him," Mr. Grayson said.

Danielle looked up at the older man. "A wife, you mean," she said, her voice soft. She didn't know why she had challenged his assertion, why she'd done anything but blandly agree. Except she knew she wasn't the woman he would have chosen for his son, and she didn't want him to pretend otherwise.

He shook his head. "I'm not talking about the ad. I know what he did. I know that he placed another ad looking for somebody he could use to get back at me. But the minute I met you, I knew you were exactly what he needed. Somebody unexpected. Somebody who would push him out of his comfort zone. It's real now, isn't it?"

It's real now.

Those words echoed inside of her. What did real mean? They were really getting married, but was their relationship real?

He didn't love her. He wanted to fix her. And somehow, through fixing her, he believed he would fix himself.

Maybe that wasn't any less real than what most people had. Maybe it was just more honest.

"Yes," she said, her voice a whisper. "It's real."

"I know that my meddling upset him. I'm not stupid. And I know he felt like I wasn't listening to him. But he has been so lost in all that pain, and I knew… I knew he just needed to love somebody again. He thought everything I did, everything I said was because I don't understand a life that goes beyond what we have here." He gestured around the living room— small, cozy, essentially a stereotype of the happy, rural family. "But that's not it. Doesn't matter what a life looks like, a man needs love. And *that* man needs love more than most. He always was stubborn, difficult. Never could get him to talk about much of anything. He needs someone he can talk to. Someone who can see the good in him so he can start to see it too."

"Love," Danielle said softly, the word a revelation she had been trying to avoid.

That was why it hurt. When she looked at him. When she was with him. When she looked away from him. When he was gone.

That was the intense, building pressure inside her that felt almost too large for her body to contain.

It was every beautiful, hopeful feeling she'd had since meeting him.

She loved him.

And he didn't love her. That absence was the cause of the dark disquiet she'd felt sometimes. He wanted to use her as a substitute for his girlfriend, the one he thought he had failed.

"Every man needs love," Todd said. "Successful businessmen and humble farmers. Trust me. It's the thing that makes life run. The thing that keeps you going when crops don't grow and the weather doesn't cooperate. The thing that pulls you up from the dark pit when you can't find the light. I'm glad he found his light."

But he hadn't.

She had found hers.

For him, she was a Band-Aid he was trying to put over a wound that would end up being fatal if he didn't do something to treat it. If he didn't do something more than simply cover it up.

She took a deep breath. "I don't…"

"Are you ready to go home?"

Danielle looked up and saw Joshua standing in front of her. And those words…

Him asking if she wanted to go home, meaning to his house, with him, like that house belonged to her. Like he belonged to her…

Well, his question allowed her to erase all the doubts that had just washed through her. Allowed her to put herself back in the fantasy she'd been living in since she'd agreed to his proposal.

"Sure," she said, pushing herself up from the couch.

She watched as he said goodbye to his family, as he collected Riley and slung the diaper bag over his shoulder. Yes. She loved him.

She was an absolute and total lost cause for him. In love. Something she had thought she could never be.

The only problem was, she was in love alone.

It was his wedding day.

Thankfully, only his family would be in attendance. A small wedding in Copper Ridge's Baptist church, which was already decorated for Christmas and so saved everyone time and hassle.

Which was a good thing, since he had already harassed local baker Alison Donnelly to the point where she was ready to assault him with a spatula over his demands related to a Pop-Tart cake.

It was the one thing Danielle had said she wanted, and even if she had been joking, he wanted to make it happen for her.

He liked doing things for her. Whether it was teaching her how to ride horses, pleasuring her in the bedroom or fixing her nice meals, she always expressed a deep and sweet gratitude that transcended anything he had ever experienced before.

Her appreciation affected him. He couldn't pretend it didn't.

She affected him.

He walked into the empty church, looking up at the steeply pitched roof and the thick, curved beams of wood that ran the length of it, currently decked with actual boughs of holly.

Everything looked like it was set up and ready, all there was to do now was wait for the ceremony to start.

Suddenly, the doors that led to the fellowship hall opened wide and in burst Danielle. If he had thought she looked ethereal before, it was nothing compared to how she looked at this moment. Her dark hair was swept back in a loose bun, sprigs of baby's breath woven into it, some tendrils hanging around her face.

And the dress…

The bodice was fitted, showing off her slim figure, and the skirt billowed out around her, shimmering with each and every step. She was holding a bouquet of dark red roses, her lips painted a deep crimson to match.

"I didn't think I was supposed to see you until the wedding?" It was a stupid thing to say, but it was about the only thing he could think of.

"Yes. I know. I was here getting ready, and I was going to hide until everything started. Stay in the dressing room." She shook her head. "I need to talk to you, though. And I was already wearing this dress, and all of the layers of underwear that you have to wear underneath it to make it do this." She kicked her foot out, causing the skirt to flare.

"To make it do what?"

"You need a crinoline. Otherwise your skirt is like a wilted tulip. That's something I learned when the wedding store lady came this morning to help me get ready. But that's not what I wanted to talk to you about."

He wasn't sure if her clarification was a relief or not. He wasn't an expert on the subject of crinolines, but it seemed like an innocuous subject. Anything else that had drawn her out of hiding before the ceremony probably wasn't.

"Then talk."

She took a deep breath, wringing her hands around the stem of her bouquet. "Okay. I will talk. I'm going to. In just a second."

He shook his head. "Danielle Kelly, you stormed into my house with a baby and pretty much refused to leave until I agreed to give you what you wanted—don't act like you're afraid of me now."

"That was different. I wasn't afraid of losing you

then." She looked up at him, her dark eyes liquid. "I'm afraid right now."

"You?" He couldn't imagine this brave, wonderfully strong woman being afraid of anything.

"I've never had anything that I wanted to keep. Or I guess, I never did before Riley. Once I had him, the thought of losing him was one of the things that scared me. It was the first time I'd ever felt anything like it. And now...it's the same with you. Do you know what you have in common with Riley?"

"The occasional tantrum?" His chest was tight. He knew that was the wrong thing to say, knew it was wrong to make light of the situation when she was so obviously serious and trembling.

"Fair enough," she said. Then she took a deep breath. "I love you. That's what you have in common with Riley. That's why I'm afraid of losing you. Because you matter. Because you more than matter. You're...everything."

Her words were like a sucker punch straight to the gut. "Danielle..."

He was such an ass. Of course she thought she was in love with him. He was her first lover, the first man to ever give her an orgasm. He had offered her a place to live and he was promising a certain amount of financial security, the kind she'd never had before.

Of course such a vulnerable, lonely woman would confuse those feelings of gratitude with love.

She frowned. "Don't use that tone with me. I know you're about to act like you're the older and wiser of the two of us. You're about to explain why I don't understand what I'm talking about. Remember when you told me about your penis?"

He looked over his shoulder, then back at Danielle. "Okay, I'm not usually a prude, but we are in a church."

She let out an exasperated sound. "Sorry. But the thing is, remember when you told me that because you had been indiscriminate you knew the difference between common, garden-variety sex—"

"Danielle, Pastor John is around here somewhere."

She straightened her arms at her sides, the flowers in her hand trembling with her unsuppressed irritation. "Who cares? This is our life. Anyway, what little I've read in the Bible was pretty honest about people. Everything I'm talking about—it's all part of being a person. I'm not embarrassed about any of it." She tilted her chin up, looking defiant. "My point is, I don't need you telling me what you think I feel. I have spent so much time alone, so much time without love, that I've had a lot of time to think about what it might feel like. About what it might mean."

He lowered his voice and took a step toward her. "Danielle, feeling cared for isn't the same as love. Pleasure isn't the same as love."

"I know that!" Her words echoed in the empty sanctuary. "Trust me. If I thought being taken care of was the same thing as love, I probably would have repeated my mother's pattern for my entire life. But I didn't. I waited. I waited until I found a man who was worth being an idiot over. Here I am in a wedding dress yelling at the man I'm supposed to marry in an hour, wanting him to understand that I love him. You can't be much more of an idiot than that, Joshua."

"It's okay if you love me," he said, even though it made his stomach feel tight. Even though it wasn't okay at all. "But I don't know what you expect me to do with that."

She stamped her foot, the sound ricocheting around them. "Love me back, dammit."

He felt like someone had grabbed hold of his heart and squeezed it hard. "Danielle, I can't do that. I can't. And honestly, it's better if you don't feel that way about me. I think we can have a partnership. I'm good with those. I'm good with making agreements, shaking hands, holding up my end of the deal. But feelings, all that stuff in between... I would tell you to call Shannon and ask her about that, but I don't think she has a phone right now, because I'm pretty sure she's homeless."

"You can't take the blame for that. You can't take the blame for her mistakes. I mean, I guess you can, you've been doing a great job of it for the past five years. And I get that. You lost a child. And then you lost your fiancée, the woman you loved. And you're holding on to that pain to try to insulate yourself from more."

He shook his head. "That's not it. It would be damned irresponsible of me not to pay attention to what I did to her. To what being with me can do to a woman." He cleared his throat. "She needed something that I couldn't give. I did love her—you're right. But it wasn't enough."

"You're wrong about that too," she said. "You loved her enough. But sometimes, Joshua, you can love somebody and love somebody, but unless they do something with that love it goes fallow. You can sow the seeds all you want, but if they don't water them, if they don't nurture them, you can't fix it for them."

"I didn't do enough," he said, tightening his jaw, hardening his heart.

"Maybe you were difficult. Maybe you did some wrong things. But at some point, she needed to reach out and tell you that. But she didn't. She shut down. Love can be everything, but it can't all be coming from one direction. The other person has to accept it. You can't love someone into being whole. They have to love themselves enough to want to be whole. And they have to love you enough to lay down their pain, to lay down their selfishness, and change—even when it's hard."

"I can't say she was selfish," he said, his voice rough. "I can't say she did anything wrong."

"What about my mother? God knows she had it hard, Joshua. I can't imagine having a baby at fourteen. It's hard enough having one at twenty-two. She has a lot of excuses. And they're valid. She went through hell, but the fact of the matter is she's choosing to go through it at this point. She has spent her whole life searching for the kind of love that either one of her children would have given her for nothing. I couldn't have loved her more. Riley is a baby, completely and totally dependent on whoever might take care of him. Could we have loved her more? Could we have made her stay?"

"That's different."

She stamped her foot again. "It is fucking not!"

He didn't bother to yell at her about them being in a church again. "I understand that all of this is new to you," he said, fighting to keep his voice steady. "And honestly? It feels good, selfishly good, to know you see all this in me. It's tempting to lie to you, Danielle.

But I can't do that. What I offered you is the begin-ning and end of what I have. Either you accept our partnership or you walk away."

She wouldn't.

She needed him too much. That was the part that made him a monster.

He knew he had all the power here, and he knew she would ultimately see things his way. She would have to.

And then what? Would she wither away living with him? Wanting something that he refused to give her?

The situation looked too familiar.

He tightened his jaw, steeling himself for her re-sponse.

What he didn't expect was to find a bouquet of flowers tossed at him. He caught them, and her petite shoulders lifted up, then lowered as she let out a shud-dering breath. "I guess you're the next one to get mar-ried, then. Congratulations. You caught the flowers."

"Of course I damn well am," he said, tightening his fist around the roses, ignoring the thorn that bit into his palm. "Our wedding is in an hour."

Her eyes filled with tears, and she shook her head. Then she turned and ran out of the room, pausing only to kick her shoes off and leave them lying on the floor like she was Cinderella.

And he just stood there, holding on to the flow-ers, a trickle of blood from the thorn dripping down his wrist as he watched the first ray of light, the first bit of hope he'd had in years, disappear from his life.

Of course, her exit didn't stop him from standing at the altar and waiting. Didn't stop him from act-ing like the wedding would continue without a hitch.

He knew she hadn't gone far, mostly because Janine was still at the church with Riley, and while Danielle's actions were painful and mystifying at the moment, he knew her well enough to know she wasn't going to leave without Riley.

But the music began to play and no bride materialized.

There he was, a giant dick in a suit, waiting for a woman who wasn't going to come.

His family looked at each other, trading expressions filled with a mix of pity and anger. But it was his father who spoke up. "What in hell did you do, boy?"

A damned good question.

Unfortunately, he knew the answer to it.

"Why are you blaming him?" Faith asked, his younger sister defending him to the bitter end, even when he didn't deserve it.

"Because that girl loves him," his father said, his tone full of confidence, "and she wouldn't have left him standing there if he hadn't done something."

Pastor John raised his hands, the gesture clearly meant to placate. "If there are any doubts about a marriage, it's definitely best to stop and consider those doubts, as it is a union meant for life."

"And she was certain," Joshua's father said. "Which means he messed it up."

"When two people love each other…" The rest of Pastor John's words were swallowed up by Joshua's family, but those first six hit Joshua and pierced him right in the chest.

When two people love each other.

Two people. Loving each other.

Love going both ways. Giving and taking.

And he understood then. He really understood.

Why she couldn't submit to living in a relationship that she thought might be one-sided. Because she had already endured it once. Because she'd already lived it with her mother.

Danielle was willing to walk away from everything he'd offered her. From the house, from the money, from the security. Even from his family. Because for some reason his love meant that much to her.

That realization nearly brought him to his knees.

He had thought his love insufficient. Had thought it destructive. And as she had stood there, pleading with him to love her back, he had thought his love unimportant.

But to her, it was everything.

How dare he question her feelings for him? Love, to Danielle, was more than a ranch and good sex. And she had proved it, because she was clearly willing to sacrifice the ranch and the sex to have him return her love.

"It was my fault," he said, his voice sounding like a stranger's as it echoed through the room. "She said she loved me. And I told her I couldn't love her back."

"Well," Faith said, "not even I can defend you now, dumbass."

His mother looked stricken, his father angry. His brothers seemed completely unsurprised.

"You do love her, though," his father said, his tone steady. "So why did you tell her you didn't?"

Of course, Joshua realized right then something else she'd been right about. He was afraid.

Afraid of wanting this life he really had always dreamed of but had written off because he messed up his first attempt so badly. Afraid because the first time had been so painful, had gone so horribly wrong.

"Because I'm a coward," he said. "But I'm not going to be one anymore."

He walked down off the stage and to the front pew, picking up the bouquet. "I'm going to go find her," he said. "I know she's not far, since Riley is here."

Suddenly, he knew exactly where she was.

"Do you have any other weddings today, Pastor?"

Pastor John shook his head. "No. This is the only thing I have on my schedule today. Not many people get married on a Thursday."

"Hopefully, if I don't mess this up, we'll need you."

Eleven

It was cold. And Danielle's bare feet were starting to ache. But there had been no way in hell she could run in those high heels. She would have broken her neck.

Of course, if she had broken her neck, she might have fully severed her spinal cord and then not been able to feel anything. A broken heart sadly didn't work that way. She felt everything. Pain, deep and unending. Pain that spread from her chest out to the tips of her fingers and toes.

She wiggled her toes. In fairness, they might just be frostbitten.

She knew she was being pathetic. Lying down on that Pendleton blanket in the loft. The place where Joshua had first made love to her. Hiding.

Facing everyone—facing Joshua again—was inevitable. She was going to have to get Riley. Pack up her things.

Figure out life without Joshua's money. Go back to working a cash register at a grocery store somewhere. Wrestling with childcare problems.

She expected terror to clutch her at the thought. Expected to feel deep sadness about her impending poverty. But those feelings didn't come.

She really didn't care about any of that.

Well, she probably would care once she was neck deep in it again, but right now all she cared about was that she wouldn't have Joshua.

If he had no money, if he was struggling just like her, she would have wanted to struggle right along with him.

But money or no money, struggle or no struggle, she needed him to love her. Otherwise…

She closed her eyes and took in a breath of sharp, cold air.

She had been bound and determined to ignore all of the little warnings she'd felt in her soul when she'd thought about their relationship. But in the end, she couldn't.

She knew far too well what it was like to pour love out and never get it back. And for a while it had been easy to pretend. That his support, and the sex, was the same as getting something back.

But they were temporary.

The kinds of things that would fade over the years.

If none of his choices were rooted in love, if none of it was founded in love, then what they had couldn't last.

She was saving herself hideous heartbreak down the road by stabbing herself in the chest now.

She snorted. Right now, she kind of wondered what the point was.

Pride?

"Screw pride," she croaked.

She heard the barn door open, heard footsteps down below, and she curled up into a ball, the crinoline under her dress scratching her legs. She buried her face in her arm, like a child. As if whoever had just walked into the barn wouldn't be able to see her as long as she couldn't see him.

Then she heard footsteps on the ladder rungs, the sound of calloused hands sliding over the metal. She knew who it was. Oh well. She had already embarrassed herself in front of him earlier. It was not like him seeing her sprawled in a tragic heap in a barn was any worse than her stamping her foot like a dramatic silent-film heroine.

"I thought I might find you here."

She didn't look up when she heard his voice. Instead, she curled into a tighter, even more resolute ball.

She felt him getting closer, which was ridiculous. She knew she couldn't actually feel the heat radiating from his body.

"I got you that Pop-Tart cake," he said. "I mean, I had Alison from Pie in the Sky make one. And I have to tell you, it looks disgusting. I mean, she did a great job, but I can't imagine that it's edible."

She uncurled as a sudden spout of rage flooded through her and she pushed herself into a sitting position. "Fuck your Pop-Tart cake, Joshua."

"I thought we both liked Pop-Tarts."

"Yes. But I don't like lies. And your Pop-Tarts would taste like lies."

"Actually," he said slowly, "I think the Pop-Tart

cake is closer to the truth than anything I said to you back in the church. You said a lot of things that were true. I'm a coward, Danielle. And guilt is a hell of a lot easier than grief."

"What the hell does that mean?" She drew her arm underneath her nose, wiping snot and tears away, tempted to ask him where his elfin princess was now. "Don't tease me. Don't talk in riddles. I'm ready to walk away from you if I need to, but I don't want to do it. So please, don't tempt me to hurt myself like that if you aren't…"

"I love you," he said, his voice rough. "And my saying so now isn't because I was afraid you were a gold digger and you proved you weren't by walking away. I realize what I'm about to say could be confused for that, but don't be confused. Because loving you has nothing to do with that. If you need my money… I've never blamed you for going after it. I've never blamed you for wanting to make your and Riley's lives easier. But the fact that you *were* willing to walk away from everything over three words… How can I pretend they aren't important? How can I pretend that I don't need your love when you demonstrated that you need my love more than financial security. More than sex. How can I doubt you and the strength of your feelings? How can I excuse my unwillingness to open myself up to you? My unwillingness to make myself bleed for you?"

He reached out, taking hold of her hands, down on his knees with her.

"You're going to get your suit dirty," she said inanely.

"Your dress is filthy," he returned.

She looked down at the dirt and smudges on the beautiful white satin. "Crap."

He took hold of her chin, tilting her face up to look at him. "I don't care. It doesn't matter. Because I would marry you in blue jeans, or I would marry you in this barn. I would sure as hell marry you in that dirty wedding dress. I… You are right about everything.

"It was easy to martyr myself over Shannon's pain. To blame myself so I didn't have to try again. So I didn't have to hurt again. Old pain is easier. The pain from that time in my life isn't gone, but it's dull. It throbs sometimes. It aches. When I look at Riley, he reminds me of my son, who never took a breath, and it hurts down deep. But I know that if I were to lose either of you now… That would be fresh pain. A fresh hell. And I have some idea of what that hell would be like because of what I've been through before.

"But it would be worse now. And… I was protecting myself from it. But now, I don't care about the pain, the fear. I want it all. I want you.

"I love you. Whatever might happen, whatever might come our way in the future… I love you. And I am going to do the hard fucking yards for you, Danielle."

His expression was so fierce, his words so raw and real, all she could do was stare at him, listening as he said all the things she had never imagined she would hear.

"I was young and stupid the last time I tried love. Selfish. I made mistakes. I can't take credit for everything that went wrong. Some of it was fate. Some of it was her choices. But when things get hard this time, you have my word I won't pull away. I'm not going to let you shut me out. If you close the door on me, I'm going to kick it down. Because what we have is special. It's real. It's hope. And I will fight with everything I have to hold on to it."

She lurched forward, wrapping her arms around his neck, making them both fall backward. "I'll never shut you out." She squeezed her eyes closed, tears tracking down her cheeks. "Finding you has been the best thing that's ever happened to me. I don't feel alone, Joshua. Can you possibly understand what that means to me?"

He nodded gravely, kissing her lips. "I do understand," he said. "Because I've been alone in my own swamp for a long damned time. And you're the first person who made me feel like it was worth it to wade out."

"I love you," she said.

"I love you too. Do you still want to marry me?"

"Hell yeah."

"Good." He maneuvered them both so they were upright, taking her hand and leading her to the ladder. They climbed down, and she hopped from foot to foot on the cold cement floor. "Come on," he said, grabbing her hand and leading her through the open double doors.

She stopped when she saw that his whole family, Janine and Riley, and Pastor John were standing out there in the gravel.

Joshua's mother was holding the bouquet of roses, and she reached out, handing it back to Danielle. Then Joshua went to Janine and took Riley from her arms, holding the baby in the crook of his own. Then Joshua went back to Danielle, taking both of her hands with his free one.

"I look bedraggled," she said.

"You look perfect to me."

She smiled, gazing at everyone, at her new family. At this new life she was going to have.

And then she looked back at the man she loved with all her heart. "Well," she said, "okay, then. Marry me, cowboy."

Epilogue

December 5, 2017
FOUND A WIFE—

Local rancher Todd Grayson and his wife, Nancy, are pleased to announce the marriage of their son, a wealthy former bachelor, Joshua Grayson (no longer irritated with his father) to Danielle Kelly, formerly of Portland, now of Copper Ridge and the daughter of their hearts. Mr. Grayson knew his son would need a partner who was strong, determined and able to handle an extremely stubborn cuss, which she does beautifully. But best of all, she loves him with her whole heart, which is all his meddling parents ever wanted for him.

* * * * *

LET'S TALK

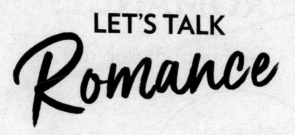

Romance

For exclusive extracts, competitions
and special offers, find us online:

 facebook.com/millsandboon

@millsandboonuk

@millsandboon

Or get in touch on 0844 844 1351*

For all the latest titles coming soon, visit
millsandboon.co.uk/nextmonth

Want even more
ROMANCE?

Join our bookclub today!

'Mills & Boon books, the perfect way to escape for an hour or so.'

Miss W. Dyer

'Excellent service, promptly delivered and very good subscription choices.'

Miss A. Pearson

'You get fantastic special offers and the chance to get books before they hit the shops'

Mrs V. Hall

Visit millsandbook.co.uk/Bookclub and save on brand new books.

MILLS & BOON